P9-EJT-774

KNIFE'S EDGE

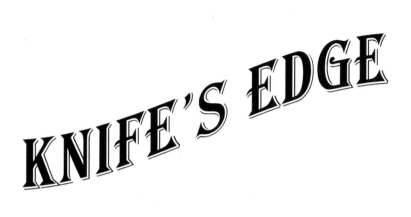

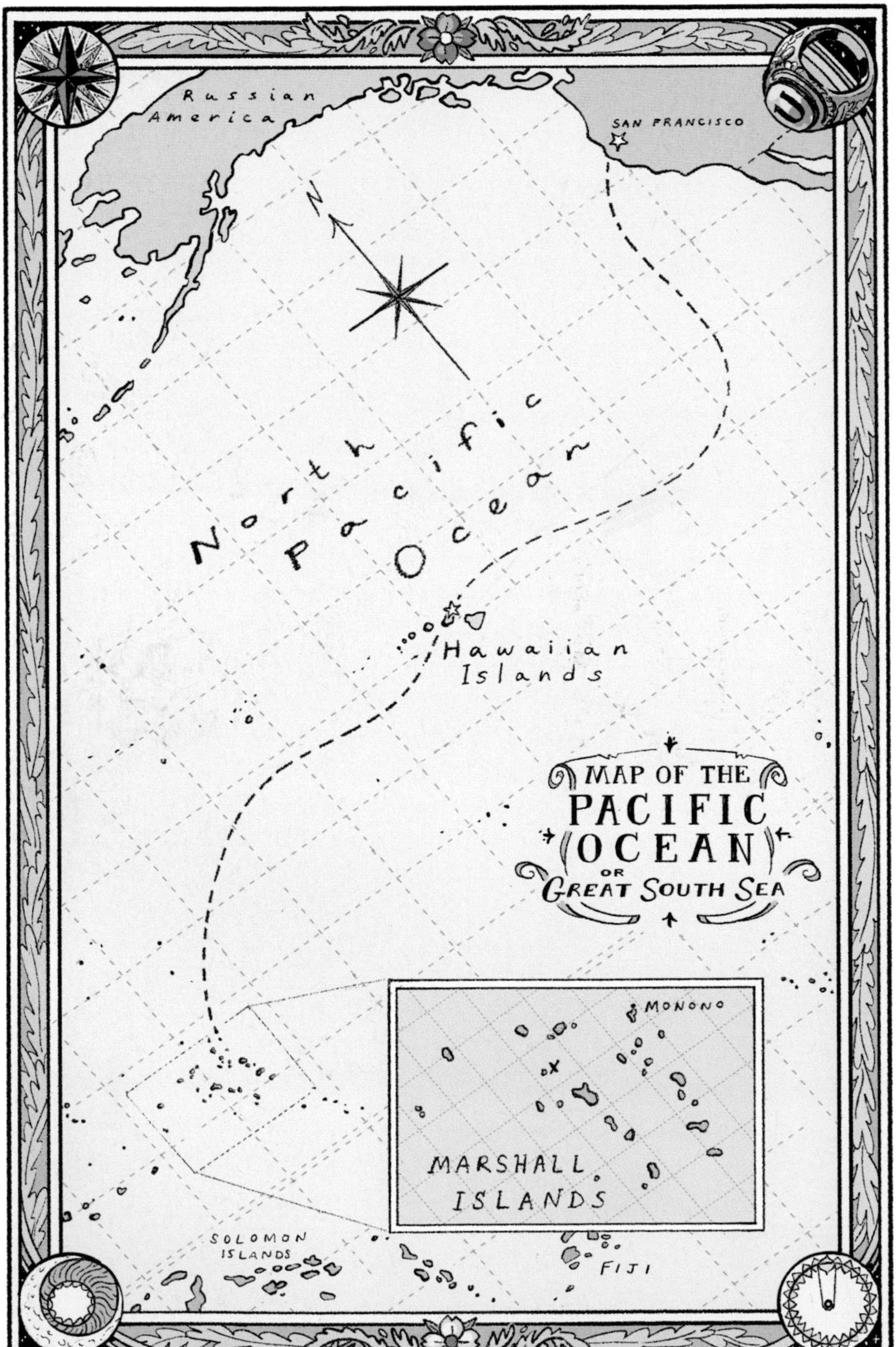
Russian America
SAN FRANCISCO
N
North Pacific Ocean
Hawaiian Islands
MAP OF THE PACIFIC OCEAN OR GREAT SOUTH SEA
MONONO
MARSHALL ISLANDS
SOLOMON ISLANDS
FIJI

HOPE LARSON

KNIFE'S EDGE

FOUR POINTS

BOOK 2

Illustrations by
REBECCA MOCK

MARGARET FERGUSON BOOKS
FARRAR STRAUS GIROUX
New York

To Sydney, Megan, and Emily
—H.L.

To my mother, Kathy, and my father, David
—R.M.

Farrar Straus Giroux Books for Young Readers
An imprint of Macmillan Publishing Group, LLC
175 Fifth Avenue, New York 10010

Text copyright © 2017 by Hope Larson
Art copyright © 2017 by Rebecca Mock
All rights reserved
Printed in China by Toppan Leefung Printing Ltd.,
Dongguan City, Guangdong Province
Designed by Andrew Arnold
First edition, 2017
1 3 5 7 9 10 8 6 4 2

mackids.com

Library of Congress Control Number: 2016951407
ISBN: 978-0-374-30044-9

Our books may be purchased in bulk for promotional, educational,
or business use. Please contact your local bookseller or the Macmillan
Corporate and Premium Sales Department at (800) 221-7945 ext. 5442
or by e-mail at MacmillanSpecialMarkets@macmillan.com.

TABLE OF CONTENTS

CHAPTER ONE
NO SAFER PLACE

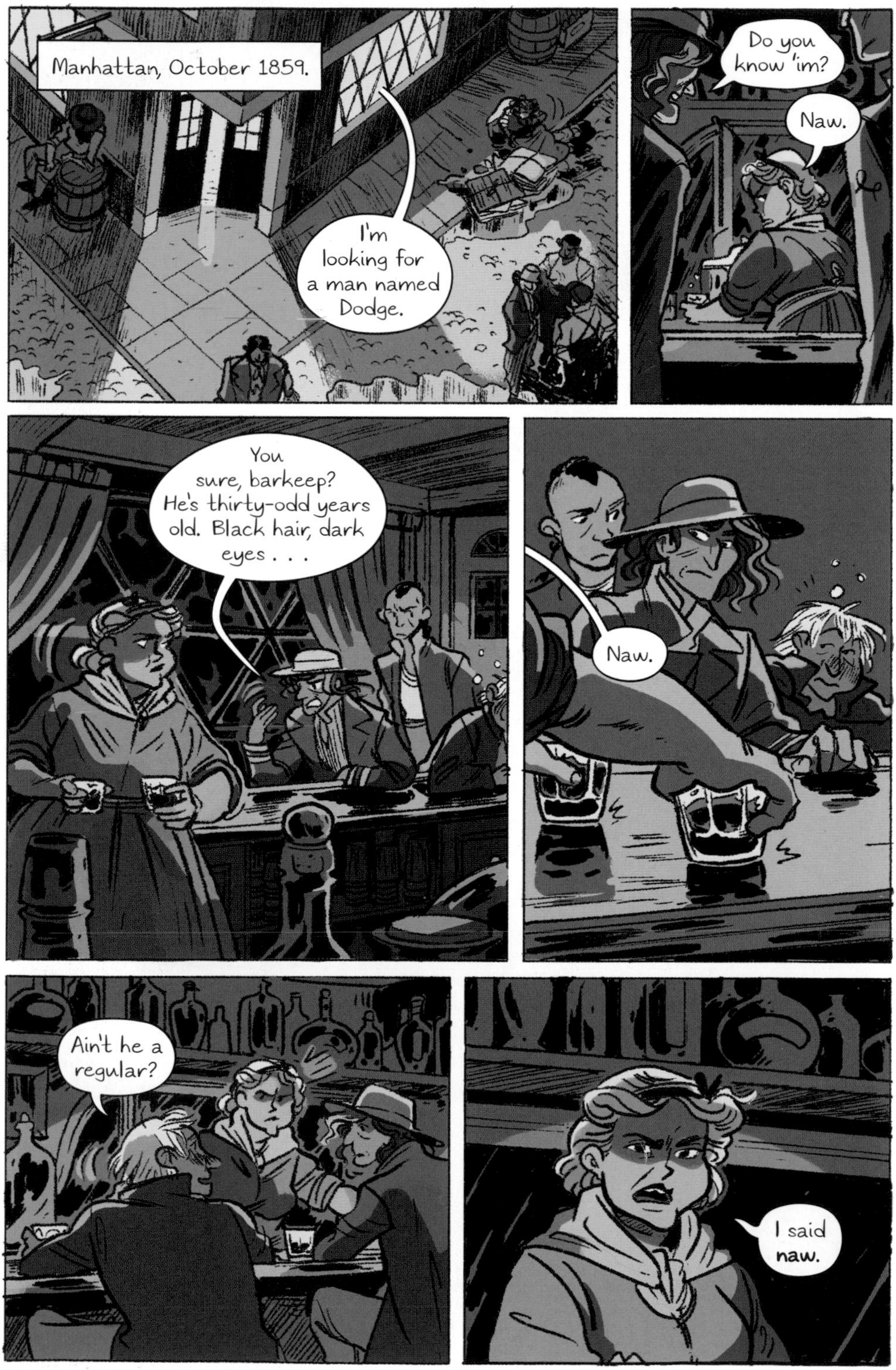
Manhattan, October 1859.
I'm looking for a man named Dodge.
Do you know 'im?
Naw.
You sure, barkeep? He's thirty-odd years old. Black hair, dark eyes . . .
Naw.
Ain't he a regular?
I said **naw.**

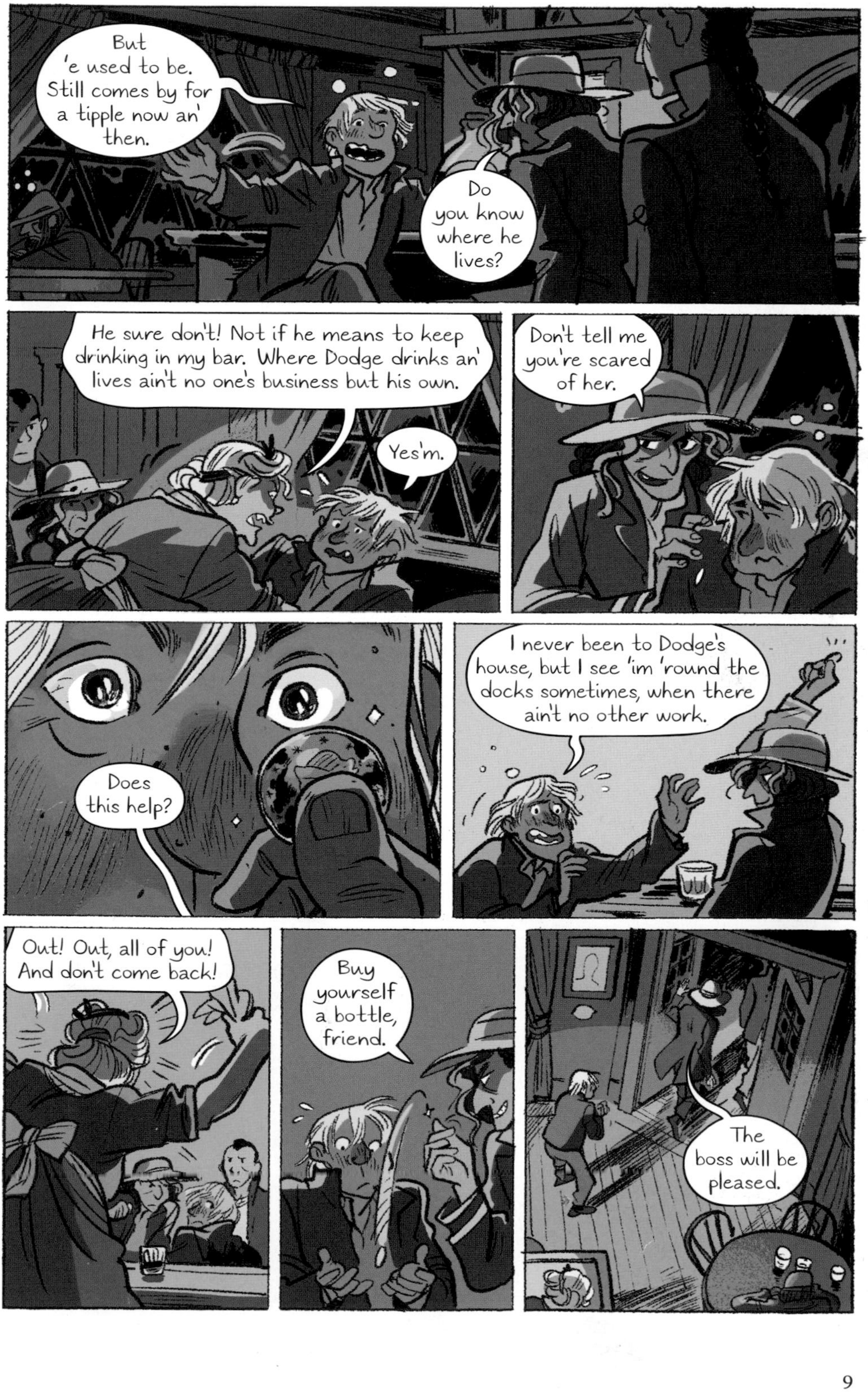

But 'e used to be. Still comes by for a tipple now an' then.
Do you know where he lives?
He sure don't! Not if he means to keep drinking in my bar. Where Dodge drinks an' lives ain't no one's business but his own.
Yes'm.
Don't tell me you're scared of her.
Does this help?
I never been to Dodge's house, but I see 'im 'round the docks sometimes, when there ain't no other work.
Out! Out, all of you! And don't come back!
Buy yourself a bottle, friend.
The boss will be pleased.

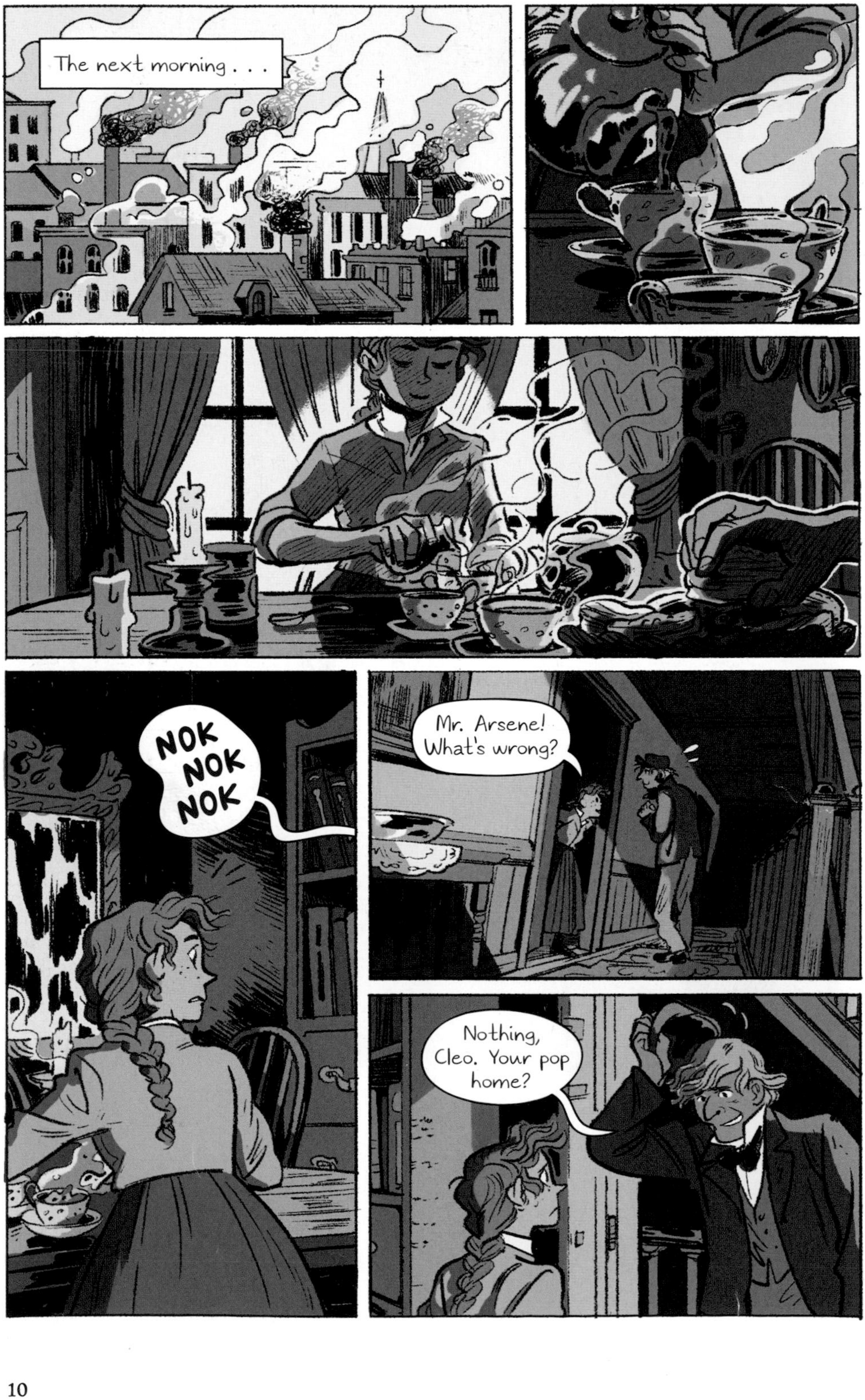
The next morning . . .
NOK NOK NOK
Mr. Arsene! What's wrong?
Nothing, Cleo. Your pop home?

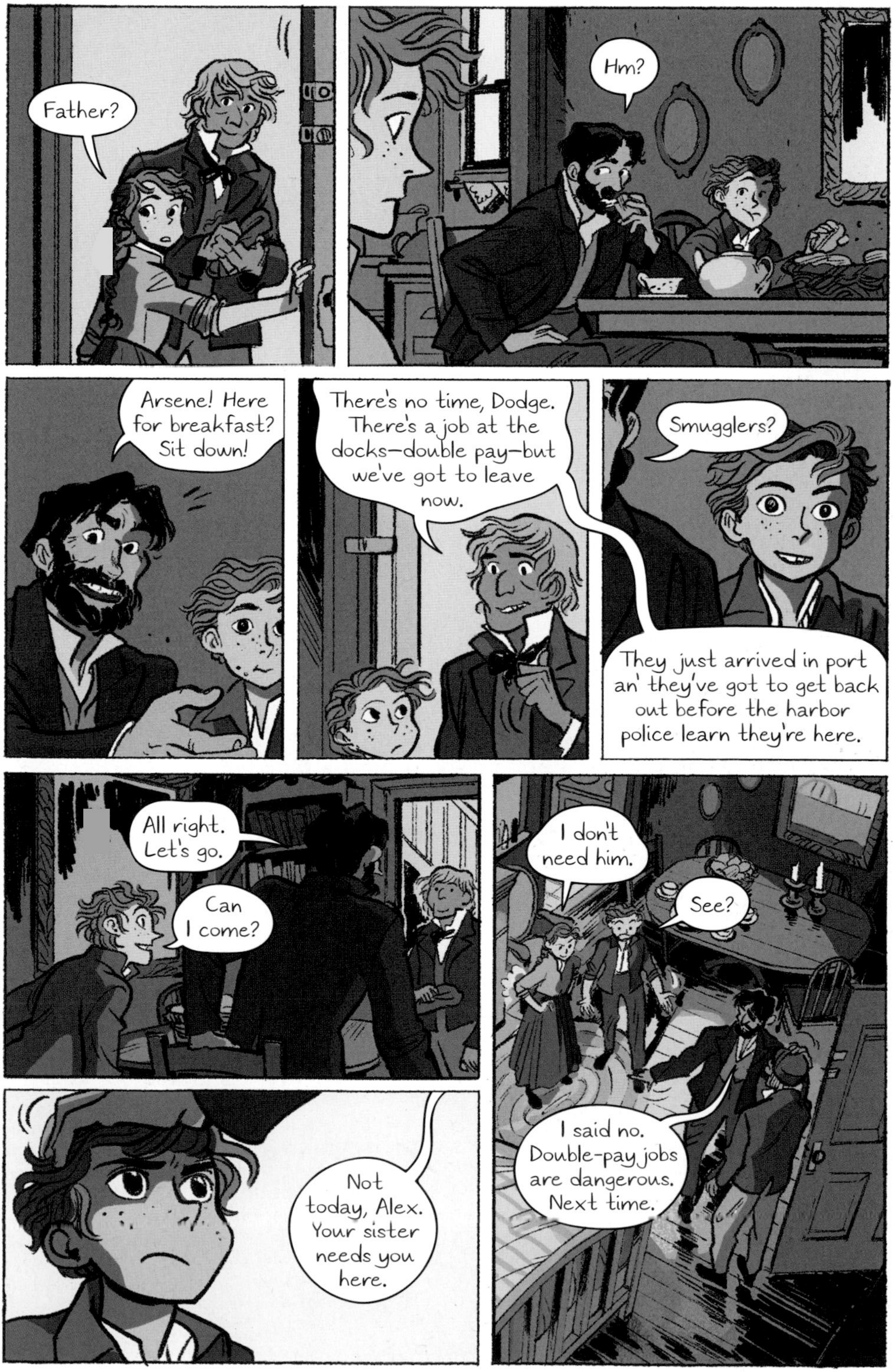
Father?
Hm?
Arsene! Here for breakfast? Sit down!
There's no time, Dodge. There's a job at the docks—double pay—but we've got to leave now.
Smugglers?
They just arrived in port an' they've got to get back out before the harbor police learn they're here.
All right. Let's go.
Can I come?
Not today, Alex. Your sister needs you here.
I don't need him.
See?
I said no. Double-pay jobs are dangerous. Next time.

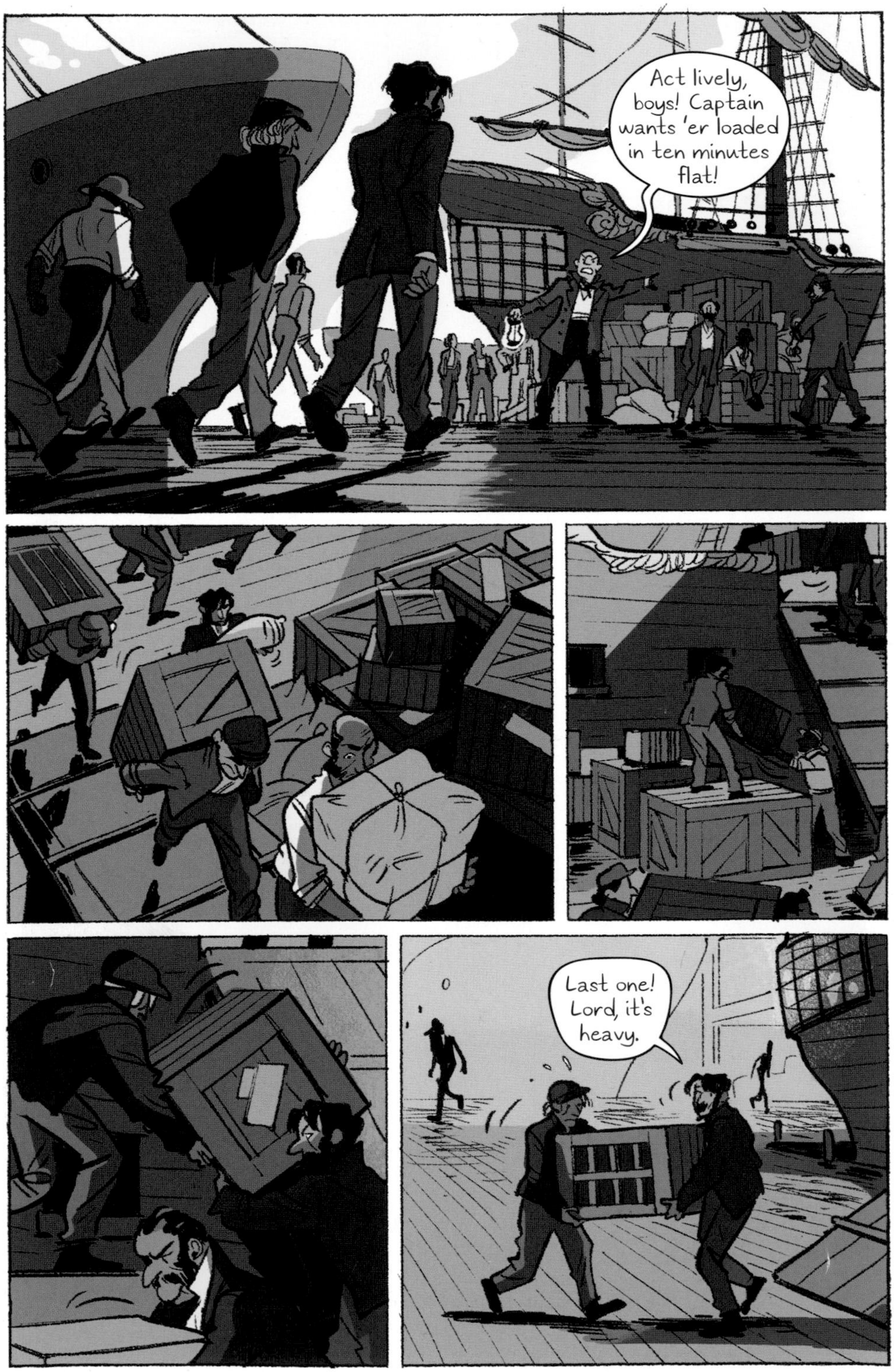
Act lively, boys! Captain wants 'er loaded in ten minutes flat!
Last one! Lord, it's heavy.

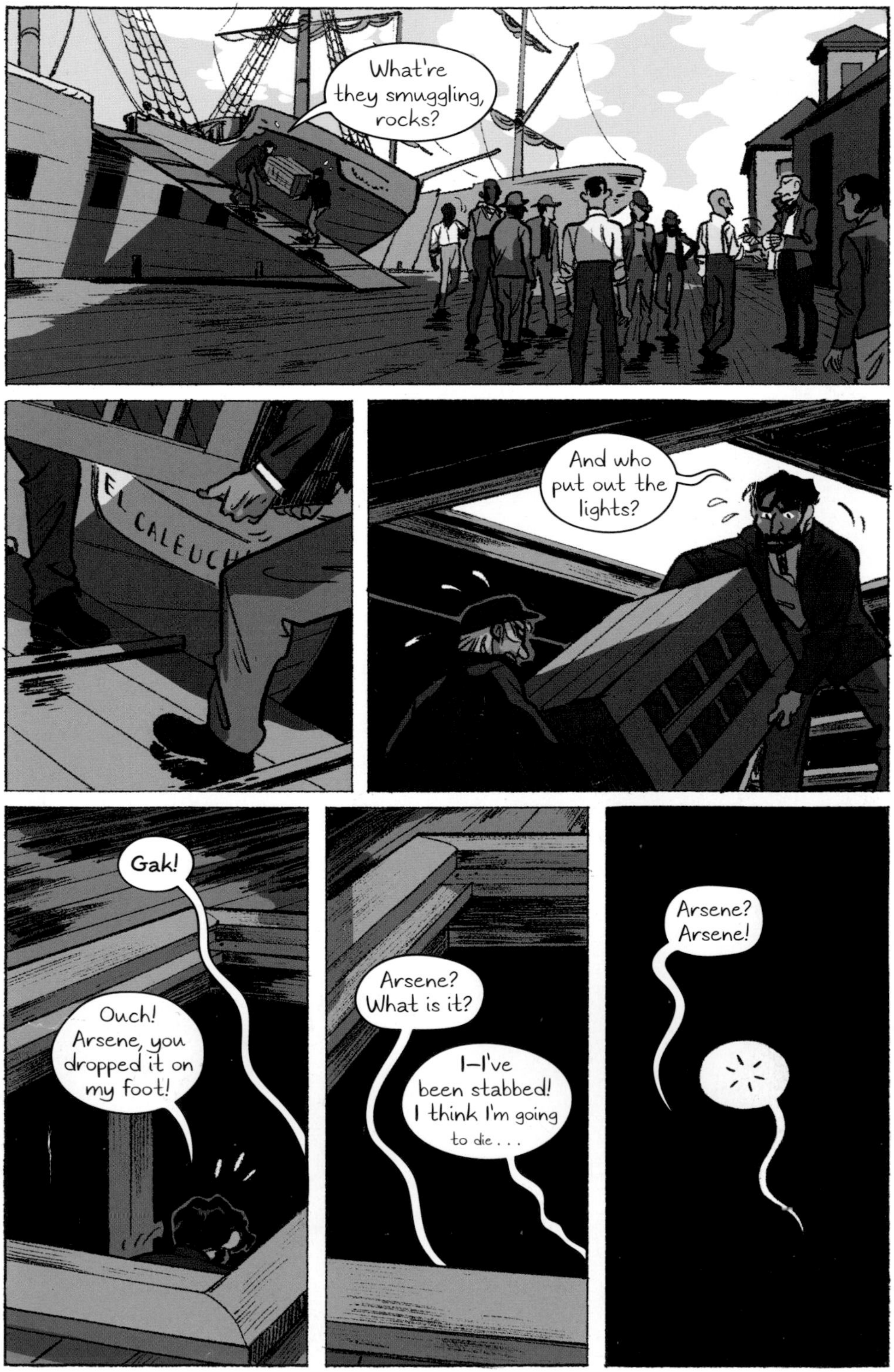
What're they smuggling, rocks?
EL CALEUCH
And who put out the lights?
Gak!
Ouch! Arsene, you dropped it on my foot!
Arsene? What is it?
I—I've been stabbed! I think I'm going to die . . .
Arsene? Arsene!

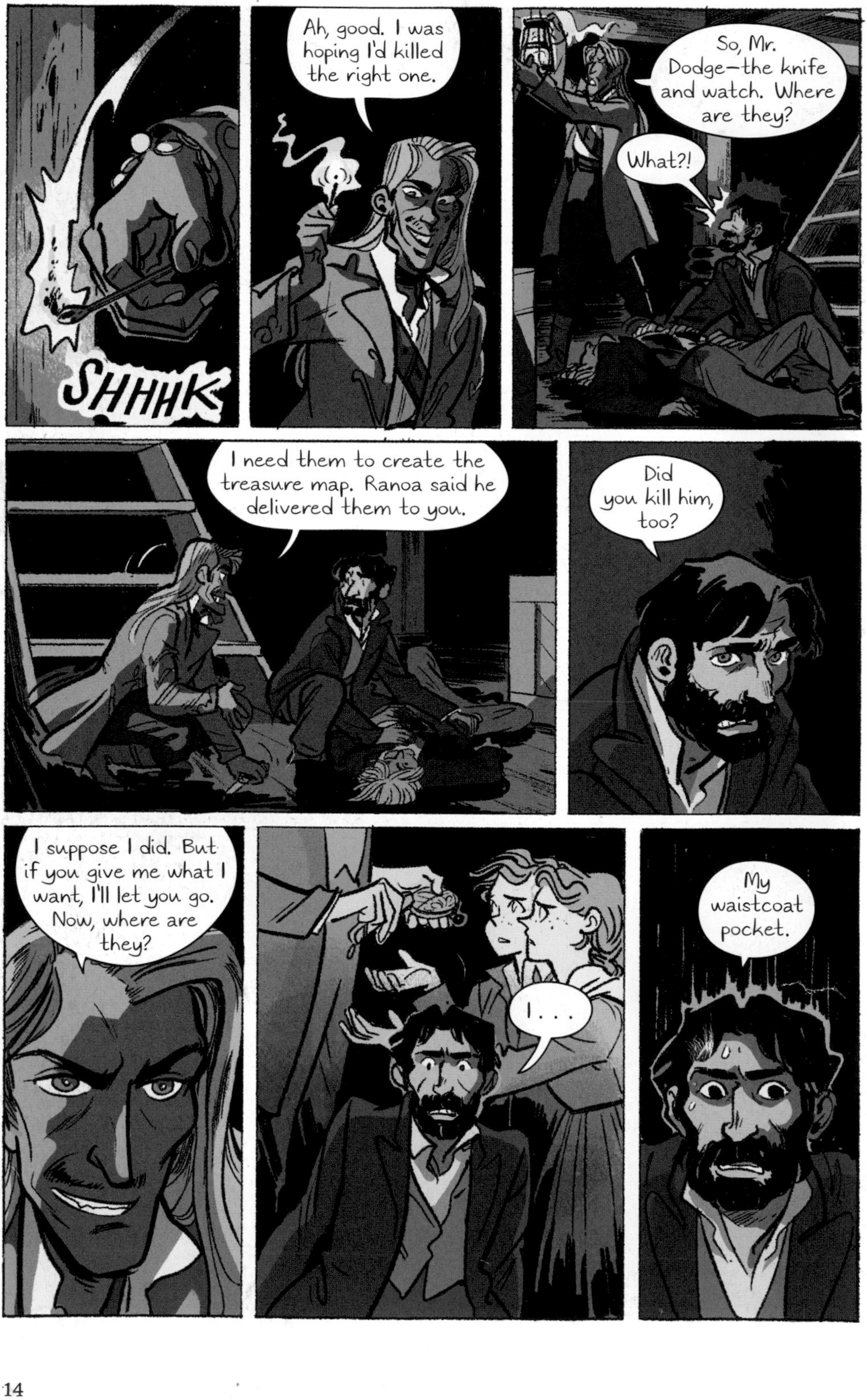
SHHHK
Ah, good. I was hoping I'd killed the right one.
So, Mr. Dodge—the knife and watch. Where are they?
What?!
I need them to create the treasure map. Ranoa said he delivered them to you.
Did you kill him, too?
I suppose I did. But if you give me what I want, I'll let you go. Now, where are they?
I . . .
My waistcoat pocket.

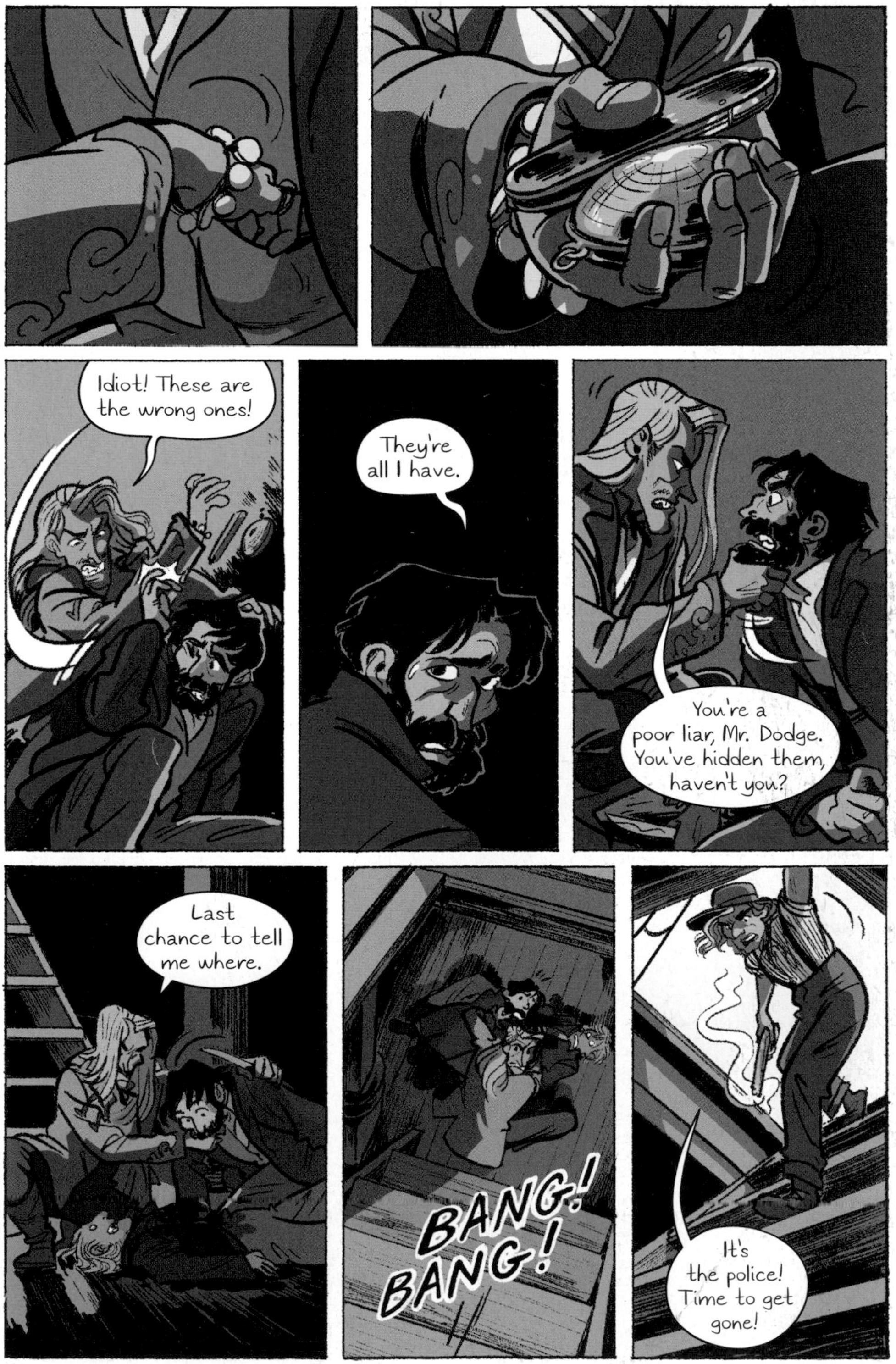
Idiot! These are the wrong ones!
They're all I have.
You're a poor liar, Mr. Dodge. You've hidden them, haven't you?
Last chance to tell me where.
BANG! BANG!
It's the police! Time to get gone!

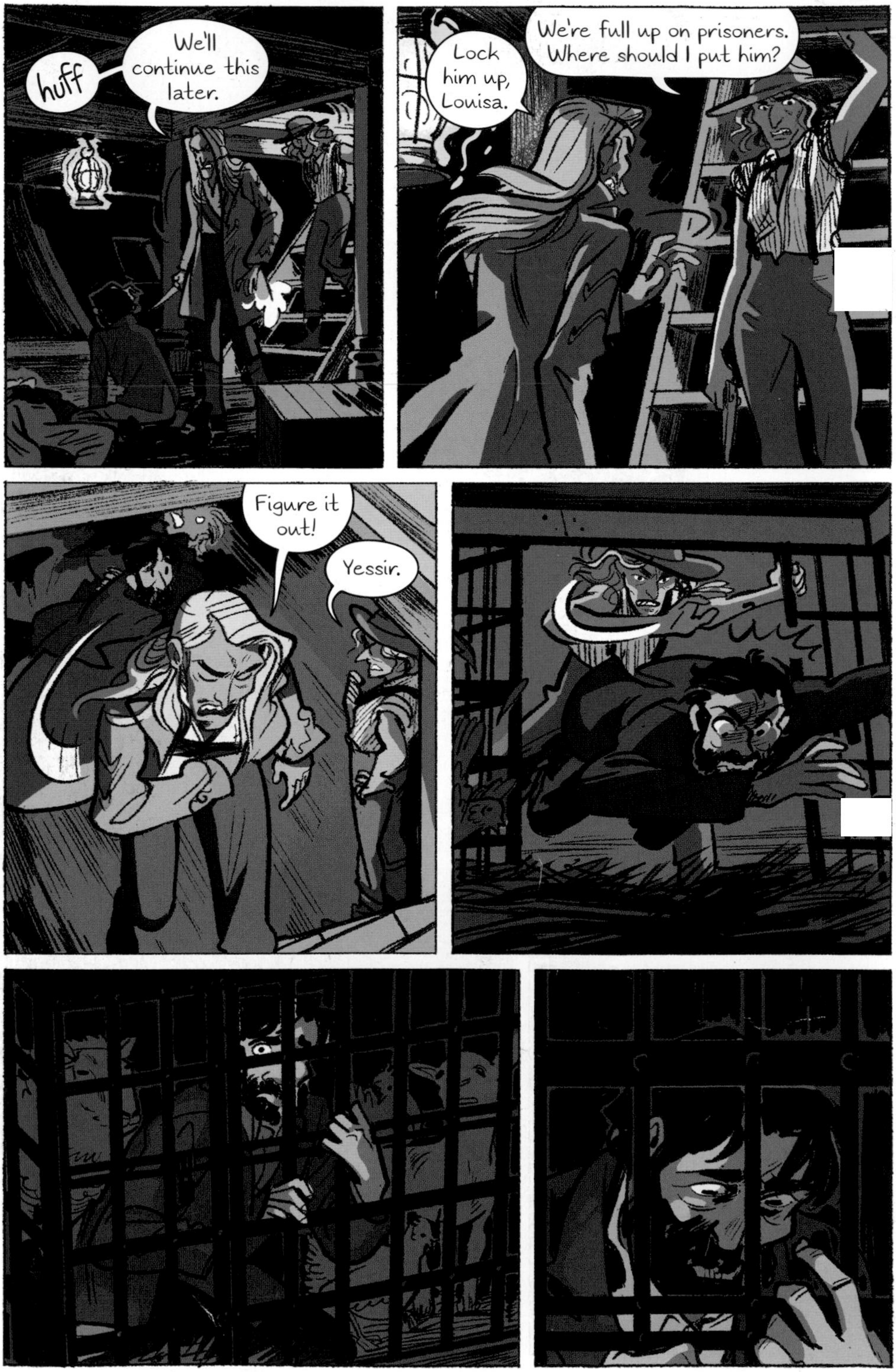
huff
We'll continue this later.
Lock him up, Louisa.
We're full up on prisoners. Where should I put him?
Figure it out!
Yessir.

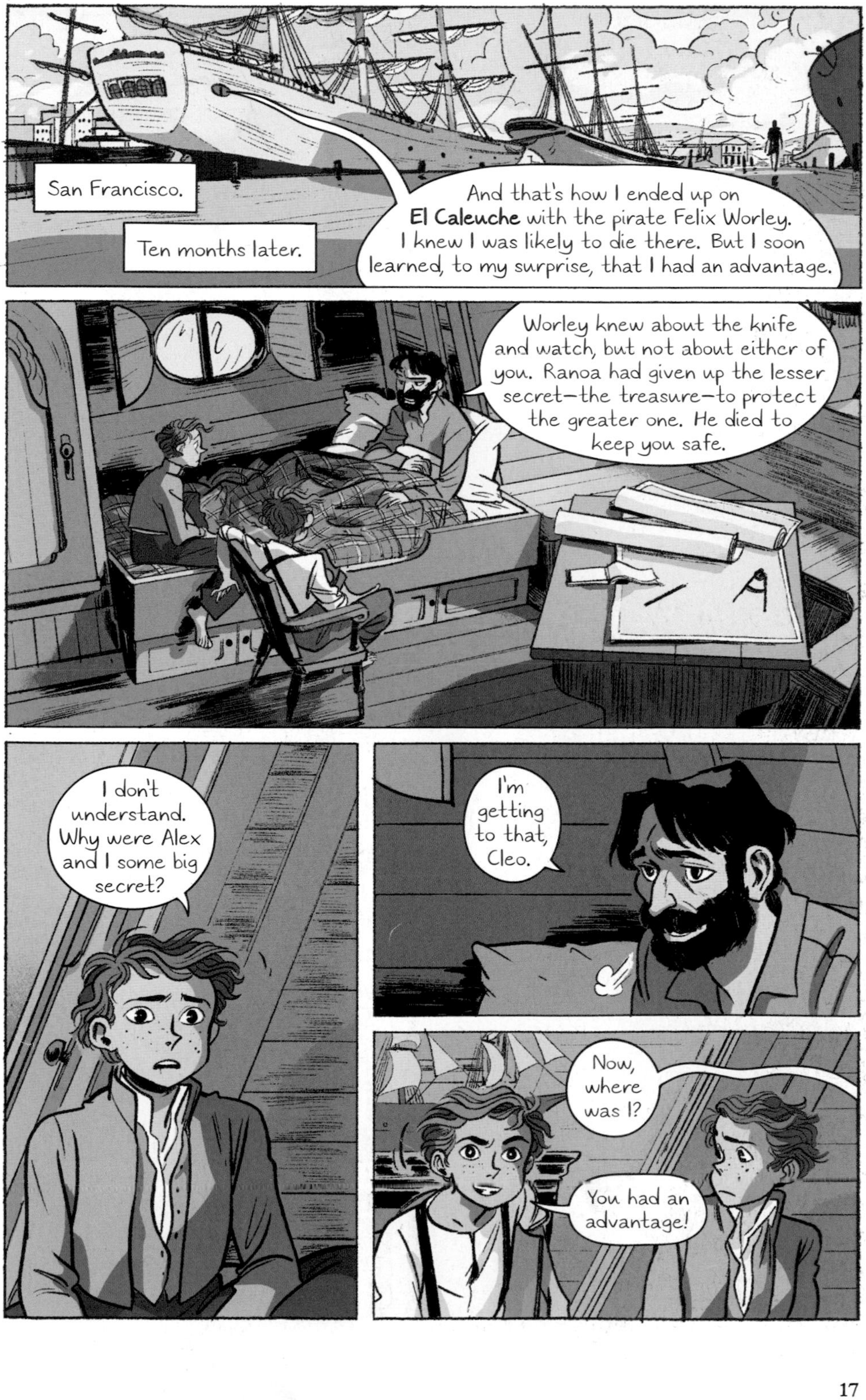
San Francisco.
Ten months later.
And that's how I ended up on **El Caleuche** with the pirate Felix Worley. I knew I was likely to die there. But I soon learned, to my surprise, that I had an advantage.
Worley knew about the knife and watch, but not about either of you. Ranoa had given up the lesser secret—the treasure—to protect the greater one. He died to keep you safe.
I don't understand. Why were Alex and I some big secret?
I'm getting to that, Cleo.
Now, where was I?
You had an advantage!

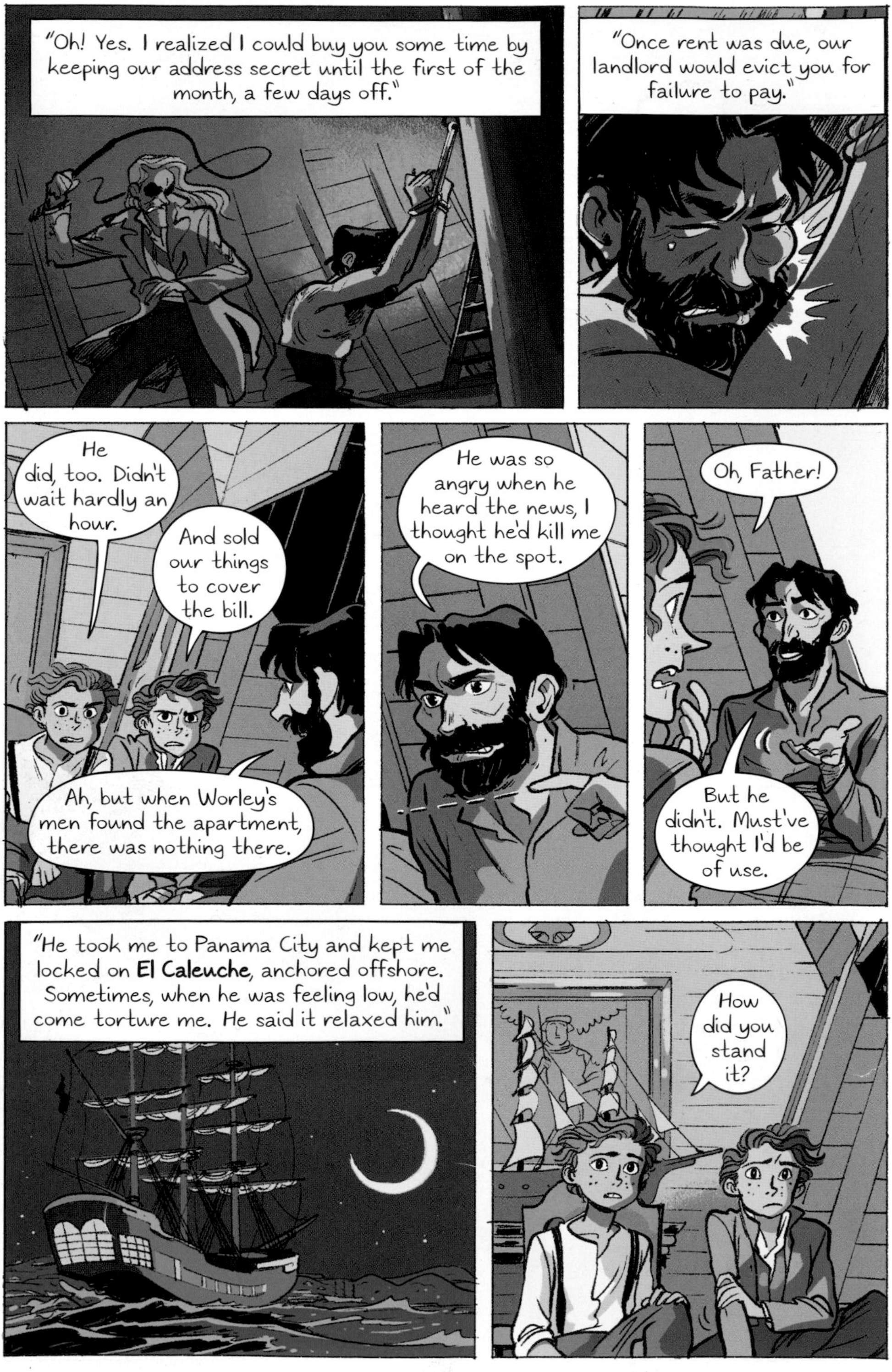
"Oh! Yes. I realized I could buy you some time by keeping our address secret until the first of the month, a few days off."
"Once rent was due, our landlord would evict you for failure to pay."
He did, too. Didn't wait hardly an hour.
And sold our things to cover the bill.
Ah, but when Worley's men found the apartment, there was nothing there.
He was so angry when he heard the news, I thought he'd kill me on the spot.
Oh, Father!
But he didn't. Must've thought I'd be of use.
"He took me to Panama City and kept me locked on El Caleuche, anchored offshore. Sometimes, when he was feeling low, he'd come torture me. He said it relaxed him."
How did you stand it?

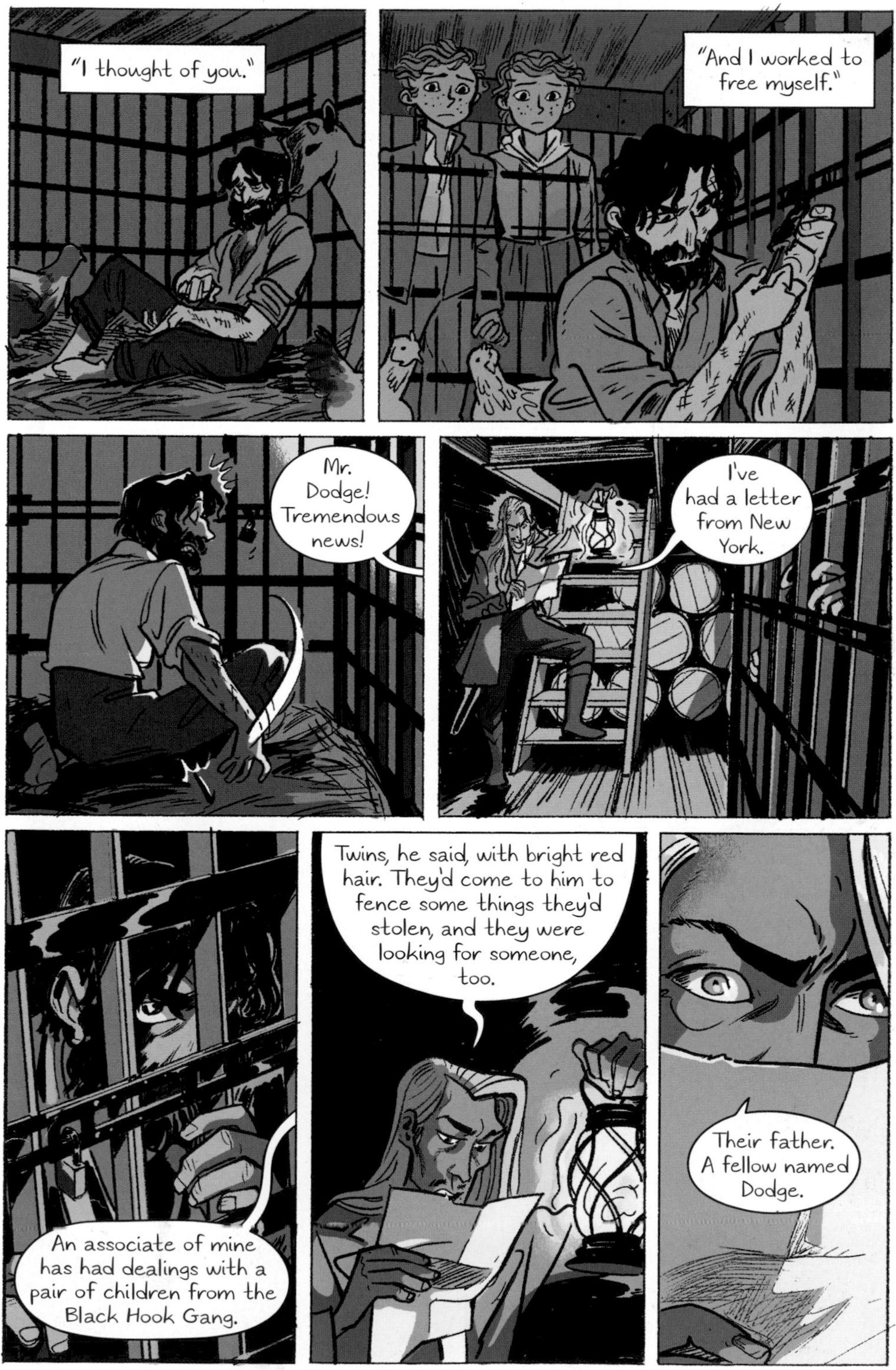
"I thought of you."
"And I worked to free myself."
Mr. Dodge! Tremendous news!
I've had a letter from New York.
An associate of mine has had dealings with a pair of children from the Black Hook Gang.
Twins, he said, with bright red hair. They'd come to him to fence some things they'd stolen, and they were looking for someone, too.
Their father. A fellow named Dodge.

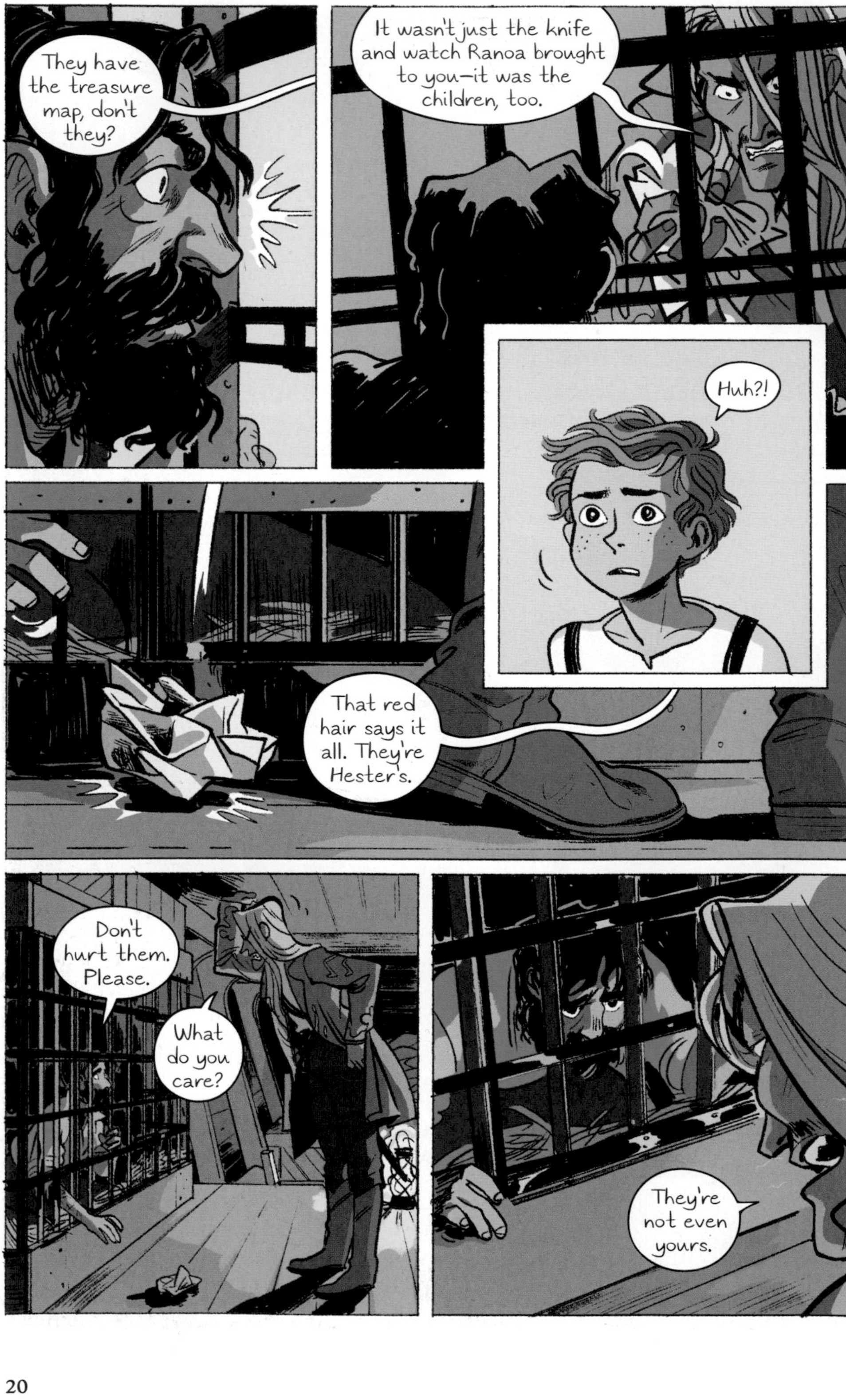

They have the treasure map, don't they?
It wasn't just the knife and watch Ranoa brought to you—it was the children, too.
Huh?!
That red hair says it all. They're Hester's.
Don't hurt them. Please.
What do you care?
They're not even yours.

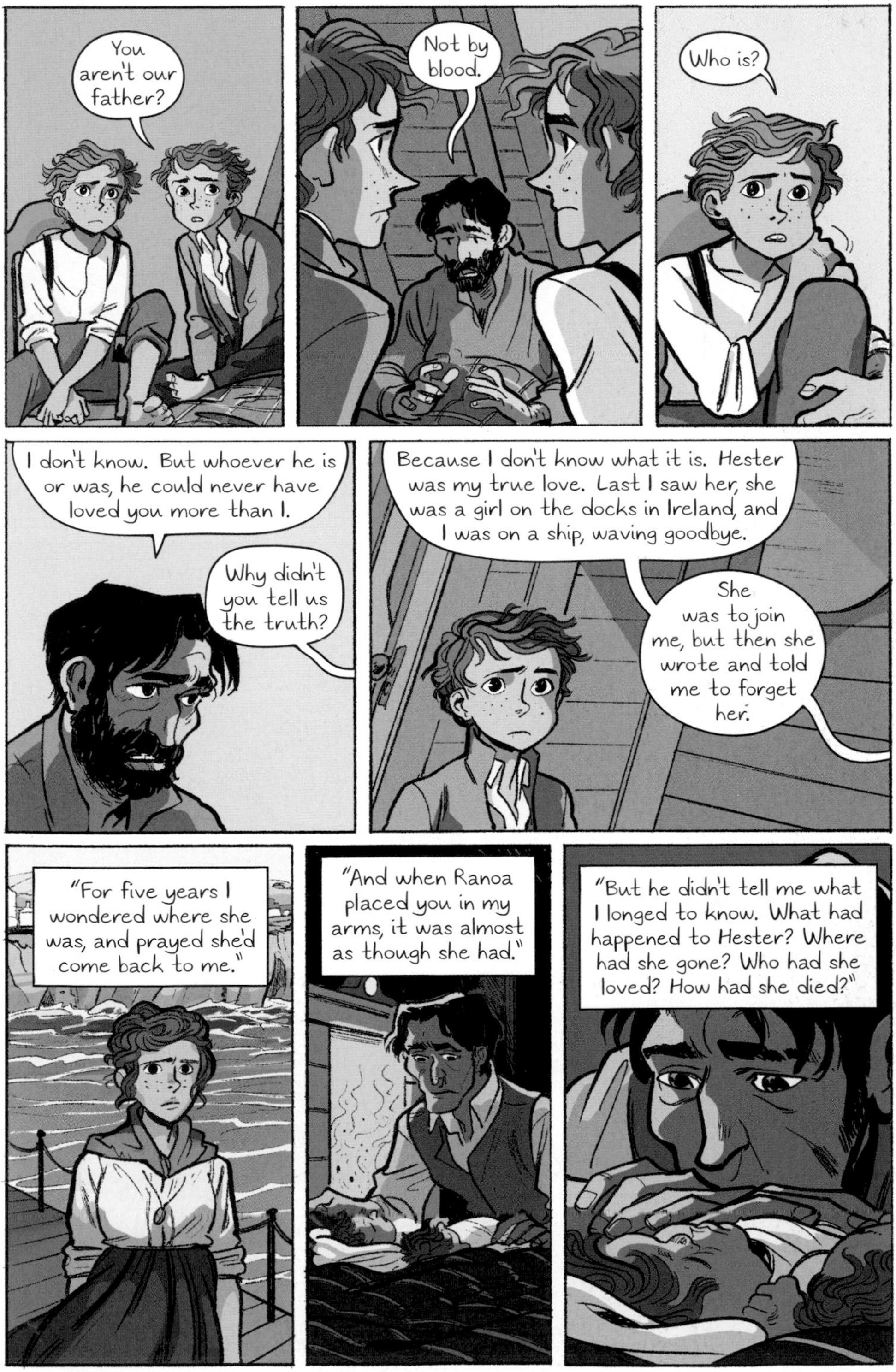
You aren't our father?
Not by blood.
Who is?
I don't know. But whoever he is or was, he could never have loved you more than I.
Why didn't you tell us the truth?
Because I don't know what it is. Hester was my true love. Last I saw her, she was a girl on the docks in Ireland, and I was on a ship, waving goodbye.
She was to join me, but then she wrote and told me to forget her.
"For five years I wondered where she was, and prayed she'd come back to me."
"And when Ranoa placed you in my arms, it was almost as though she had."
"But he didn't tell me what I longed to know. What had happened to Hester? Where had she gone? Who had she loved? How had she died?"

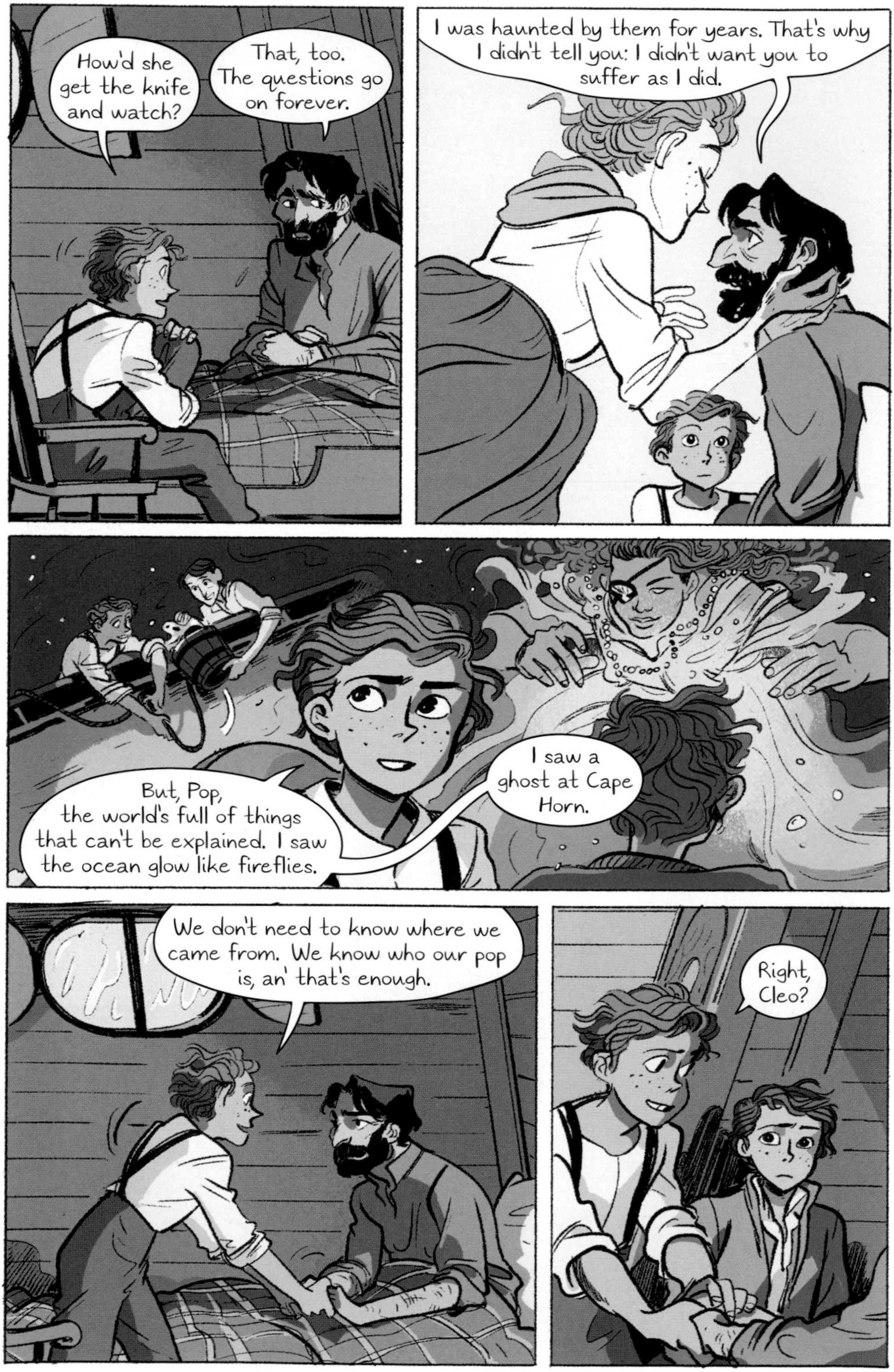
How'd she get the knife and watch?
That, too. The questions go on forever.
I was haunted by them for years. That's why I didn't tell you: I didn't want you to suffer as I did.
But, Pop, the world's full of things that can't be explained. I saw the ocean glow like fireflies.
I saw a ghost at Cape Horn.
We don't need to know where we came from. We know who our pop is, an' that's enough.
Right, Cleo?

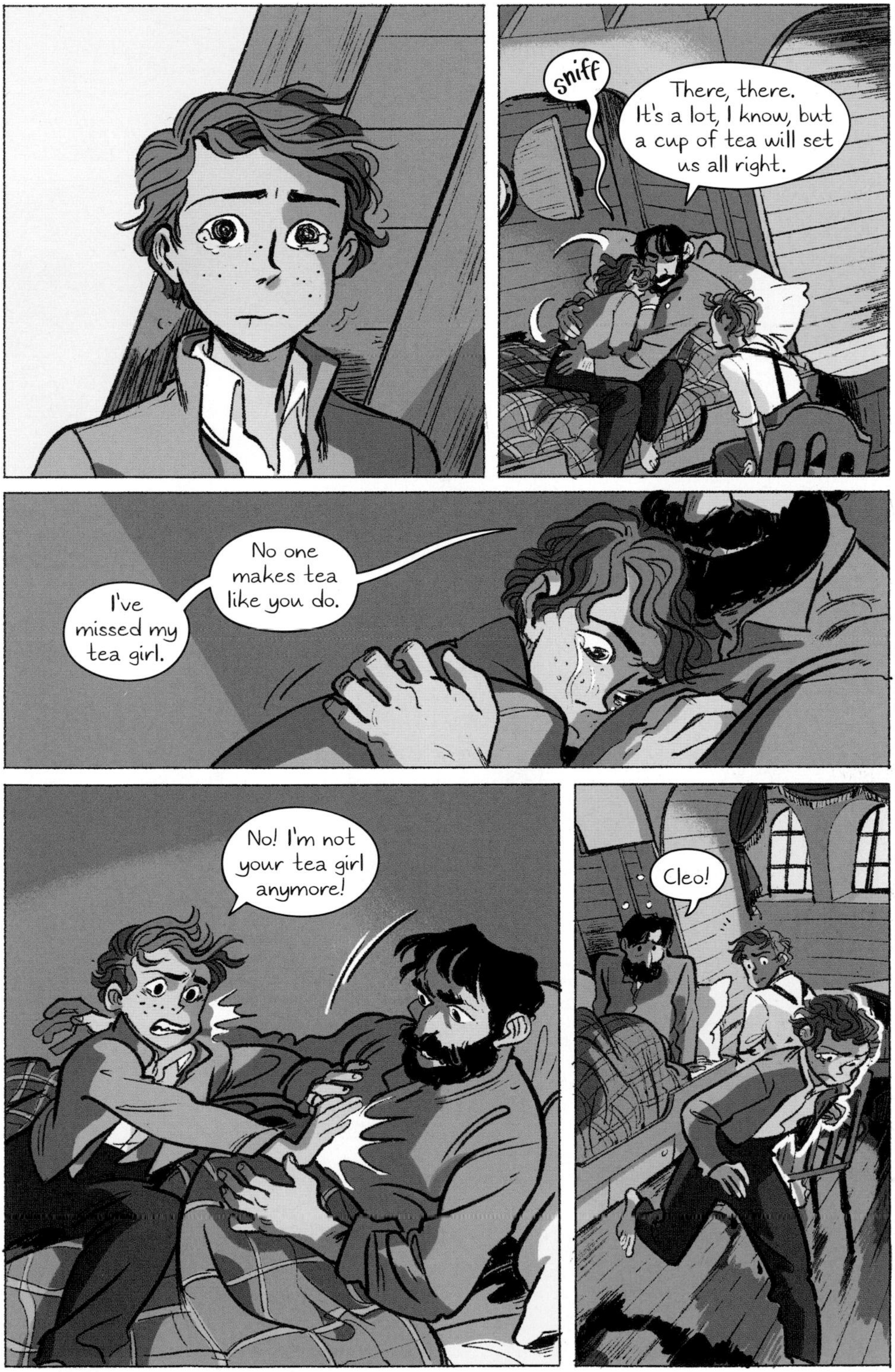

sniff
There, there. It's a lot, I know, but a cup of tea will set us all right.
No one makes tea like you do.
I've missed my tea girl.
No! I'm not your tea girl anymore!
Cleo!

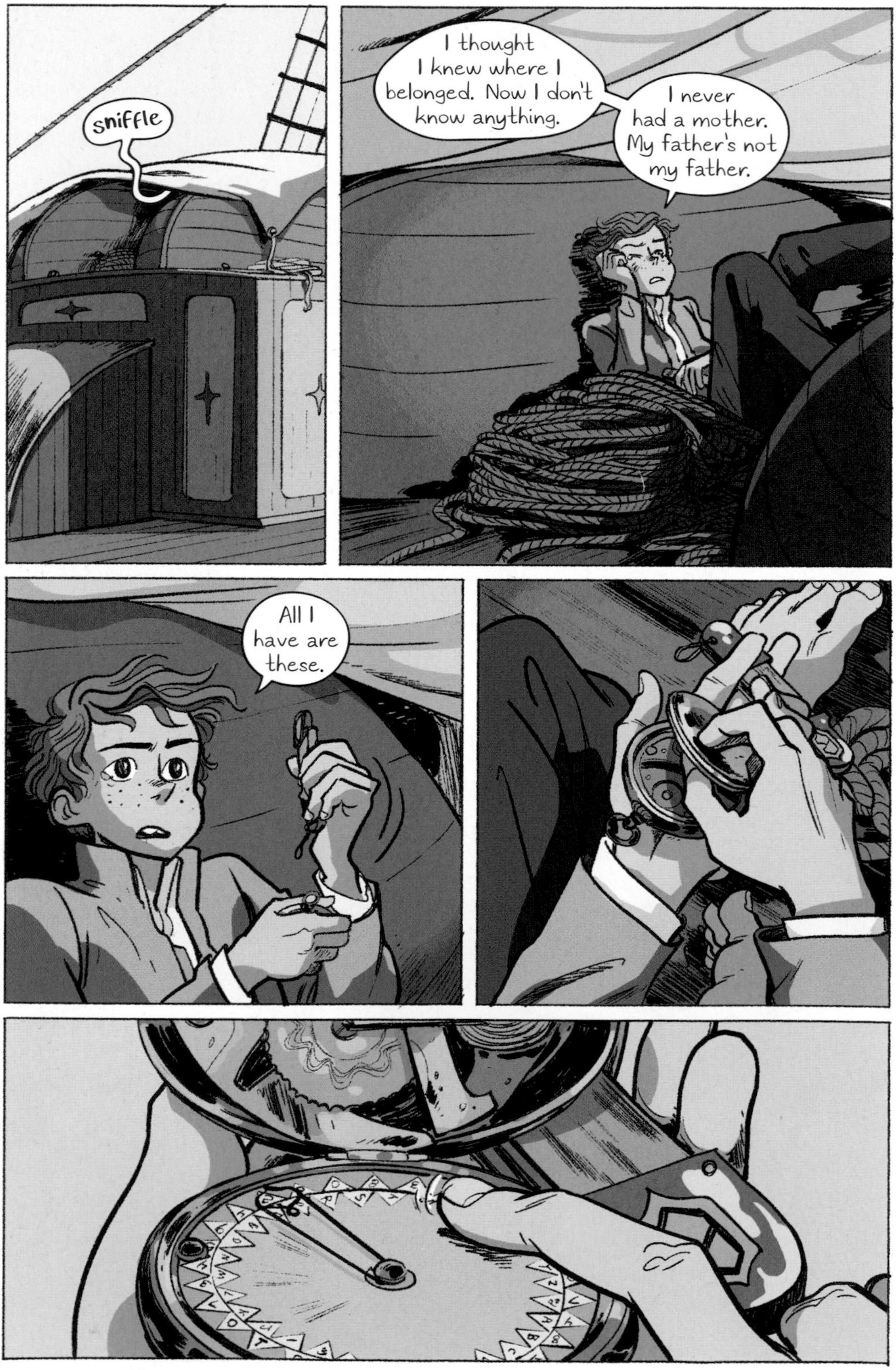
sniffle
I thought I knew where I belonged. Now I don't know anything.
I never had a mother. My father's not my father.
All I have are these.

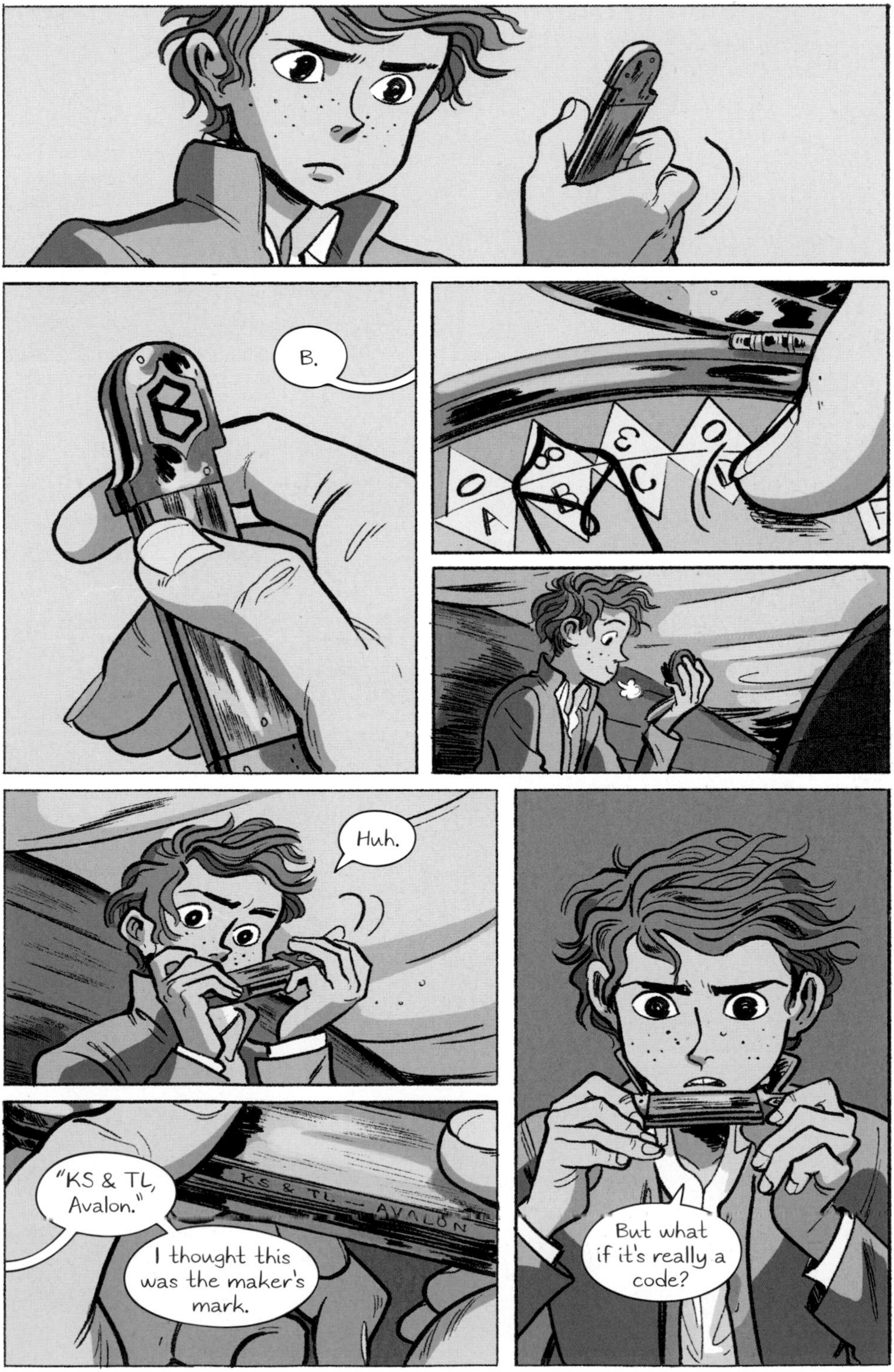
B.
Huh.
"KS & TL, Avalon."
I thought this was the maker's mark.
But what if it's really a code?

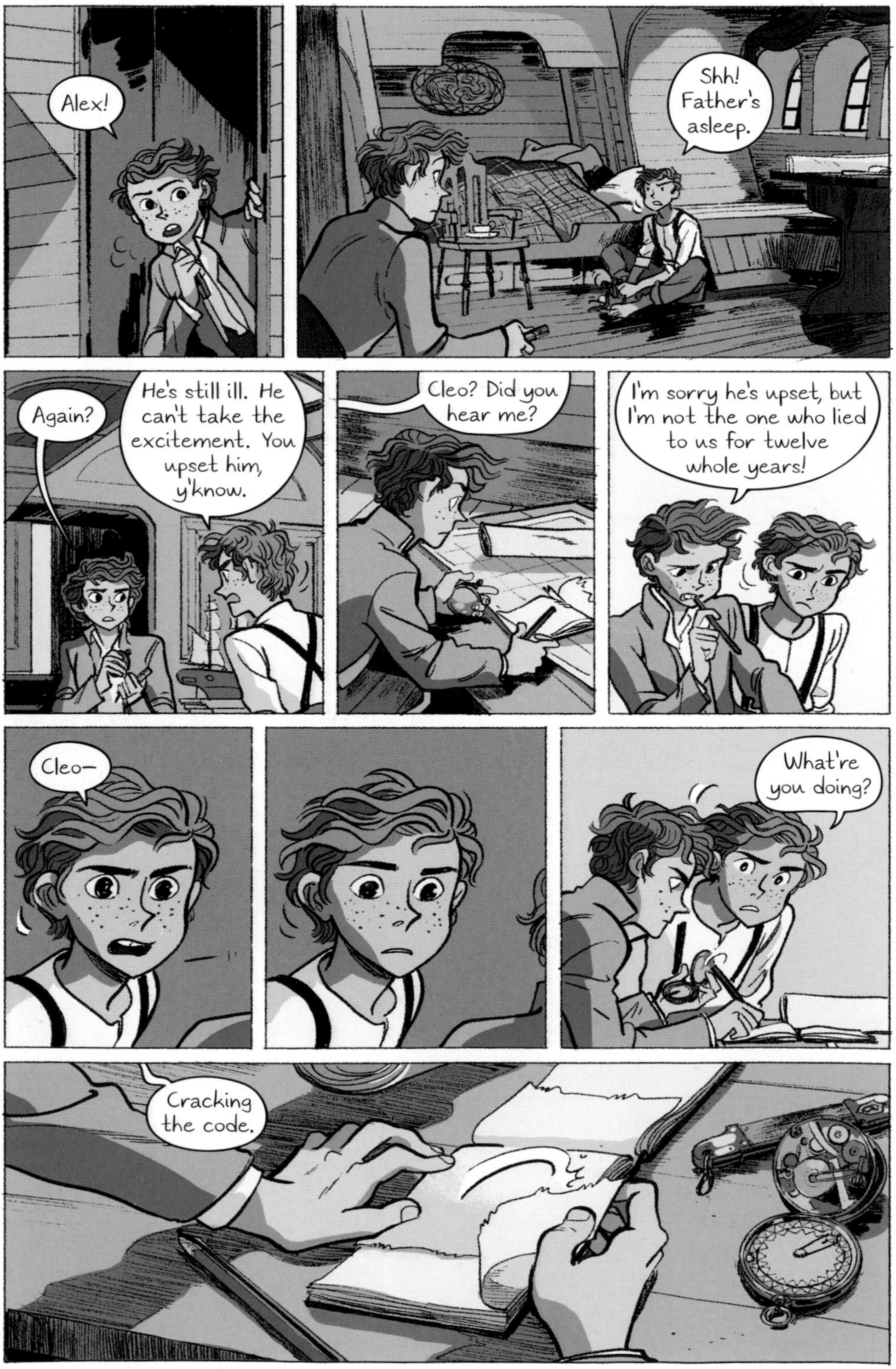
Alex!
Shh! Father's asleep.
Again?
He's still ill. He can't take the excitement. You upset him, y'know.
Cleo? Did you hear me?
I'm sorry he's upset, but I'm not the one who lied to us for twelve whole years!
Cleo—
What're you doing?
Cracking the code.

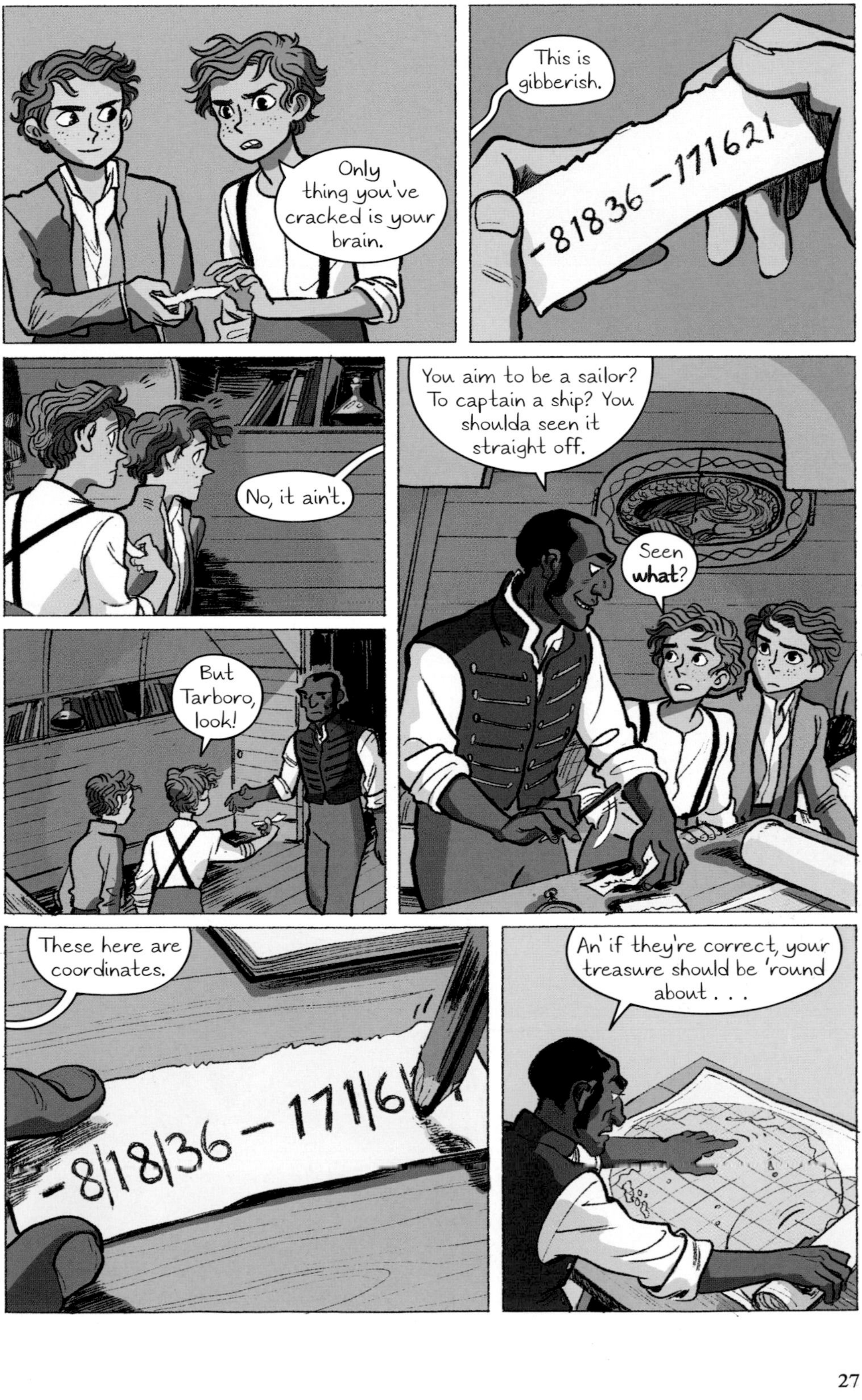
Only thing you've cracked is your brain.
This is gibberish.
-81836-171621
No, it ain't.
But Tarboro, look!
You aim to be a sailor? To captain a ship? You shoulda seen it straight off.
Seen **what**?
These here are coordinates.
-8|18|36 - 17|1|6
An' if they're correct, your treasure should be 'round about . . .

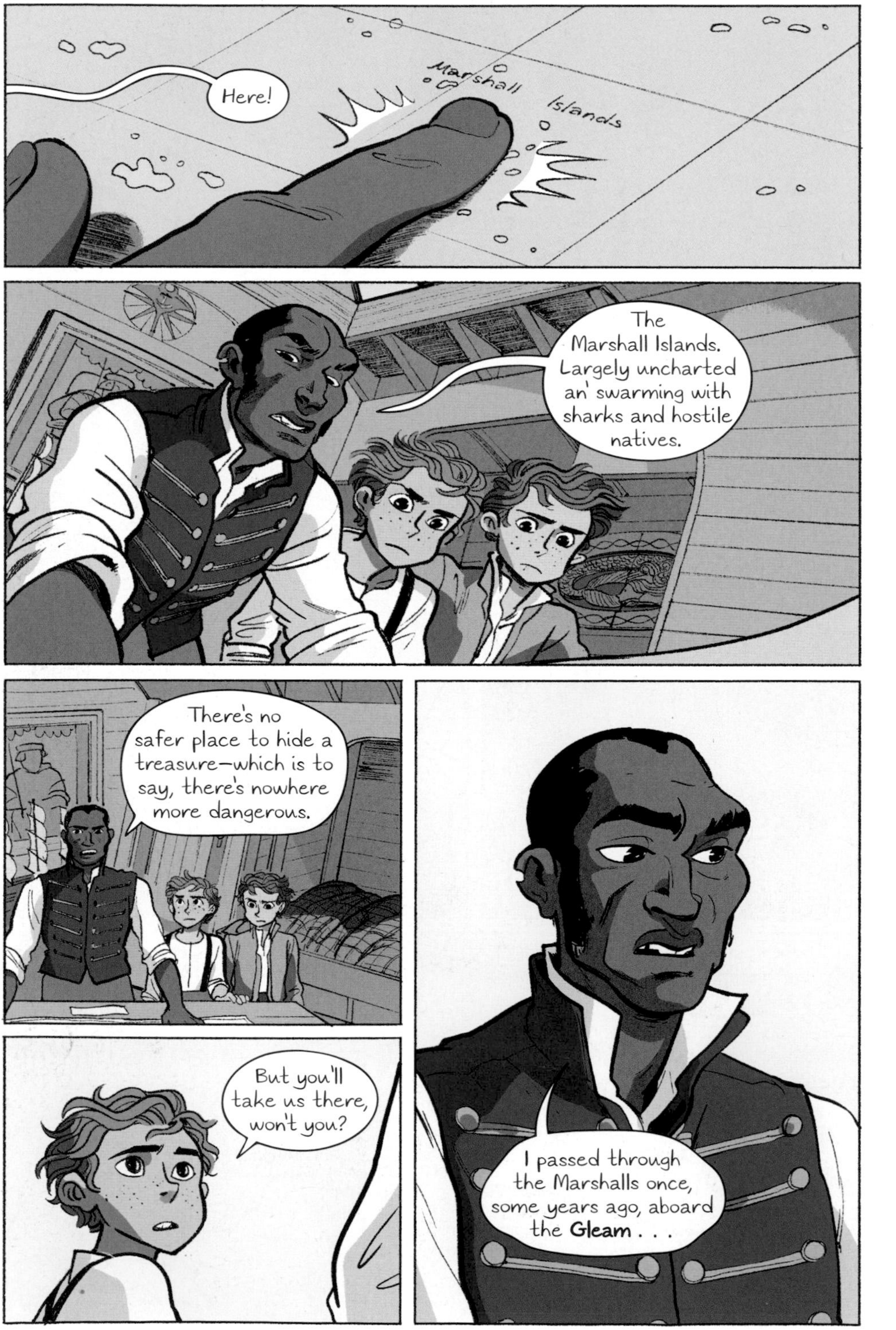
Here!
Marshall Islands
The Marshall Islands. Largely uncharted an' swarming with sharks and hostile natives.
There's no safer place to hide a treasure—which is to say, there's nowhere more dangerous.
But you'll take us there, won't you?
I passed through the Marshalls once, some years ago, aboard the **Gleam** . . .

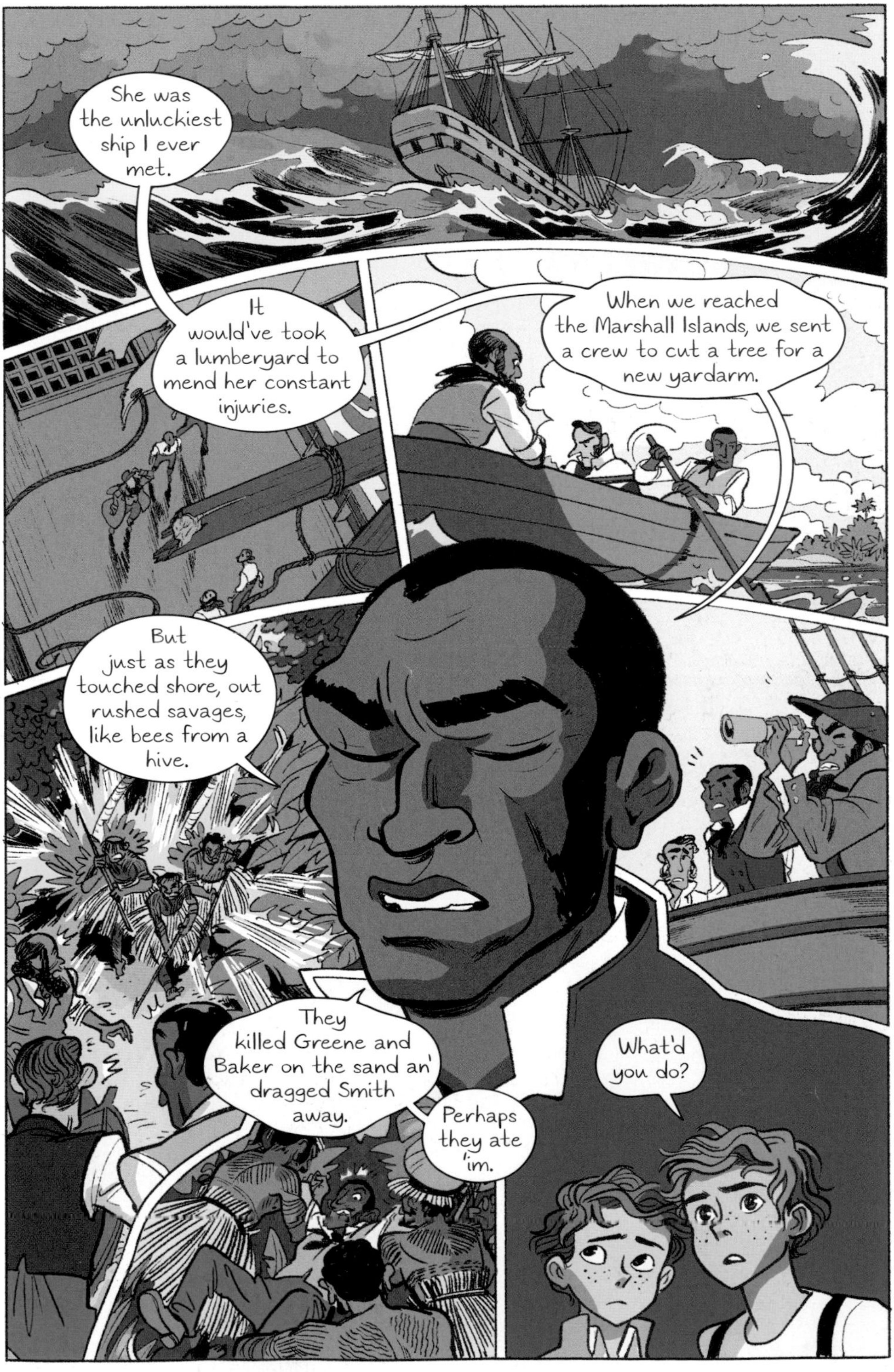
She was the unluckiest ship I ever met.
It would've took a lumberyard to mend her constant injuries.
When we reached the Marshall Islands, we sent a crew to cut a tree for a new yardarm.
But just as they touched shore, out rushed savages, like bees from a hive.
They killed Greene and Baker on the sand an' dragged Smith away.
Perhaps they ate 'im.
What'd you do?

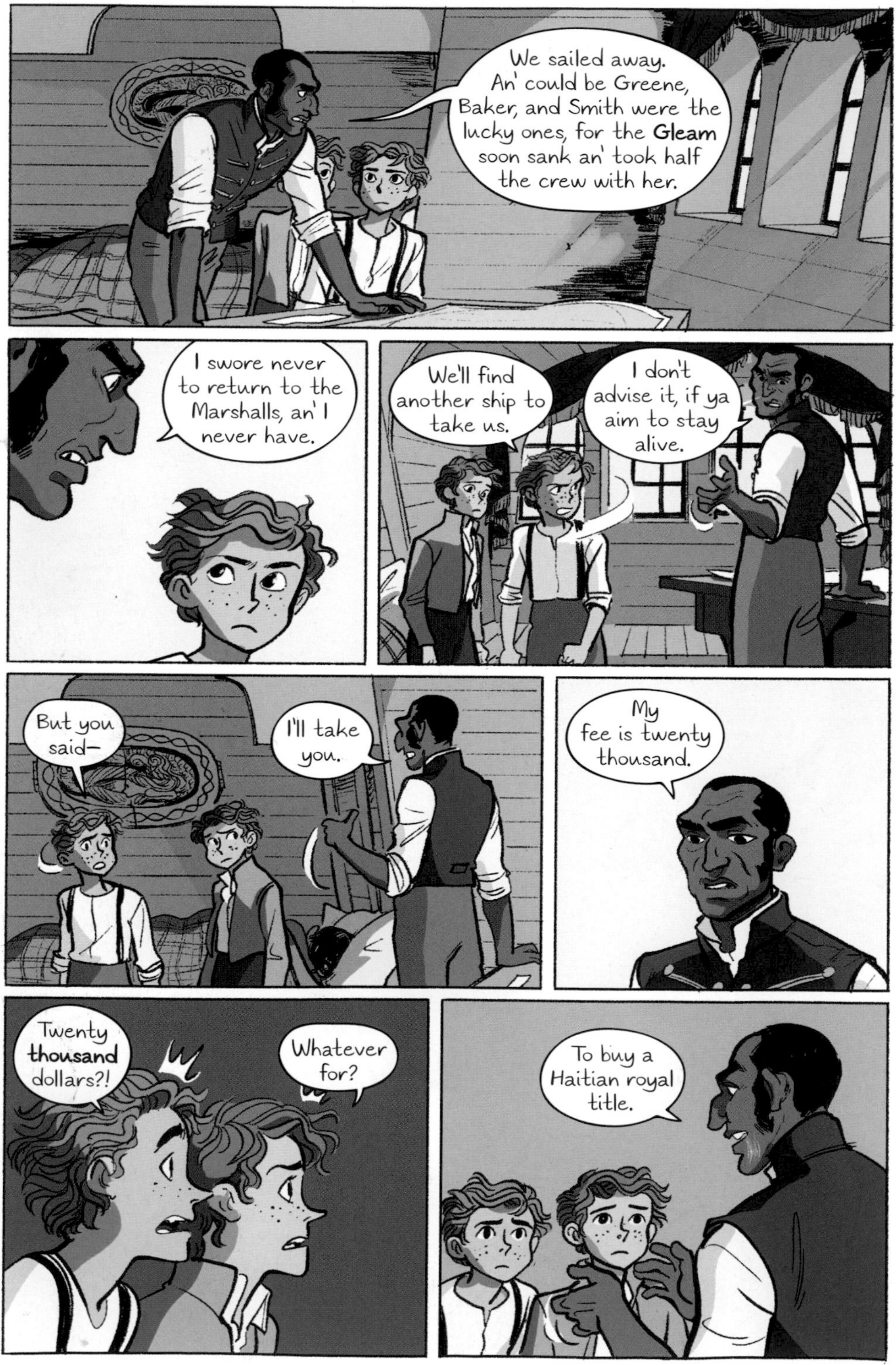
We sailed away. An' could be Greene, Baker, and Smith were the lucky ones, for the **Gleam** soon sank an' took half the crew with her.
I swore never to return to the Marshalls, an' I never have.
We'll find another ship to take us.
I don't advise it, if ya aim to stay alive.
But you said—
I'll take you.
My fee is twenty thousand.
Twenty **thousand** dollars?!
Whatever for?
To buy a Haitian royal title.

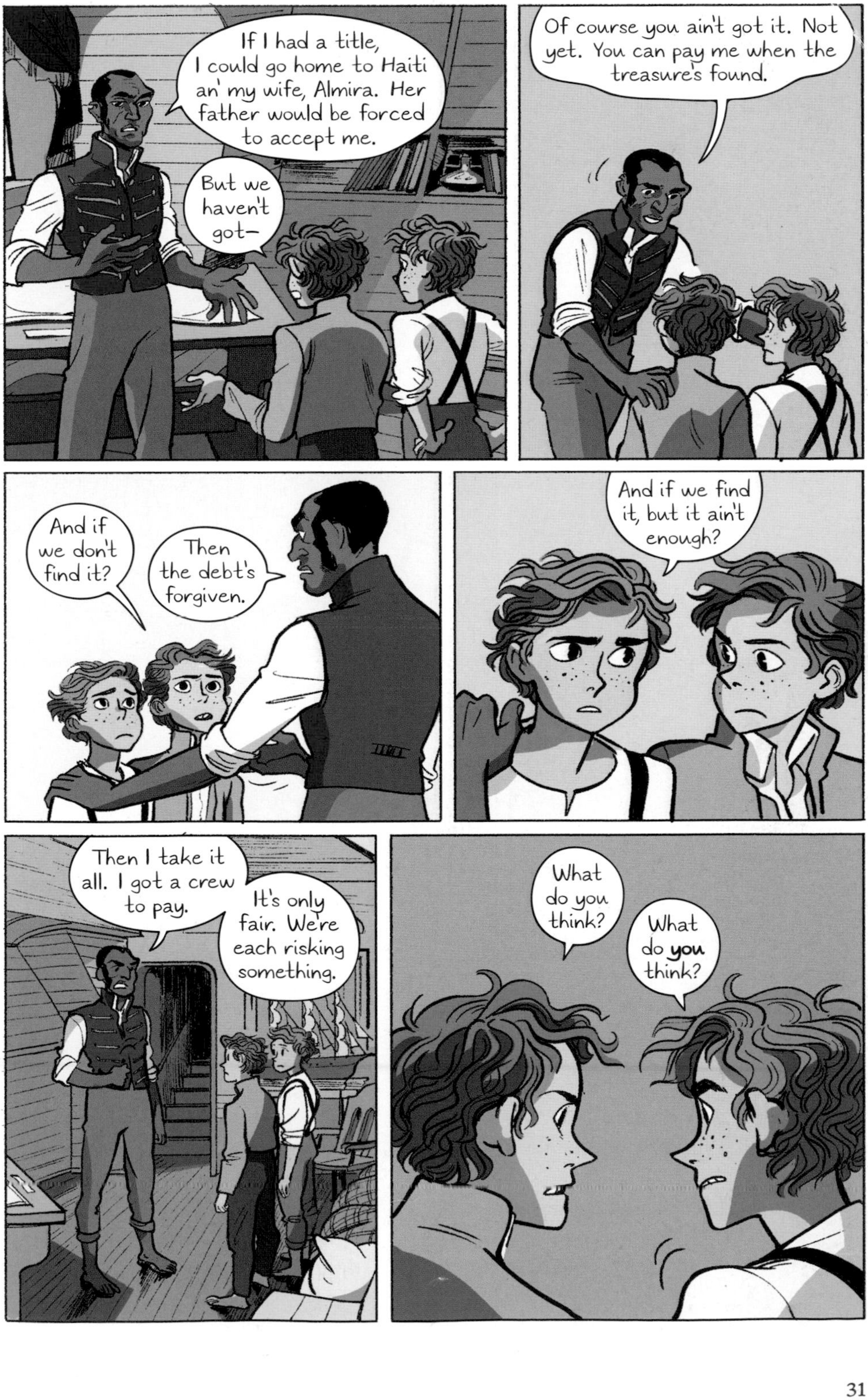
If I had a title, I could go home to Haiti an' my wife, Almira. Her father would be forced to accept me.
But we haven't got—
Of course you ain't got it. Not yet. You can pay me when the treasure's found.
And if we don't find it?
Then the debt's forgiven.
And if we find it, but it ain't enough?
Then I take it all. I got a crew to pay.
It's only fair. We're each risking something.
What do you think?
What do **you** think?

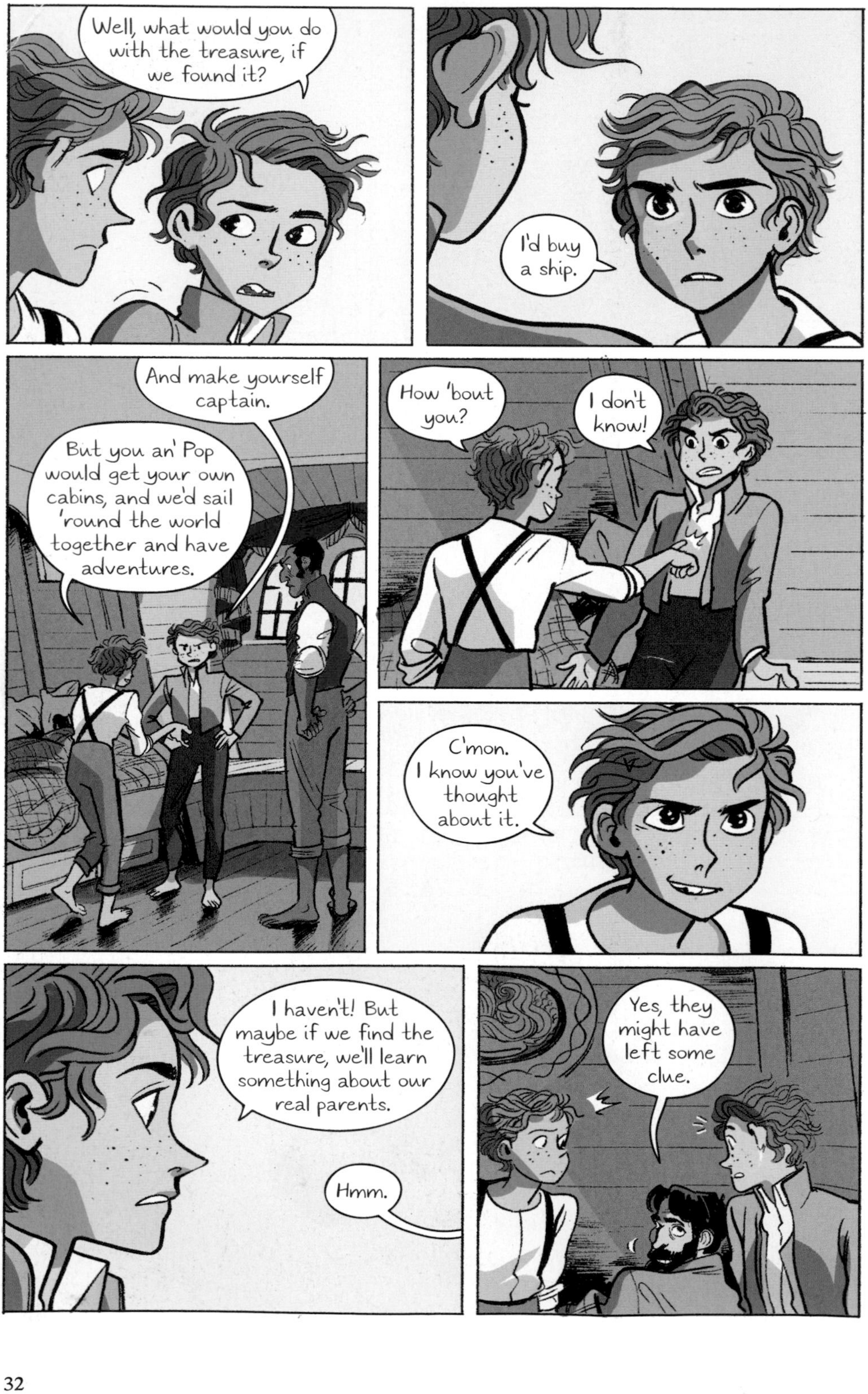

Well, what would you do with the treasure, if we found it?
I'd buy a ship.
And make yourself captain.
But you an' Pop would get your own cabins, and we'd sail 'round the world together and have adventures.
How 'bout you?
I don't know!
C'mon. I know you've thought about it.
I haven't! But maybe if we find the treasure, we'll learn something about our real parents.
Hmm.
Yes, they might have left some clue.

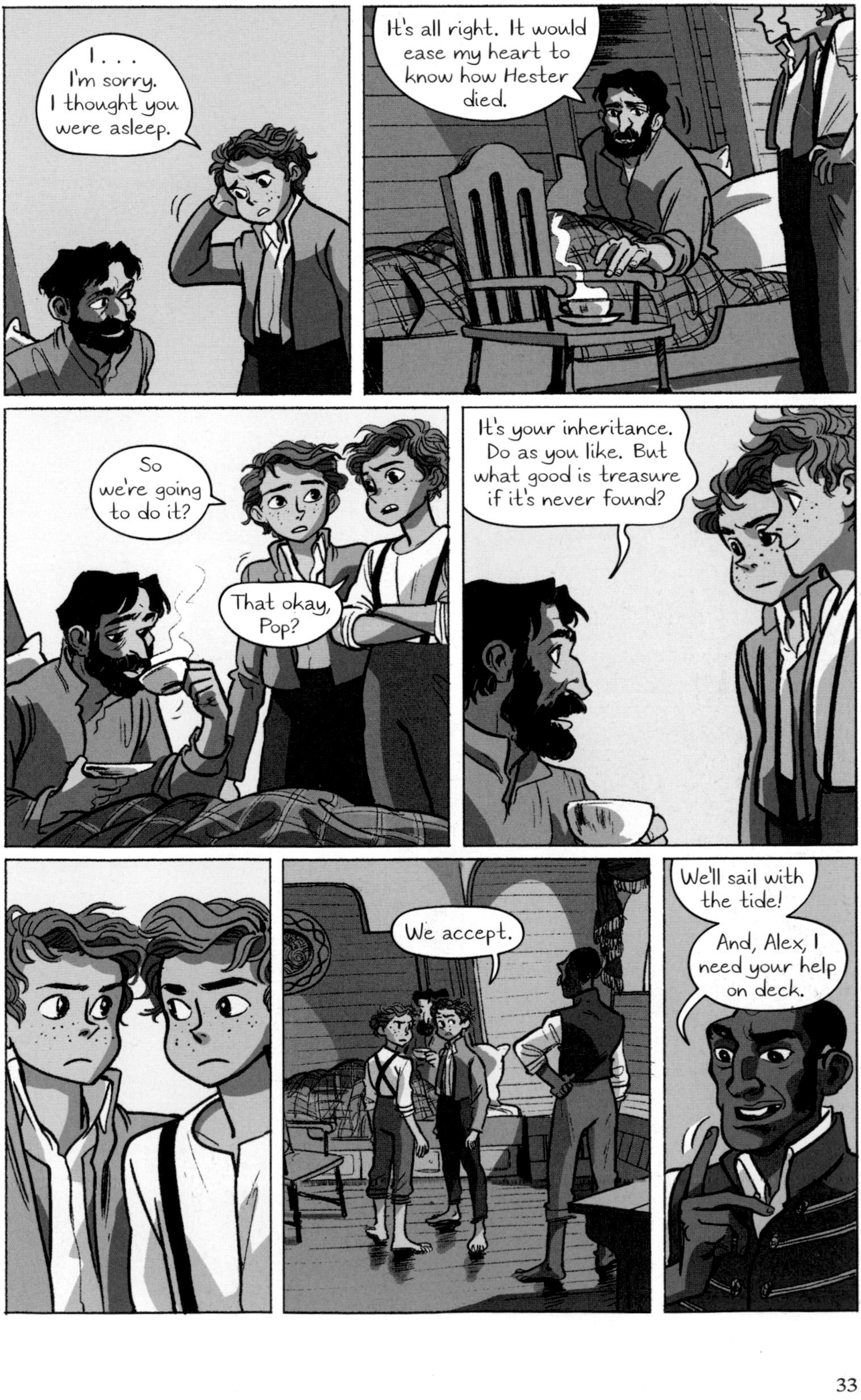
I . . .
I'm sorry.
I thought you
were asleep.
It's all right. It would
ease my heart to
know how Hester
died.
So
we're going
to do it?
That okay,
Pop?
It's your inheritance.
Do as you like. But
what good is treasure
if it's never found?
We accept.
We'll sail with
the tide!
And, Alex, I
need your help
on deck.

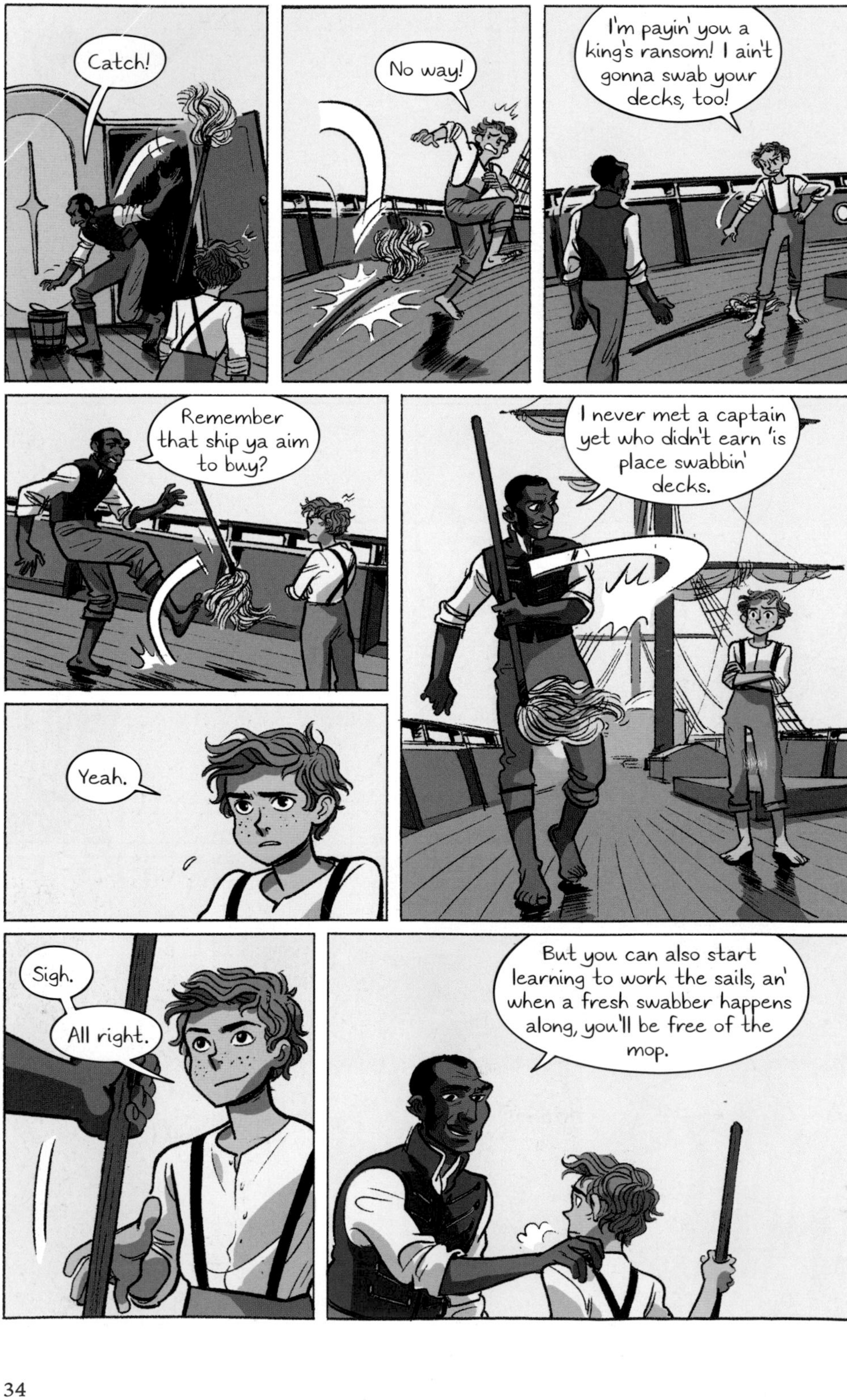
Catch!
No way!
I'm payin' you a king's ransom! I ain't gonna swab your decks, too!
Remember that ship ya aim to buy?
I never met a captain yet who didn't earn 'is place swabbin' decks.
Yeah.
Sigh.
All right.
But you can also start learning to work the sails, an' when a fresh swabber happens along, you'll be free of the mop.

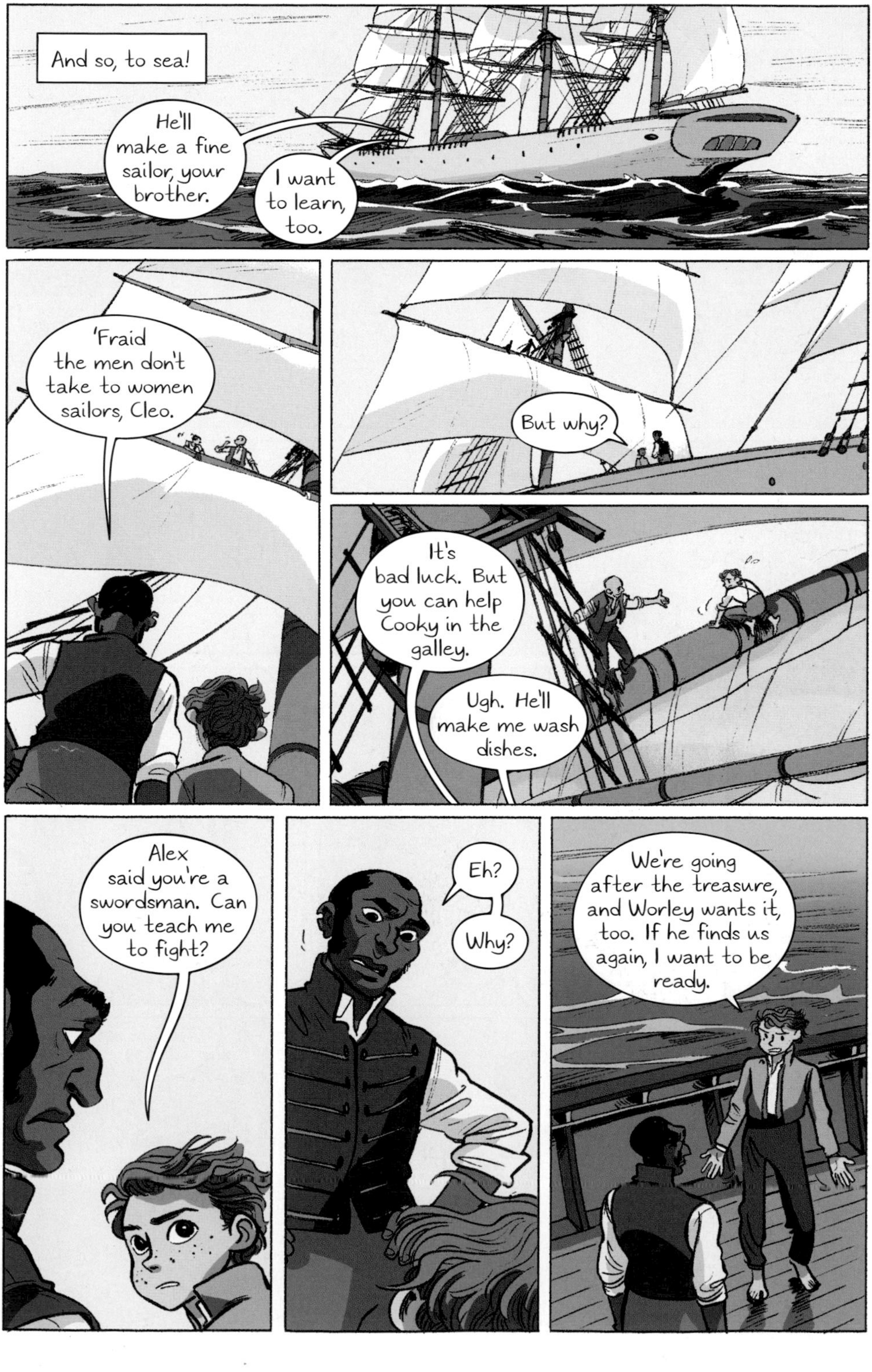
And so, to sea!
He'll make a fine sailor, your brother.
I want to learn, too.
'Fraid the men don't take to women sailors, Cleo.
But why?
It's bad luck. But you can help Cooky in the galley.
Ugh. He'll make me wash dishes.
Alex said you're a swordsman. Can you teach me to fight?
Eh?
Why?
We're going after the treasure, and Worley wants it, too. If he finds us again, I want to be ready.

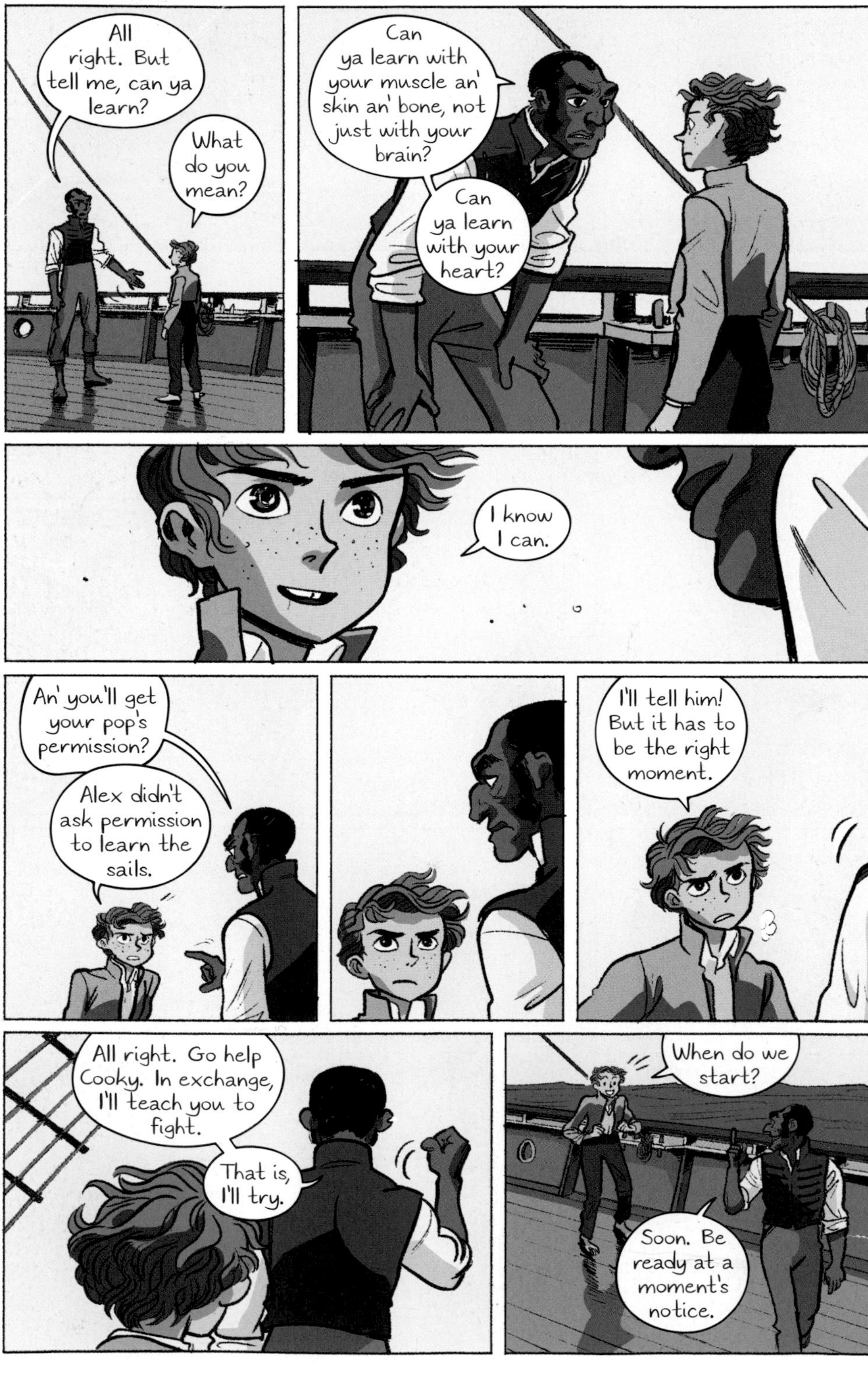
All right. But tell me, can ya learn?
What do you mean?
Can ya learn with your muscle an' skin an' bone, not just with your brain?
Can ya learn with your heart?
I know I can.
An' you'll get your pop's permission?
Alex didn't ask permission to learn the sails.
I'll tell him! But it has to be the right moment.
All right. Go help Cooky. In exchange, I'll teach you to fight.
That is, I'll try.
When do we start?
Soon. Be ready at a moment's notice.

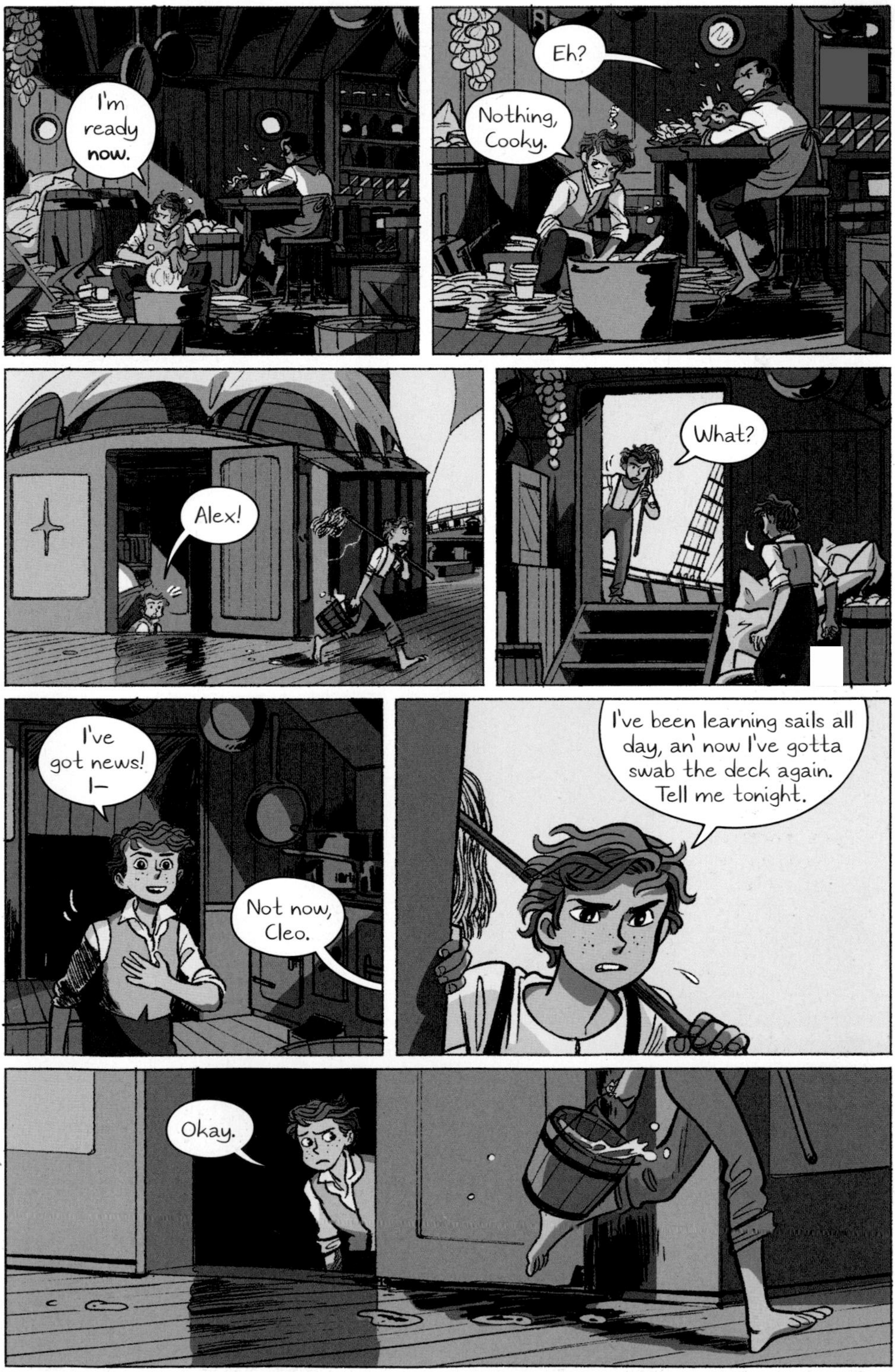
I'm ready now.
Eh?
Nothing, Cooky.
Alex!
What?
I've got news! I—
Not now, Cleo.
I've been learning sails all day, an' now I've gotta swab the deck again. Tell me tonight.
Okay.

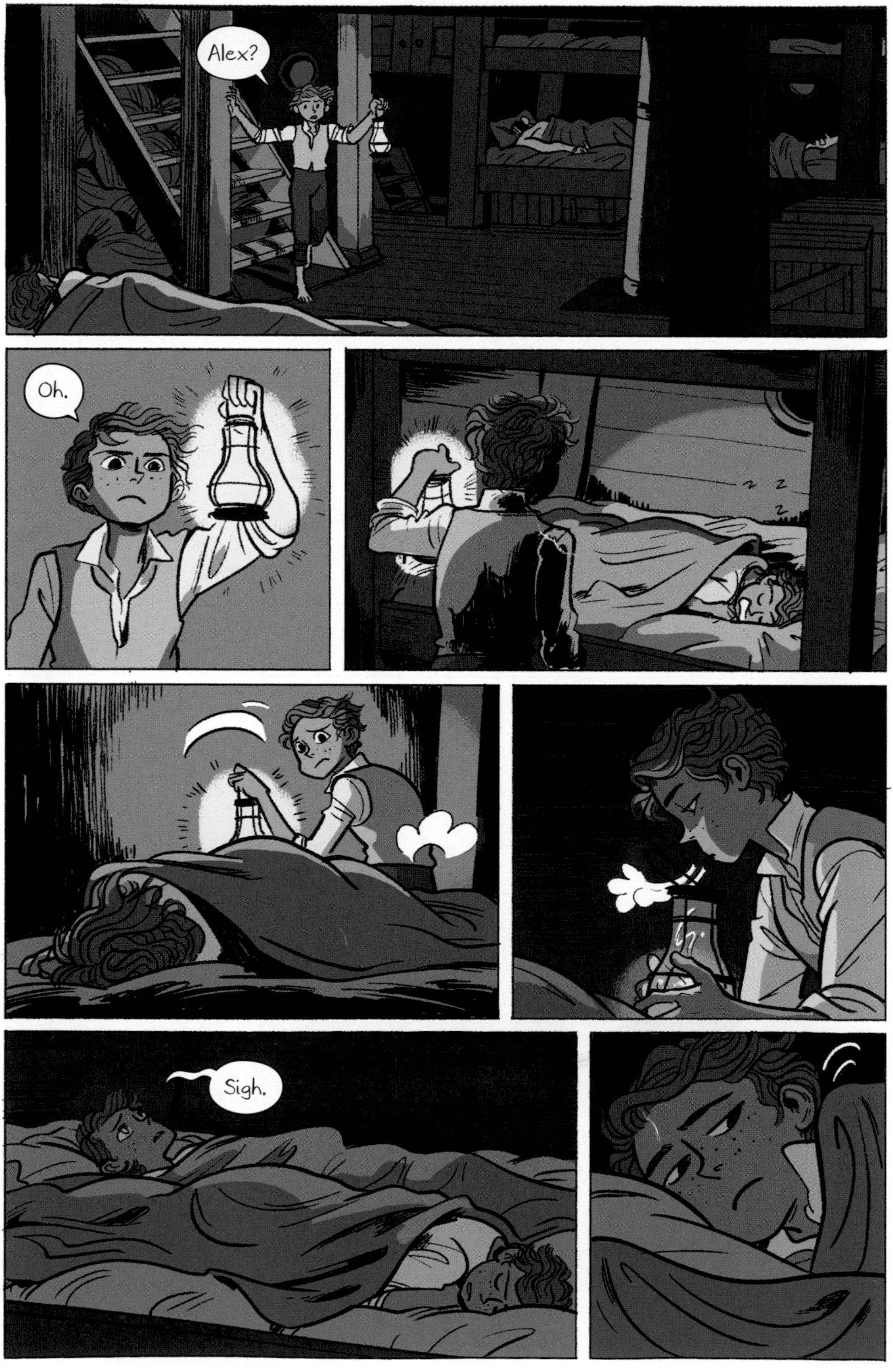
Alex?
Oh.
Sigh.

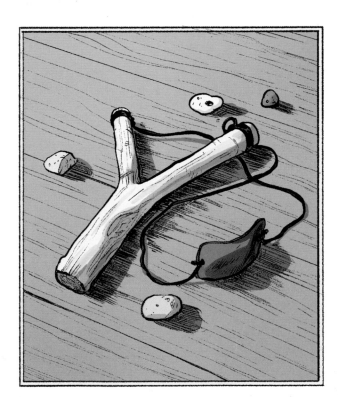

CHAPTER TWO
MERCY

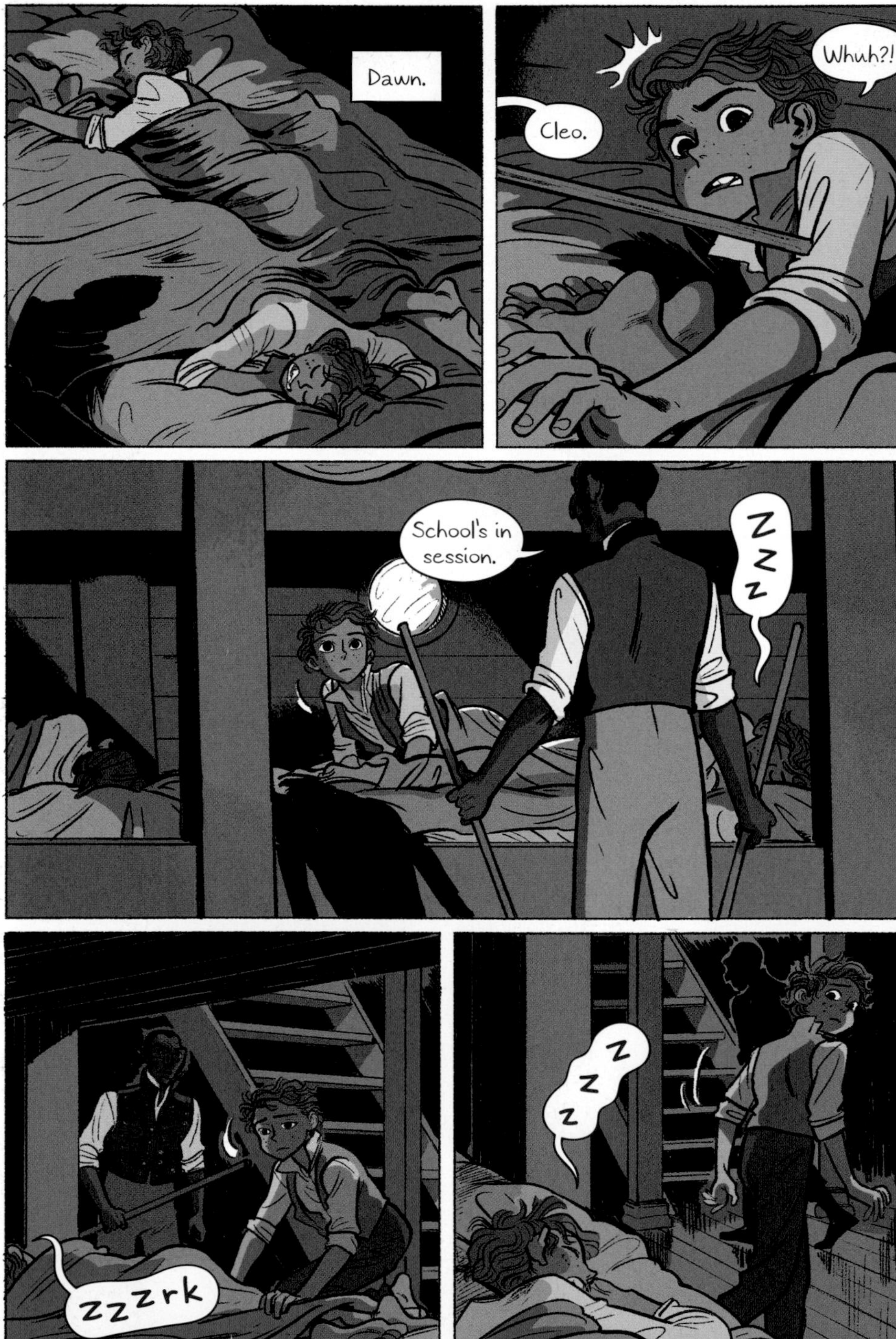
Dawn.
Cleo.
Whuh?!
School's in session.
ZZZ
zzzrk
ZZZ

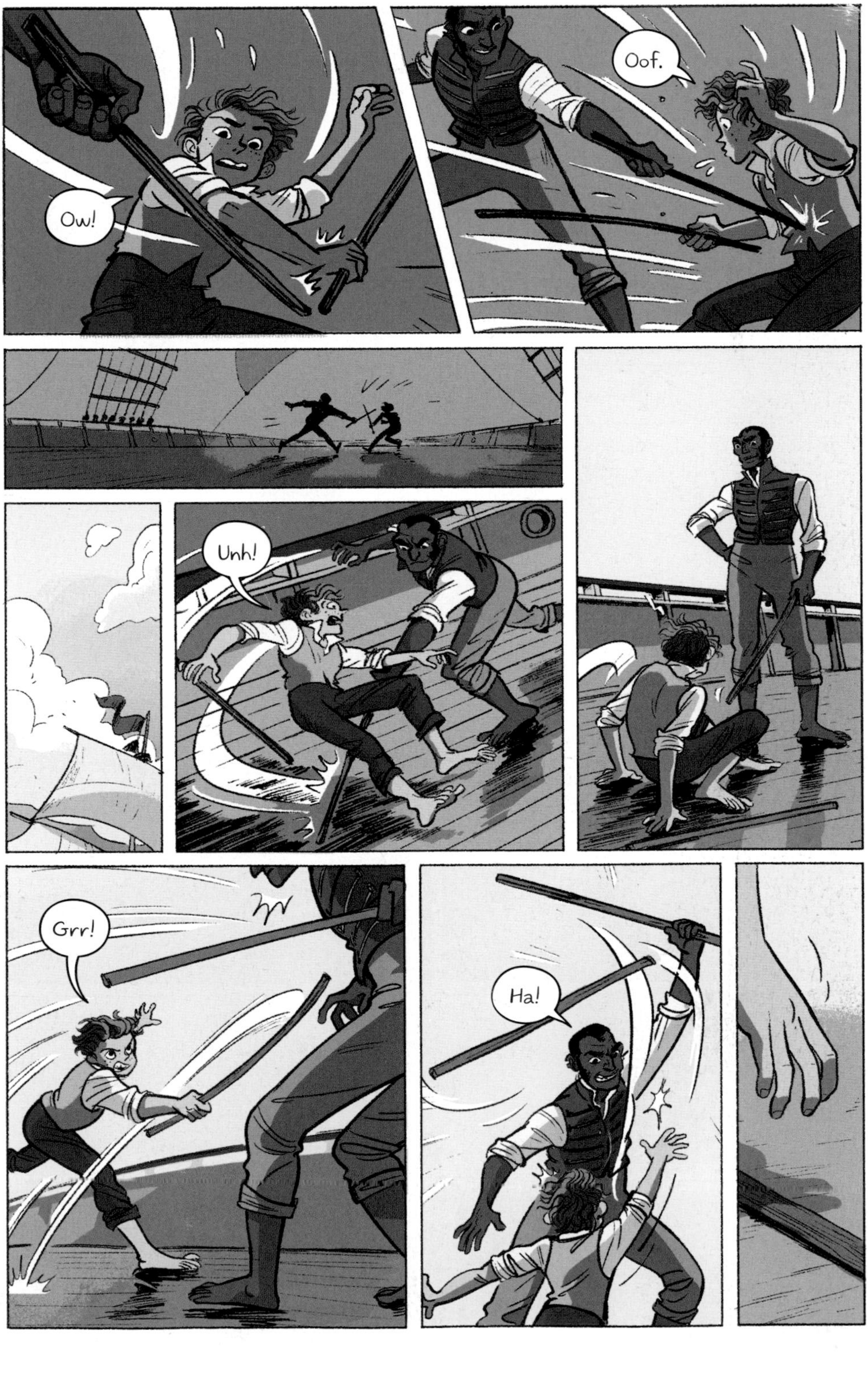
Ow!
Oof.
Unh!
Grr!
Ha!

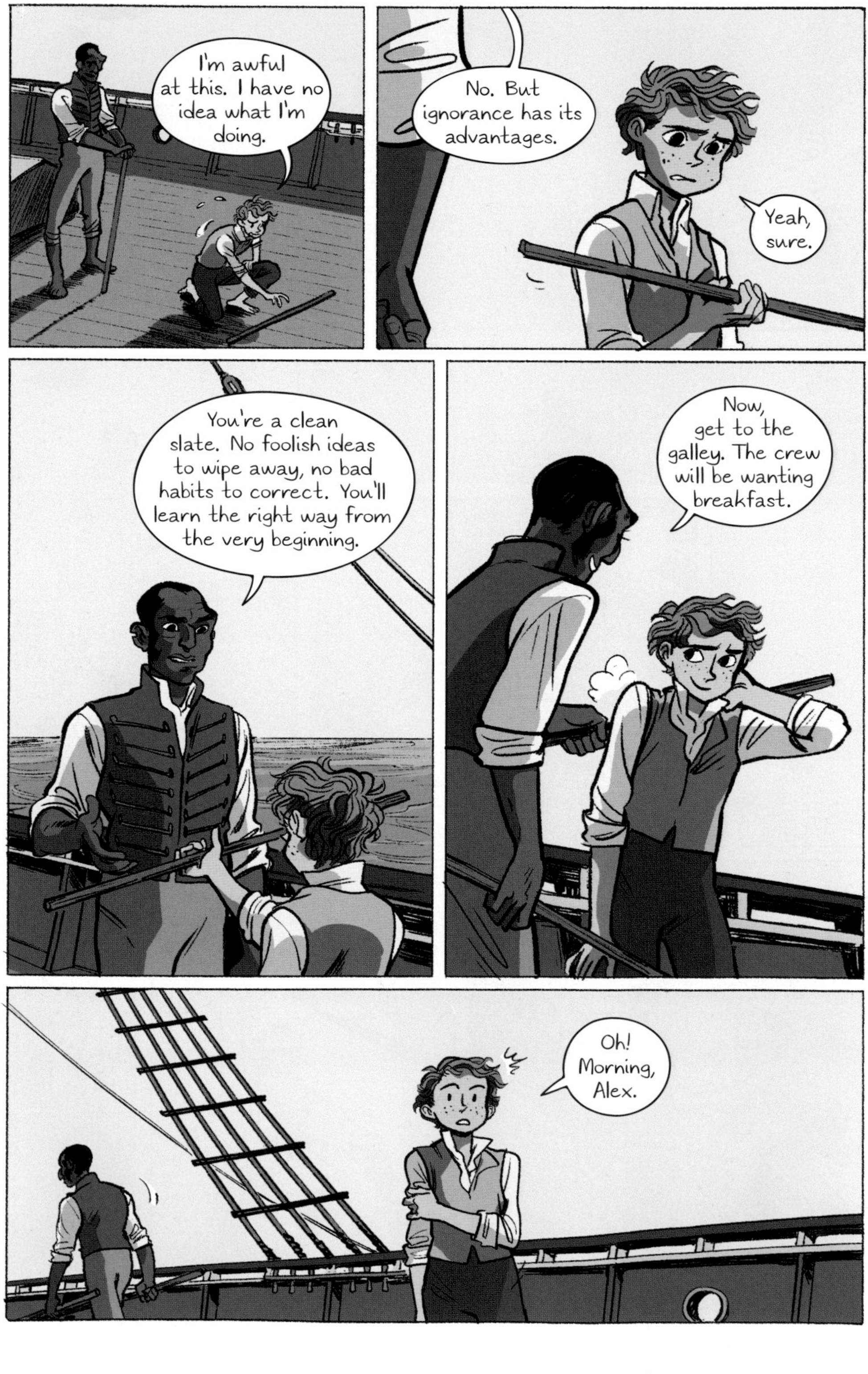
I'm awful at this. I have no idea what I'm doing.
No. But ignorance has its advantages.
Yeah, sure.
You're a clean slate. No foolish ideas to wipe away, no bad habits to correct. You'll learn the right way from the very beginning.
Now, get to the galley. The crew will be wanting breakfast.
Oh! Morning, Alex.

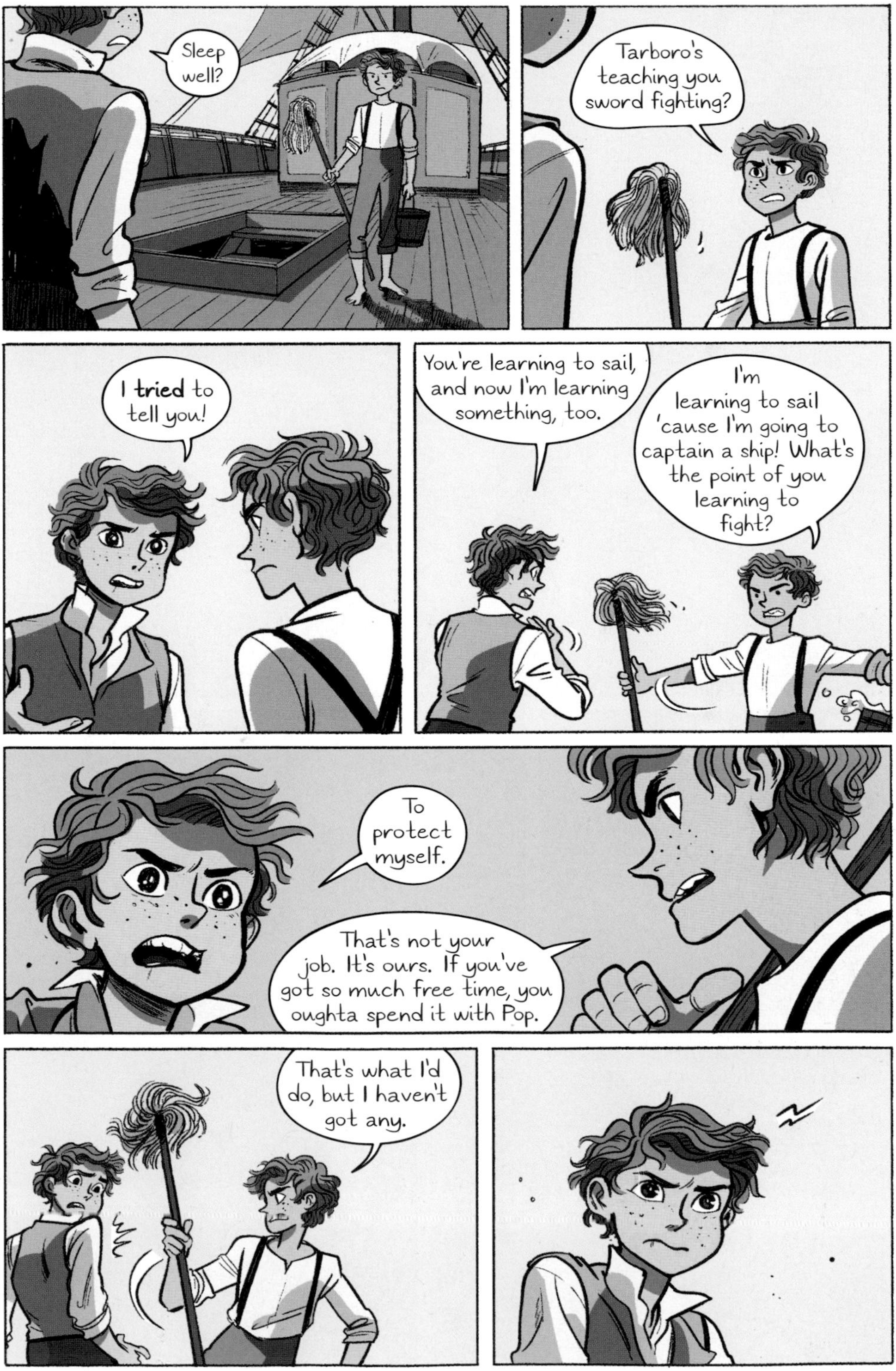
Sleep well?
Tarboro's teaching you sword fighting?
I **tried** to tell you!
You're learning to sail, and now I'm learning something, too.
I'm learning to sail 'cause I'm going to captain a ship! What's the point of you learning to fight?
To protect myself.
That's not your job. It's ours. If you've got so much free time, you oughta spend it with Pop.
That's what I'd do, but I haven't got any.

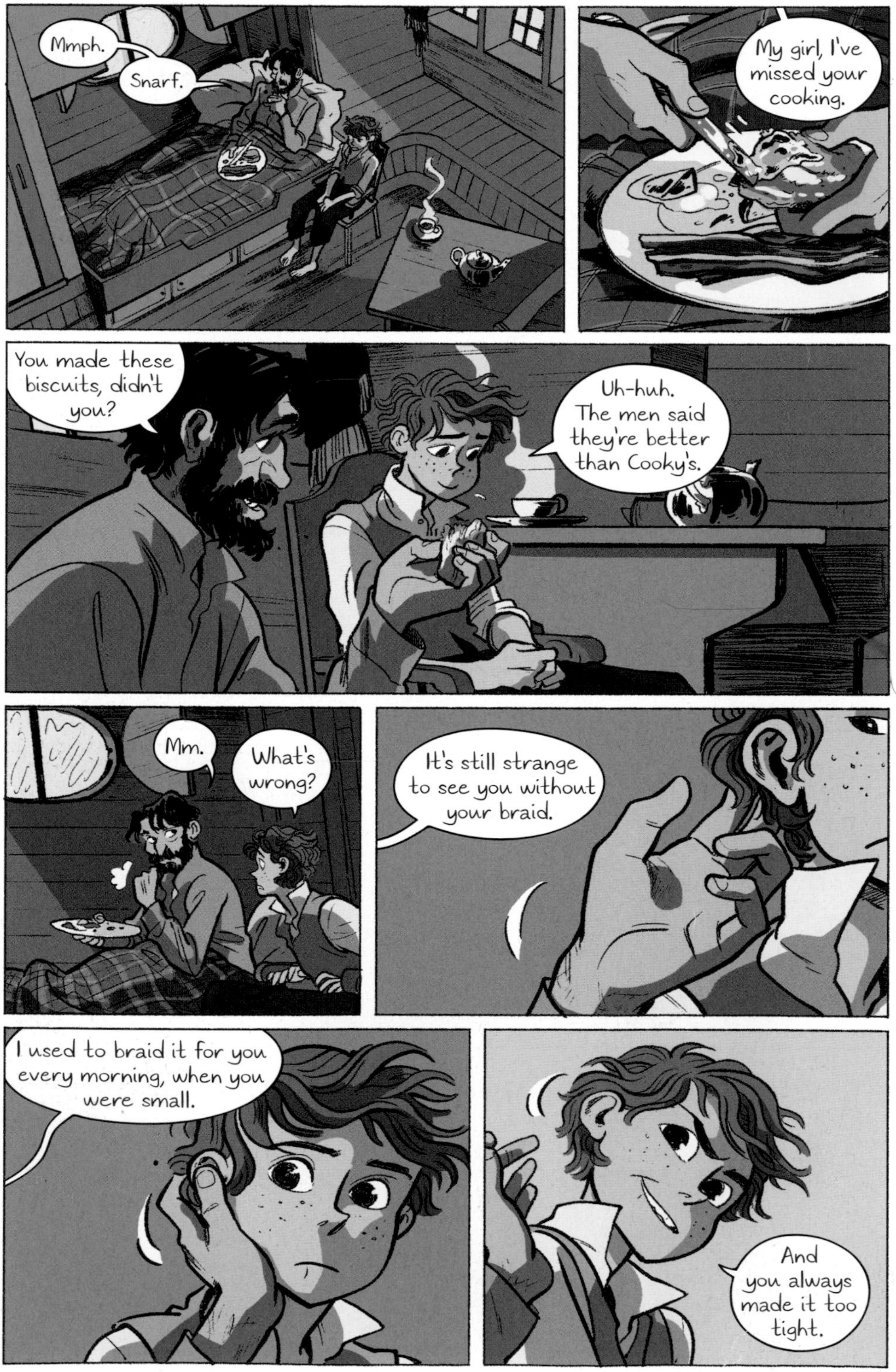
Mmph.
Snarf.
My girl, I've missed your cooking.
You made these biscuits, didn't you?
Uh-huh. The men said they're better than Cooky's.
Mm.
What's wrong?
It's still strange to see you without your braid.
I used to braid it for you every morning, when you were small.
And you always made it too tight.

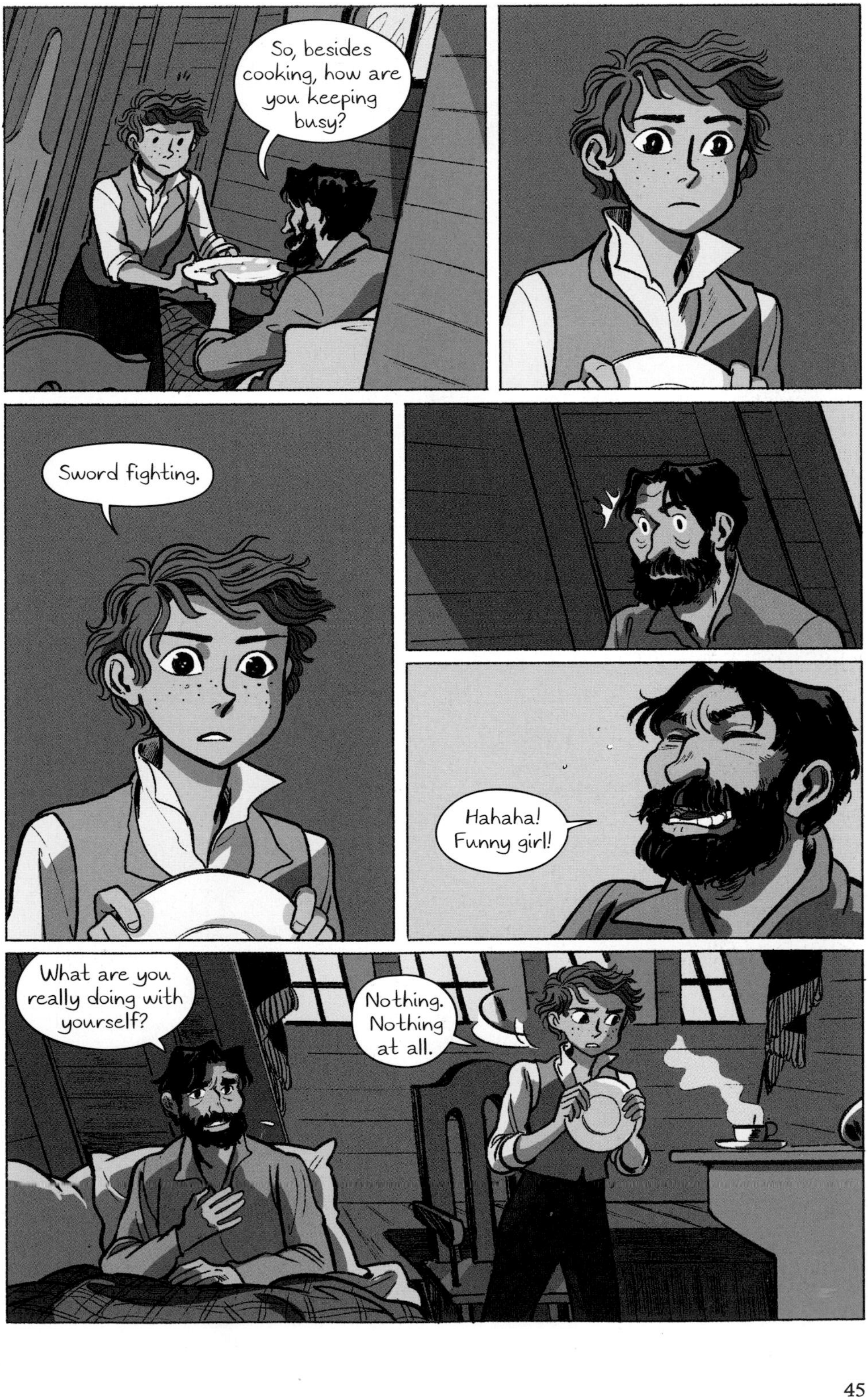
So, besides cooking, how are you keeping busy?
Sword fighting.
Hahaha! Funny girl!
What are you really doing with yourself?
Nothing. Nothing at all.

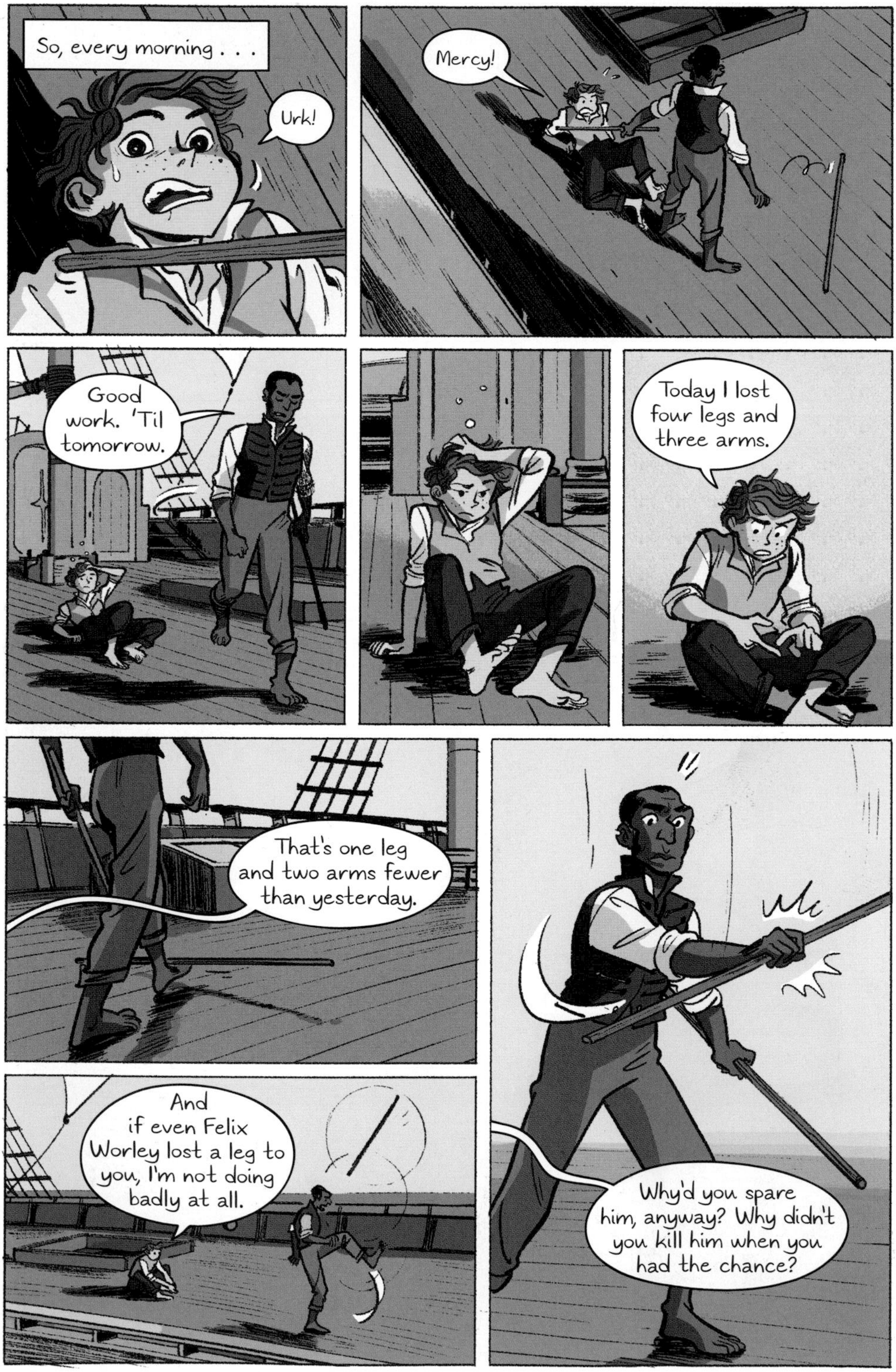
So, every morning . . .
Urk!
Mercy!
Good work. 'Til tomorrow.
Today I lost four legs and three arms.
That's one leg and two arms fewer than yesterday.
And if even Felix Worley lost a leg to you, I'm not doing badly at all.
Why'd you spare him, anyway? Why didn't you kill him when you had the chance?

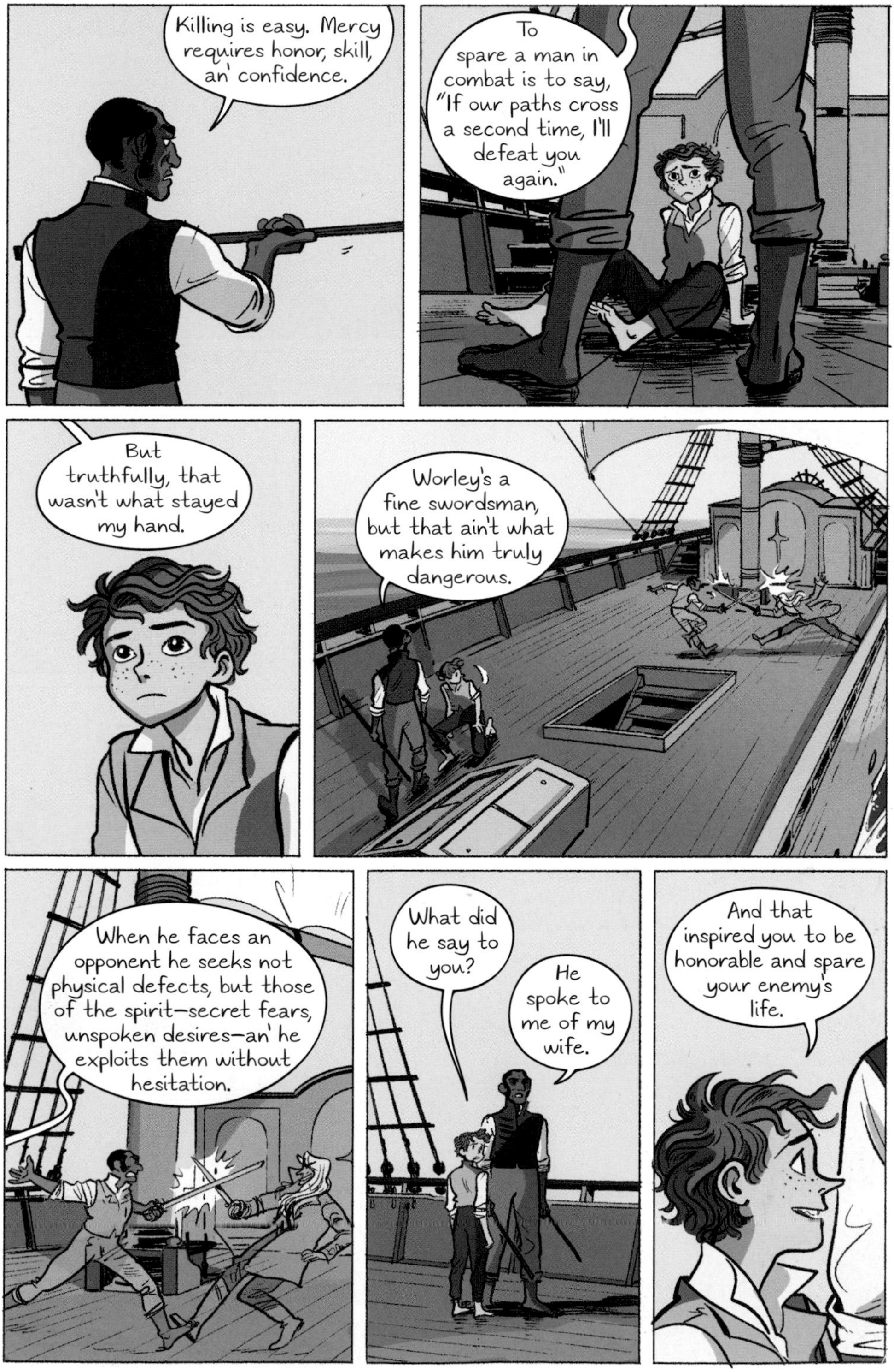
Killing is easy. Mercy requires honor, skill, an' confidence.
To spare a man in combat is to say, "If our paths cross a second time, I'll defeat you again."
But truthfully, that wasn't what stayed my hand.
Worley's a fine swordsman, but that ain't what makes him truly dangerous.
When he faces an opponent he seeks not physical defects, but those of the spirit—secret fears, unspoken desires—an' he exploits them without hesitation.
What did he say to you?
He spoke to me of my wife.
And that inspired you to be honorable and spare your enemy's life.

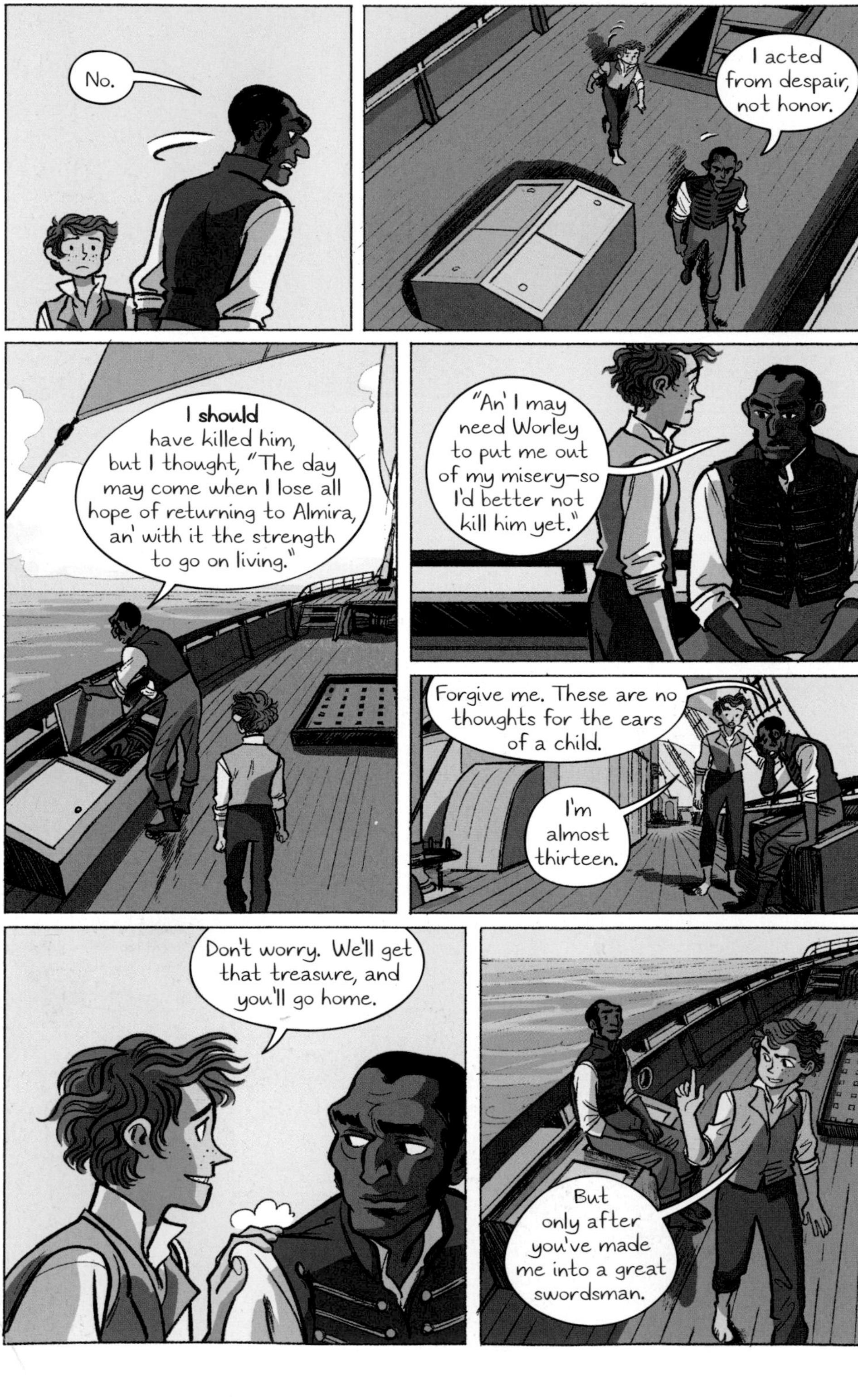
No.
I acted from despair, not honor.
I should have killed him, but I thought, "The day may come when I lose all hope of returning to Almira, an' with it the strength to go on living."
"An' I may need Worley to put me out of my misery—so I'd better not kill him yet."
Forgive me. These are no thoughts for the ears of a child.
I'm almost thirteen.
Don't worry. We'll get that treasure, and you'll go home.
But only after you've made me into a great swordsman.

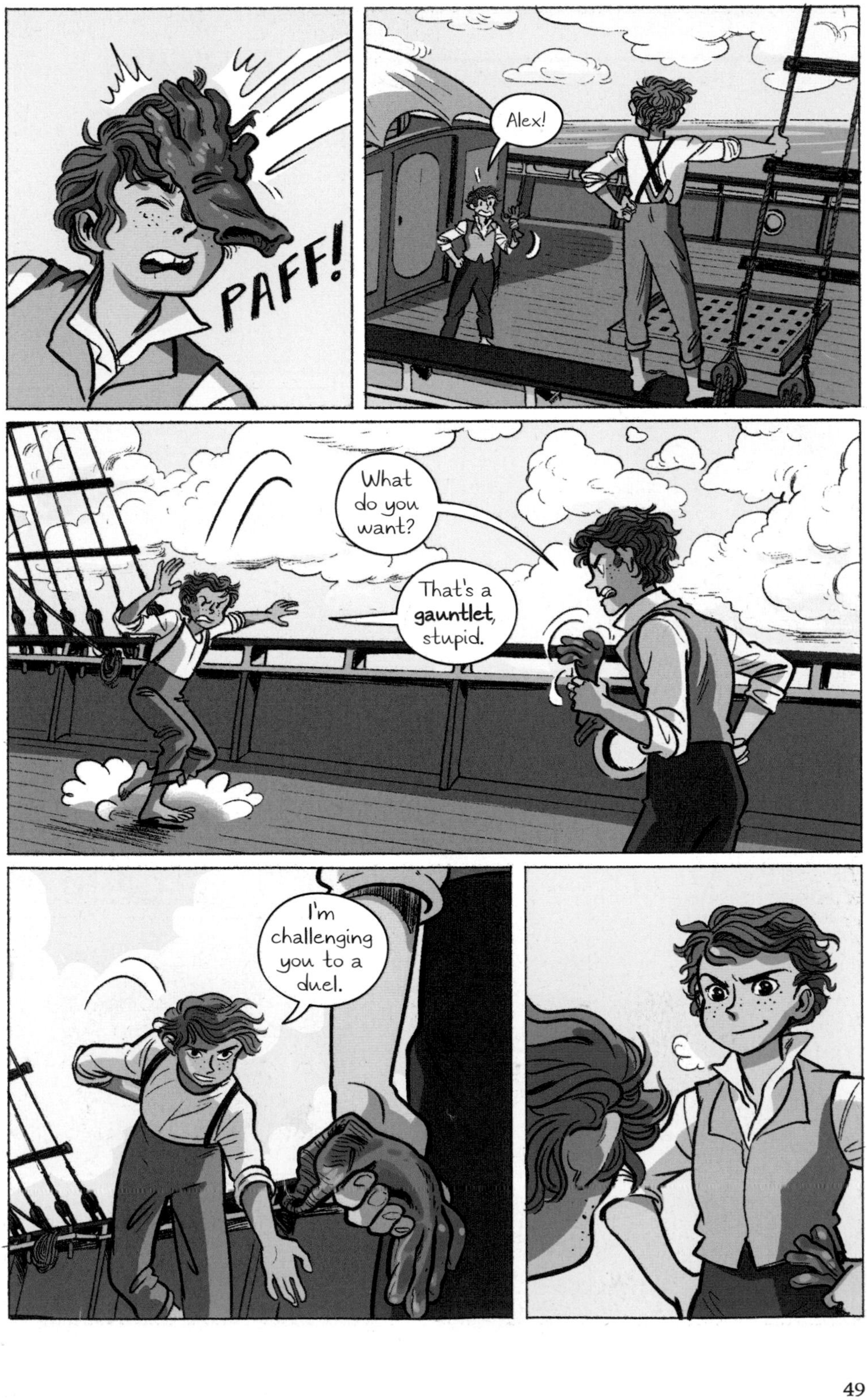
PAFF!
Alex!
What do you want?
That's a **gauntlet**, stupid.
I'm challenging you to a duel.

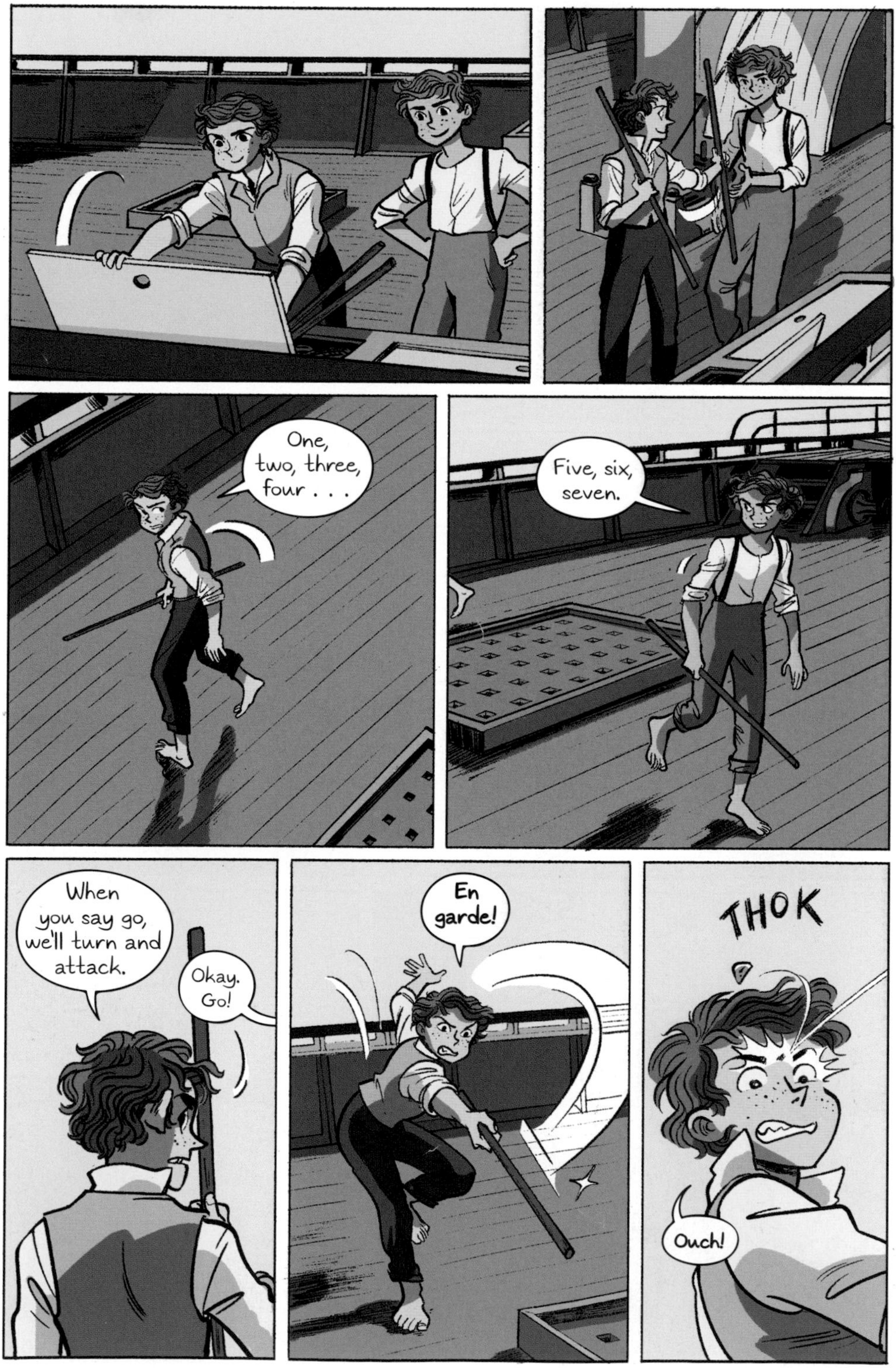
One, two, three, four . . .
Five, six, seven.
When you say go, we'll turn and attack.
Okay. Go!
En garde!
THOK
Ouch!

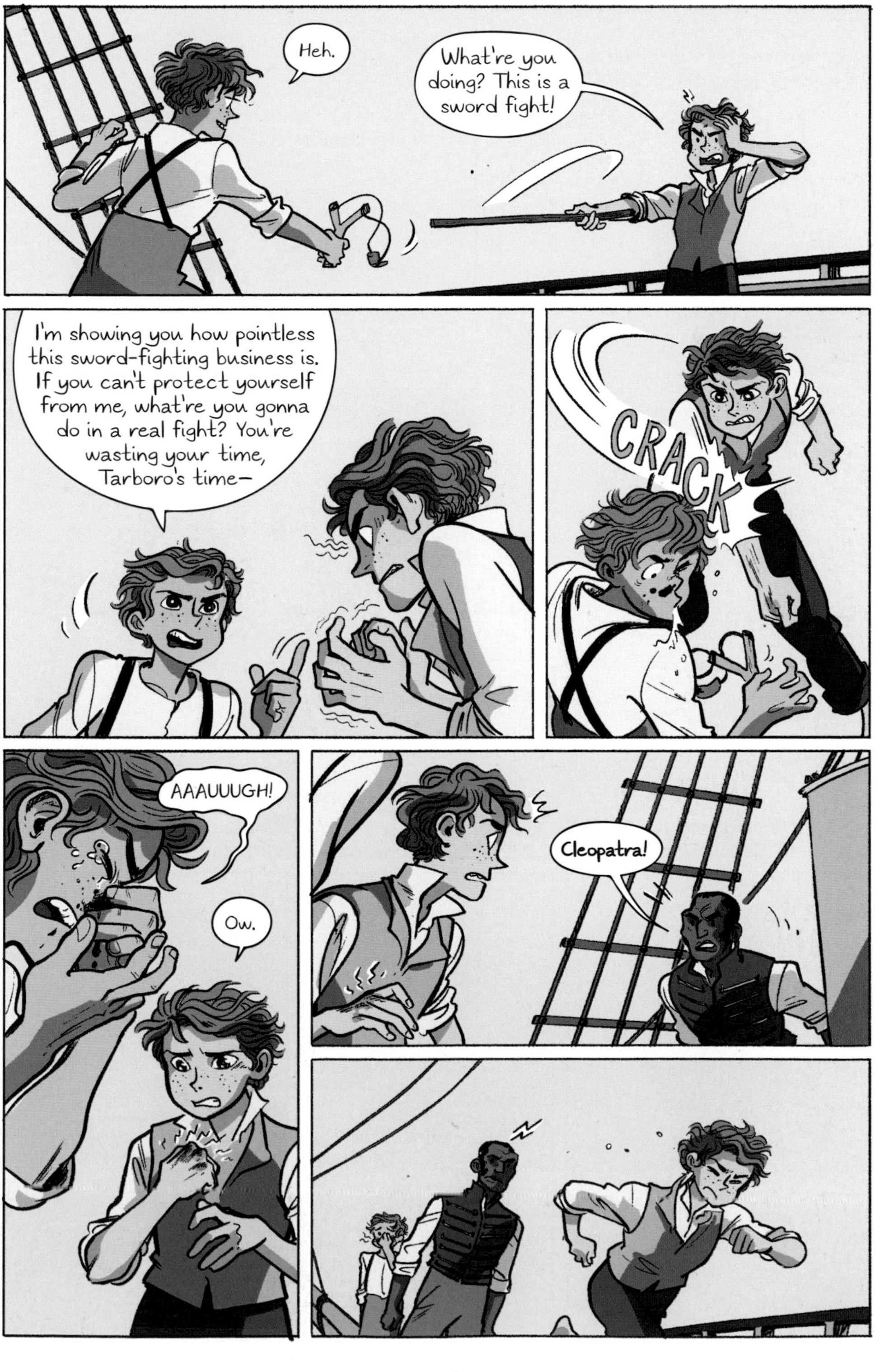

Heh.
What're you doing? This is a sword fight!
I'm showing you how pointless this sword-fighting business is. If you can't protect yourself from me, what're you gonna do in a real fight? You're wasting your time, Tarboro's time—
CRACK
AAAUUUGH!
Ow.
Cleopatra!

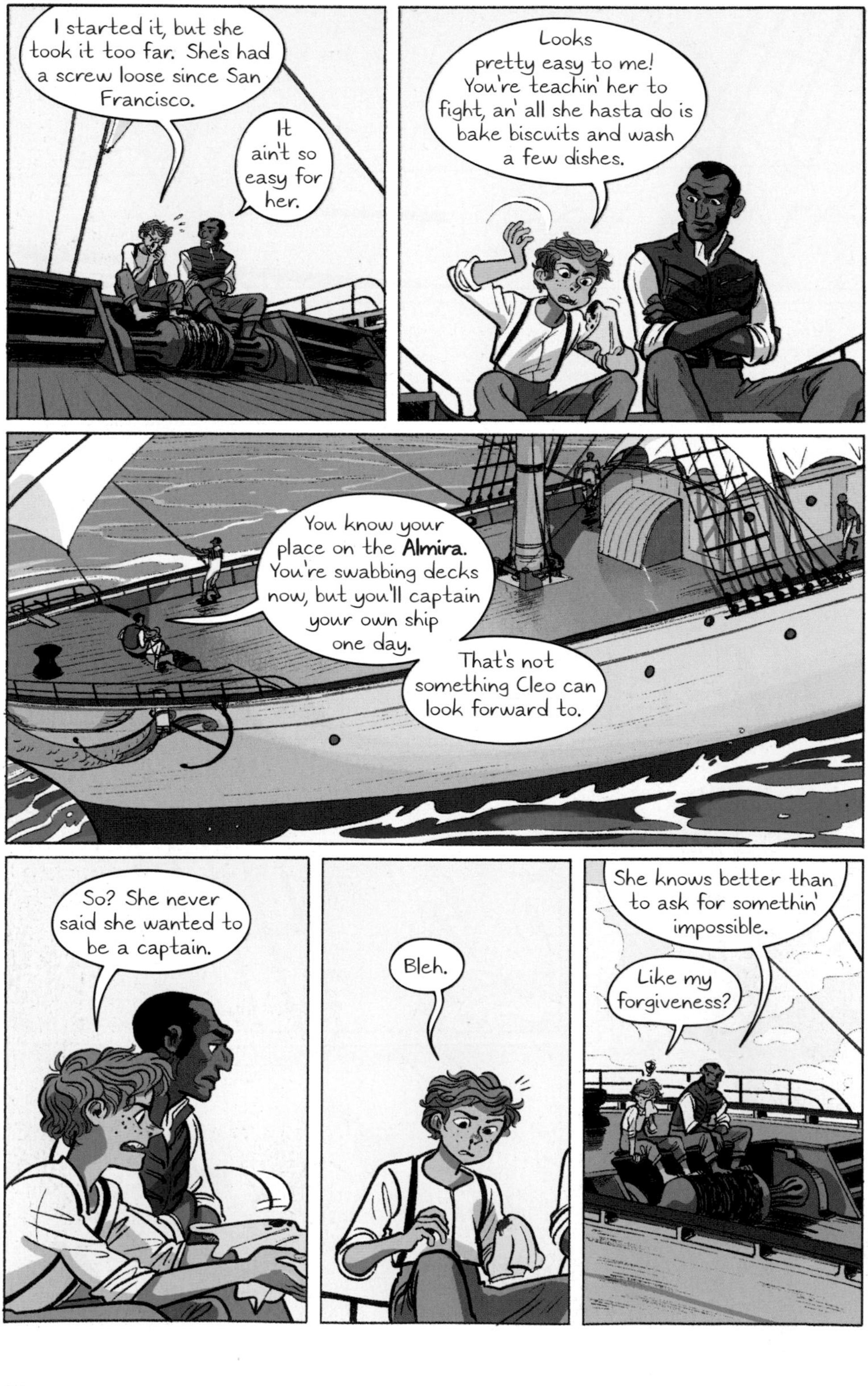
I started it, but she took it too far. She's had a screw loose since San Francisco.
It ain't so easy for her.
Looks pretty easy to me! You're teachin' her to fight, an' all she hasta do is bake biscuits and wash a few dishes.
You know your place on the **Almira**. You're swabbing decks now, but you'll captain your own ship one day.
That's not something Cleo can look forward to.
So? She never said she wanted to be a captain.
Bleh.
She knows better than to ask for somethin' impossible.
Like my forgiveness?

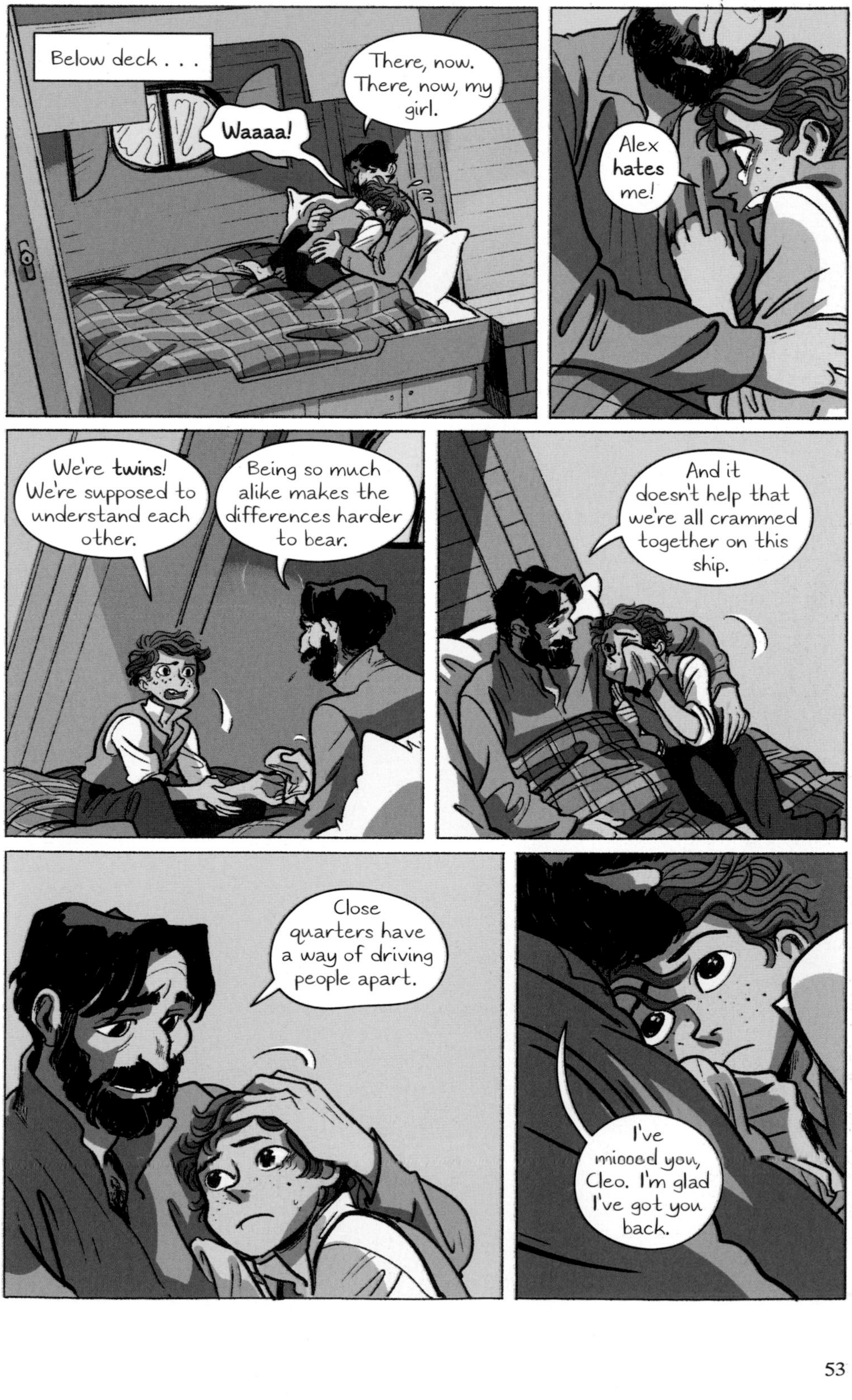
Below deck . . .
Waaaa!
There, now. There, now, my girl.
Alex hates me!
We're twins! We're supposed to understand each other.
Being so much alike makes the differences harder to bear.
And it doesn't help that we're all crammed together on this ship.
Close quarters have a way of driving people apart.
I've mioood you, Cleo. I'm glad I've got you back.

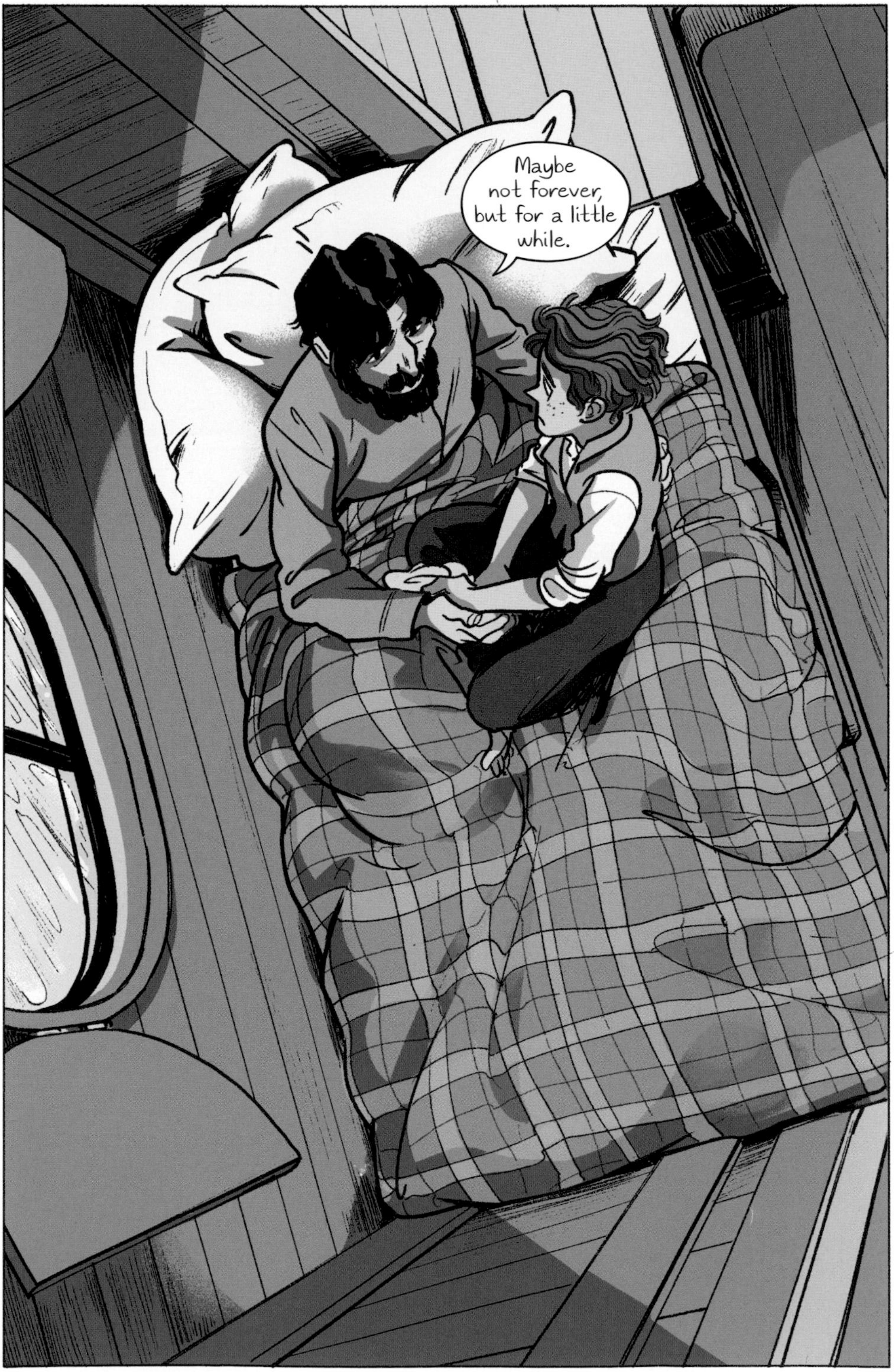
Maybe not forever, but for a little while.

CHAPTER THREE
B IS FOR BRANDEL

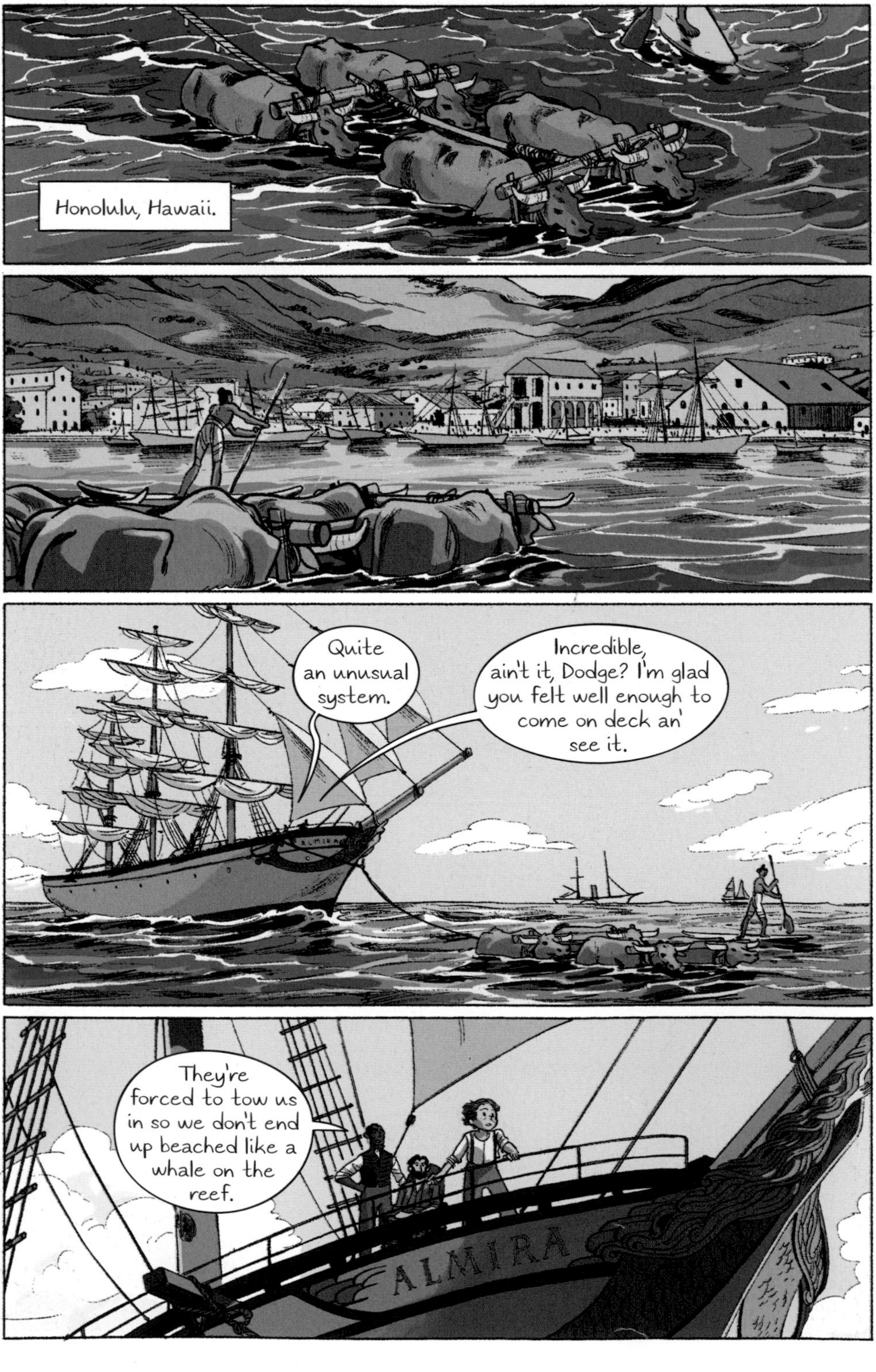
Honolulu, Hawaii.
Quite an unusual system.
Incredible, ain't it, Dodge? I'm glad you felt well enough to come on deck an' see it.
They're forced to tow us in so we don't end up beached like a whale on the reef.
ALMIRA

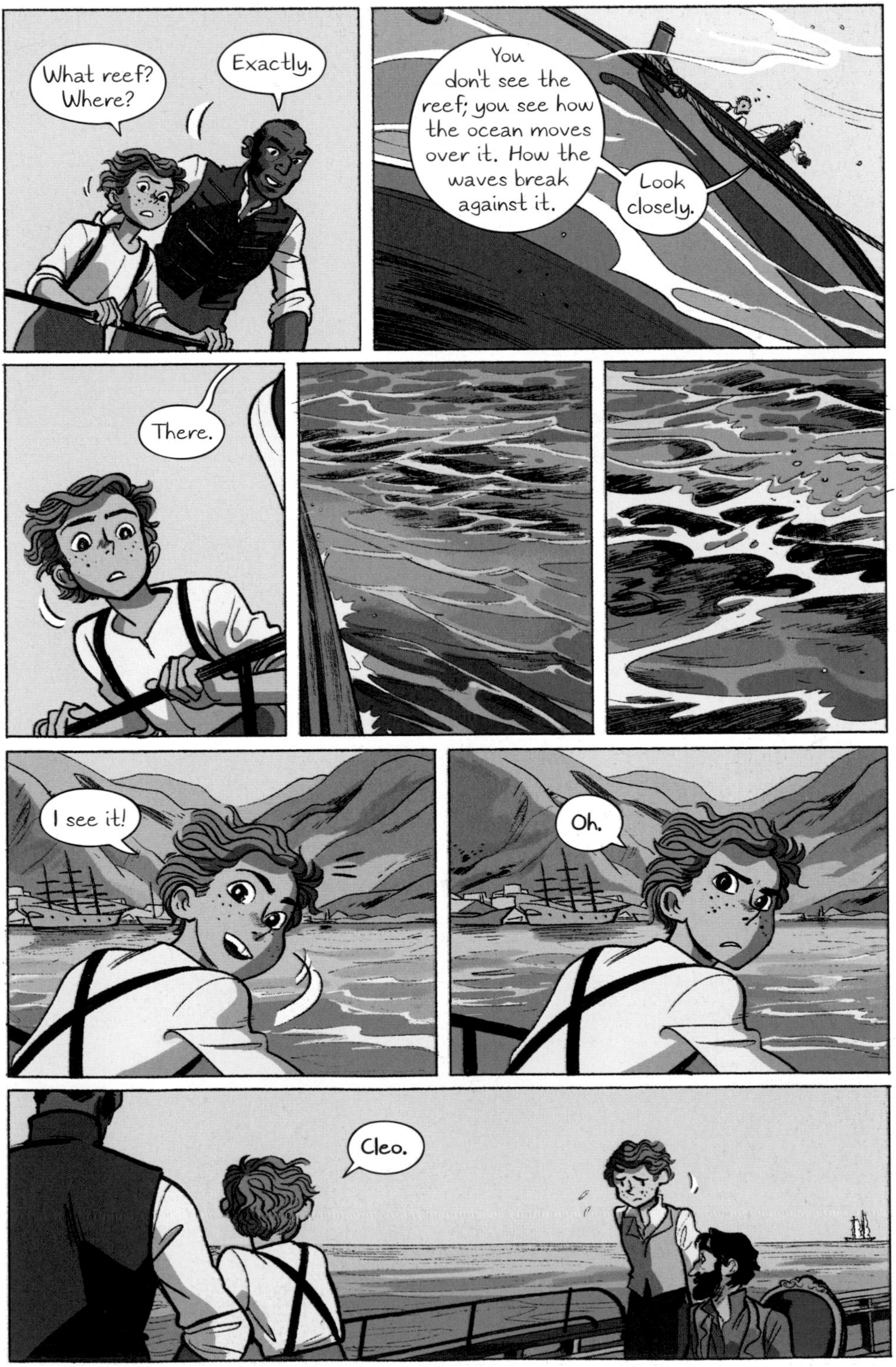
What reef? Where?
Exactly.
You don't see the reef; you see how the ocean moves over it. How the waves break against it.
Look closely.
There.
I see it!
Oh.
Cleo.

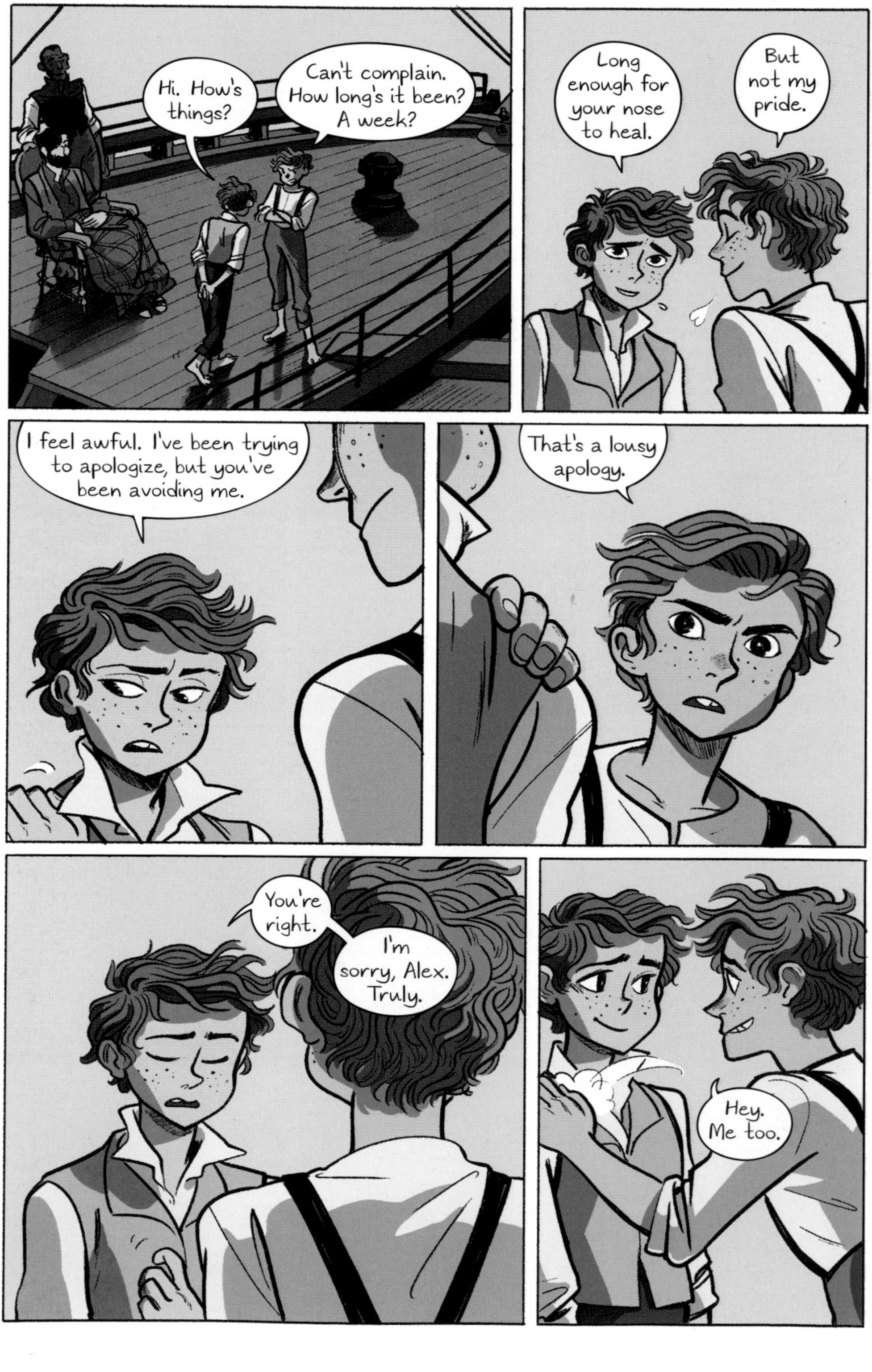
Hi. How's things?
Can't complain. How long's it been? A week?
Long enough for your nose to heal.
But not my pride.
I feel awful. I've been trying to apologize, but you've been avoiding me.
That's a lousy apology.
You're right.
I'm sorry, Alex. Truly.
Hey. Me too.

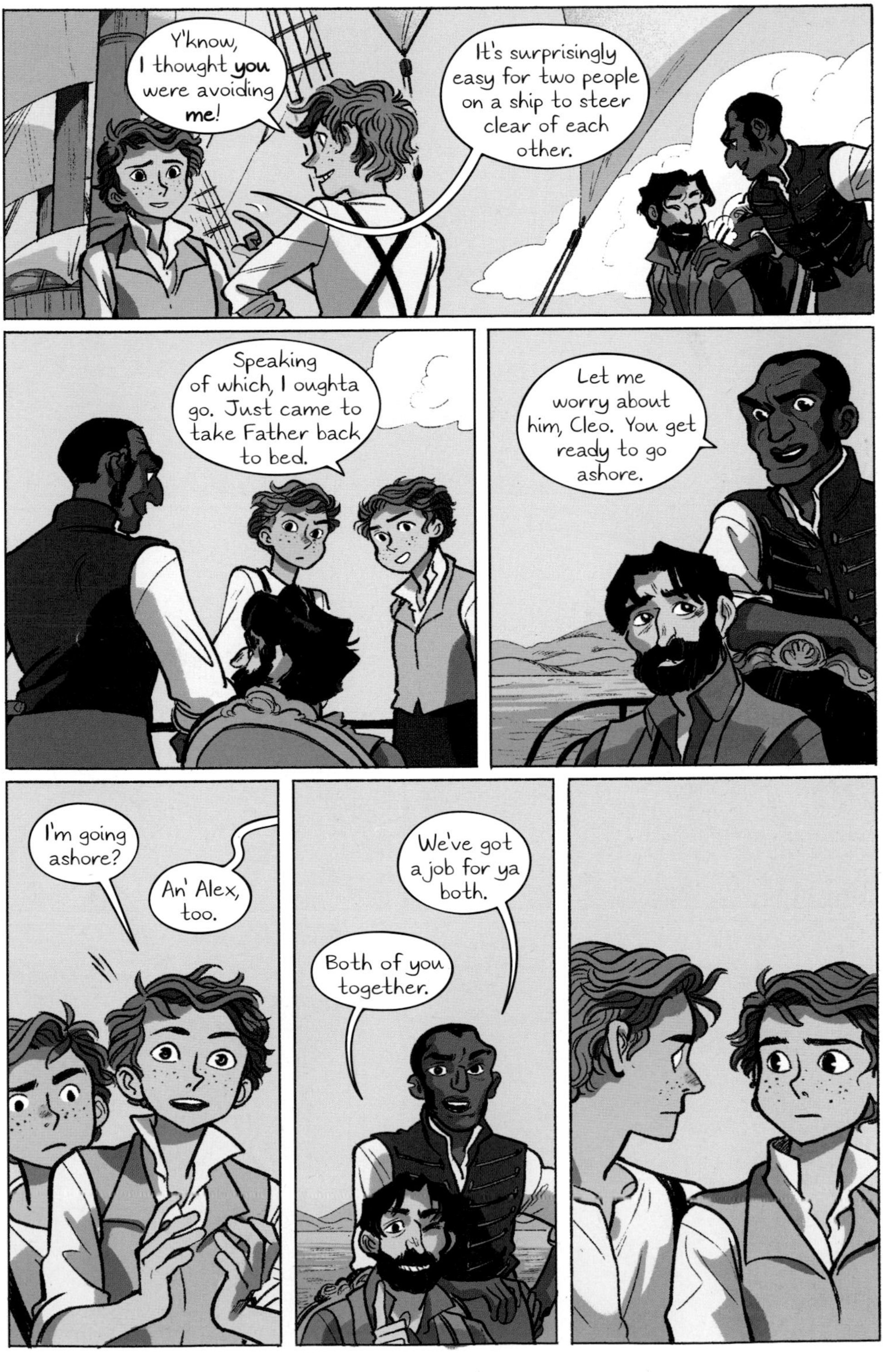
Y'know, I thought **you** were avoiding **me**!
It's surprisingly easy for two people on a ship to steer clear of each other.
Speaking of which, I oughta go. Just came to take Father back to bed.
Let me worry about him, Cleo. You get ready to go ashore.
I'm going ashore?
An' Alex, too.
We've got a job for ya both.
Both of you together.

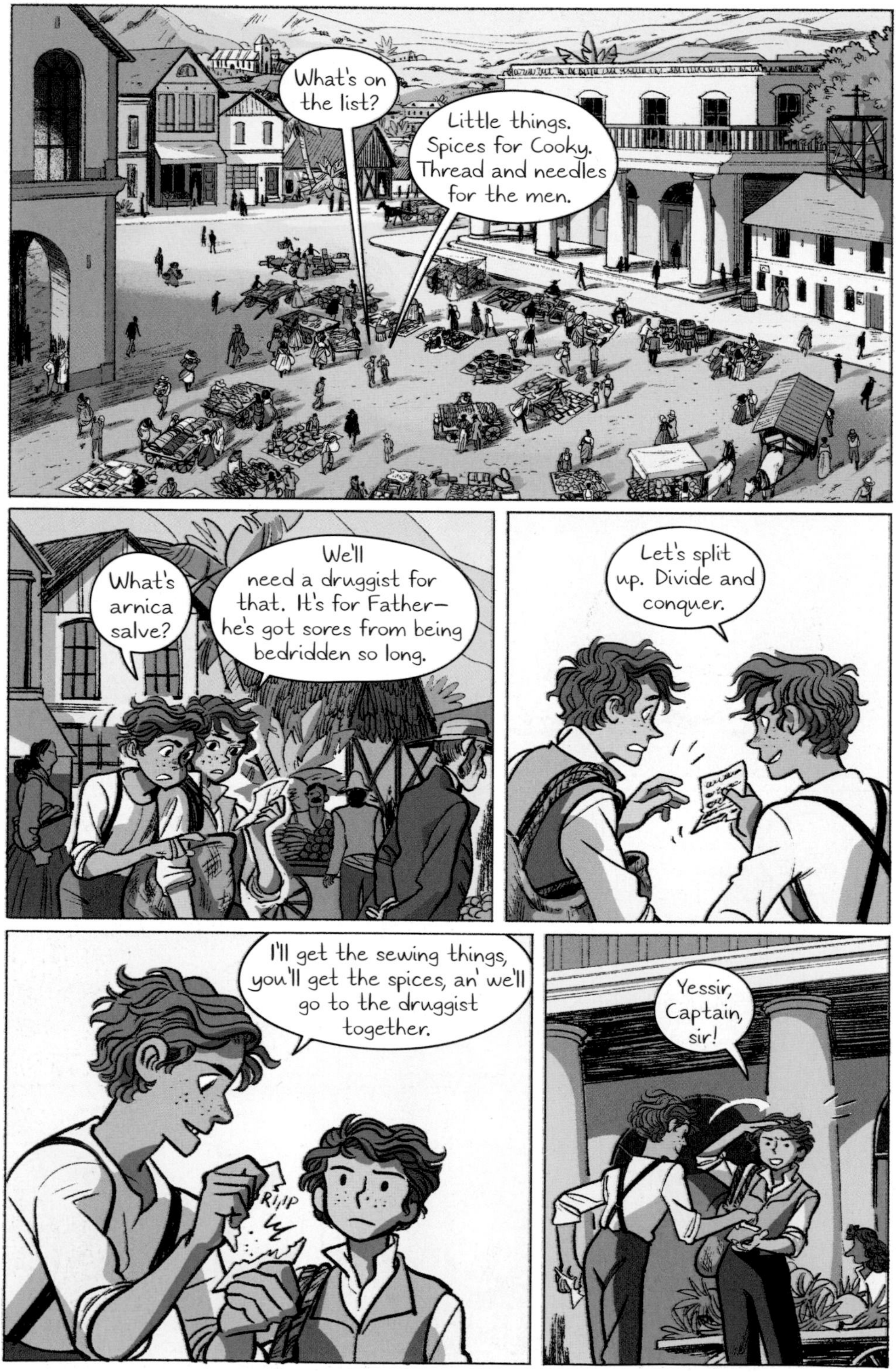
What's on the list?
Little things. Spices for Cooky. Thread and needles for the men.
What's arnica salve?
We'll need a druggist for that. It's for Father— he's got sores from being bedridden so long.
Let's split up. Divide and conquer.
I'll get the sewing things, you'll get the spices, an' we'll go to the druggist together.
RIIP
Yessir, Captain, sir!

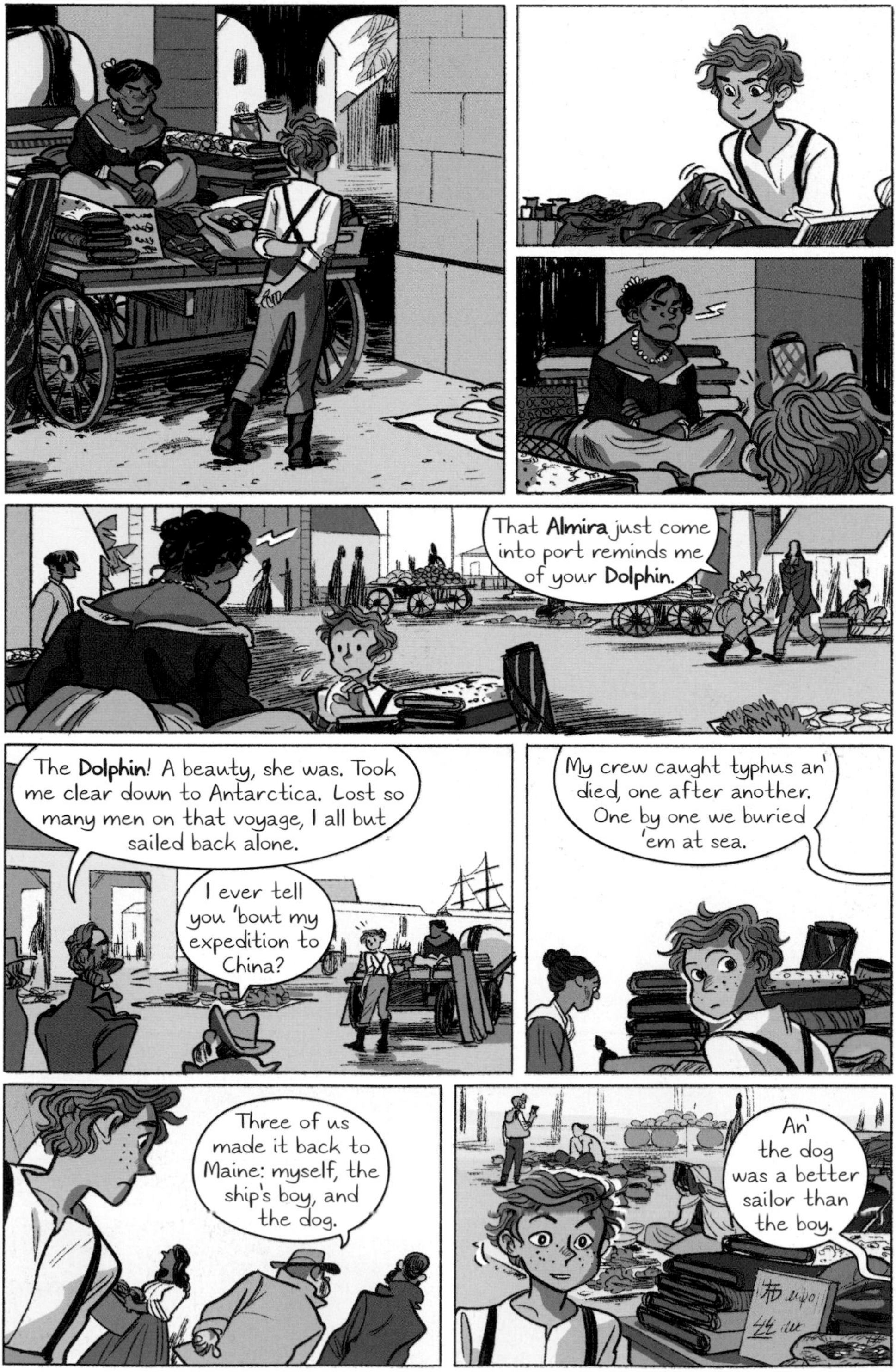
That **Almira** just come into port reminds me of your **Dolphin**.
The **Dolphin**! A beauty, she was. Took me clear down to Antarctica. Lost so many men on that voyage, I all but sailed back alone.
I ever tell you 'bout my expedition to China?
My crew caught typhus an' died, one after another. One by one we buried 'em at sea.
Three of us made it back to Maine: myself, the ship's boy, and the dog.
An' the dog was a better sailor than the boy.

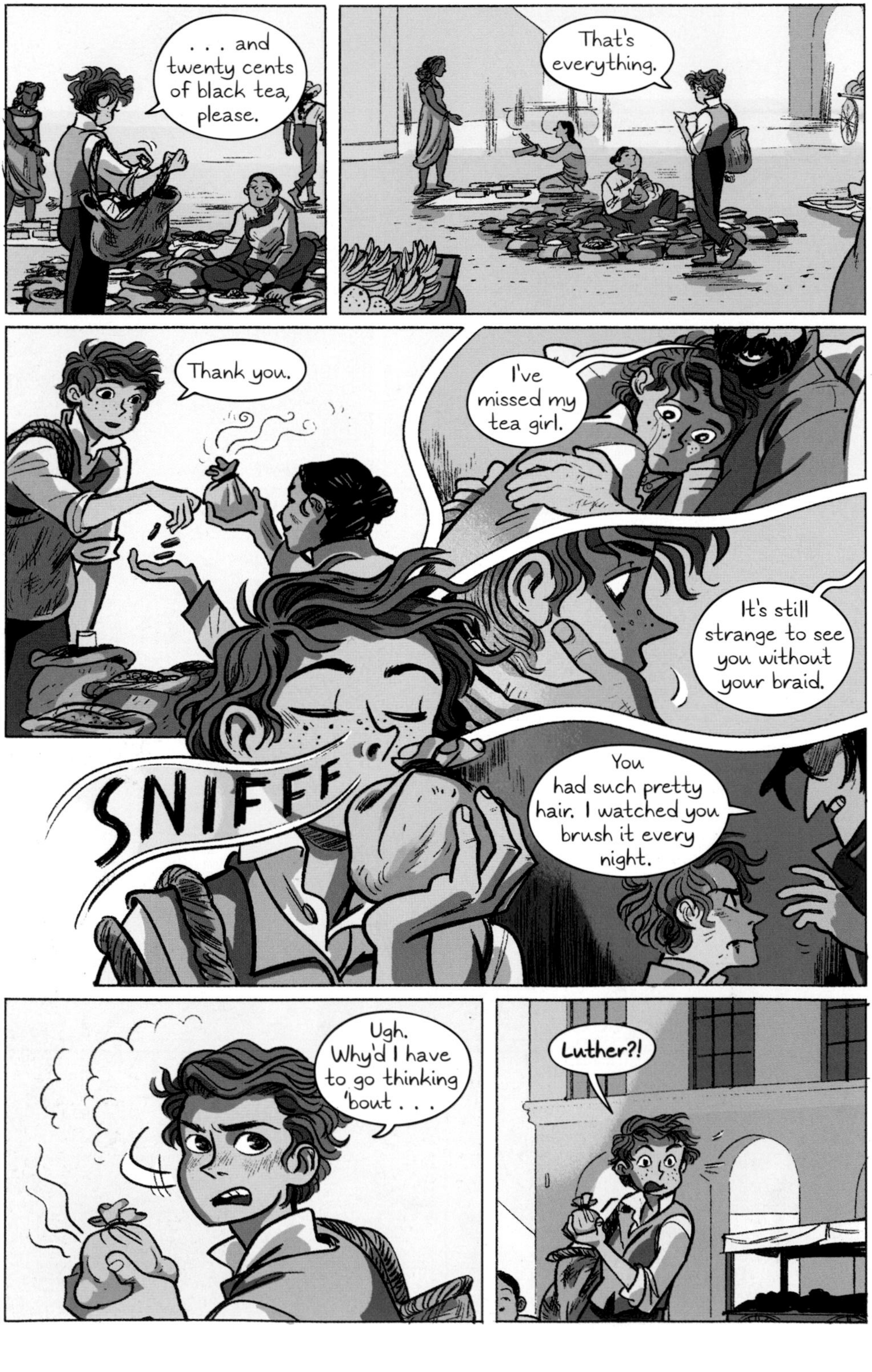
. . . and twenty cents of black tea, please.
That's everything.
Thank you.
I've missed my tea girl.
It's still strange to see you without your braid.
SNIFFF
You had such pretty hair. I watched you brush it every night.
Ugh. Why'd I have to go thinking 'bout . . .
Luther?!

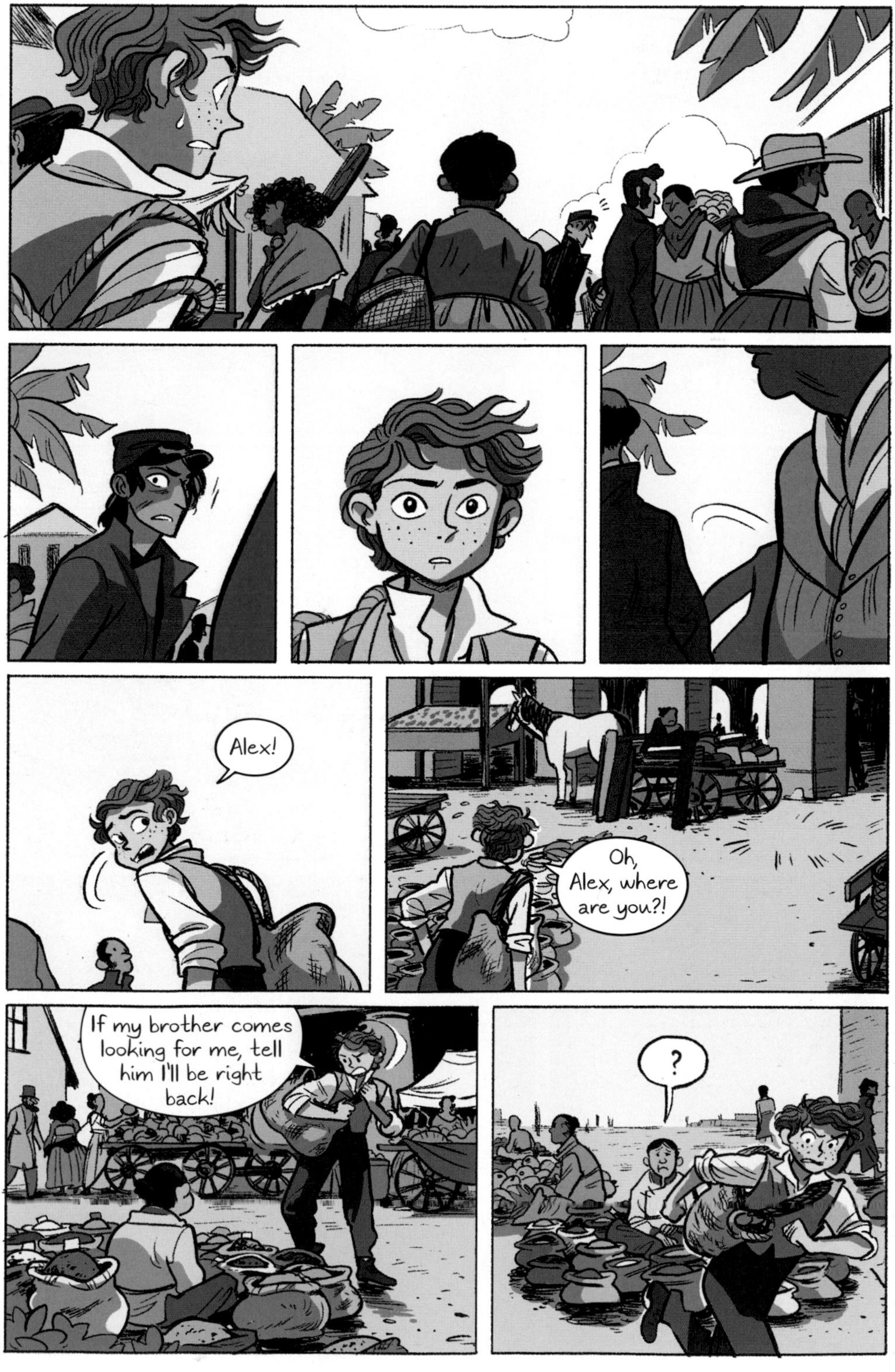
Alex!
Oh, Alex, where are you?!
If my brother comes looking for me, tell him I'll be right back!
?

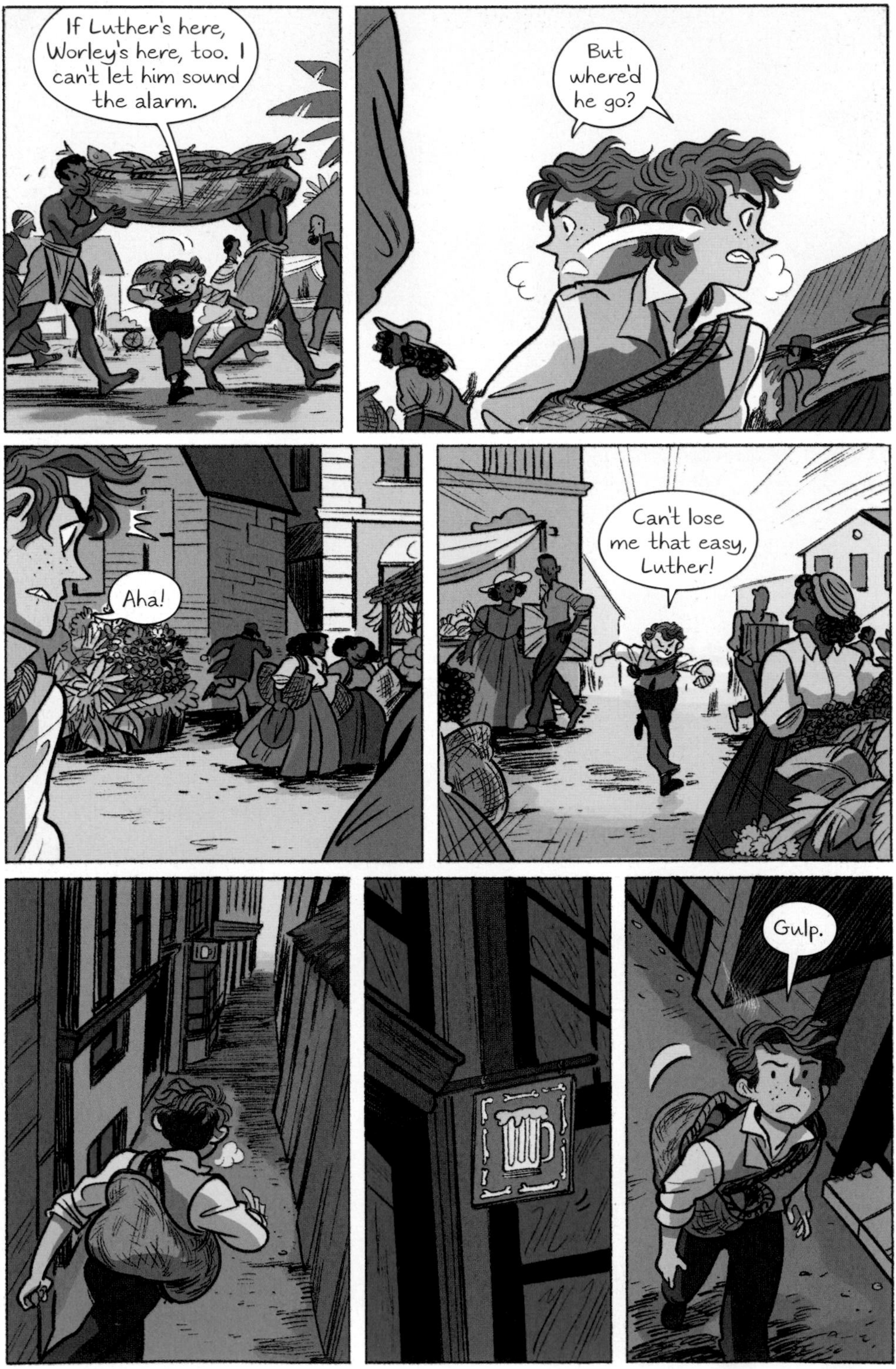
If Luther's here, Worley's here, too. I can't let him sound the alarm.
But where'd he go?
Aha!
Can't lose me that easy, Luther!
Gulp.

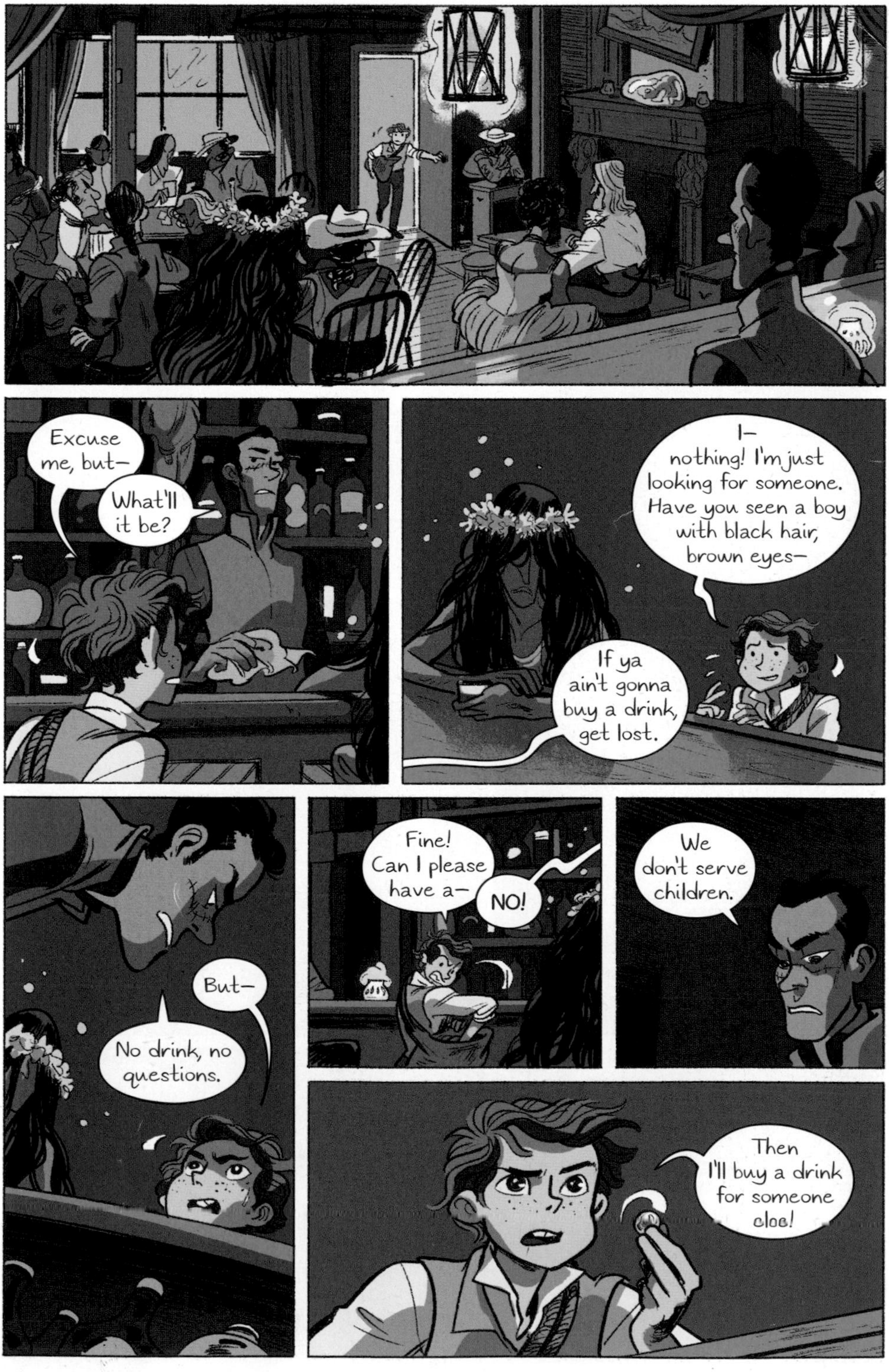
Excuse me, but—
What'll it be?
I— nothing! I'm just looking for someone. Have you seen a boy with black hair, brown eyes—
If ya ain't gonna buy a drink, get lost.
But—
No drink, no questions.
Fine! Can I please have a—
NO!
We don't serve children.
Then I'll buy a drink for someone else!

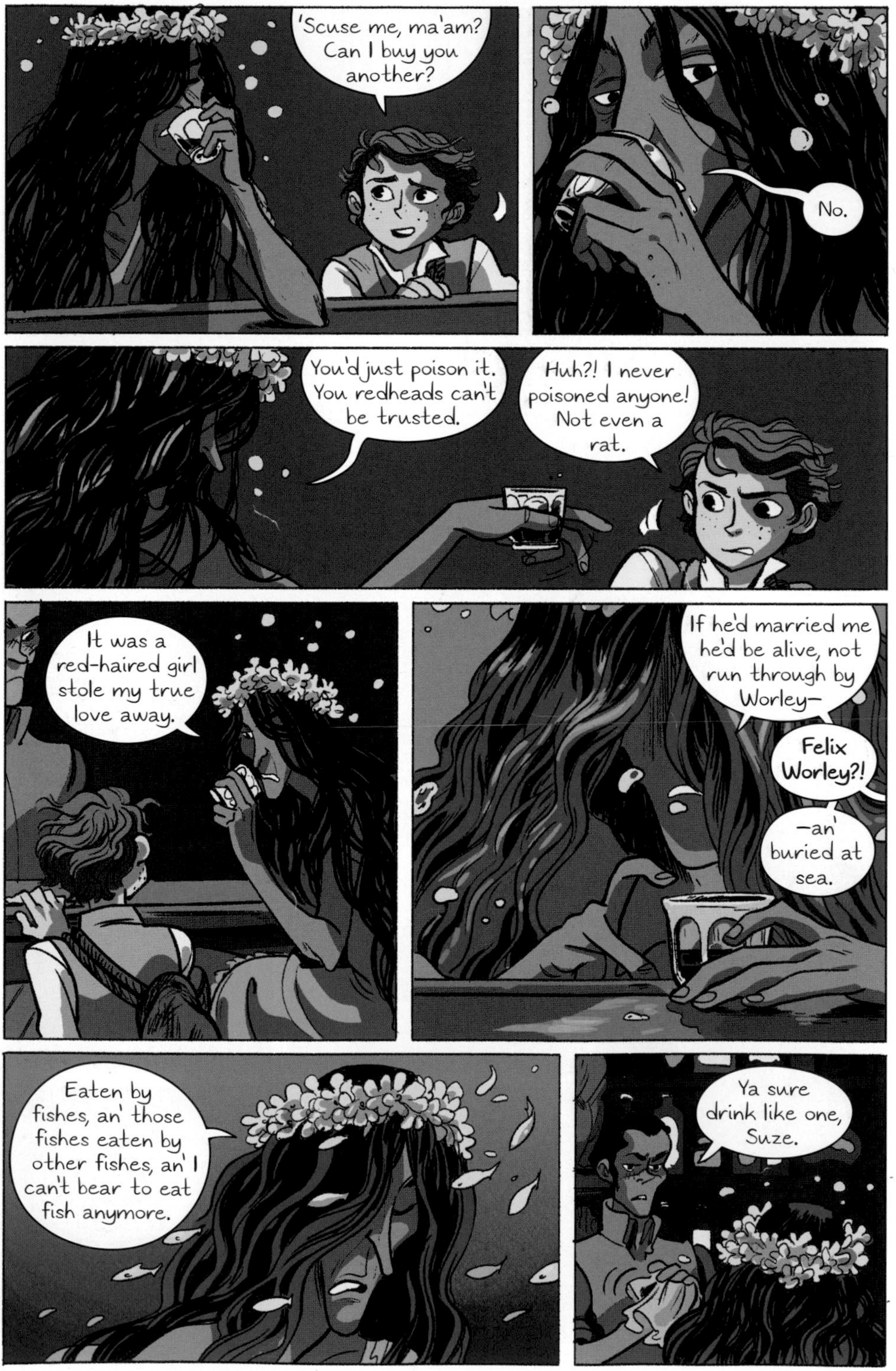
'Scuse me, ma'am? Can I buy you another?
No.
You'd just poison it. You redheads can't be trusted.
Huh?! I never poisoned anyone! Not even a rat.
It was a red-haired girl stole my true love away.
If he'd married me he'd be alive, not run through by Worley—
Felix Worley?!
—an' buried at sea.
Eaten by fishes, an' those fishes eaten by other fishes, an' I can't bear to eat fish anymore.
Ya sure drink like one, Suze.

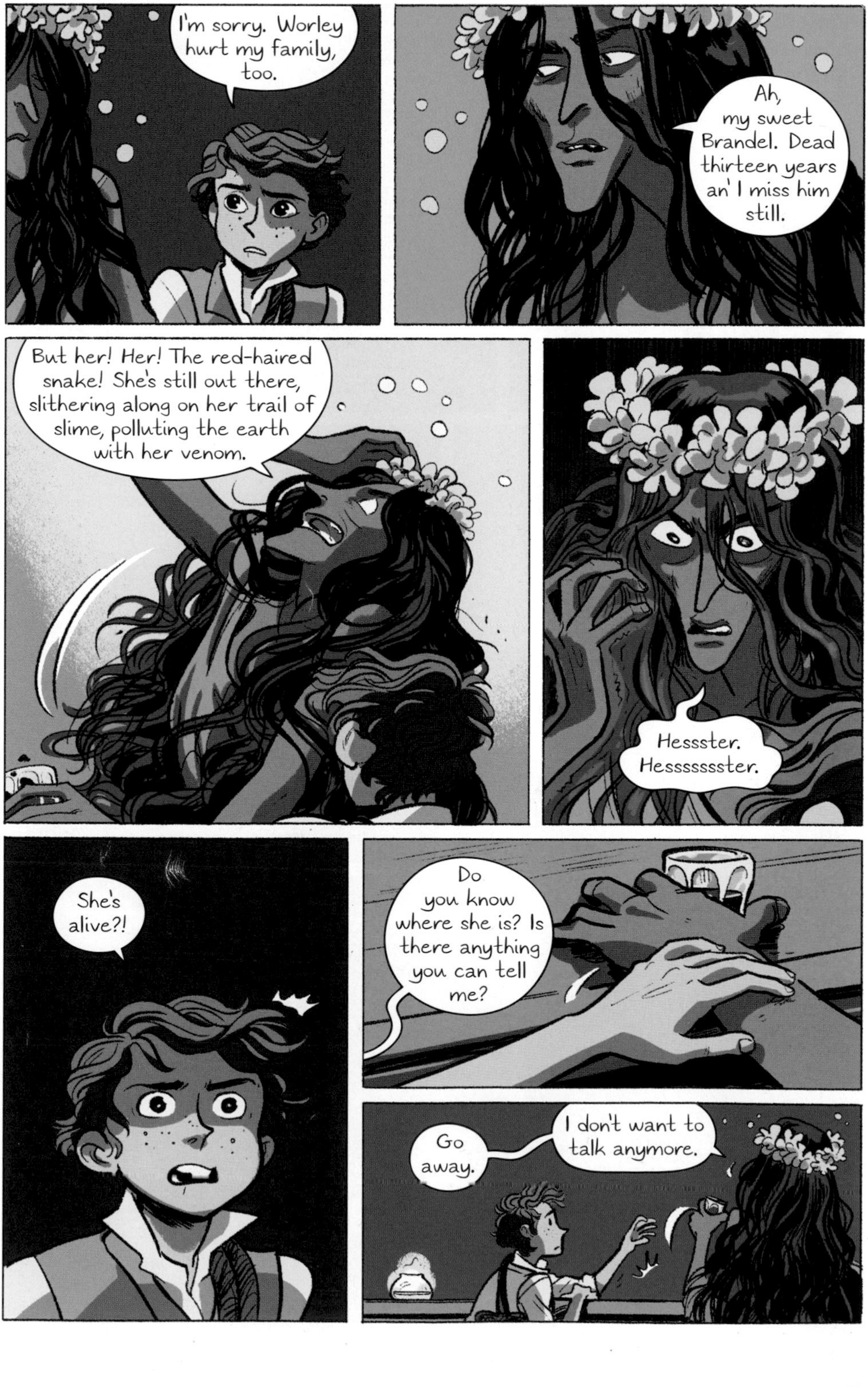
I'm sorry. Worley hurt my family, too.
Ah, my sweet Brandel. Dead thirteen years an' I miss him still.
But her! Her! The red-haired snake! She's still out there, slithering along on her trail of slime, polluting the earth with her venom.
Hessster. Hesssssssster.
She's alive?!
Do you know where she is? Is there anything you can tell me?
Go away.
I don't want to talk anymore.

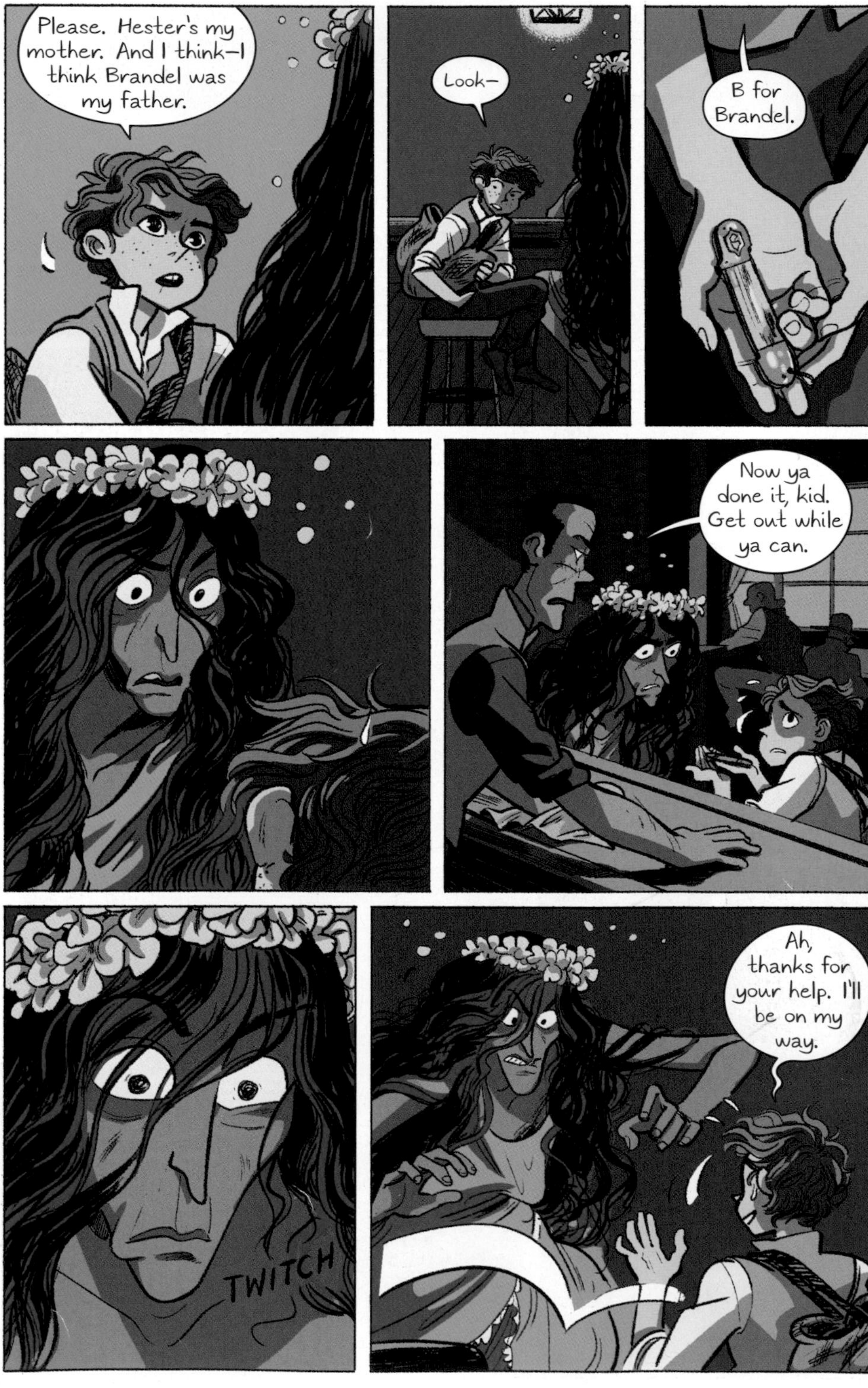
Please. Hester's my mother. And I think—I think Brandel was my father.
Look—
B for Brandel.
Now ya done it, kid. Get out while ya can.
TWITCH
Ah, thanks for your help. I'll be on my way.

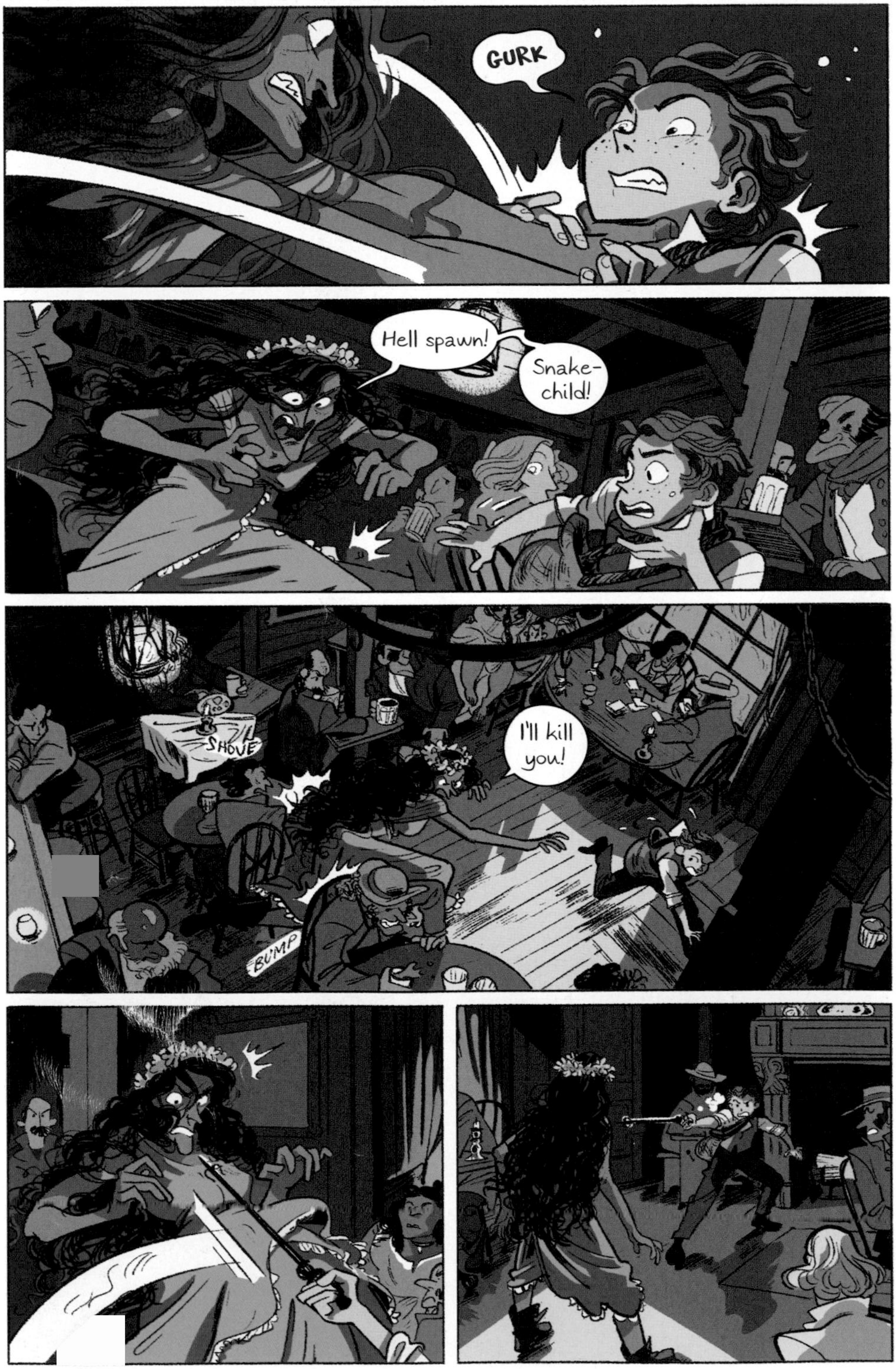
GURK
Hell spawn!
Snake-child!
SHOVE
I'll kill you!
BUMP

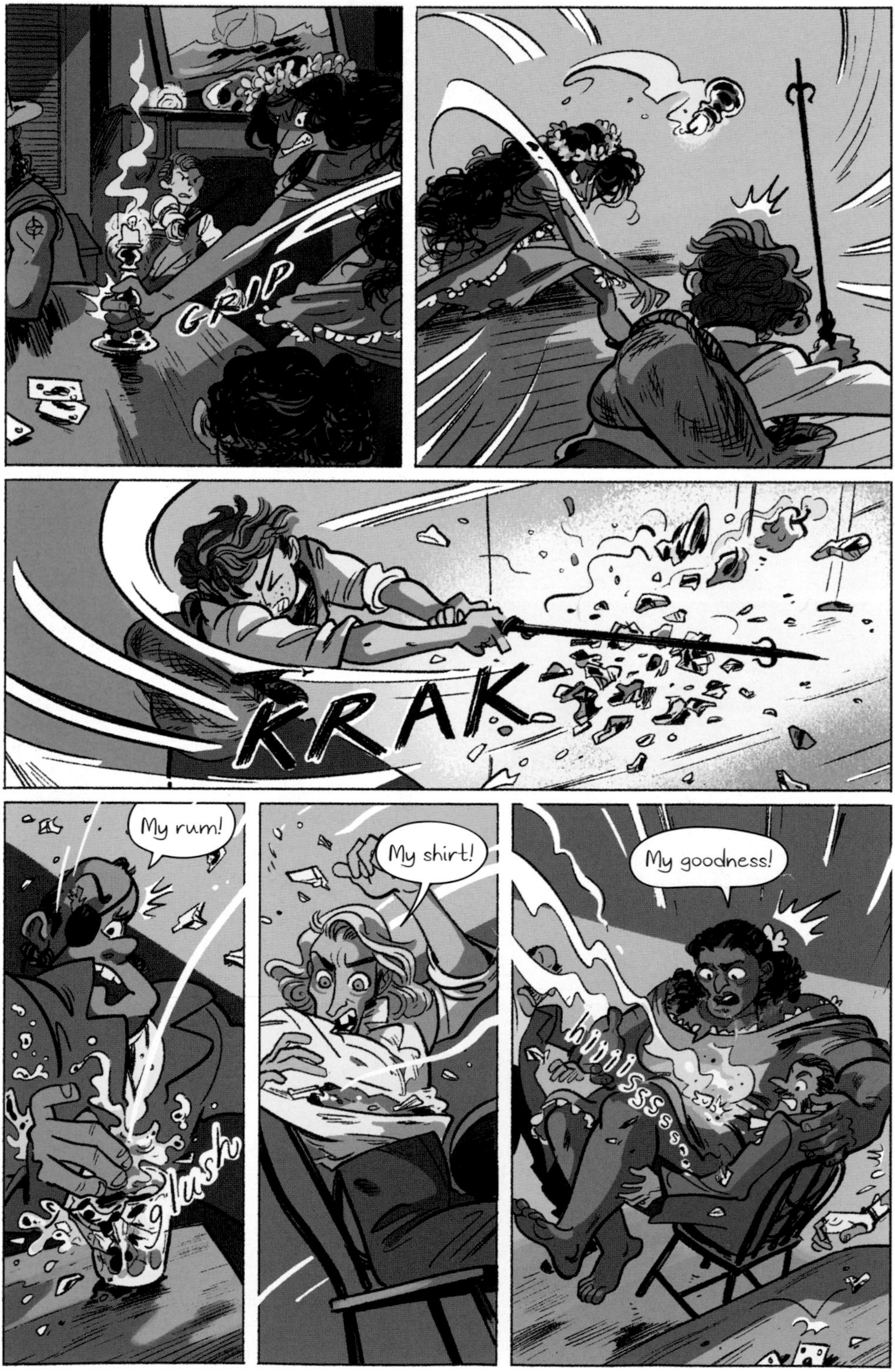
GRIP
KRAK
My rum!
glush
My shirt!
My goodness!
hiiiisssssss

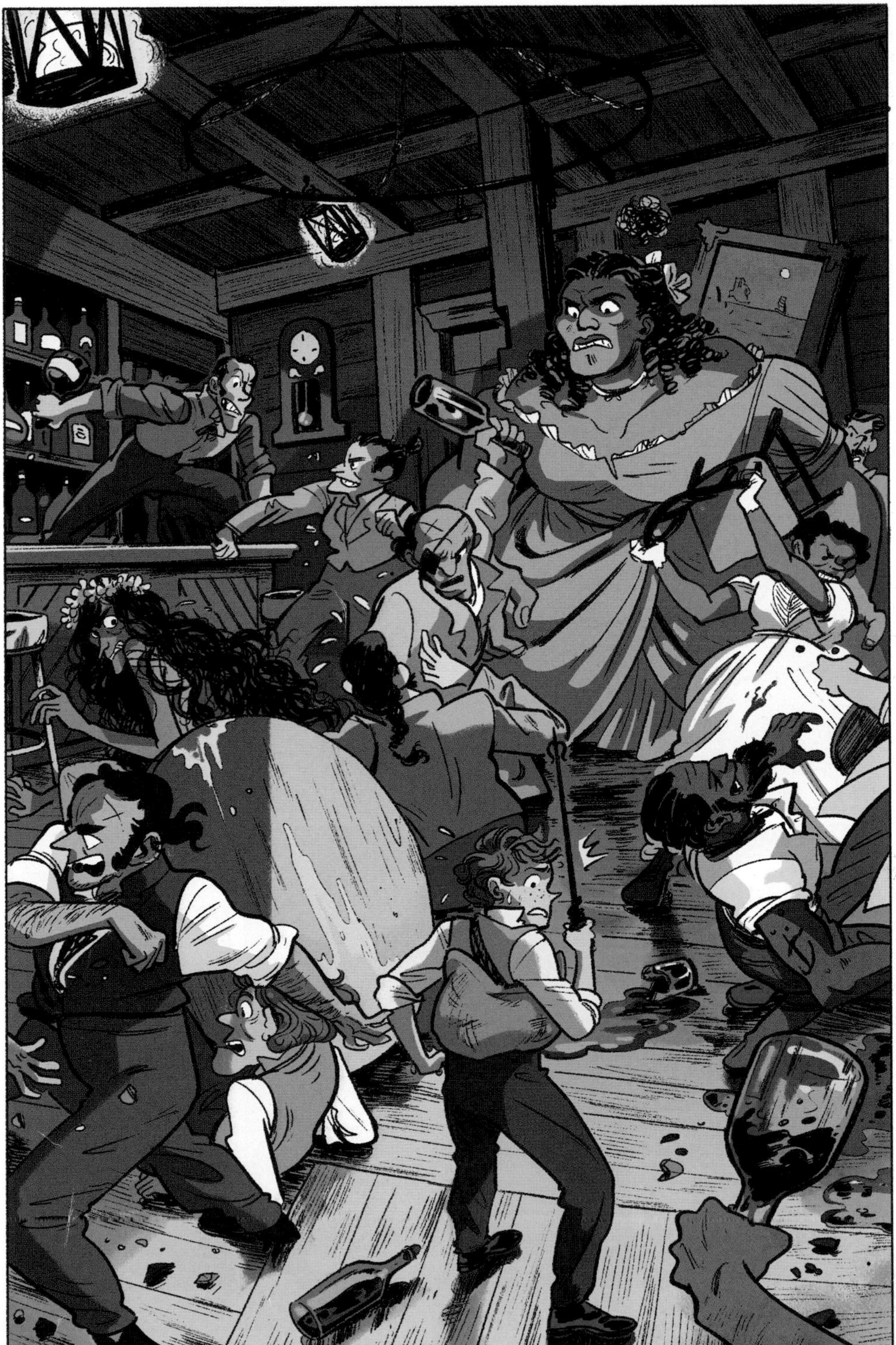

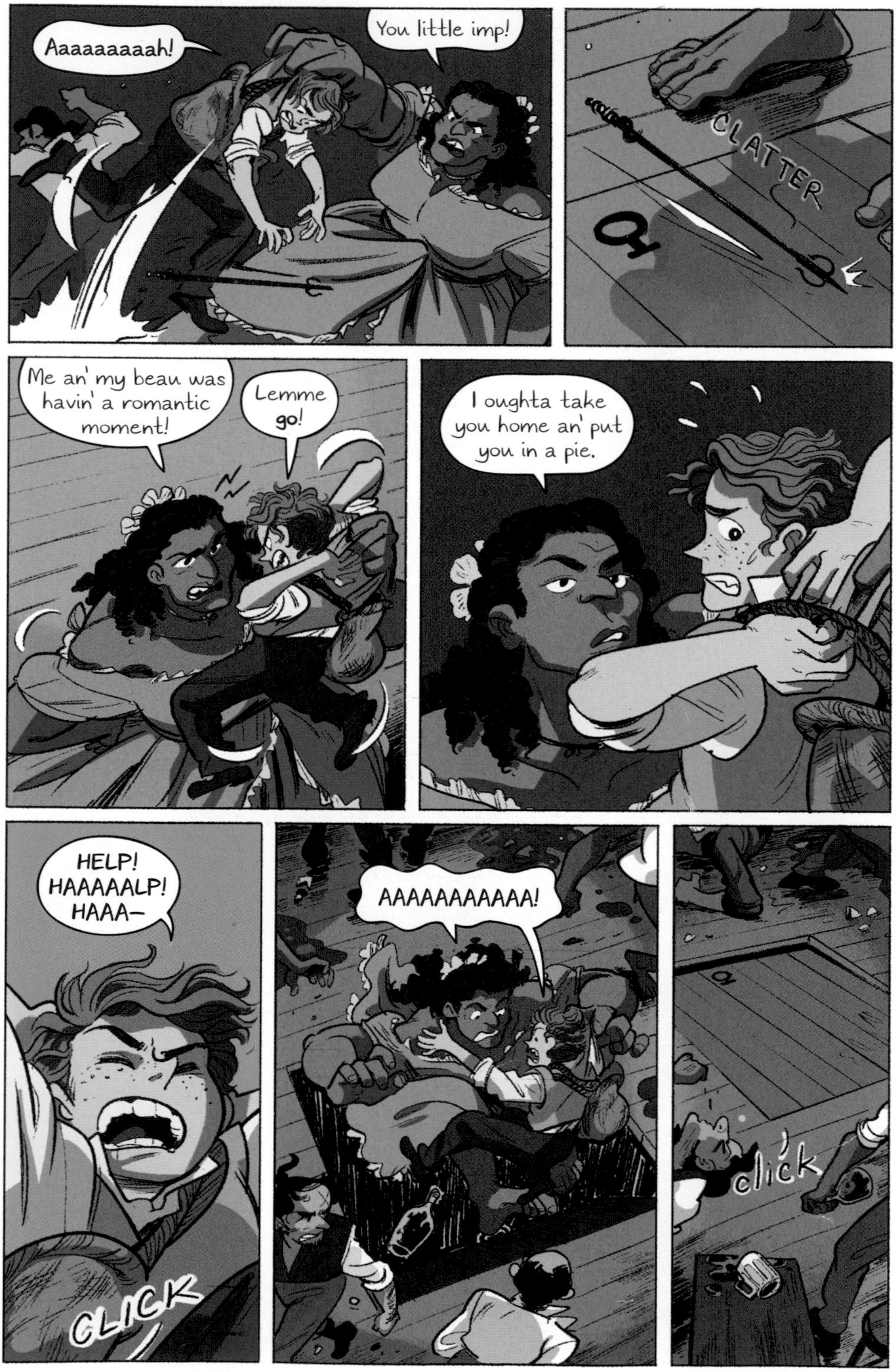
Aaaaaaaaah!
You little imp!
CLATTER
Me an' my beau was havin' a romantic moment!
Lemme go!
I oughta take you home an' put you in a pie.
HELP! HAAAAALP! HAAA—
CLICK
AAAAAAAAAAA!
click

CHAPTER FOUR
A MARKED MAN

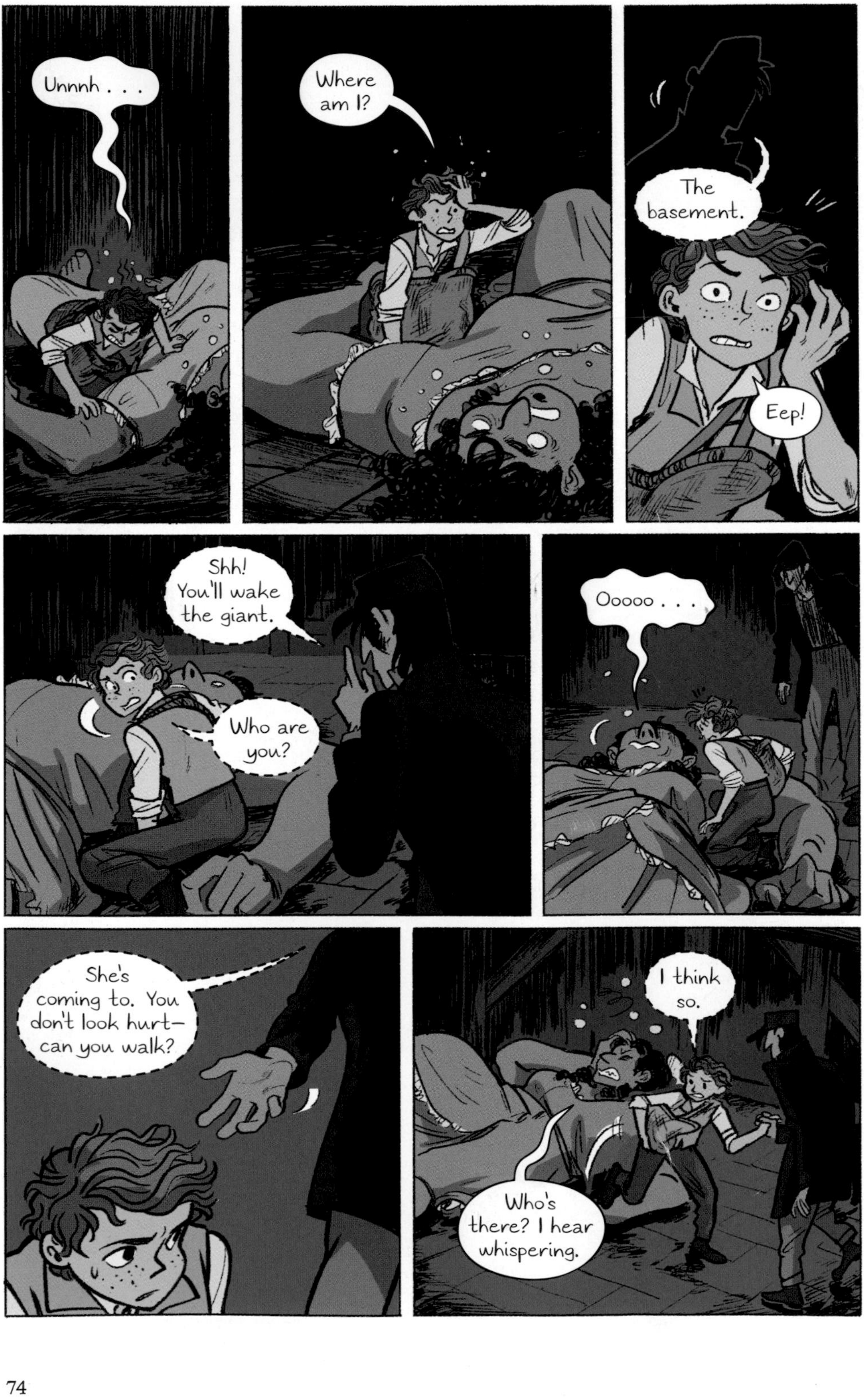
Unnnh . . .
Where am I?
The basement.
Eep!
Shh! You'll wake the giant.
Who are you?
Ooooo . . .
She's coming to. You don't look hurt—can you walk?
I think so.
Who's there? I hear whispering.

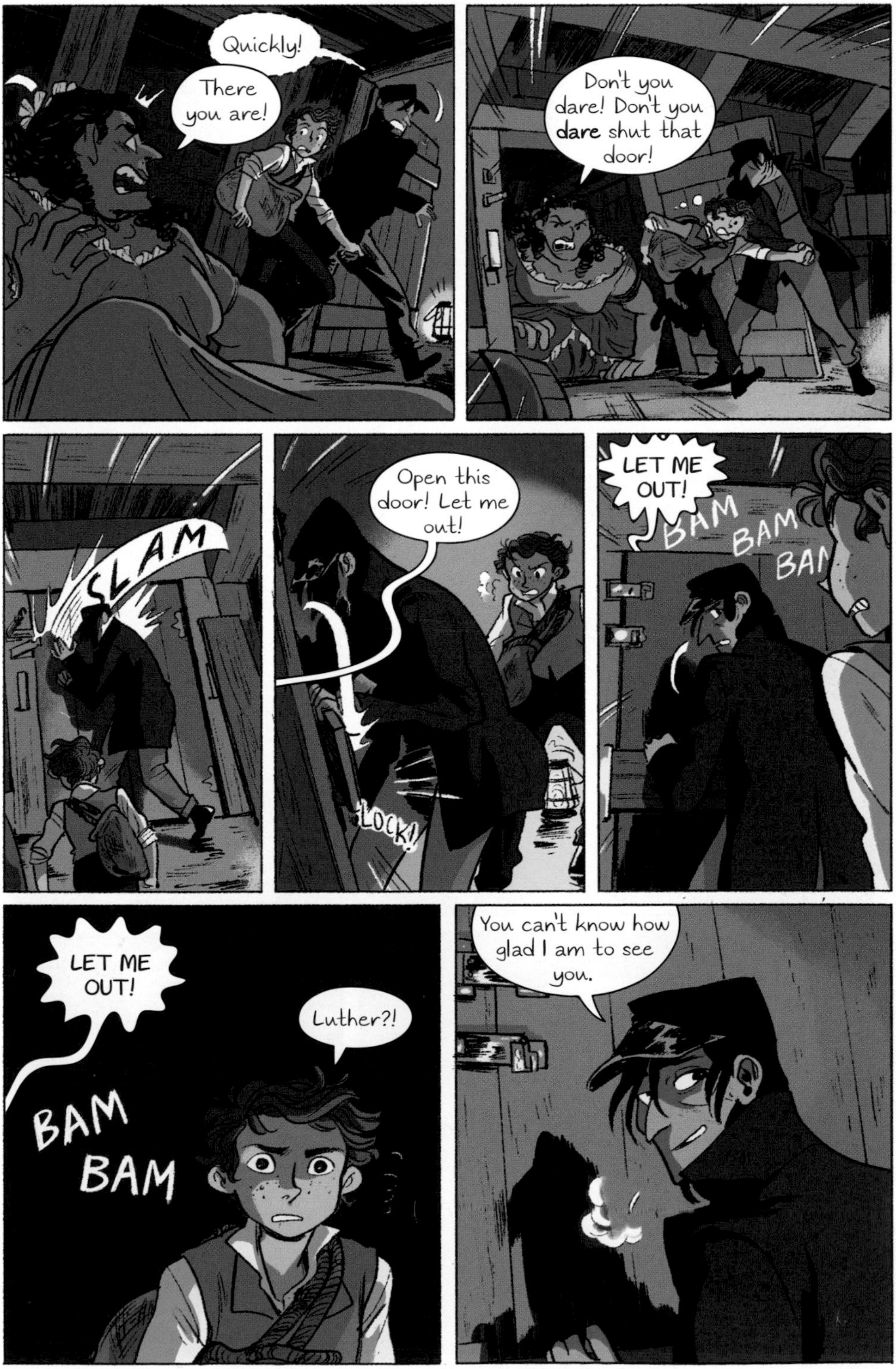
Quickly!
There you are!
Don't you dare! Don't you **dare** shut that door!
SLAM
Open this door! Let me out!
LOCK!
LET ME OUT!
BAM BAM BAM
LET ME OUT!
BAM BAM
Luther?!
You can't know how glad I am to see you.

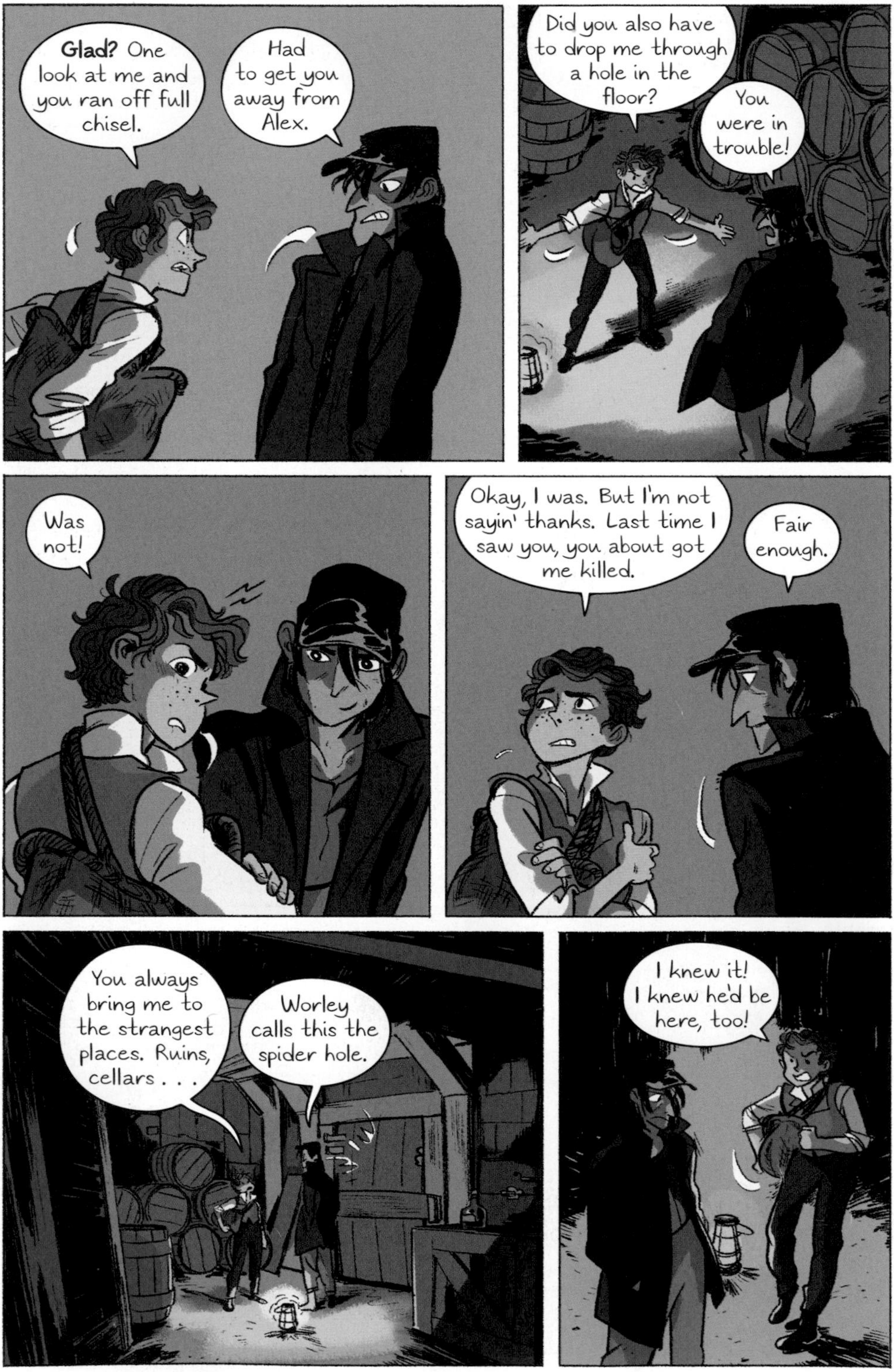
Glad? One look at me and you ran off full chisel.
Had to get you away from Alex.
Did you also have to drop me through a hole in the floor?
You were in trouble!
Was not!
Okay, I was. But I'm not sayin' thanks. Last time I saw you, you about got me killed.
Fair enough.
You always bring me to the strangest places. Ruins, cellars . . .
Worley calls this the spider hole.
I knew it! I knew he'd be here, too!

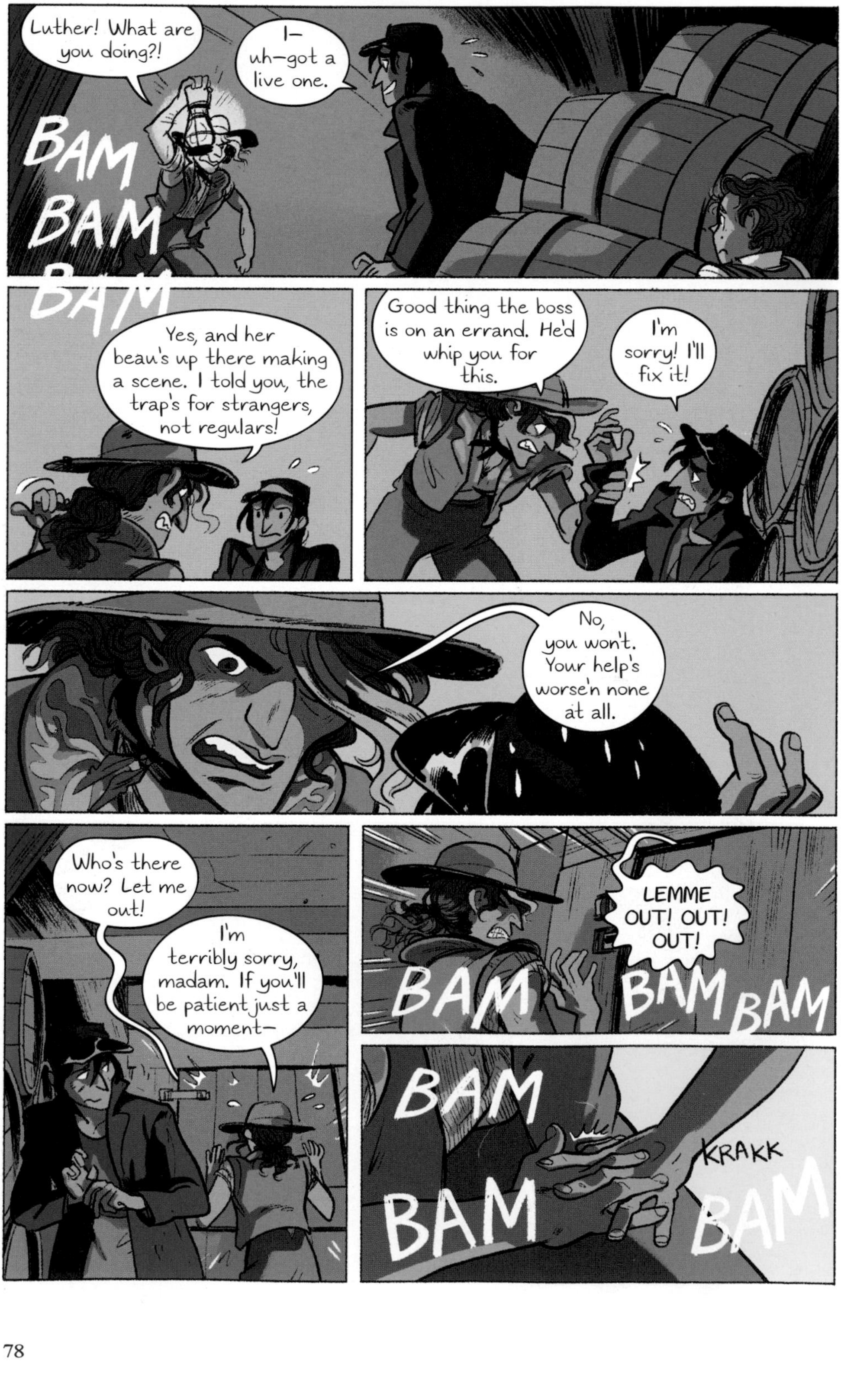
Luther! What are you doing?!
I— uh—got a live one.
BAM BAM BAM
Yes, and her beau's up there making a scene. I told you, the trap's for strangers, not regulars!
Good thing the boss is on an errand. He'd whip you for this.
I'm sorry! I'll fix it!
No, you won't. Your help's worse'n none at all.
Who's there now? Let me out!
I'm terribly sorry, madam. If you'll be patient just a moment—
LEMME OUT! OUT! OUT!
BAM BAM BAM
BAM
KRAKK
BAM BAM

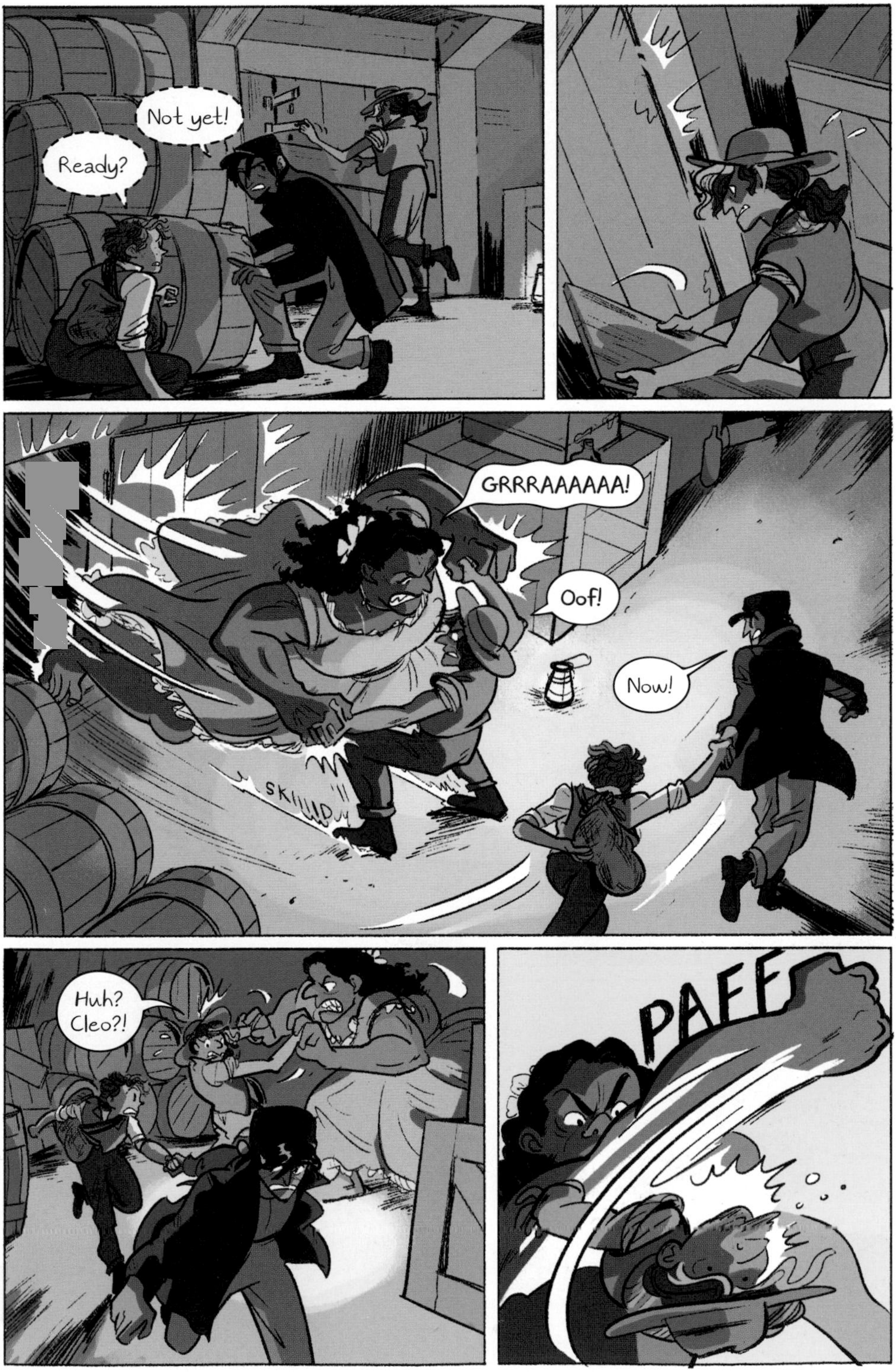
Ready?
Not yet!
GRRRAAAAAA!
Oof!
Now!
Huh? Cleo?!
PAFF

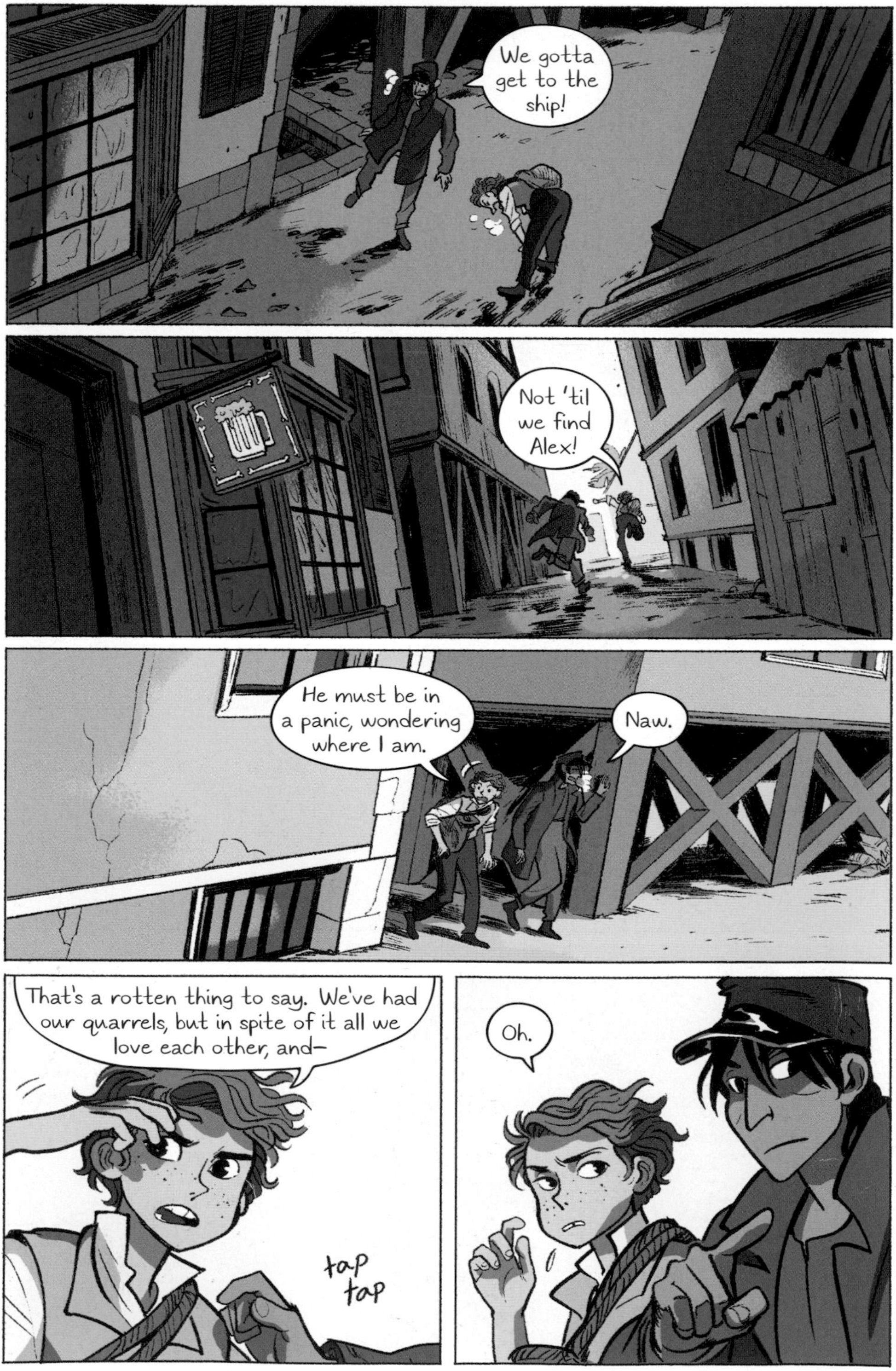
We gotta get to the ship!
Not 'til we find Alex!
He must be in a panic, wondering where I am.
Naw.
That's a rotten thing to say. We've had our quarrels, but in spite of it all we love each other, and–
tap tap
Oh.

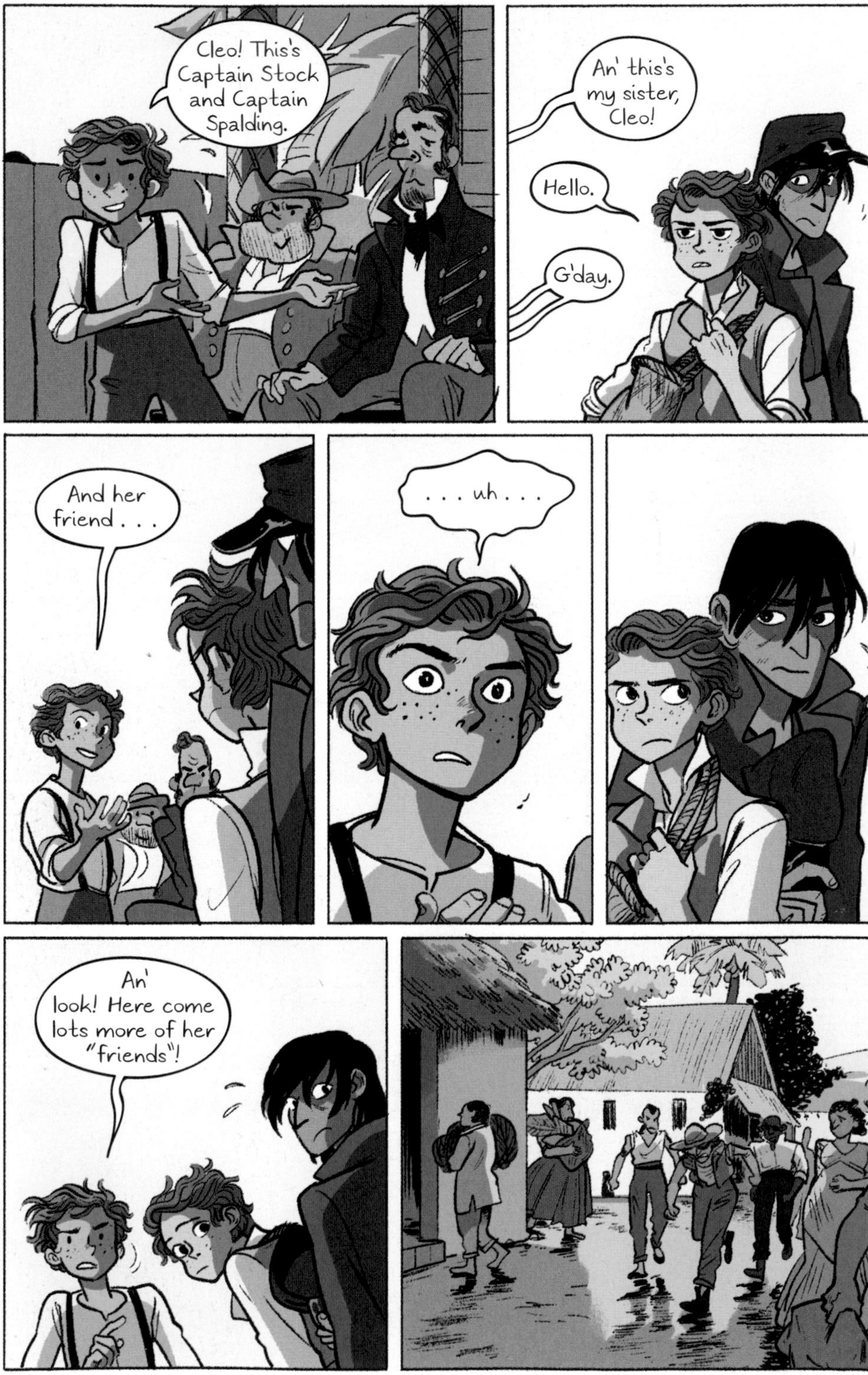
Cleo! This's Captain Stock and Captain Spalding.
An' this's my sister, Cleo!
Hello.
G'day.
And her friend . . .
. . . uh . . .
An' look! Here come lots more of her "friends"!

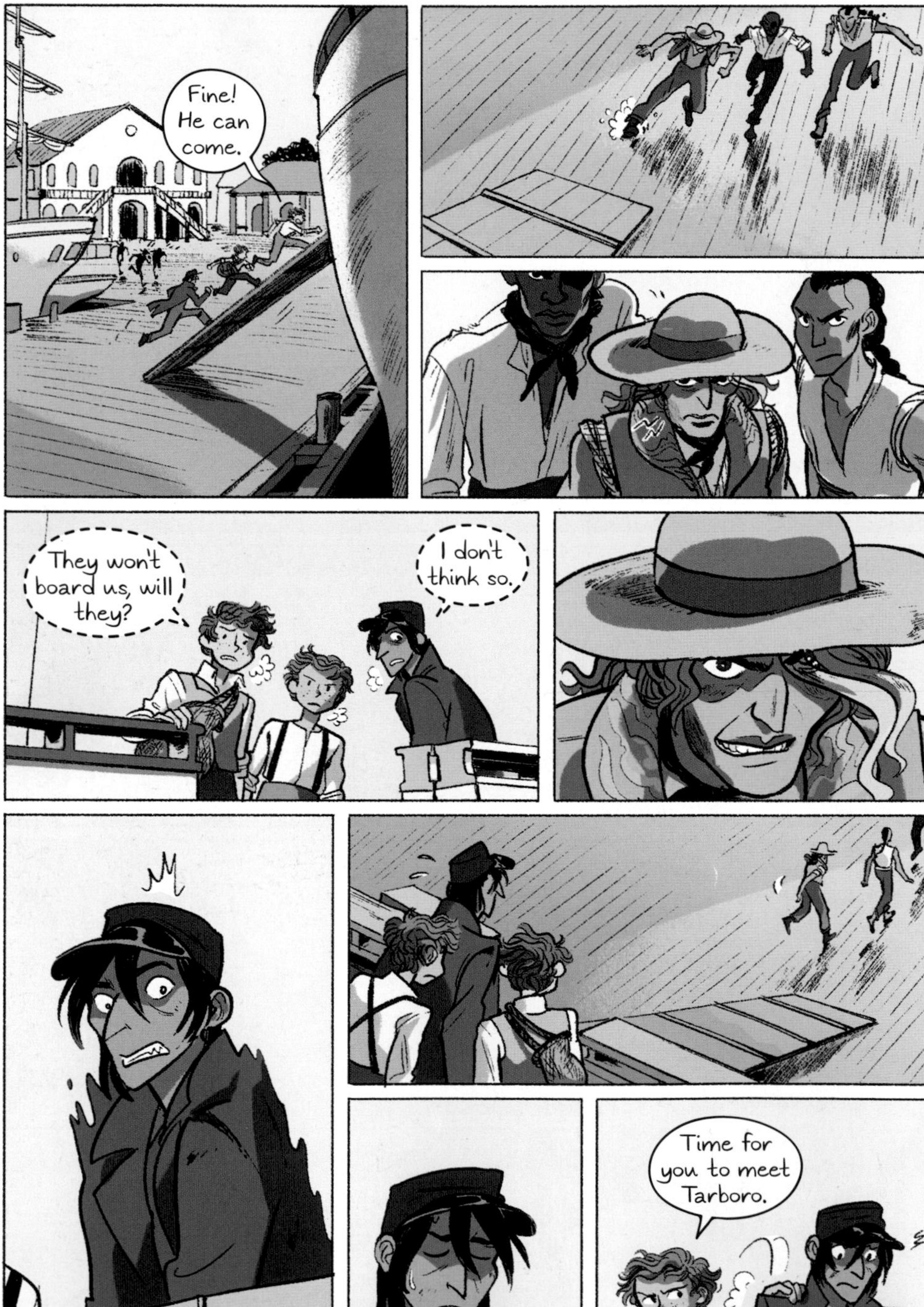
Fine! He can come.
They won't board us, will they?
I don't think so.
Time for you to meet Tarboro.

CHAPTER FIVE
THE SHIP AND HER MASTER

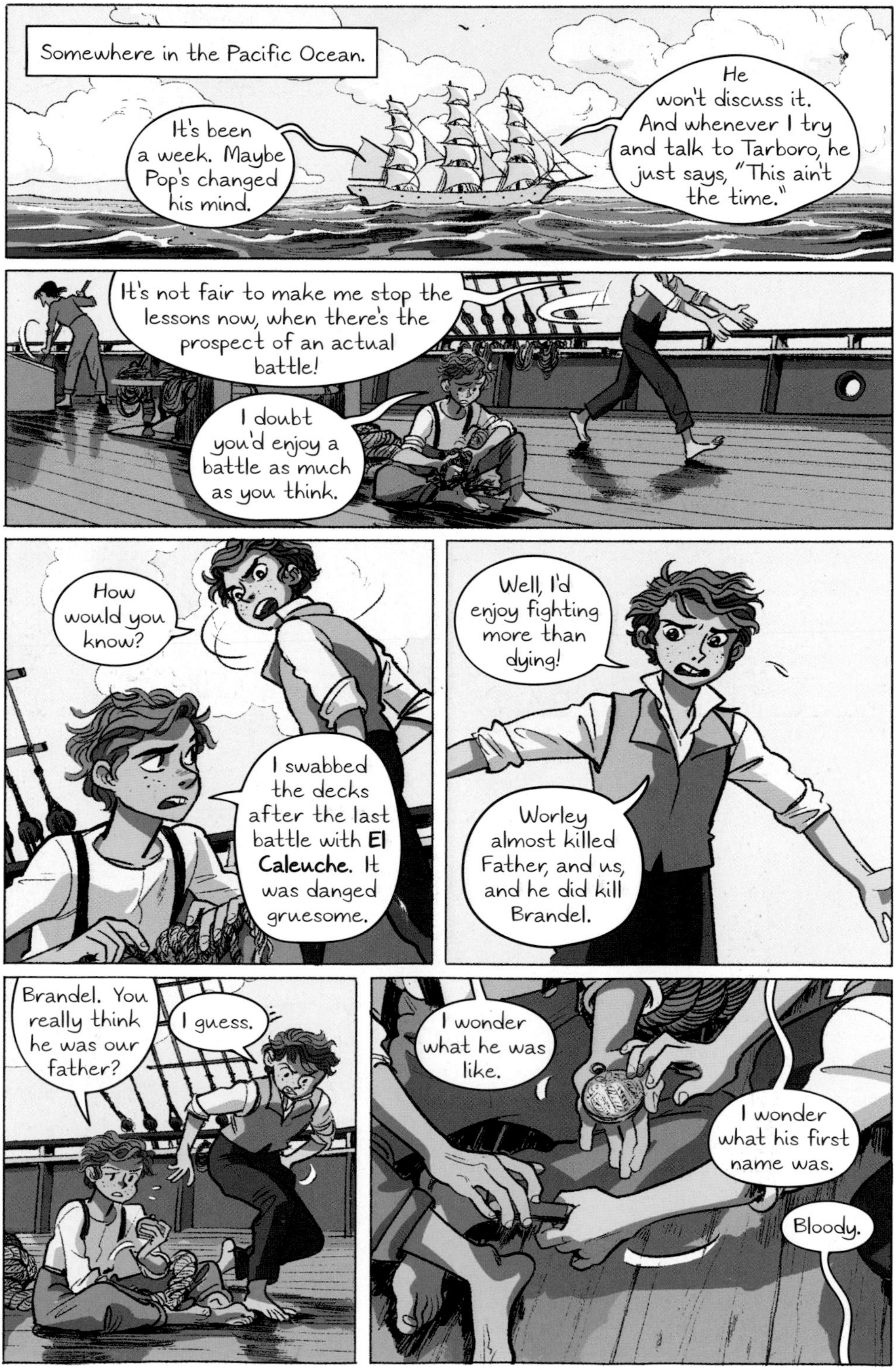
Somewhere in the Pacific Ocean.
It's been a week. Maybe Pop's changed his mind.
He won't discuss it. And whenever I try and talk to Tarboro, he just says, "This ain't the time."
It's not fair to make me stop the lessons now, when there's the prospect of an actual battle!
I doubt you'd enjoy a battle as much as you think.
How would you know?
I swabbed the decks after the last battle with El Caleuche. It was danged gruesome.
Well, I'd enjoy fighting more than dying!
Worley almost killed Father, and us, and he did kill Brandel.
Brandel. You really think he was our father?
I guess.
I wonder what he was like.
I wonder what his first name was.
Bloody.

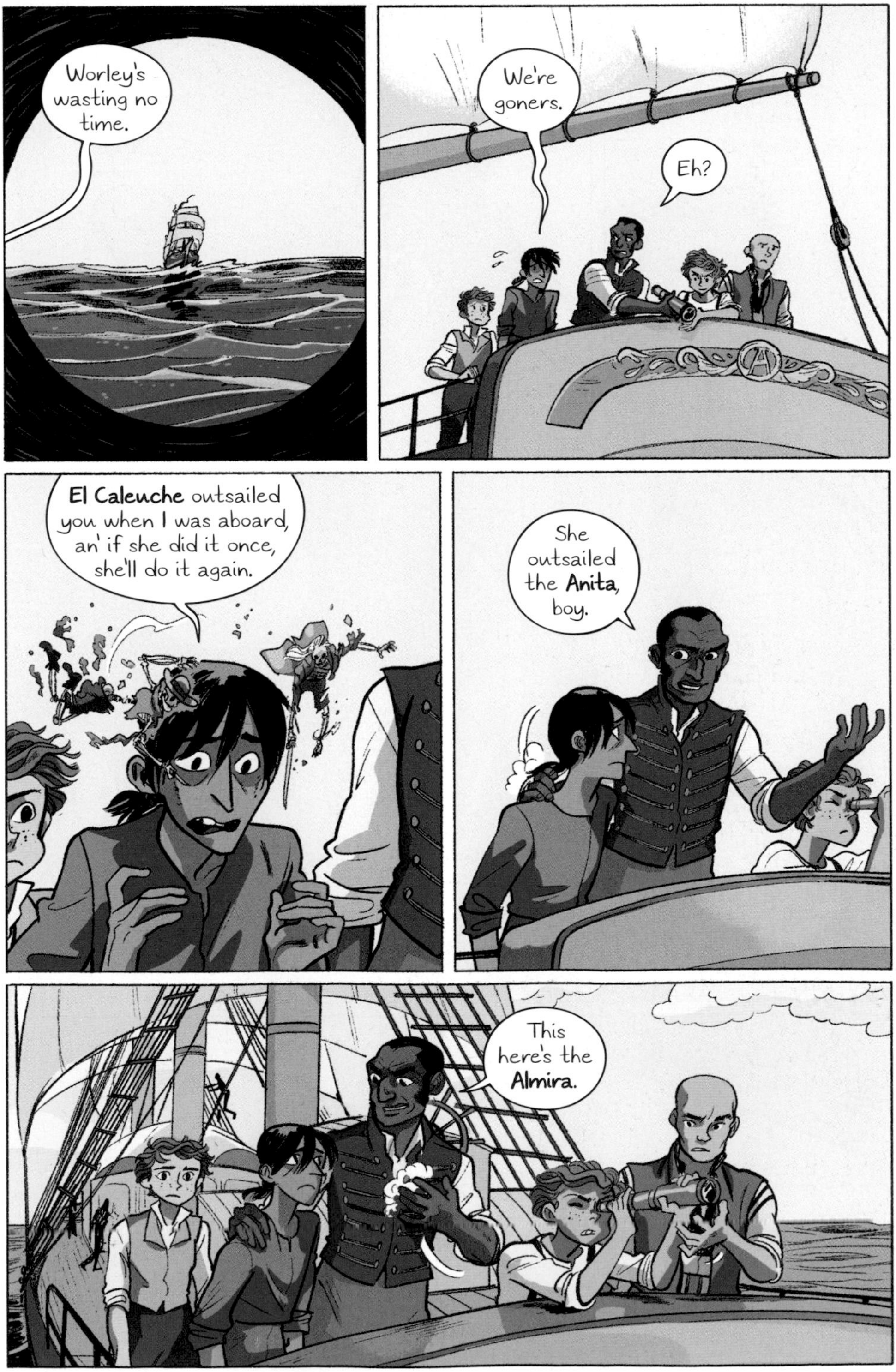
Worley's wasting no time.
We're goners.
Eh?
El Caleuche outsailed you when I was aboard, an' if she did it once, she'll do it again.
She outsailed the Anita, boy.
This here's the Almira.

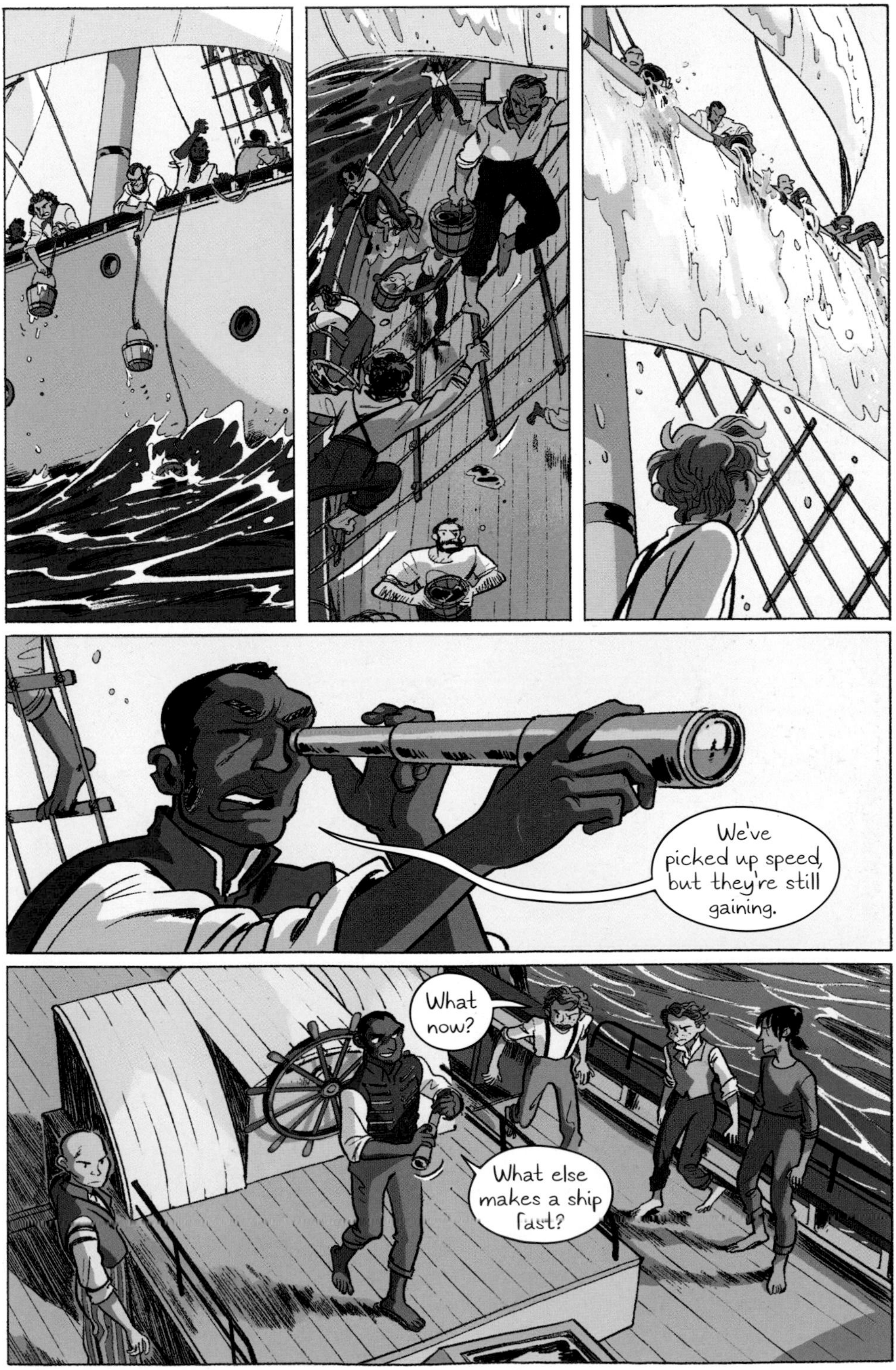
We've picked up speed, but they're still gaining.
What now?
What else makes a ship fast?

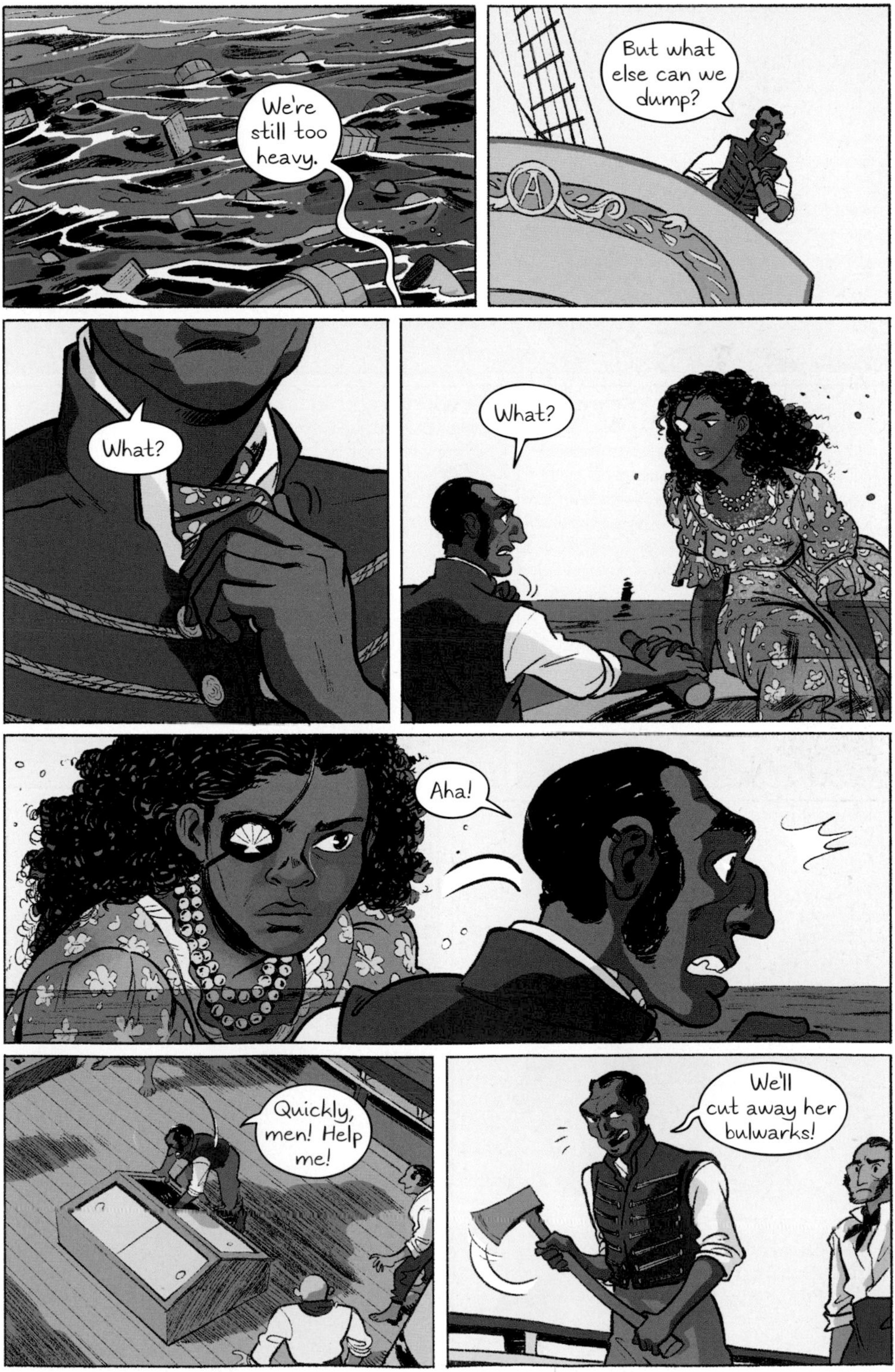
We're still too heavy.
But what else can we dump?
What?
What?
Aha!
Quickly, men! Help me!
We'll cut away her bulwarks!

CHAPTER SIX
RECONSTRUCTION

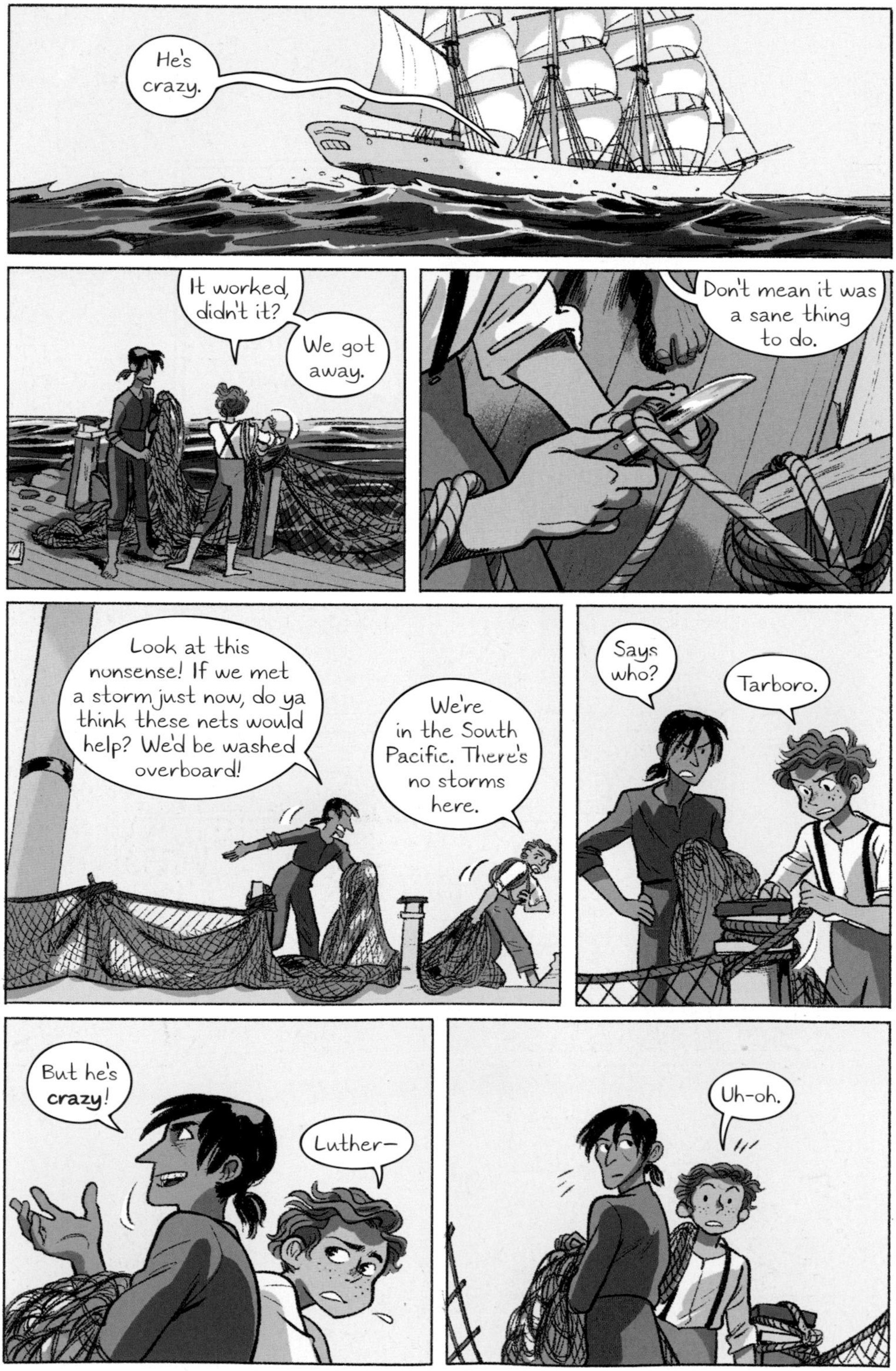
He's crazy.
It worked, didn't it?
We got away.
Don't mean it was a sane thing to do.
Look at this nonsense! If we met a storm just now, do ya think these nets would help? We'd be washed overboard!
We're in the South Pacific. There's no storms here.
Says who?
Tarboro.
But he's **crazy**!
Luther—
Uh-oh.

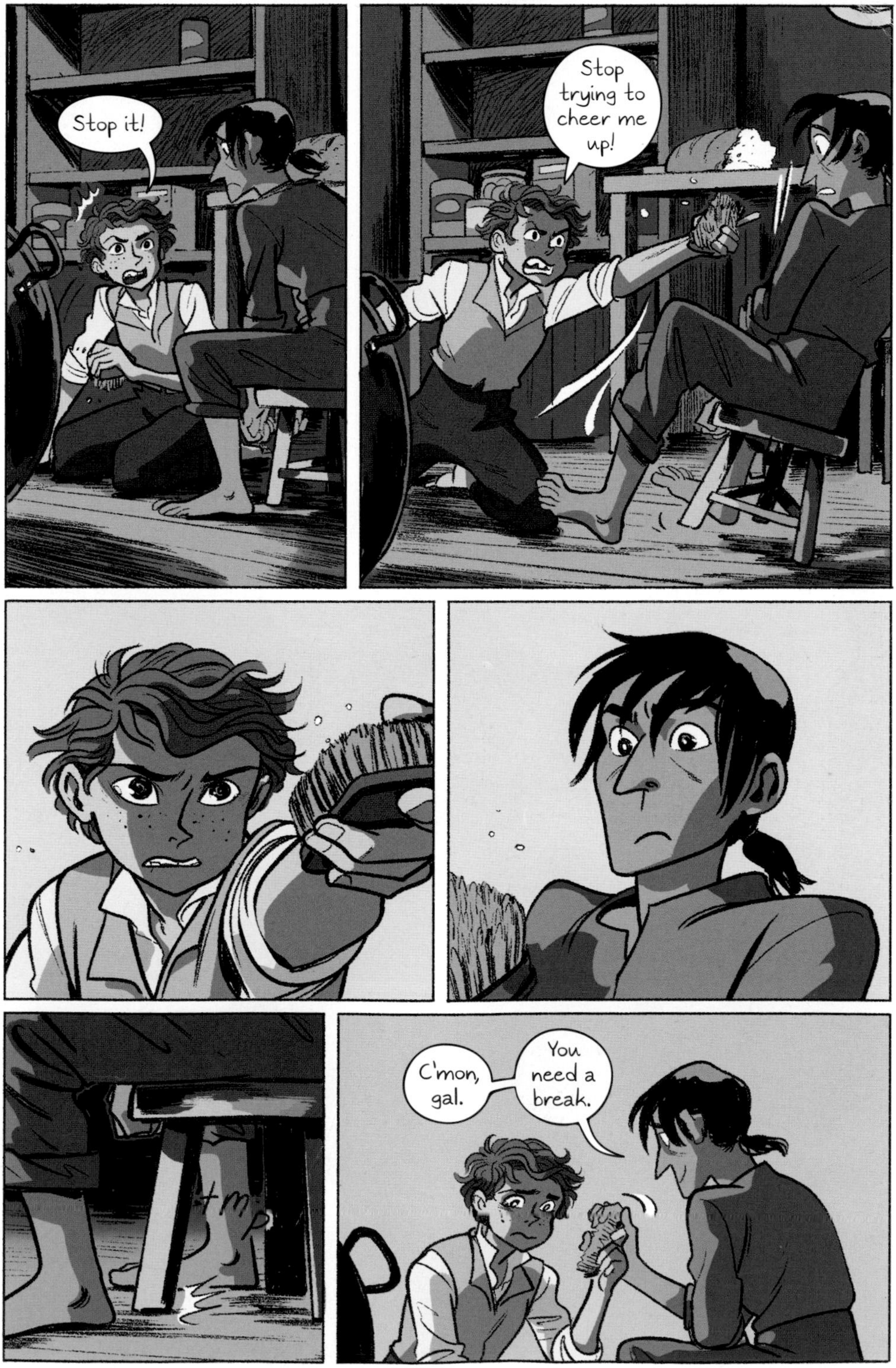
Stop it!
Stop trying to cheer me up!
C'mon, gal.
You need a break.

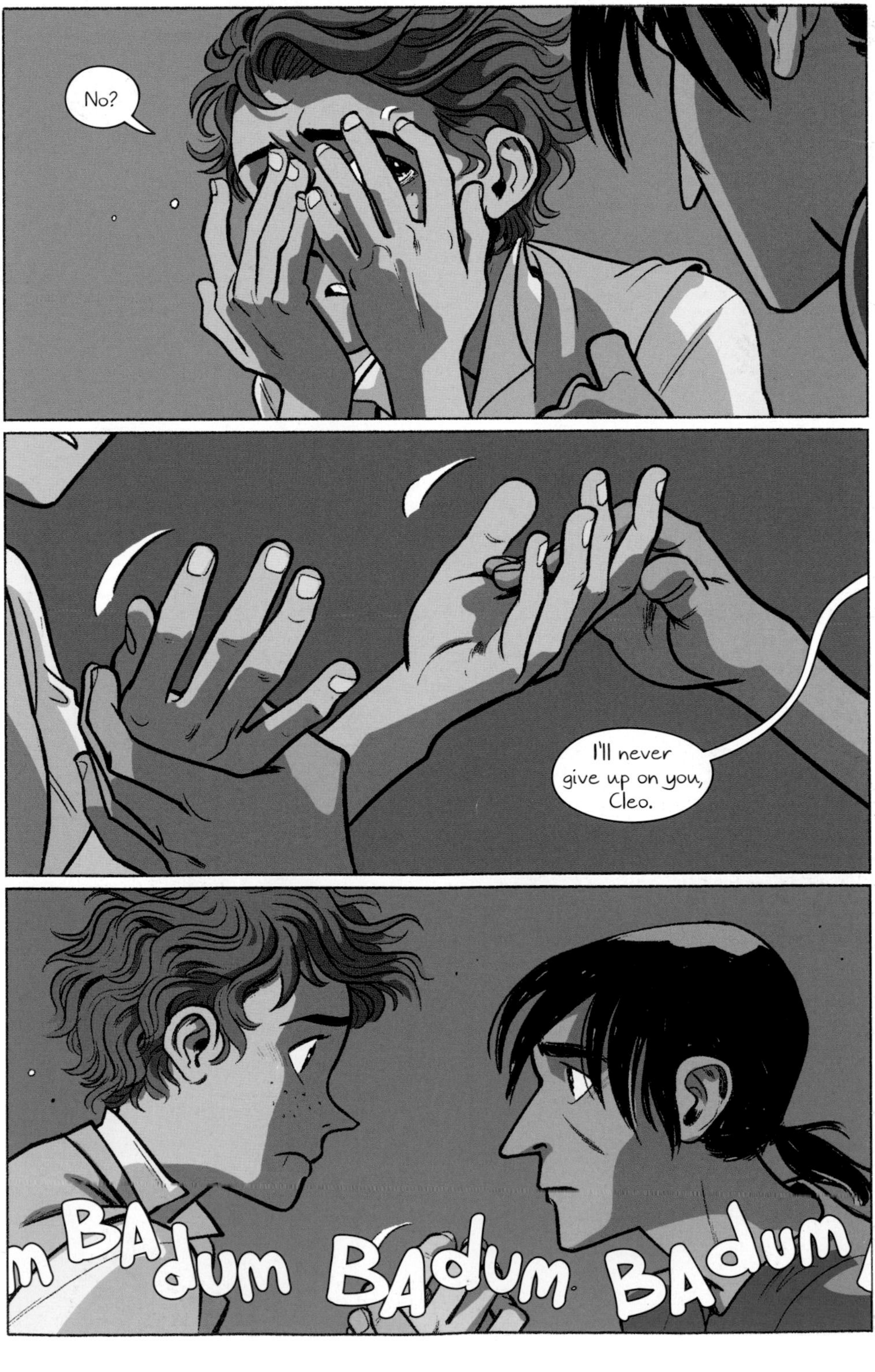
No?
I'll never give up on you, Cleo.
m BA dum BAdum BAdum

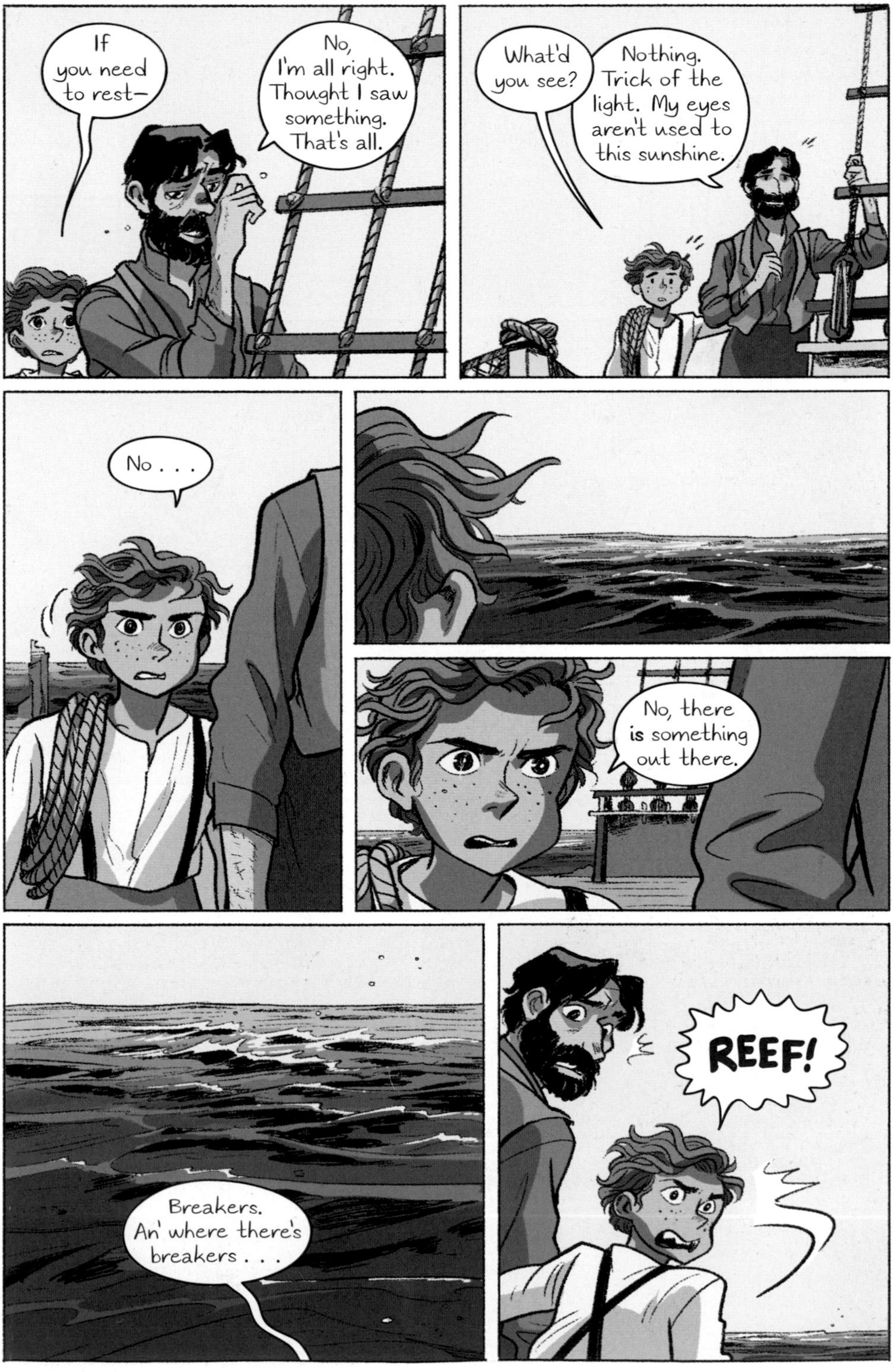

If you need to rest—
No, I'm all right. Thought I saw something. That's all.
What'd you see?
Nothing. Trick of the light. My eyes aren't used to this sunshine.
No . . .
No, there **is** something out there.
Breakers. An' where there's breakers . . .
REEF!

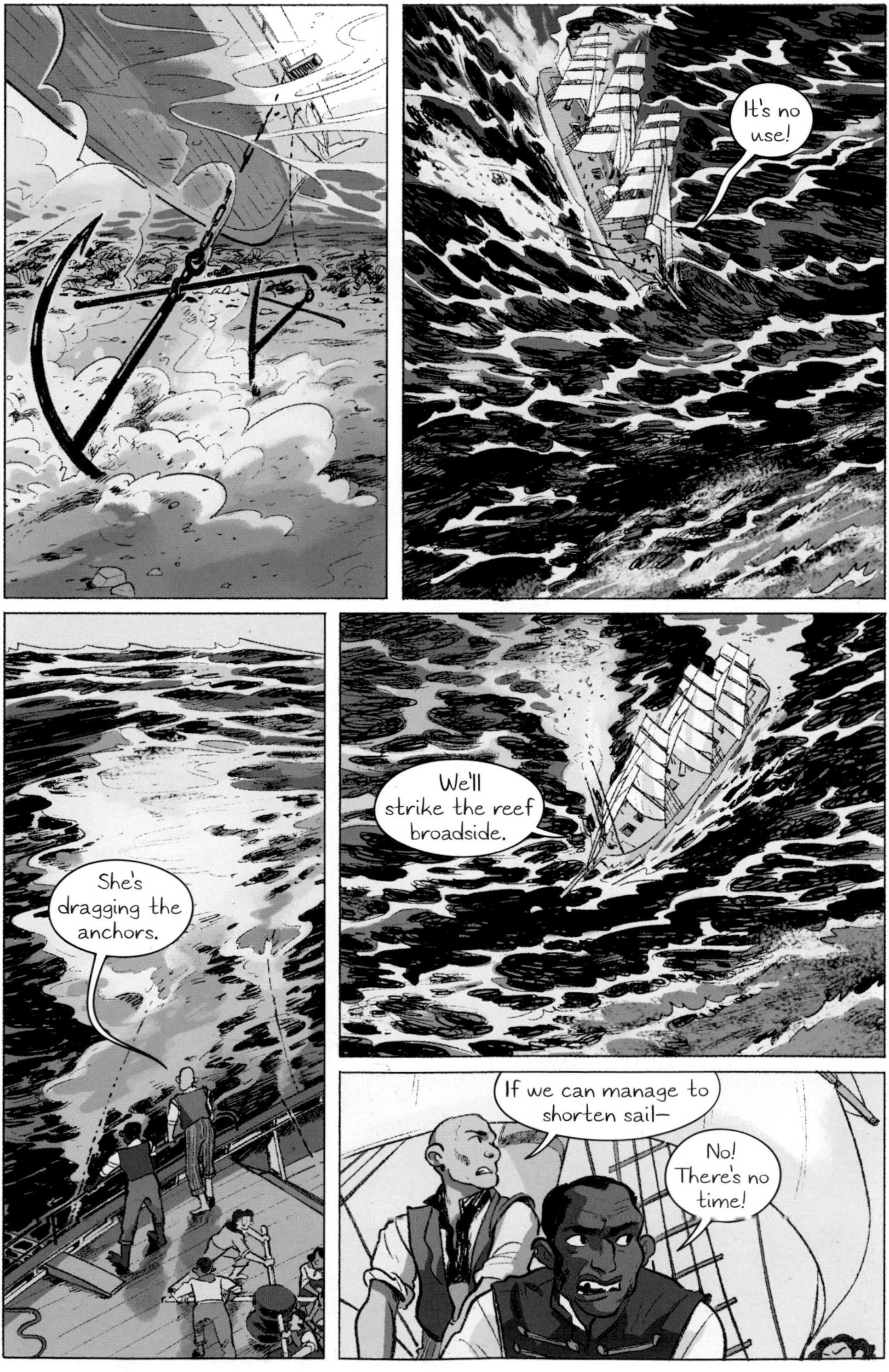
It's no use!
She's dragging the anchors.
We'll strike the reef broadside.
If we can manage to shorten sail—
No! There's no time!

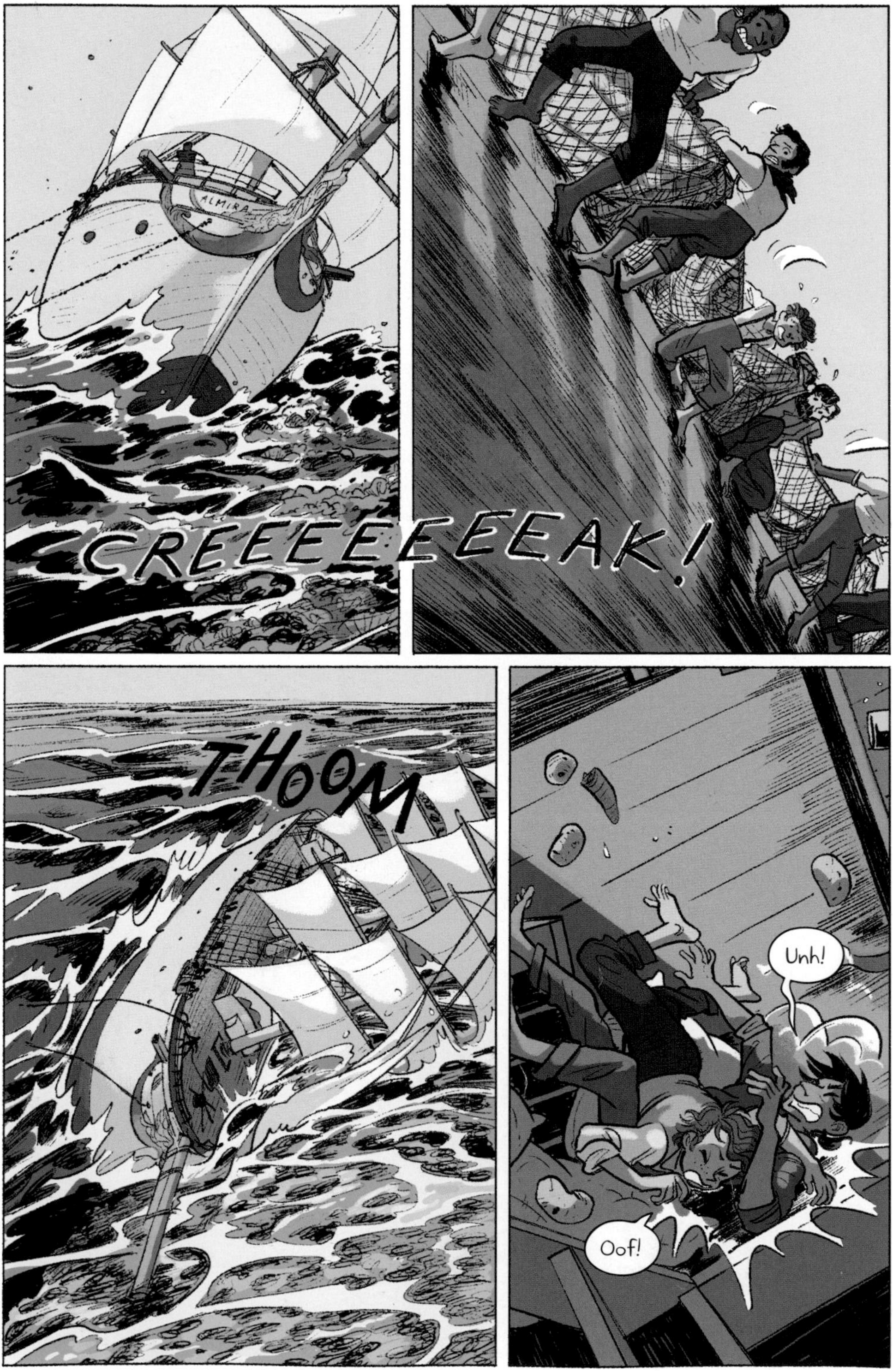
ALMIRA
CREEEEEEEEAK!
THOOM
Unh!
Oof!

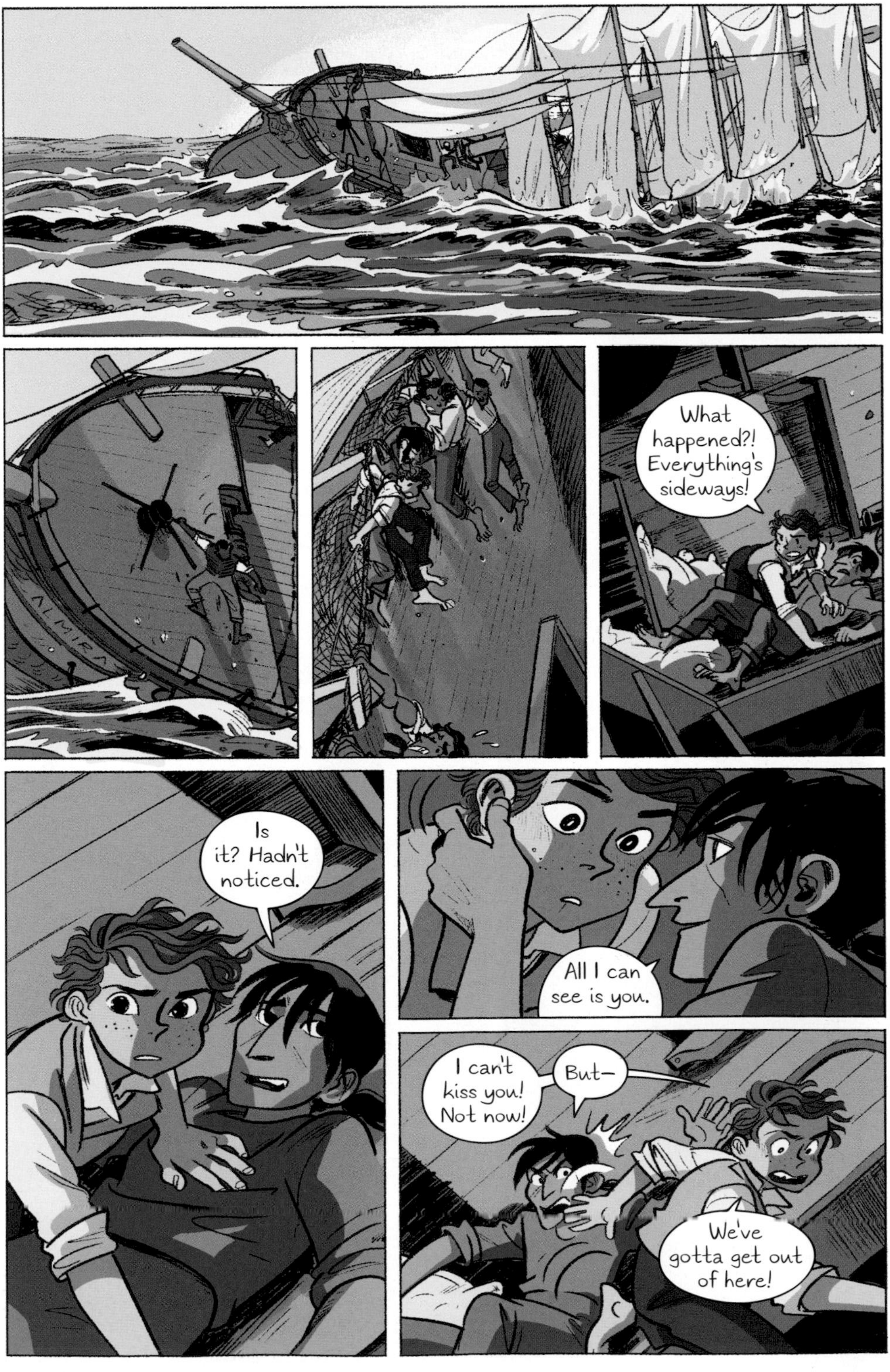
What happened?! Everything's sideways!
Is it? Hadn't noticed.
All I can see is you.
I can't kiss you! Not now!
But—
We've gotta get out of here!

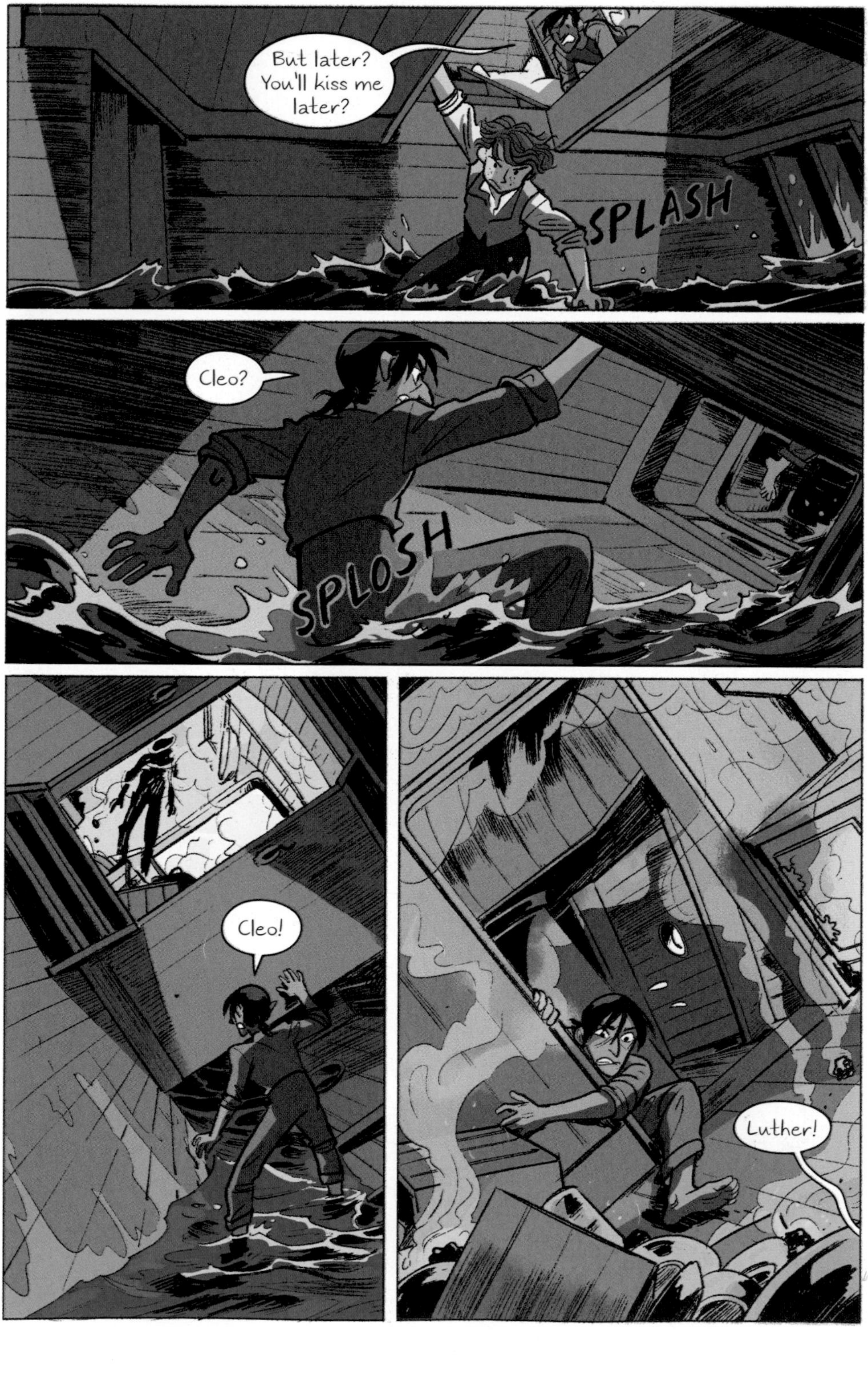
But later? You'll kiss me later?
SPLASH
Cleo?
SPLOSH
Cleo!
Luther!

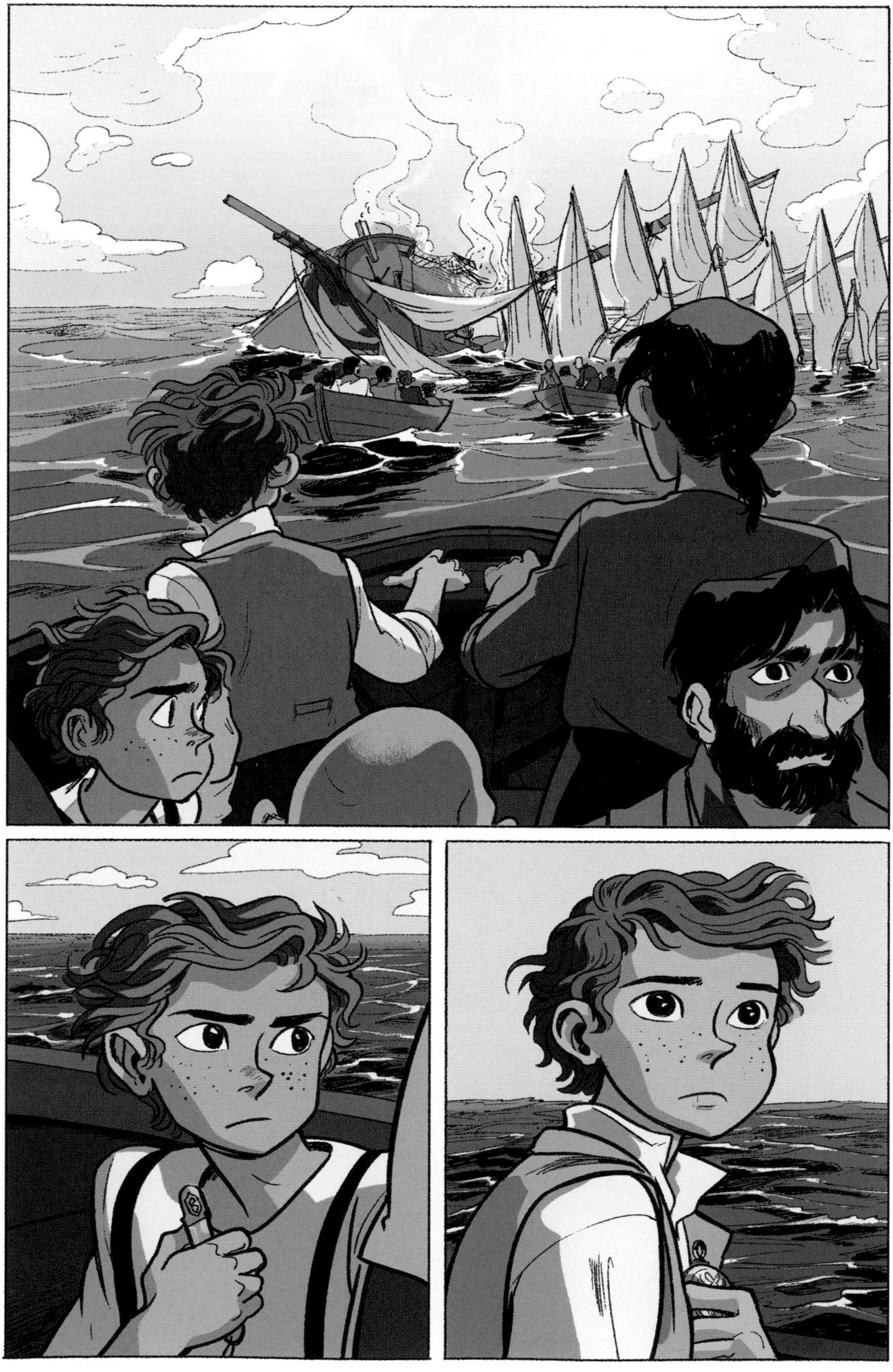

CHAPTER SEVEN
MONONO

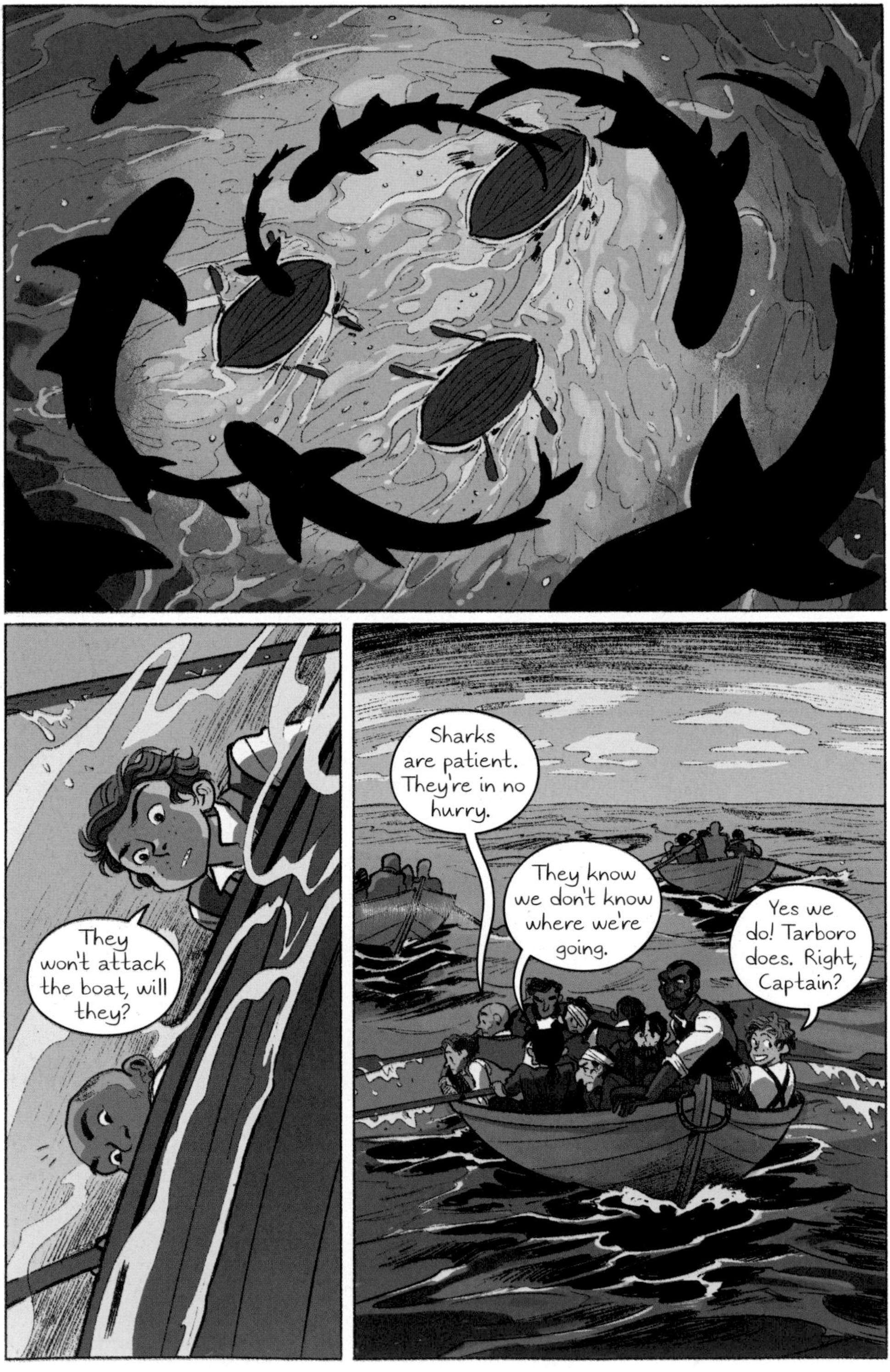
They won't attack the boat, will they?
Sharks are patient. They're in no hurry.
They know we don't know where we're going.
Yes we do! Tarboro does. Right, Captain?

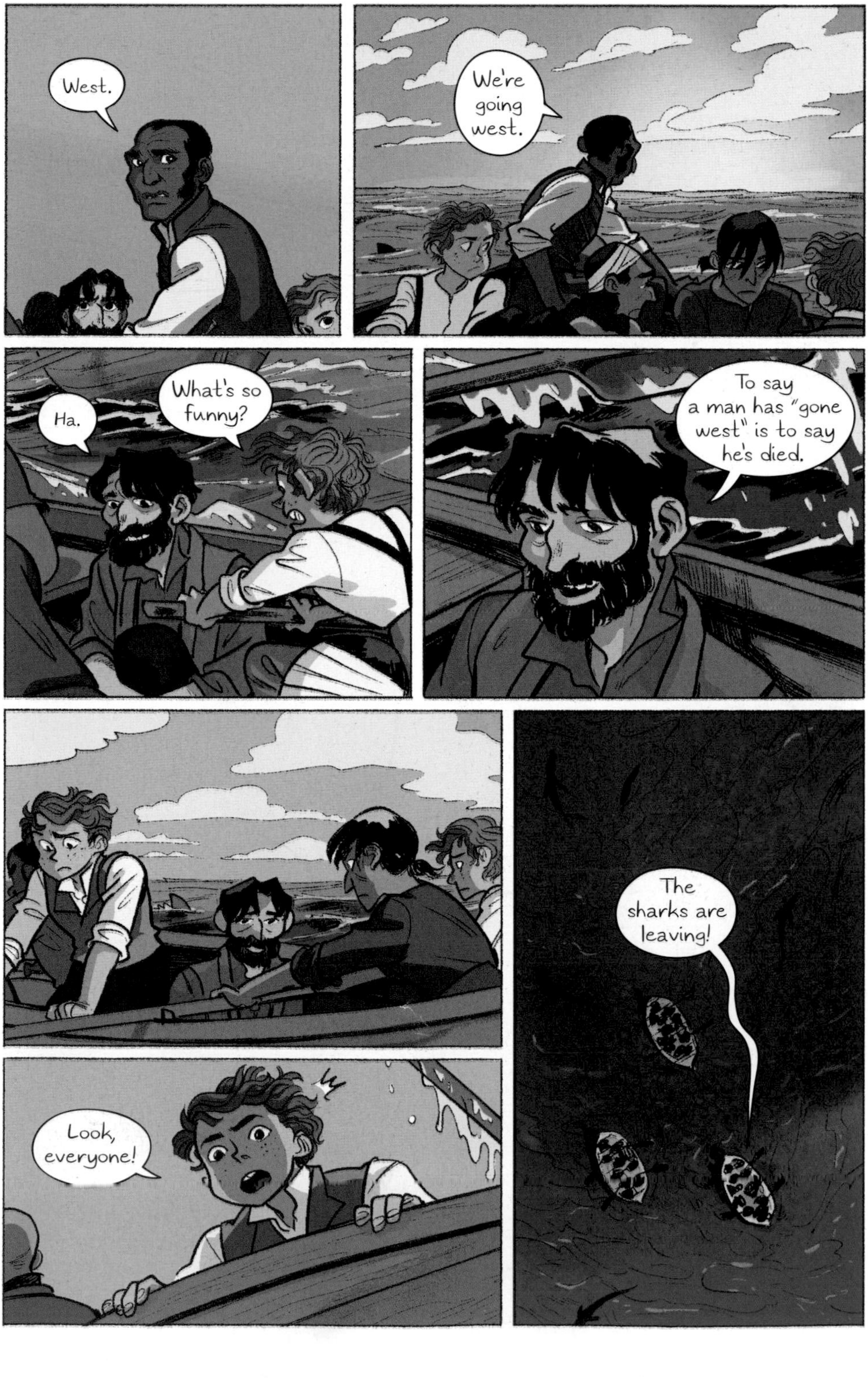
West.
We're going west.
Ha.
What's so funny?
To say a man has "gone west" is to say he's died.
Look, everyone!
The sharks are leaving!

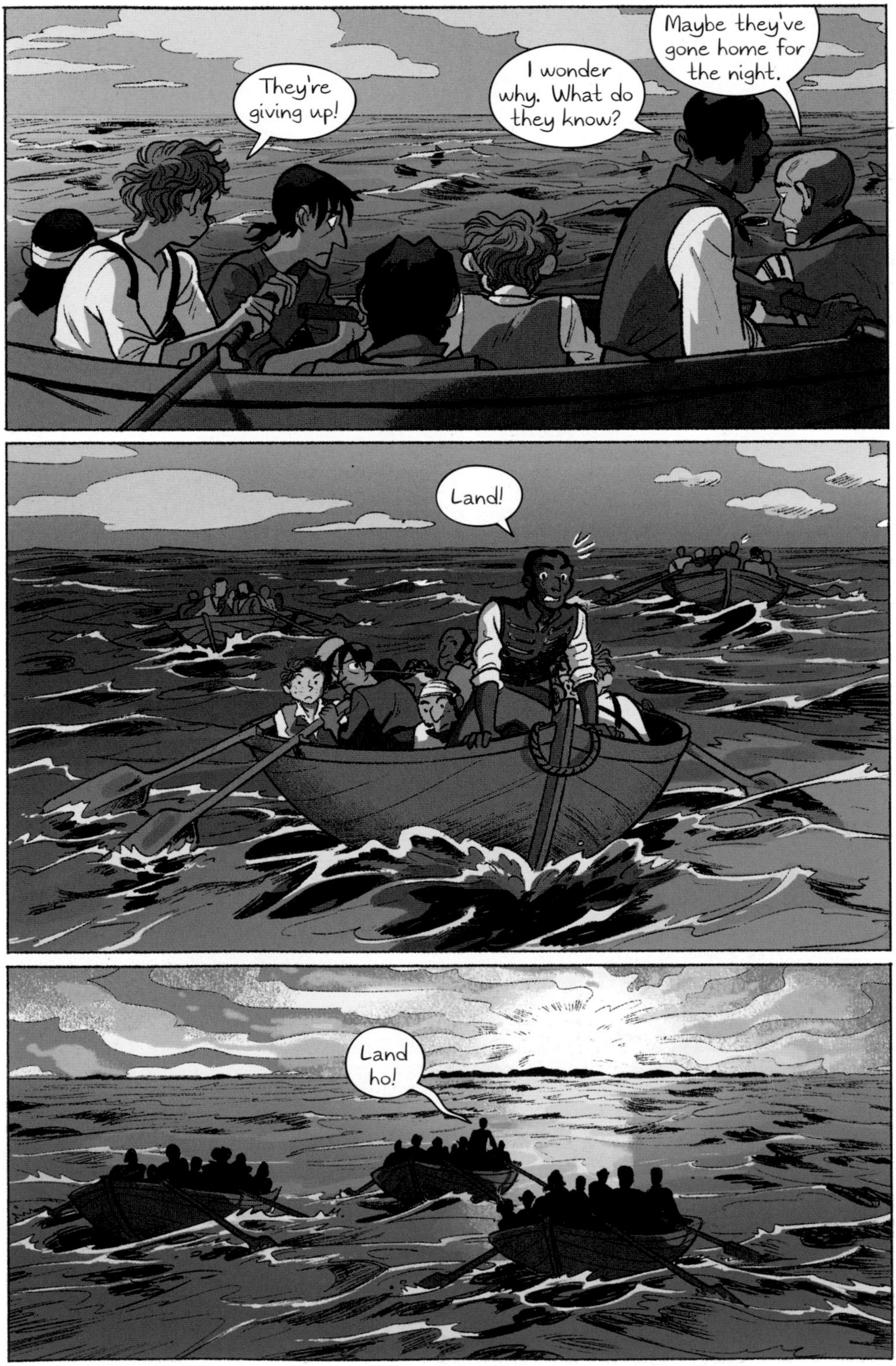
They're giving up!
I wonder why. What do they know?
Maybe they've gone home for the night.
Land!
Land ho!

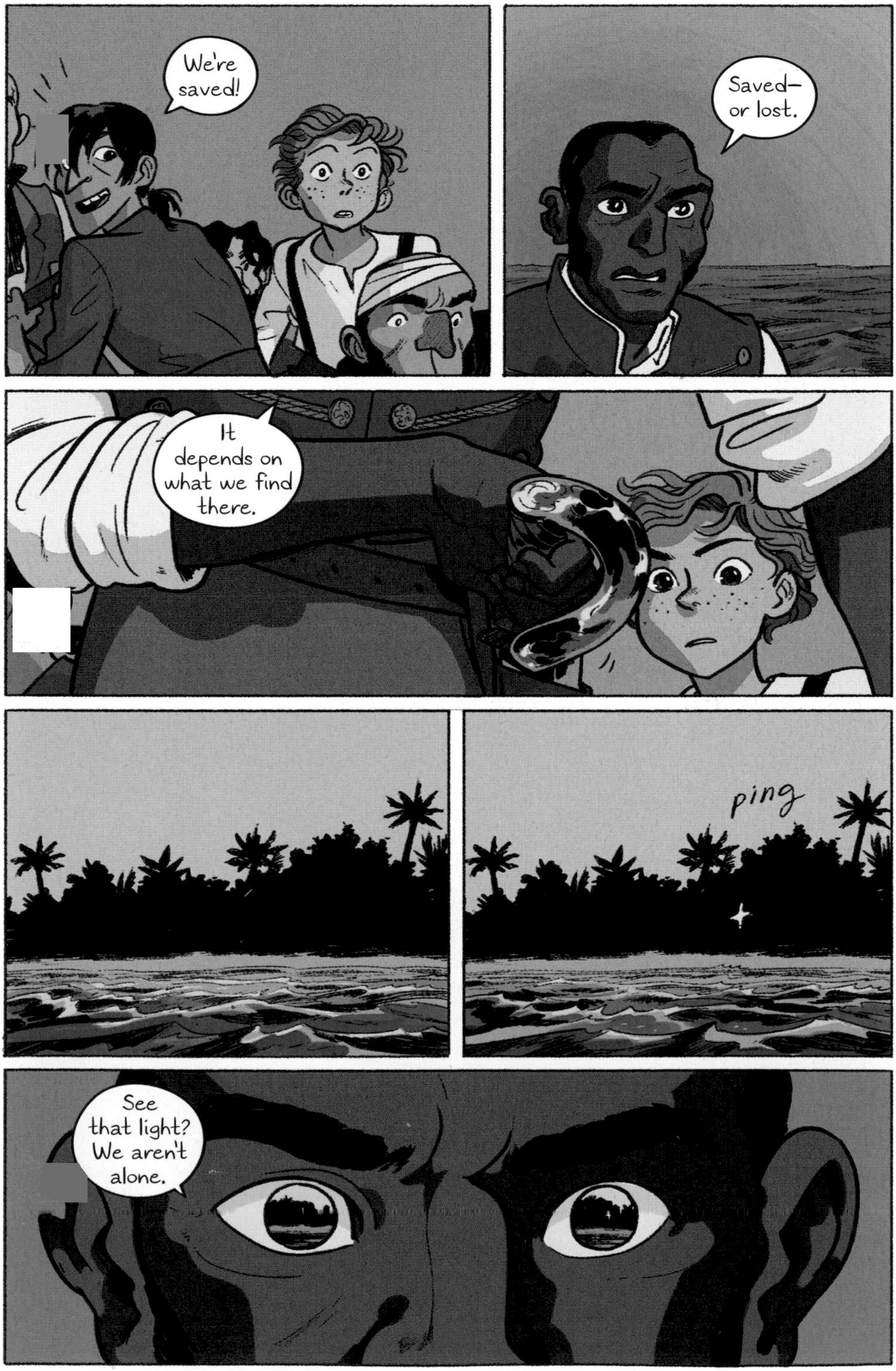
We're saved!
Saved—or lost.
It depends on what we find there.
ping
See that light? We aren't alone.

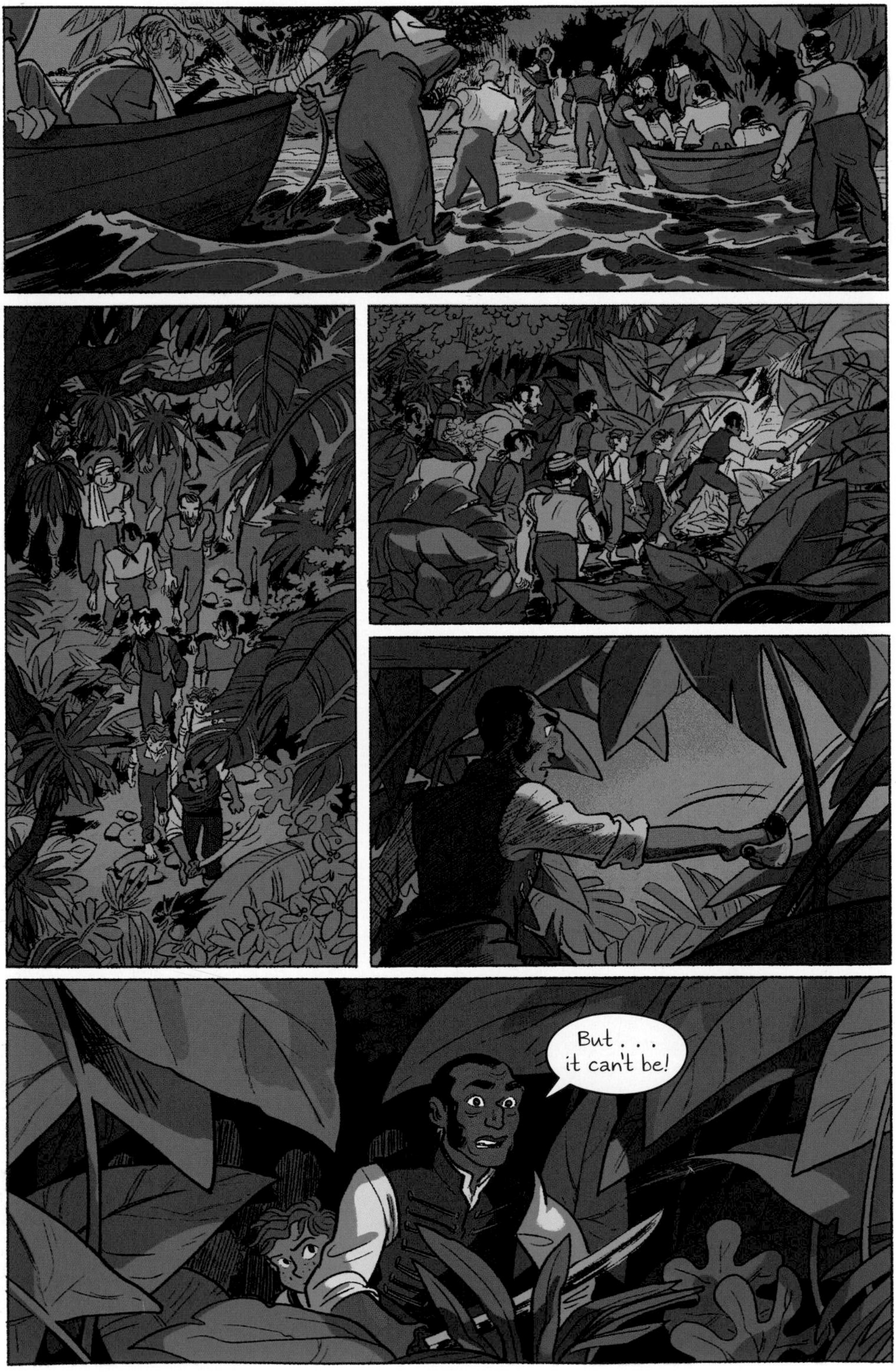
But . . .
it can't be!

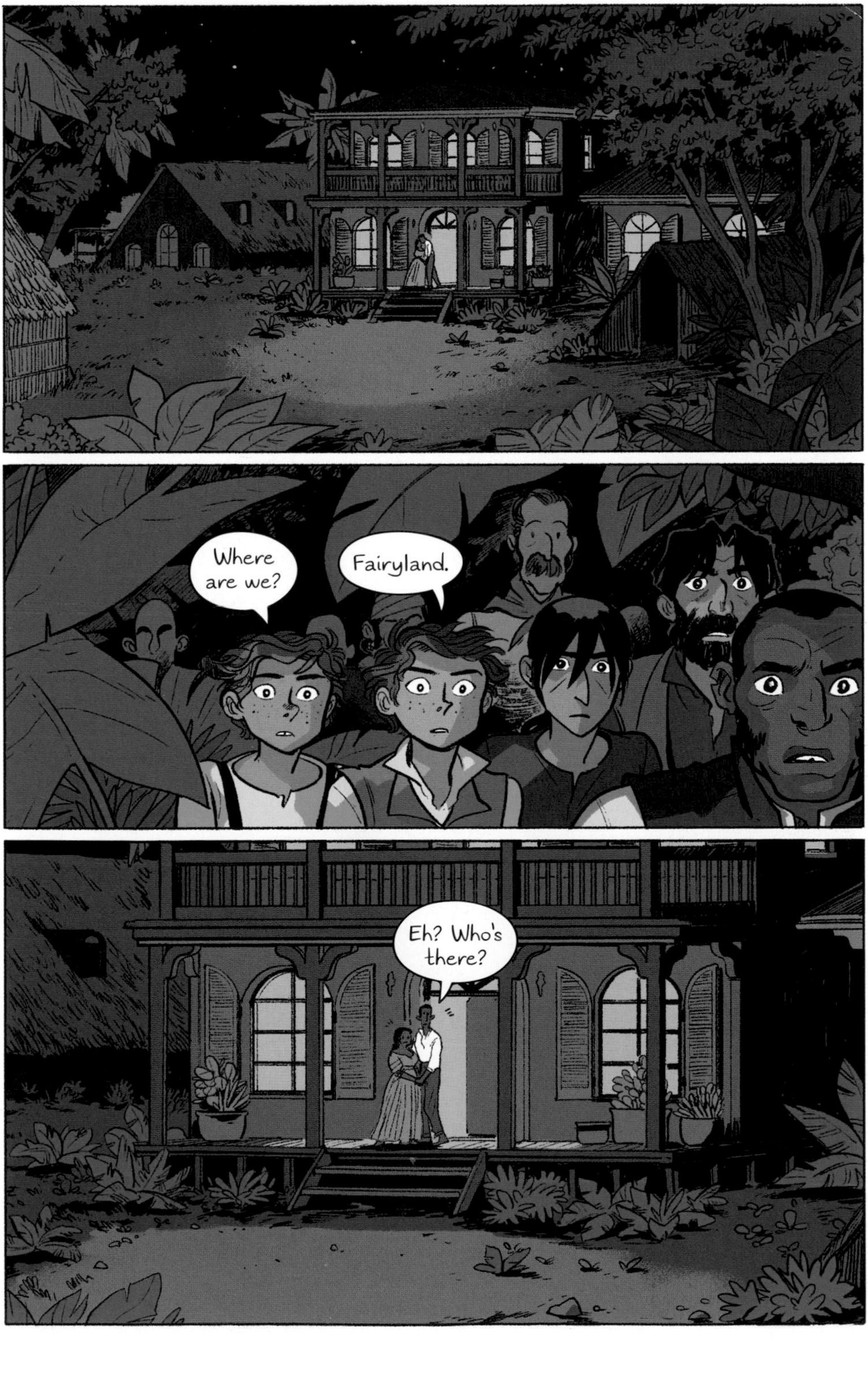
Where are we?
Fairyland.
Eh? Who's there?

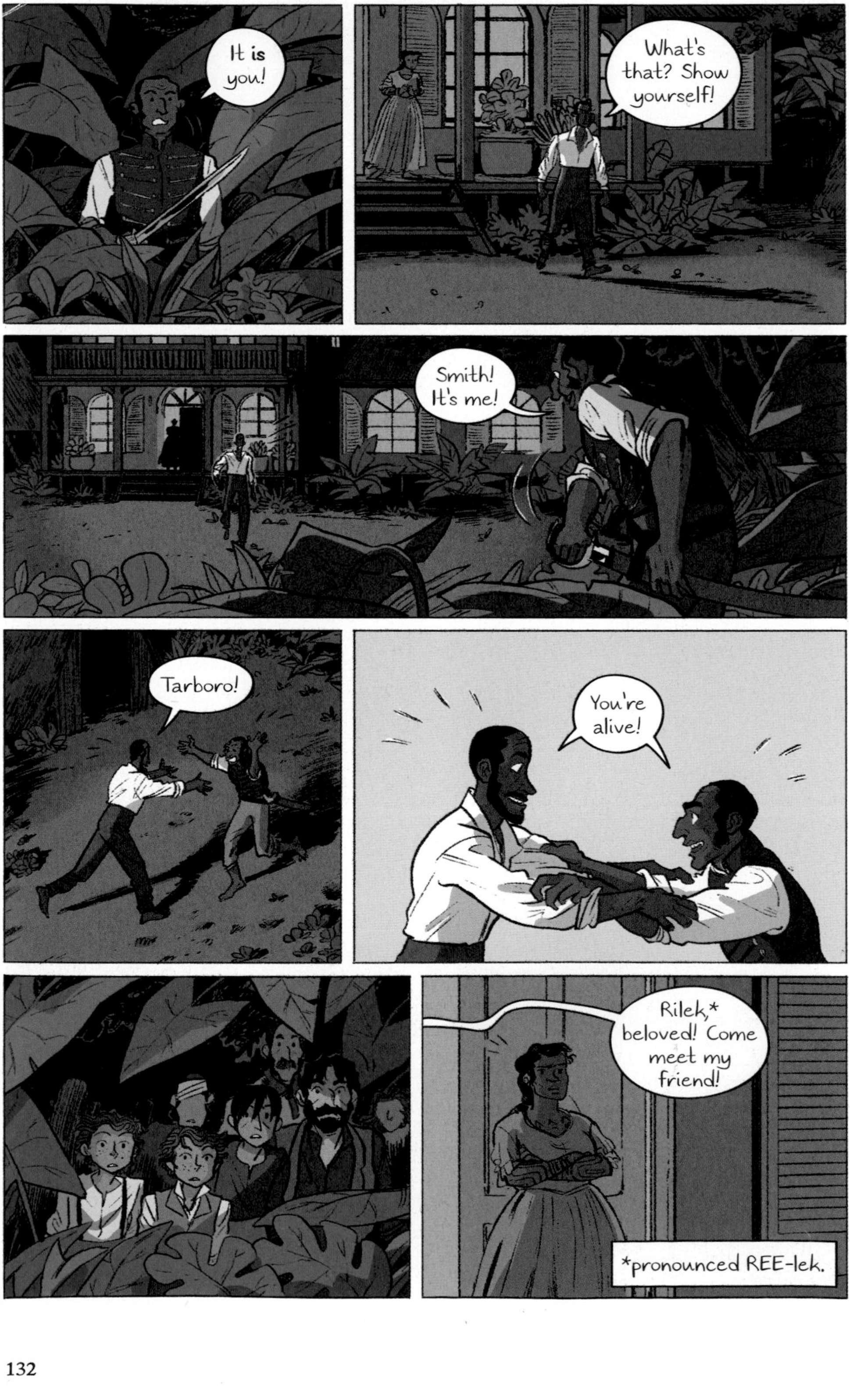
It is you!
What's that? Show yourself!
Smith! It's me!
Tarboro!
You're alive!
Rilek,* beloved! Come meet my friend!
*pronounced REE-lek.

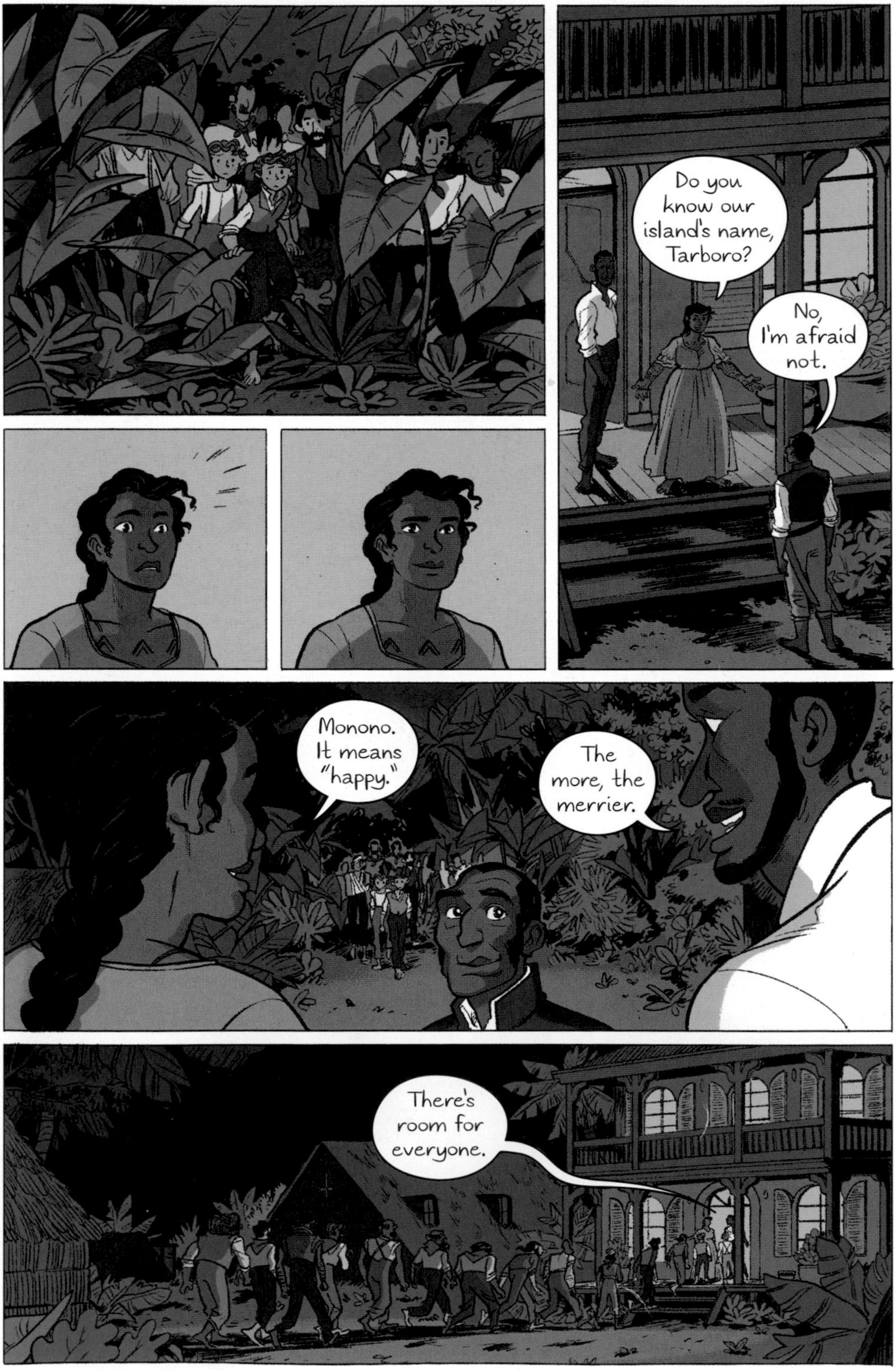
Do you know our island's name, Tarboro?
No, I'm afraid not.
Monono. It means "happy."
The more, the merrier.
There's room for everyone.

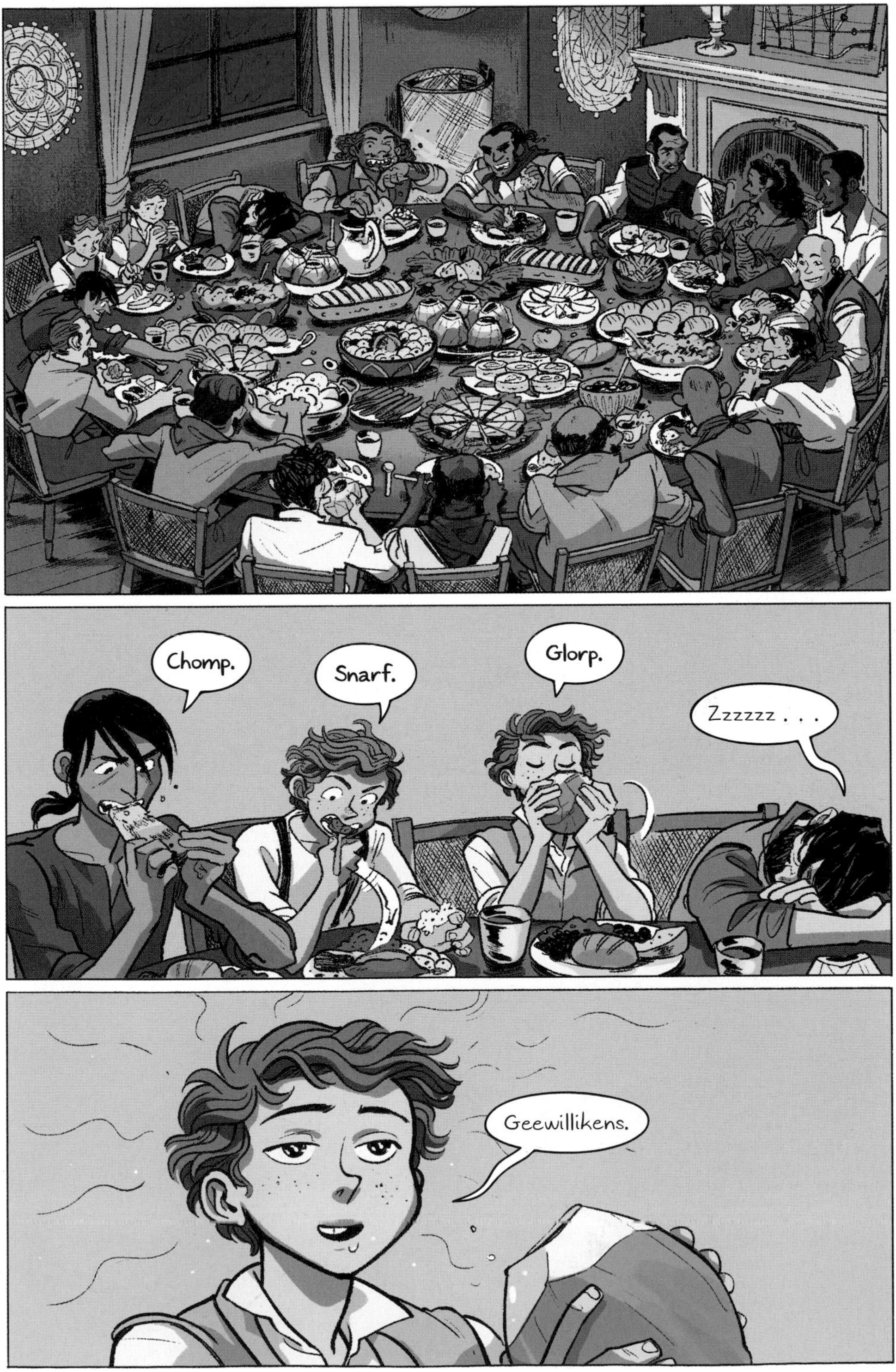
Chomp.
Snarf.
Glorp.
Zzzzzz . . .
Geewillikens.

140

141

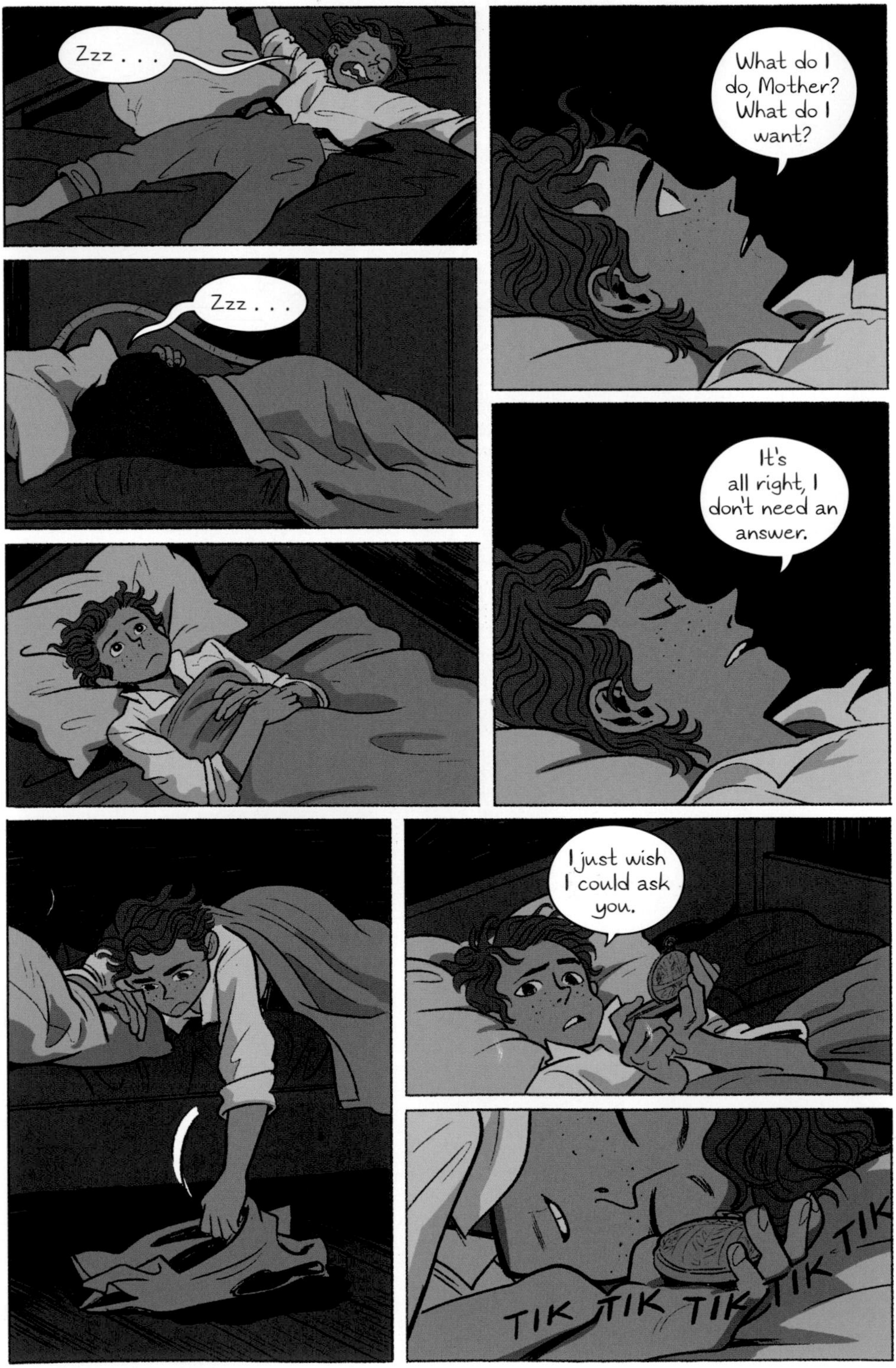
Zzz . . .
What do I do, Mother? What do I want?
Zzz . . .
It's all right, I don't need an answer.
I just wish I could ask you.
TIK TIK TIK TIK TIK

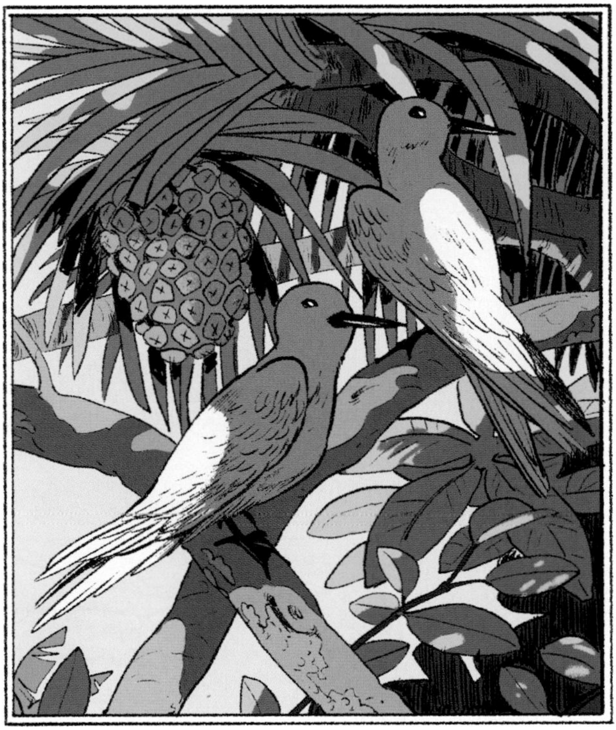

CHAPTER EIGHT

TRUCE

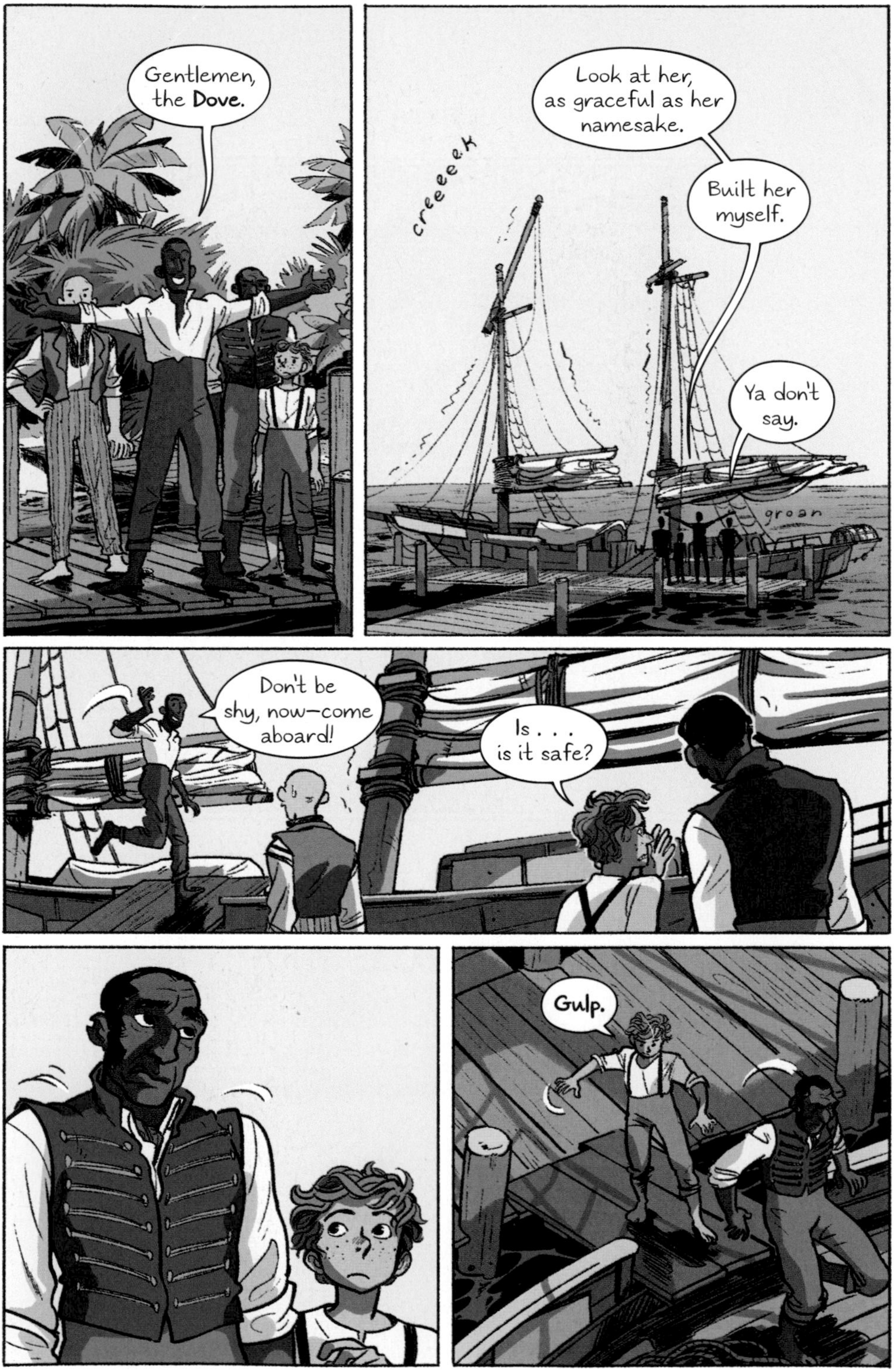
Gentlemen, the **Dove.**
Look at her, as graceful as her namesake.
creeeeek
Built her myself.
Ya don't say.
groan
Don't be shy, now—come aboard!
Is . . . is it safe?
Gulp.

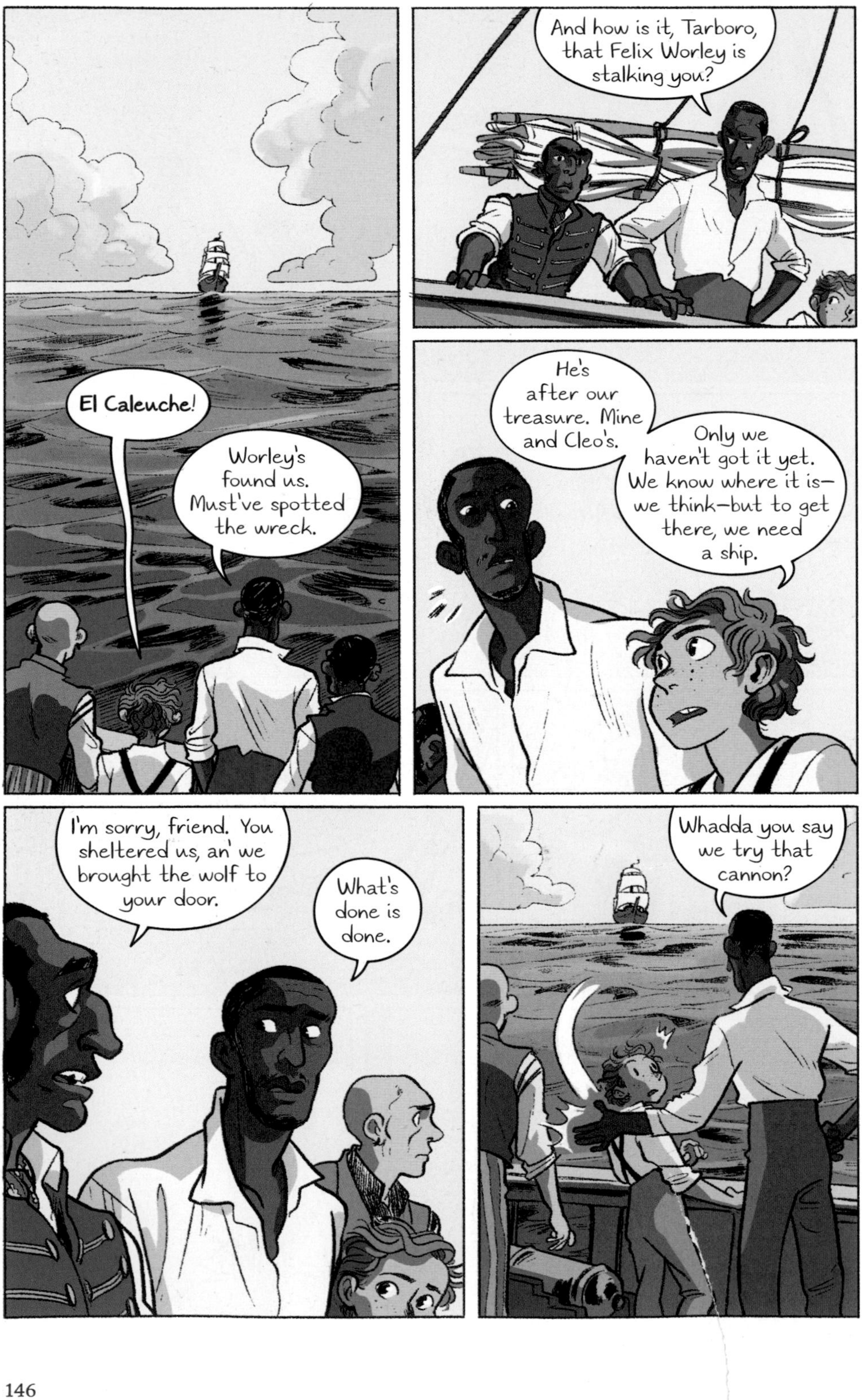
El Caleuche!
Worley's found us. Must've spotted the wreck.
And how is it, Tarboro, that Felix Worley is stalking you?
He's after our treasure. Mine and Cleo's.
Only we haven't got it yet. We know where it is—we think—but to get there, we need a ship.
I'm sorry, friend. You sheltered us, an' we brought the wolf to your door.
What's done is done.
Whadda you say we try that cannon?

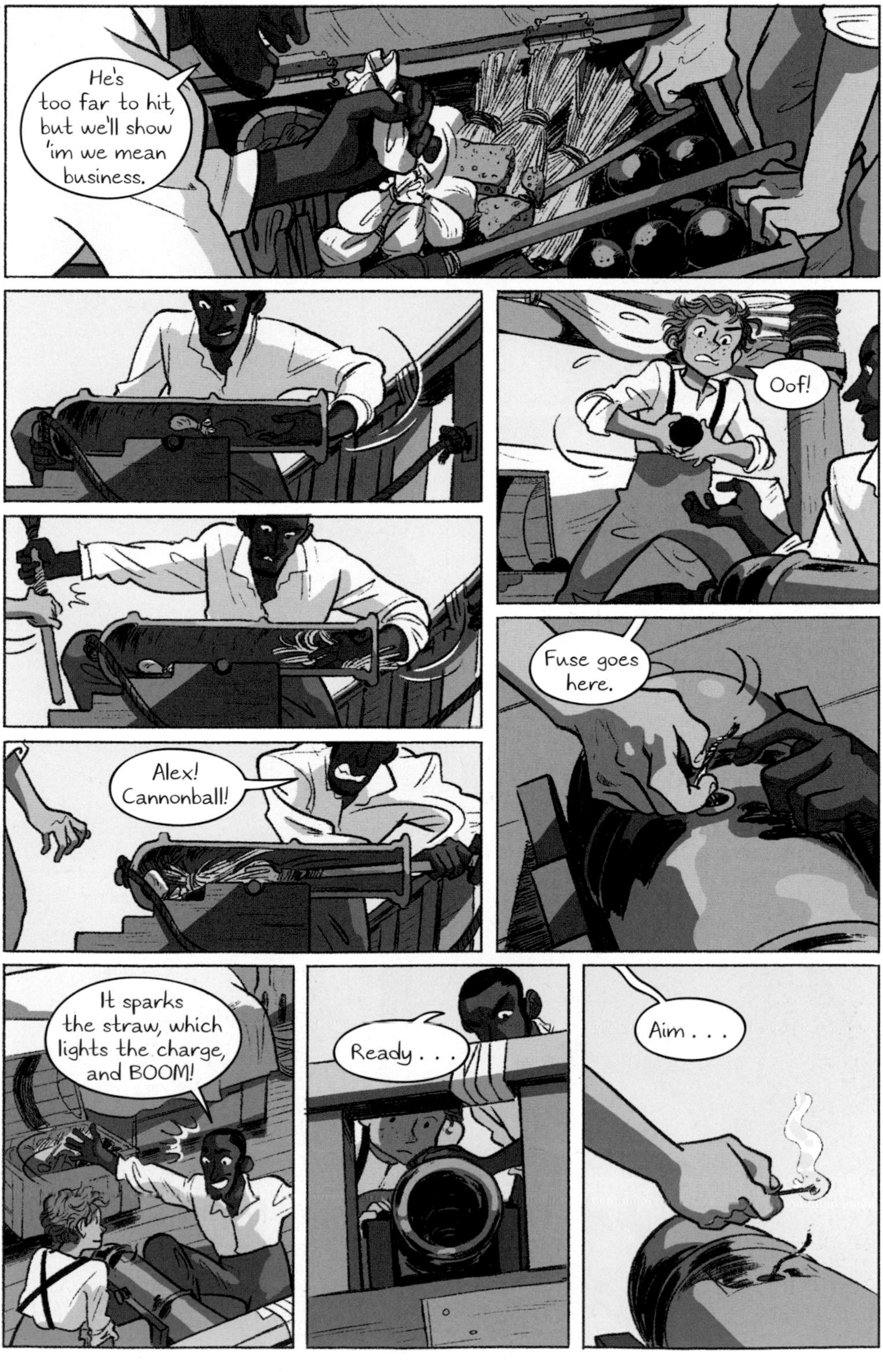
He's too far to hit, but we'll show 'im we mean business.
Oof!
Alex! Cannonball!
Fuse goes here.
It sparks the straw, which lights the charge, and BOOM!
Ready . . .
Aim . . .

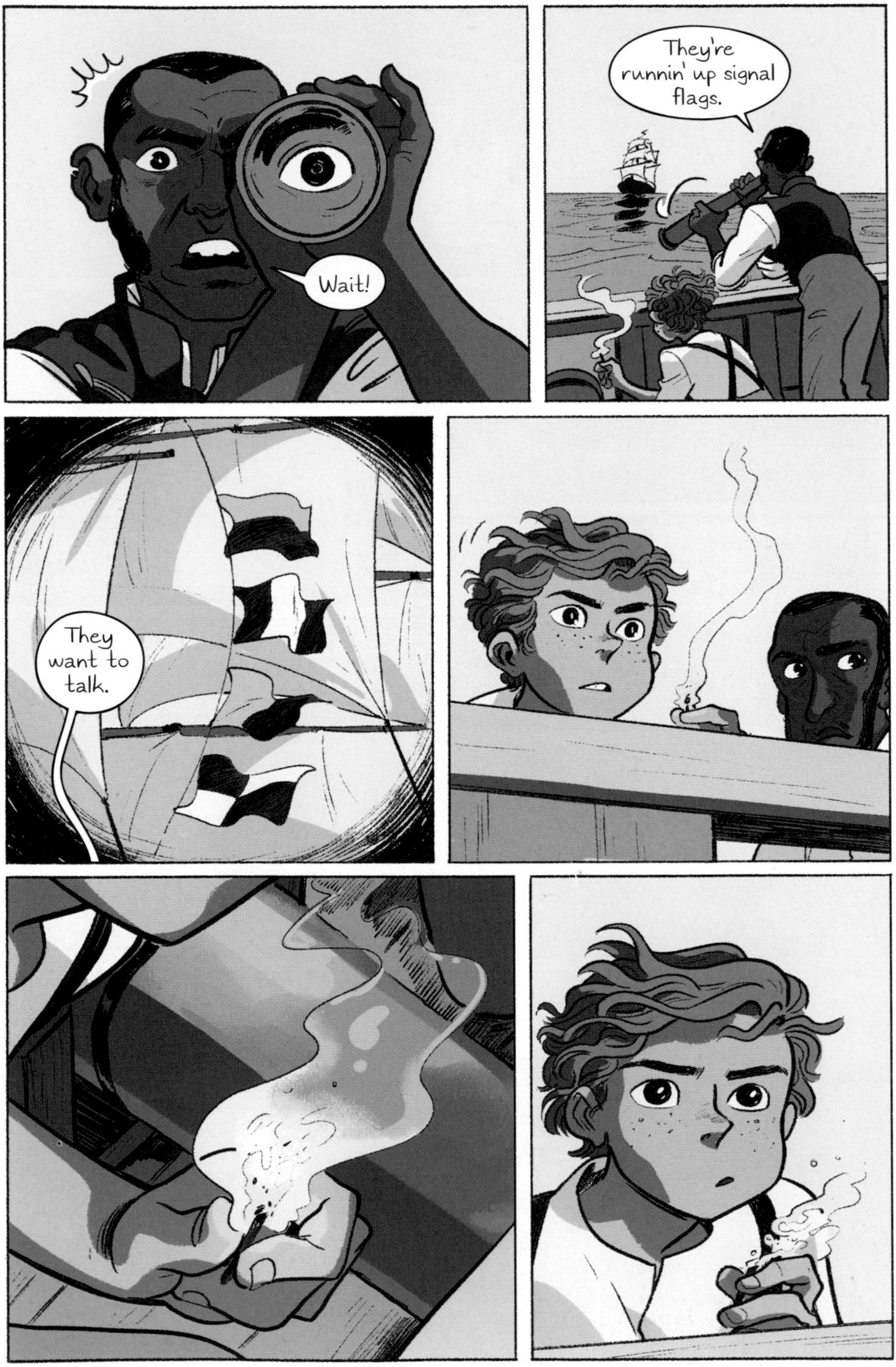
Wait!
They're runnin' up signal flags.
They want to talk.

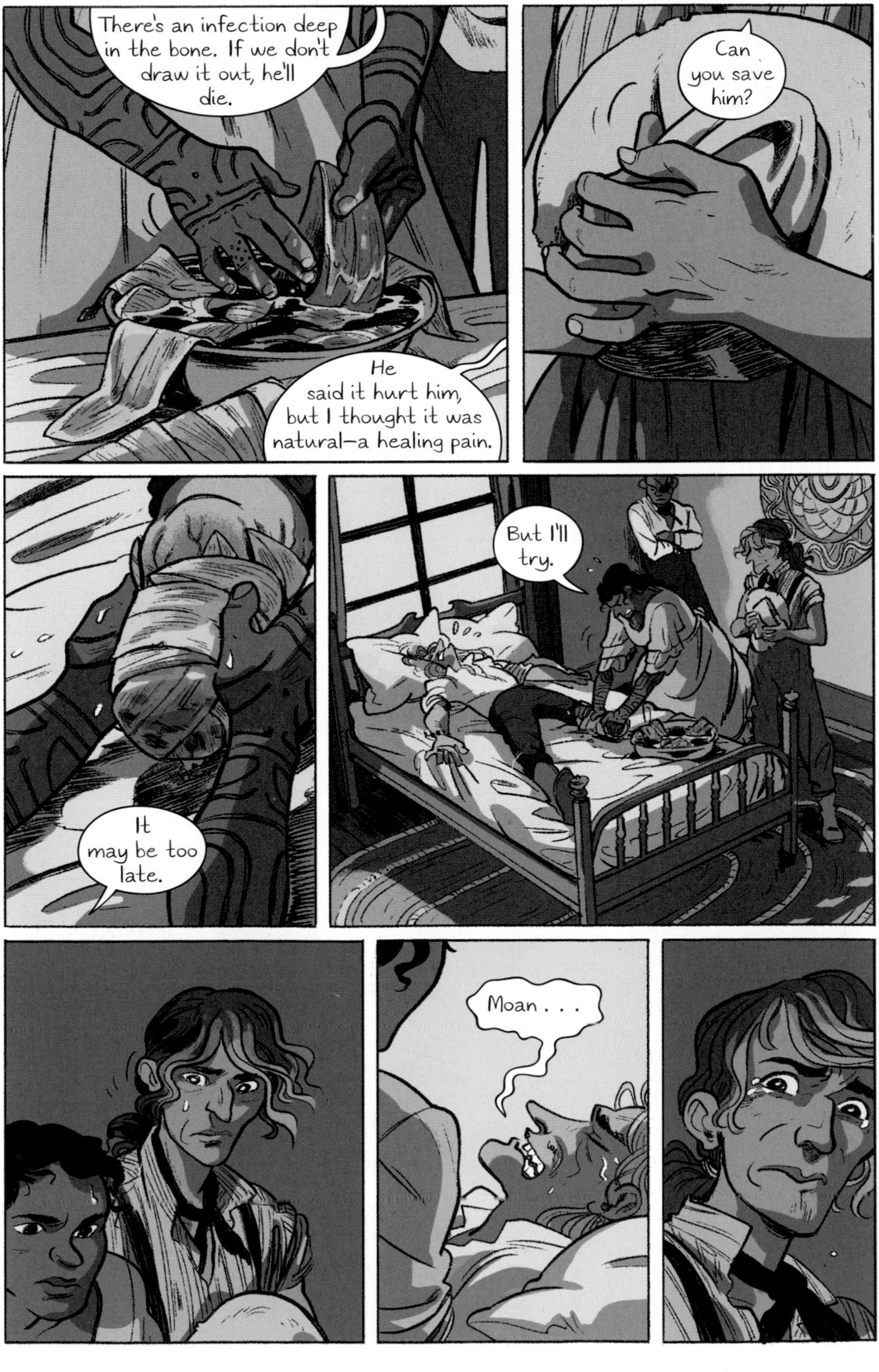

There's an infection deep in the bone. If we don't draw it out, he'll die.
He said it hurt him, but I thought it was natural—a healing pain.
Can you save him?
It may be too late.
But I'll try.
Moan . . .

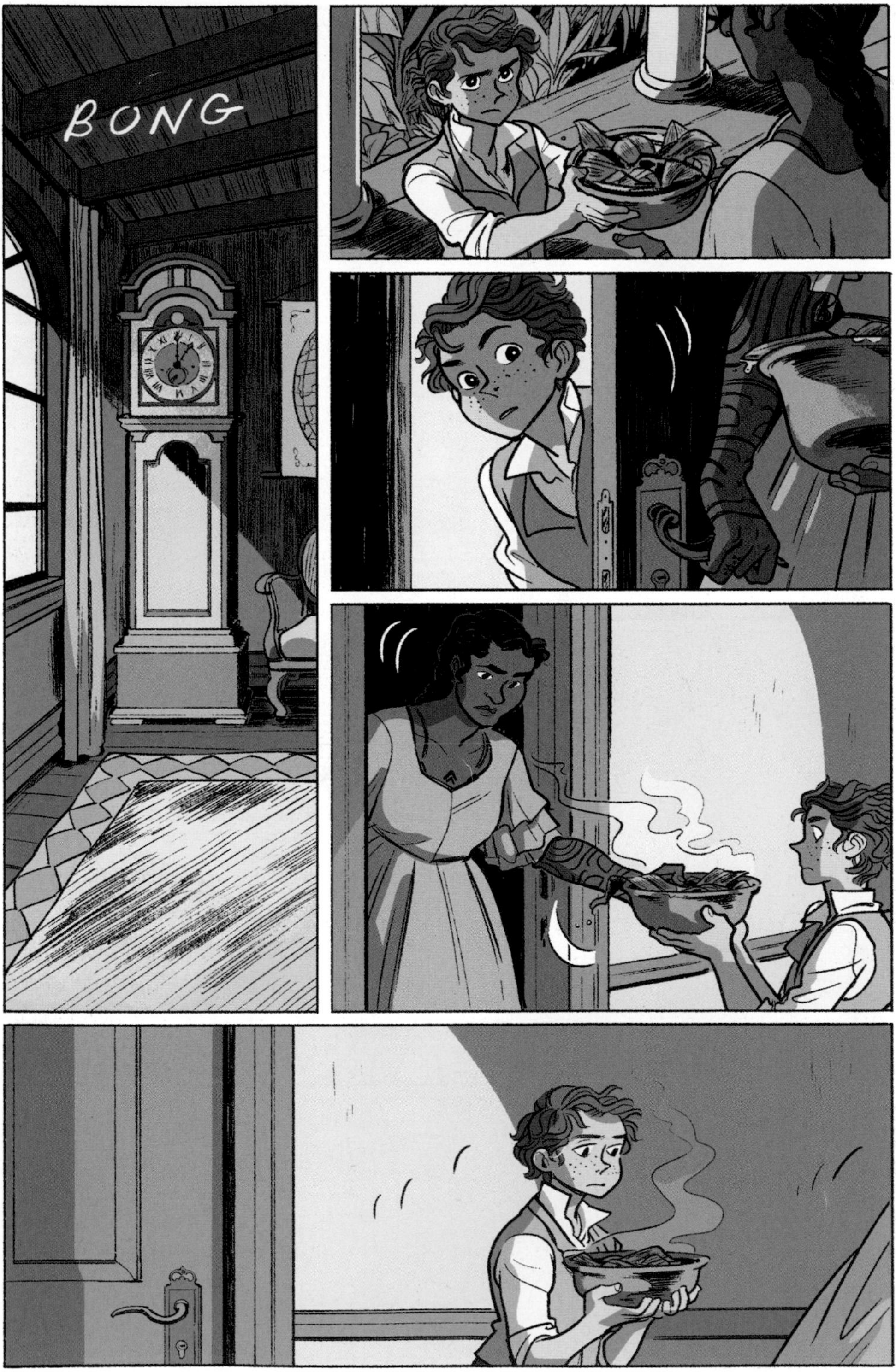
BONG

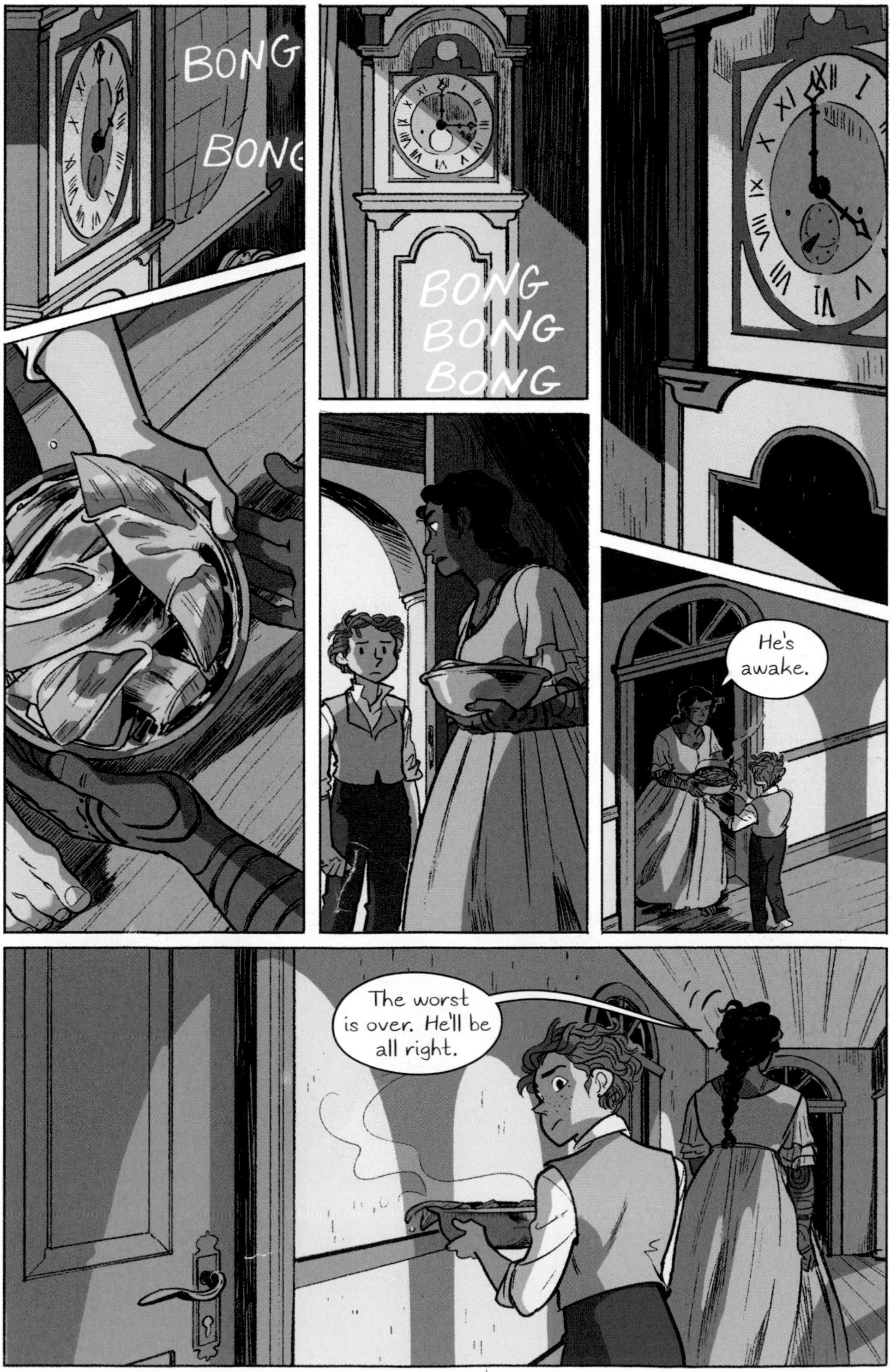
BONG
BONG
BONG
BONG
BONG
He's awake.
The worst is over. He'll be all right.

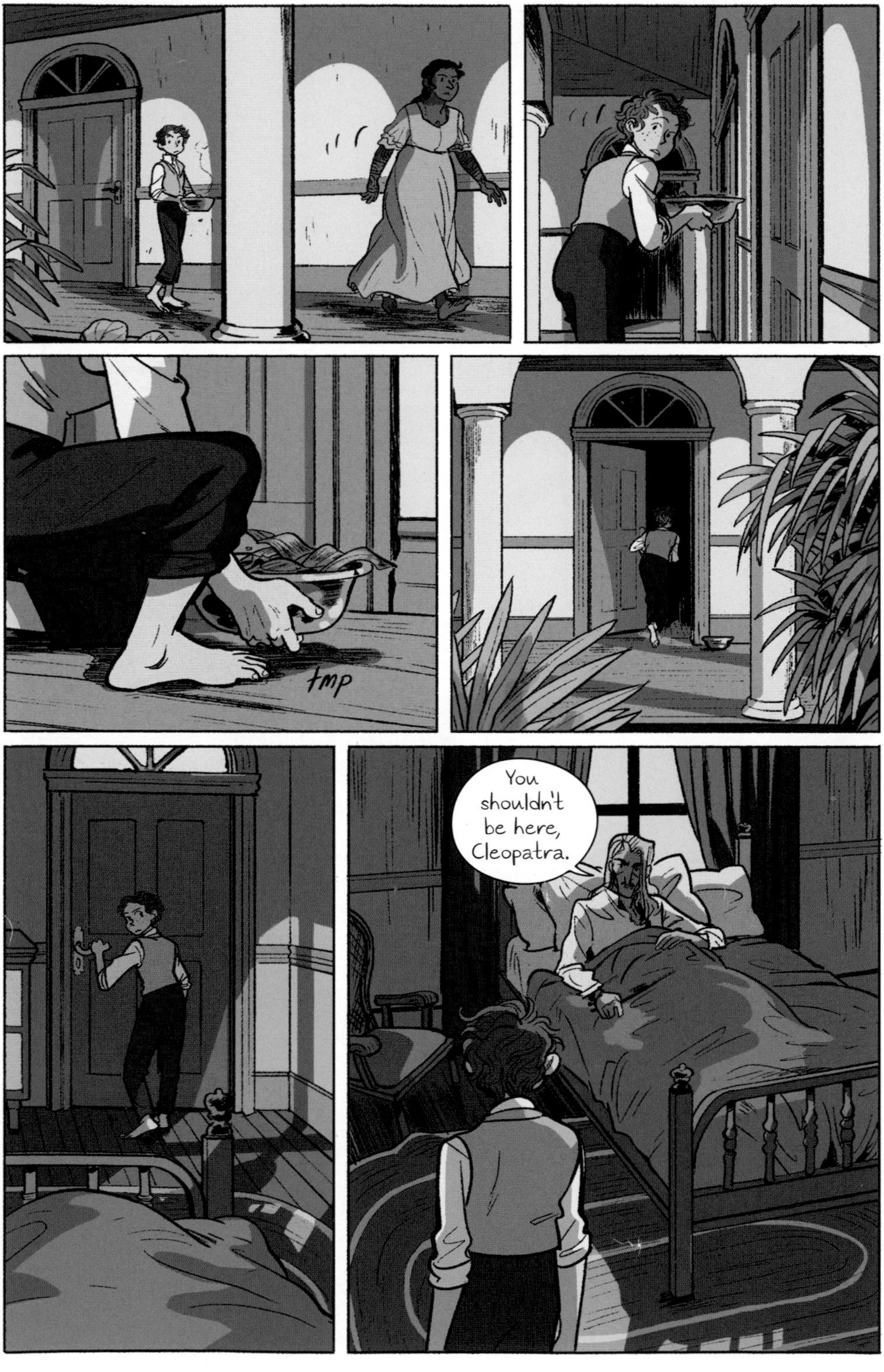
tmp
You shouldn't be here, Cleopatra.

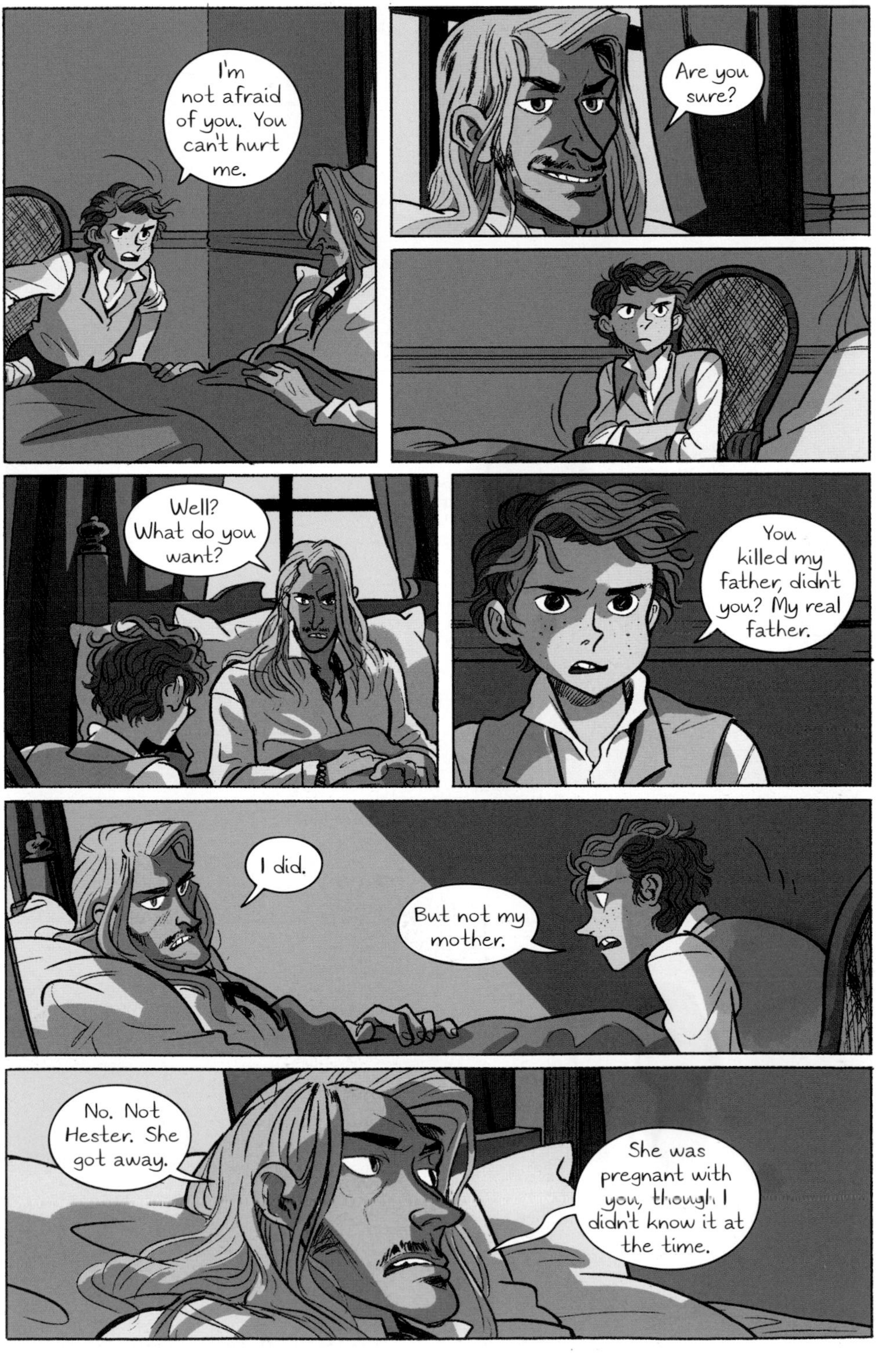
I'm not afraid of you. You can't hurt me.
Are you sure?
Well? What do you want?
You killed my father, didn't you? My real father.
I did.
But not my mother.
No. Not Hester. She got away.
She was pregnant with you, though I didn't know it at the time.

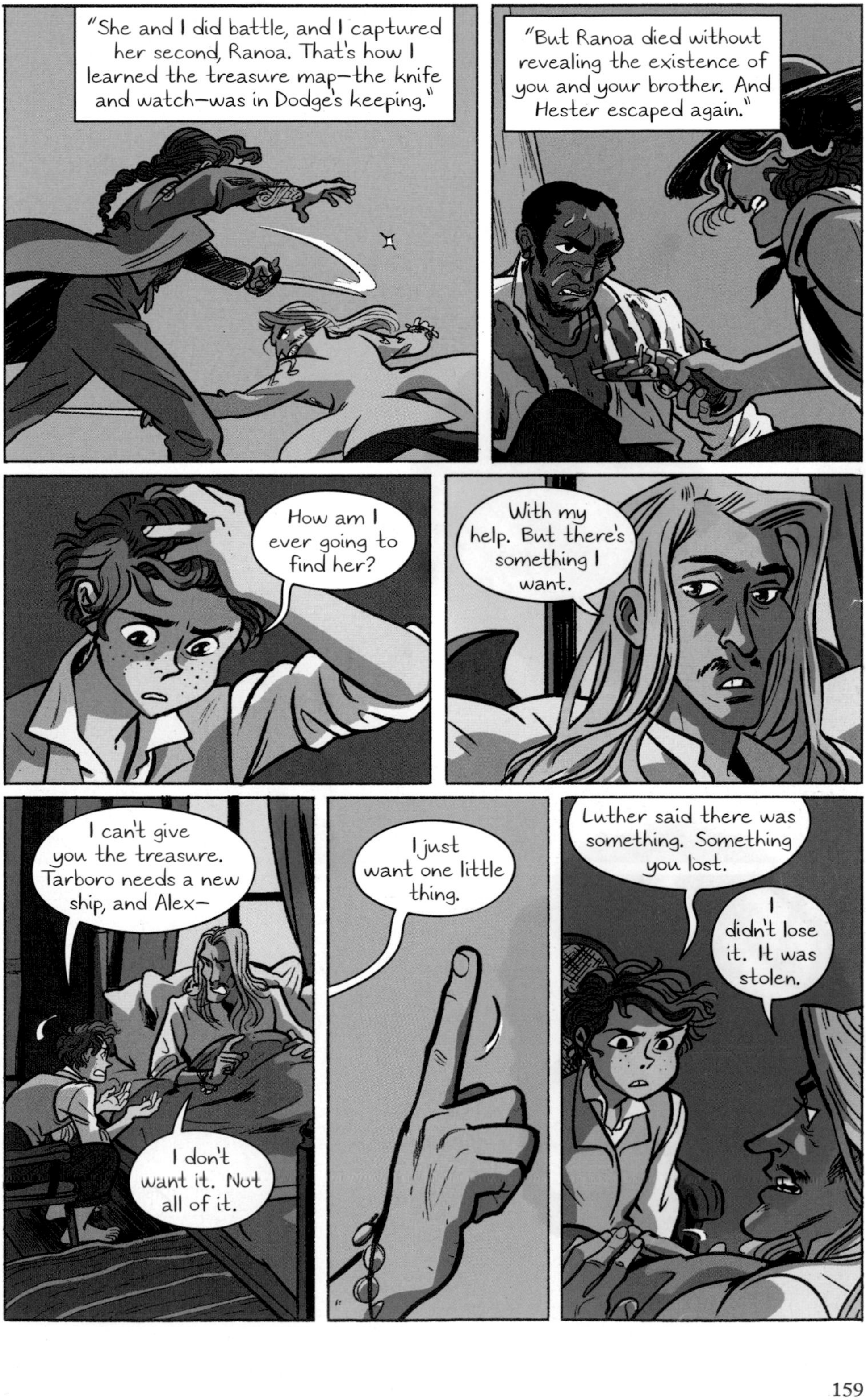
"She and I did battle, and I captured her second, Ranoa. That's how I learned the treasure map—the knife and watch—was in Dodge's keeping."
"But Ranoa died without revealing the existence of you and your brother. And Hester escaped again."
How am I ever going to find her?
With my help. But there's something I want.
I can't give you the treasure. Tarboro needs a new ship, and Alex—
I don't want it. Not all of it.
I just want one little thing.
Luther said there was something. Something you lost.
I didn't lose it. It was stolen.

CHAPTER NINE
A TASTE OF SUNSHINE

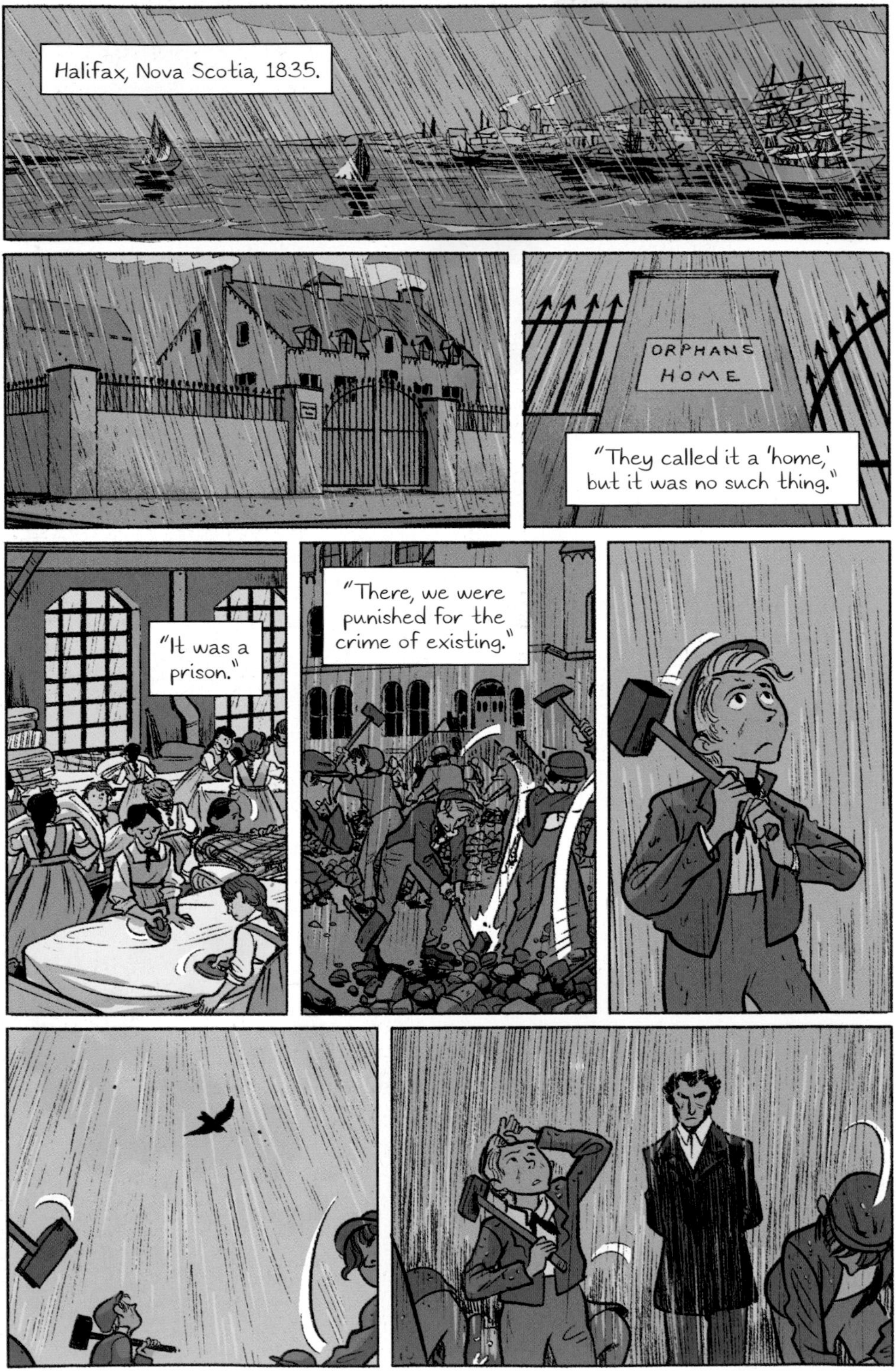
Halifax, Nova Scotia, 1835.
ORPHANS HOME
"They called it a 'home,' but it was no such thing."
"It was a prison."
"There, we were punished for the crime of existing."

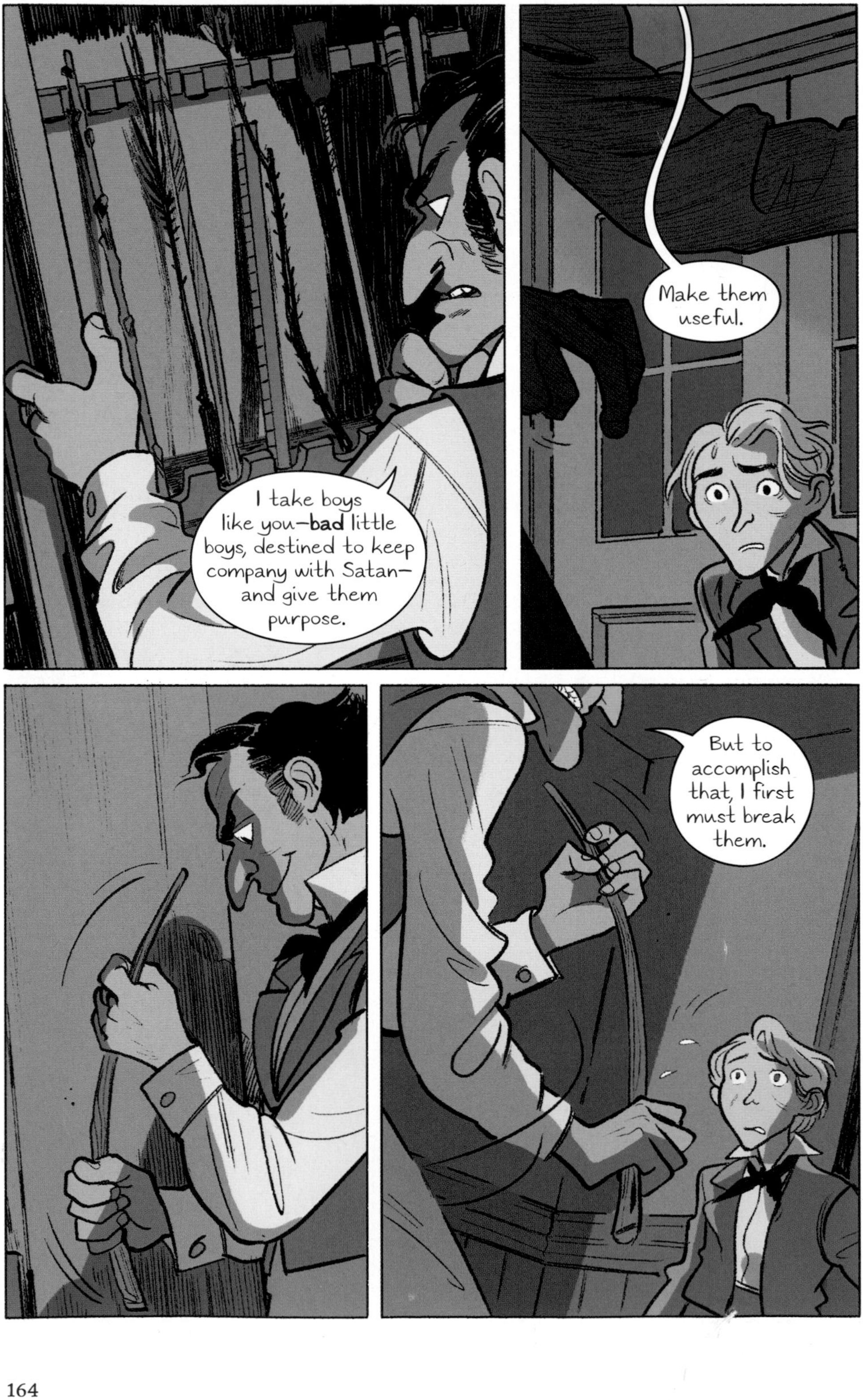
I take boys like you—**bad** little boys, destined to keep company with Satan—and give them purpose.
Make them useful.
But to accomplish that, I first must break them.

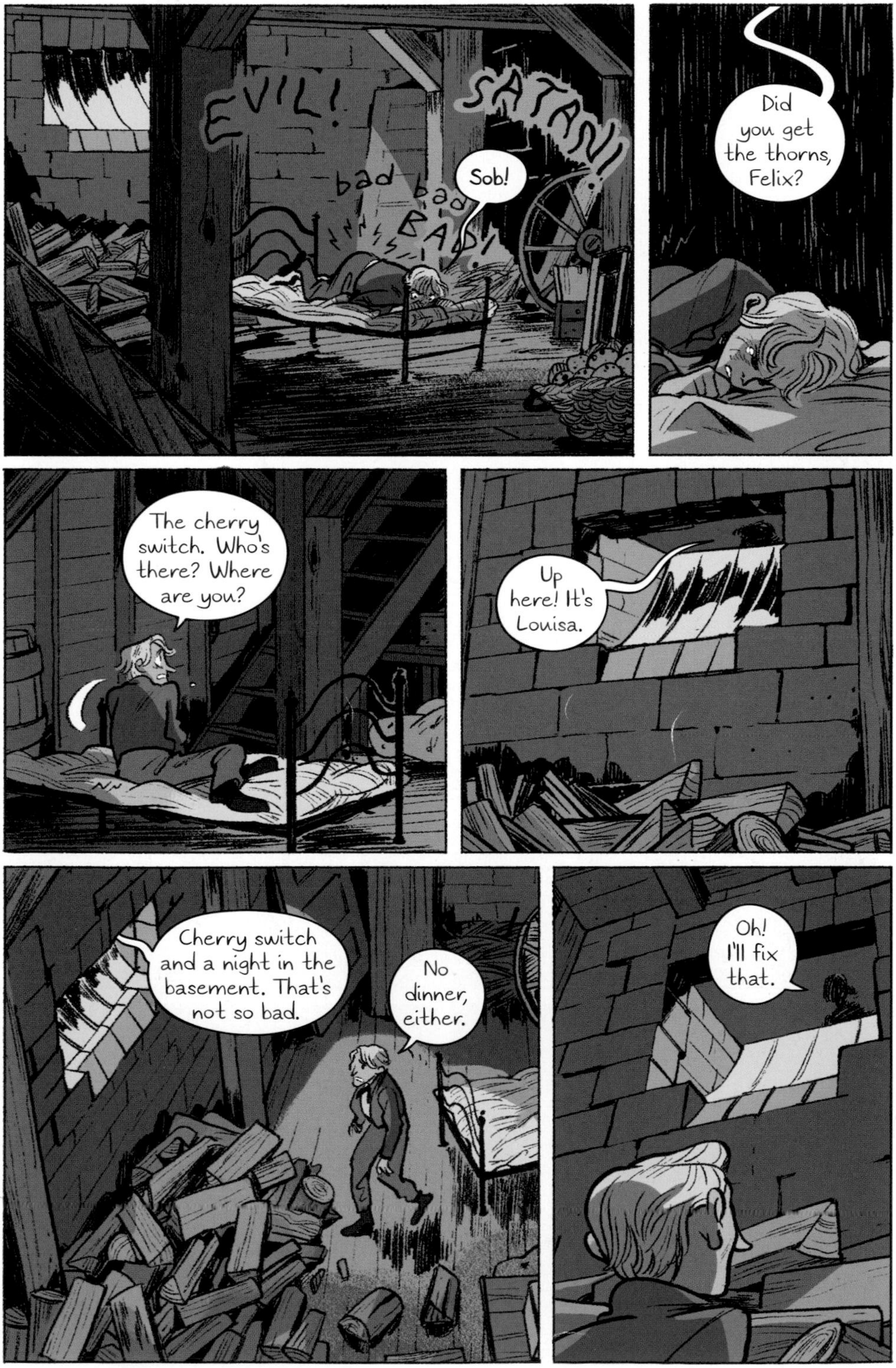
EVIL!
SATAN!
bad bad BAD!
Sob!
Did you get the thorns, Felix?
The cherry switch. Who's there? Where are you?
Up here! It's Louisa.
Cherry switch and a night in the basement. That's not so bad.
No dinner, either.
Oh! I'll fix that.

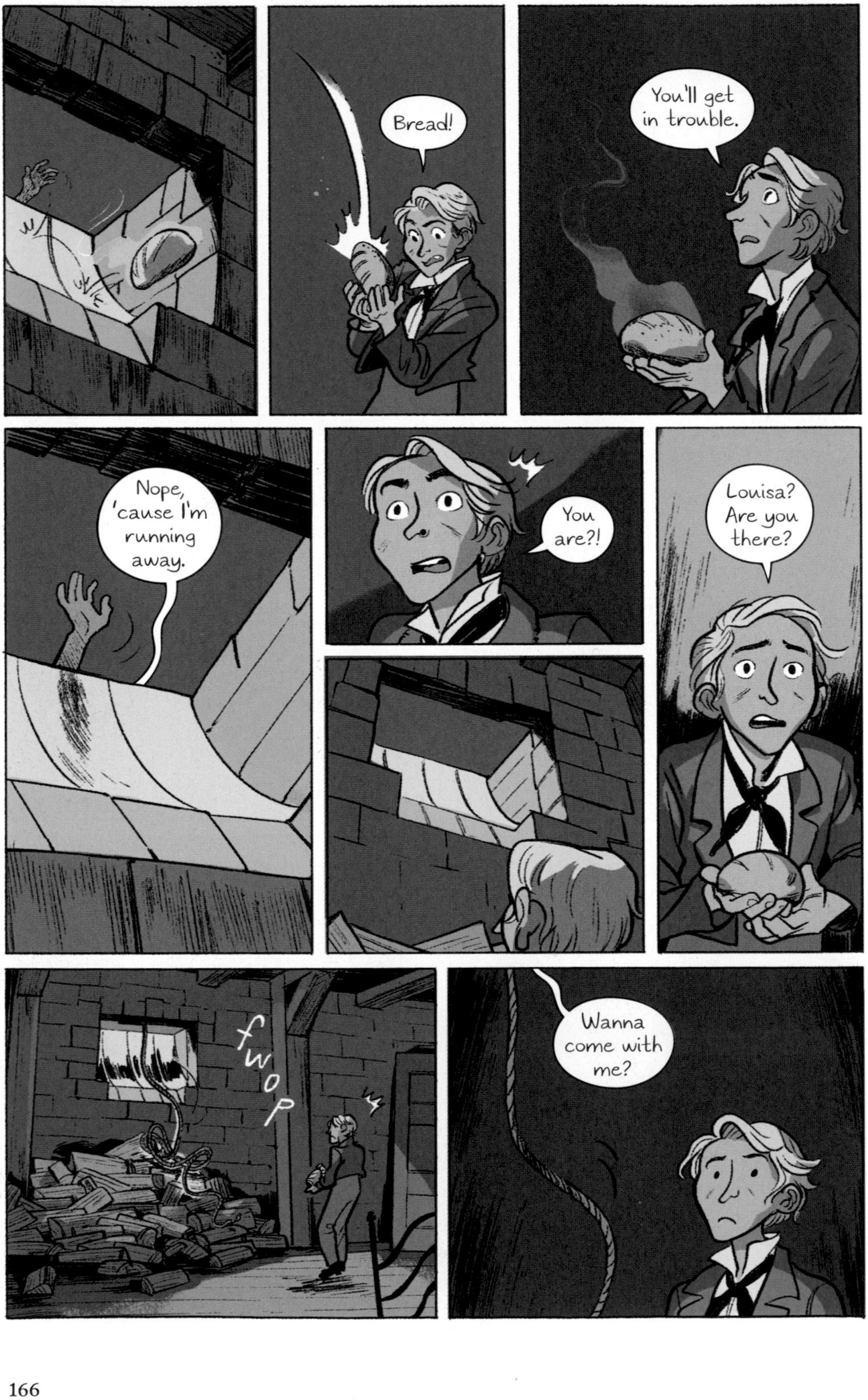
Bread!
You'll get in trouble.
Nope, 'cause I'm running away.
You are?!
Louisa? Are you there?
FWOP
Wanna come with me?

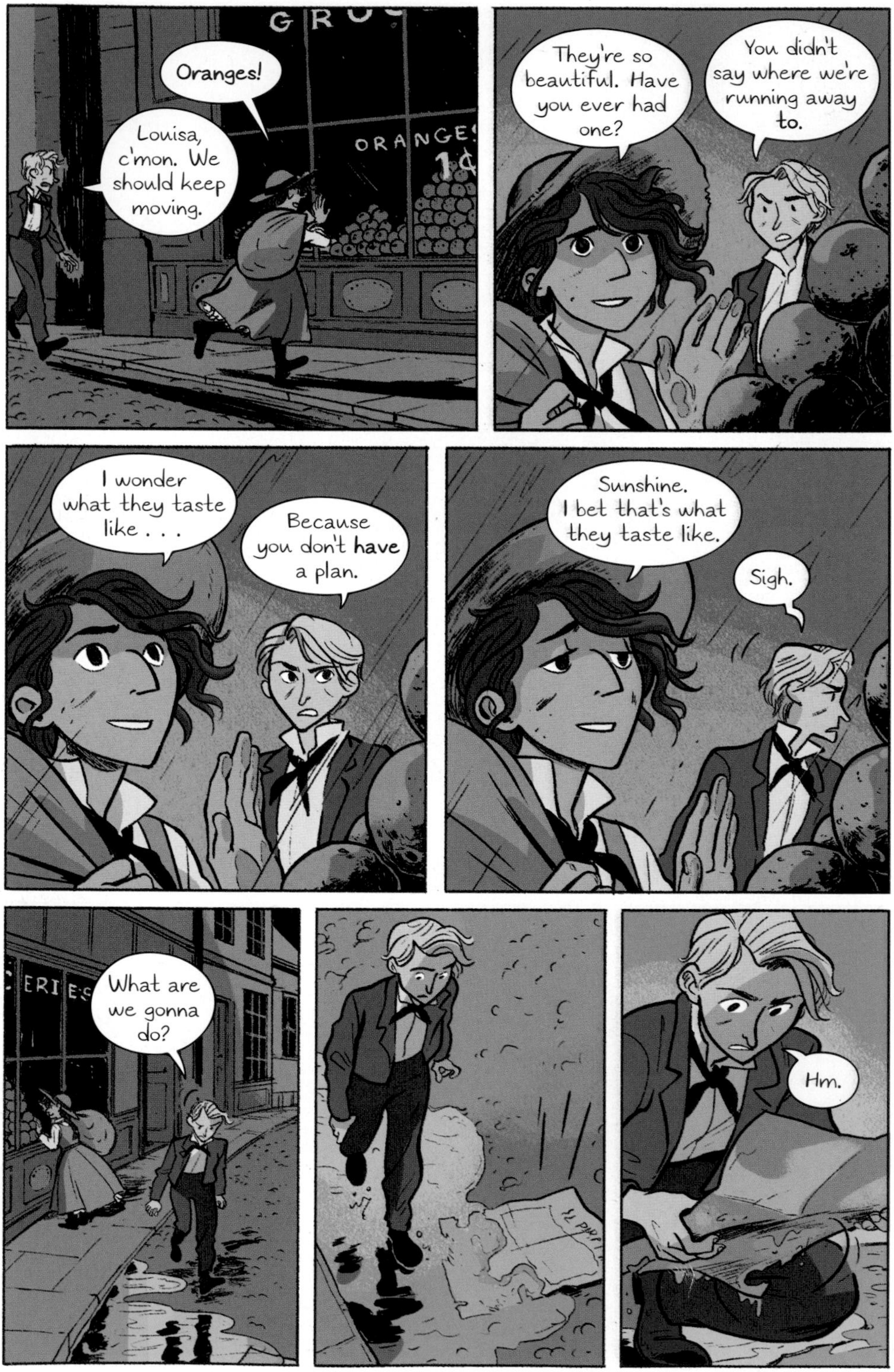
GRO
Oranges!
Louisa, c'mon. We should keep moving.
ORANGES 1¢
They're so beautiful. Have you ever had one?
You didn't say where we're running away to.
I wonder what they taste like . . .
Because you don't have a plan.
Sunshine. I bet that's what they taste like.
Sigh.
ERIES
What are we gonna do?
Hm.

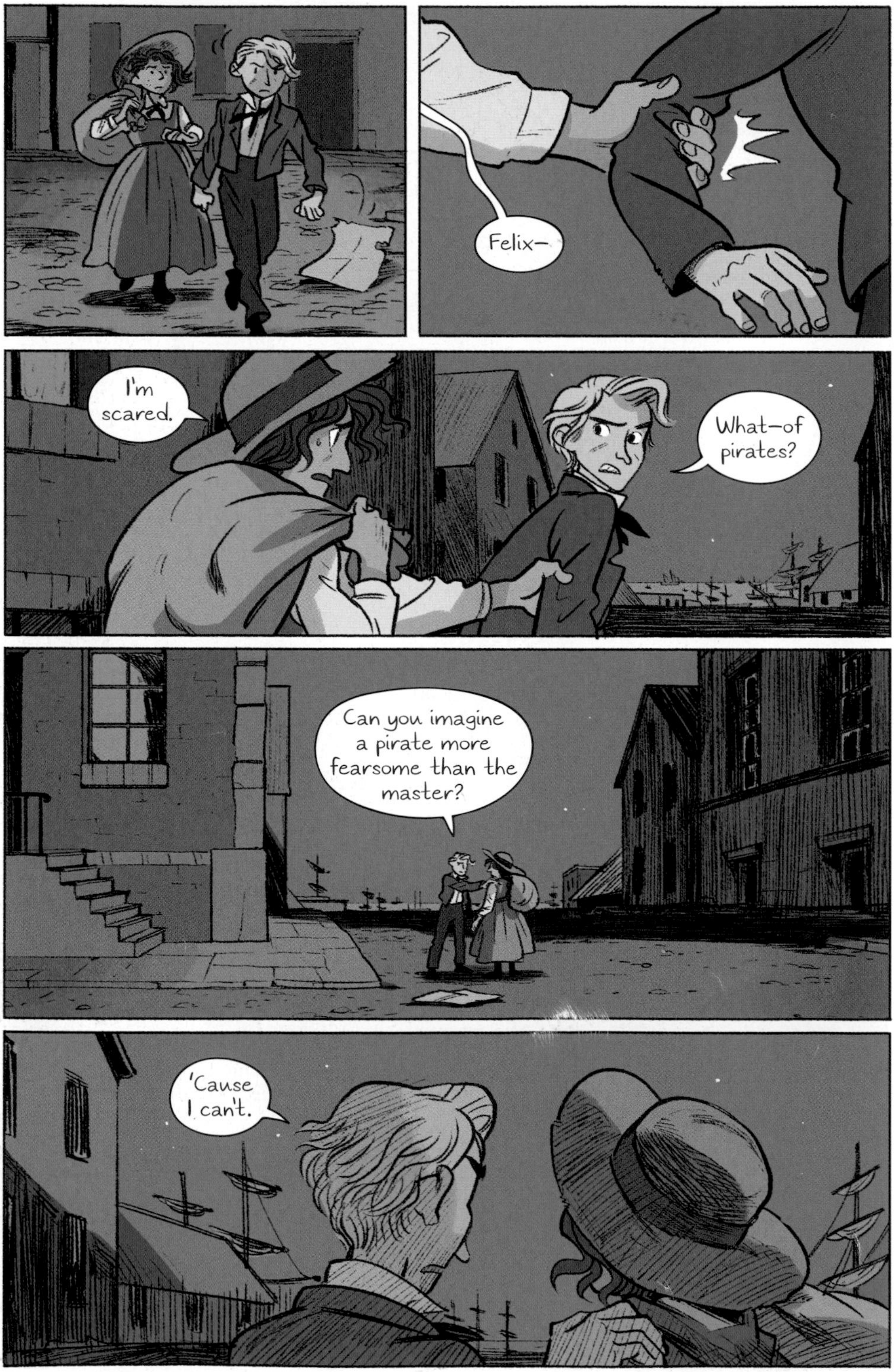
Felix—
I'm scared.
What—of pirates?
Can you imagine a pirate more fearsome than the master?
'Cause I can't.

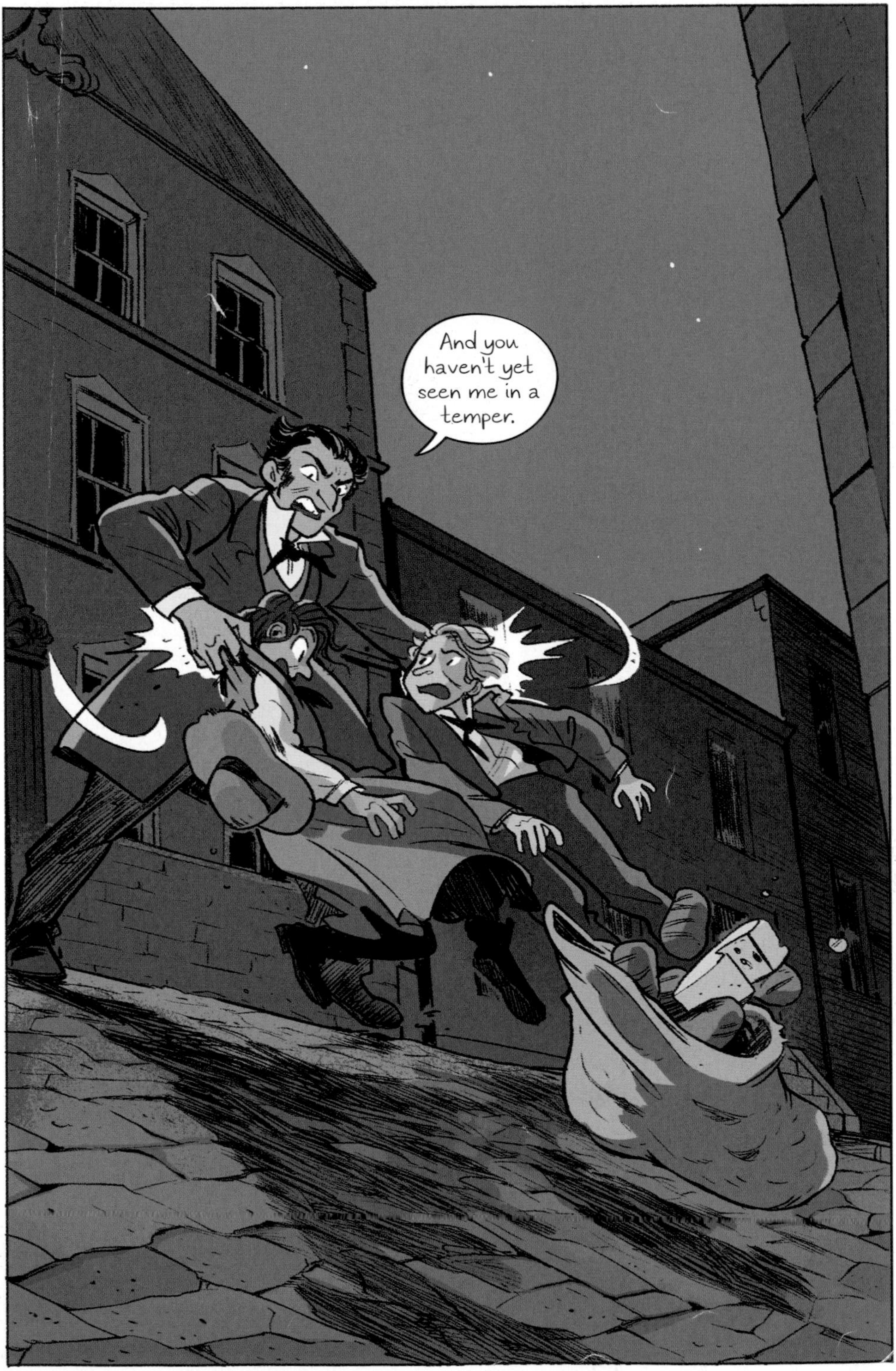
And you haven't yet seen me in a temper.

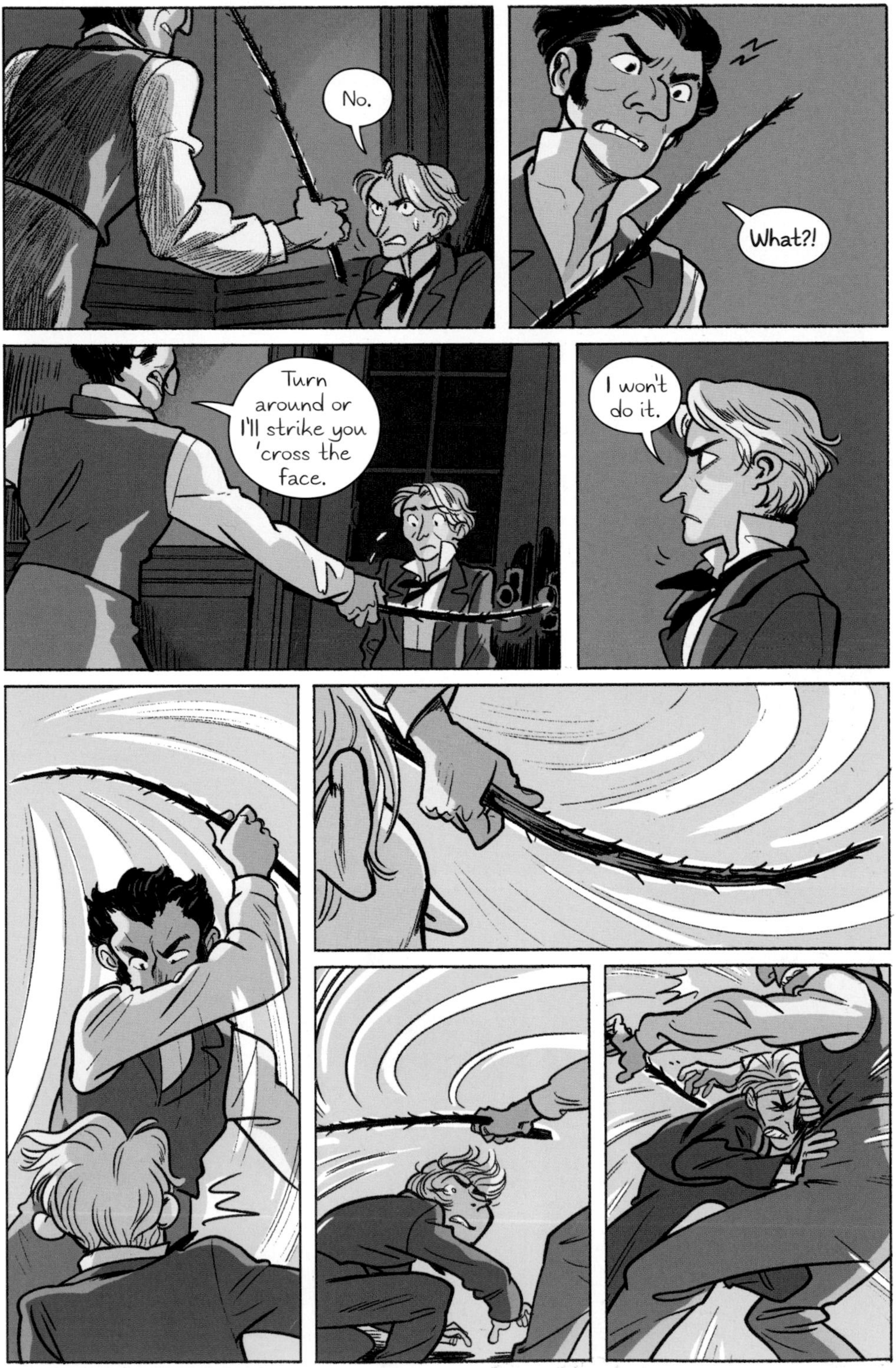
No.
What?!
Turn around or I'll strike you 'cross the face.
I won't do it.

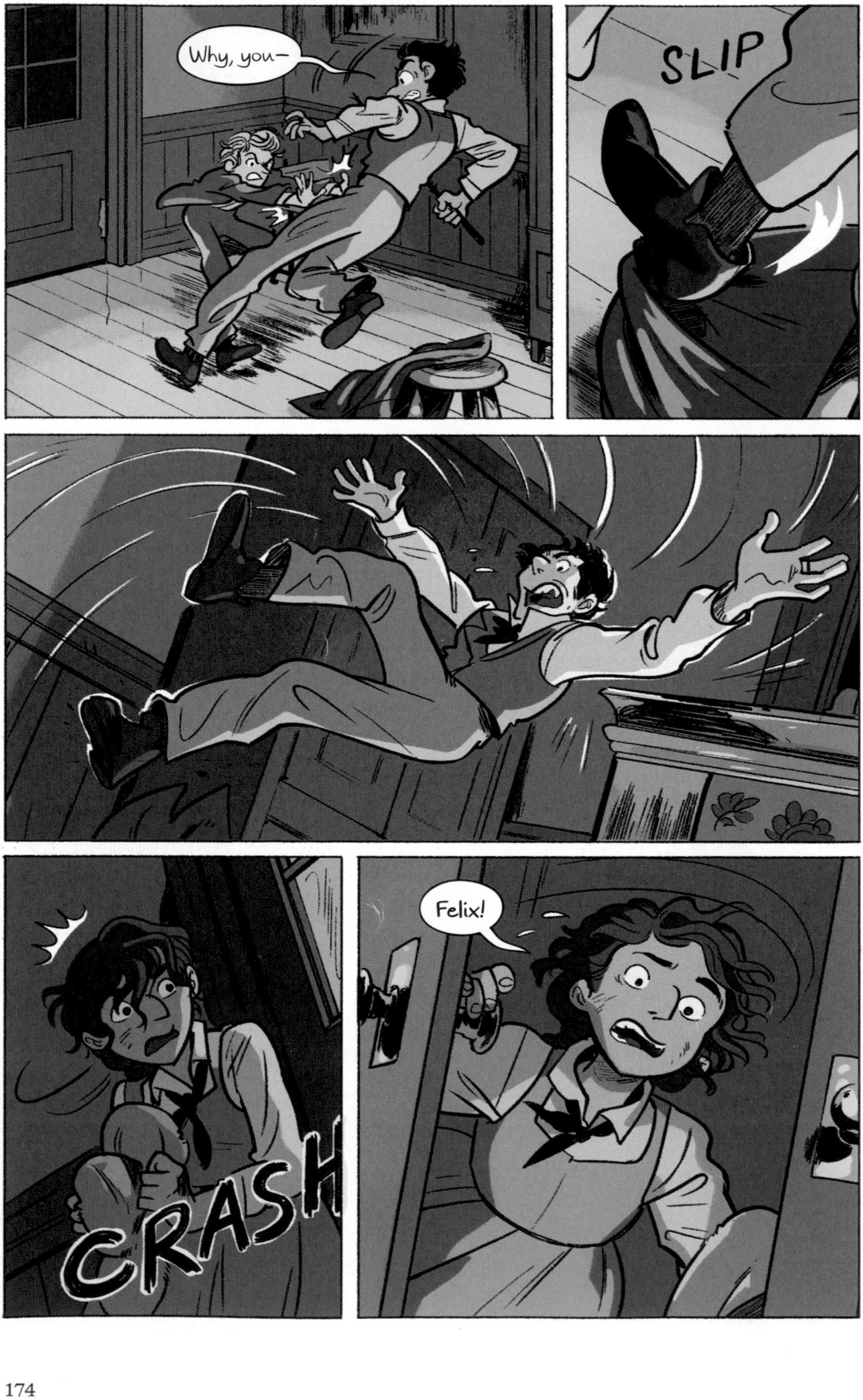
Why, you–
SLIP
Felix!
CRASH

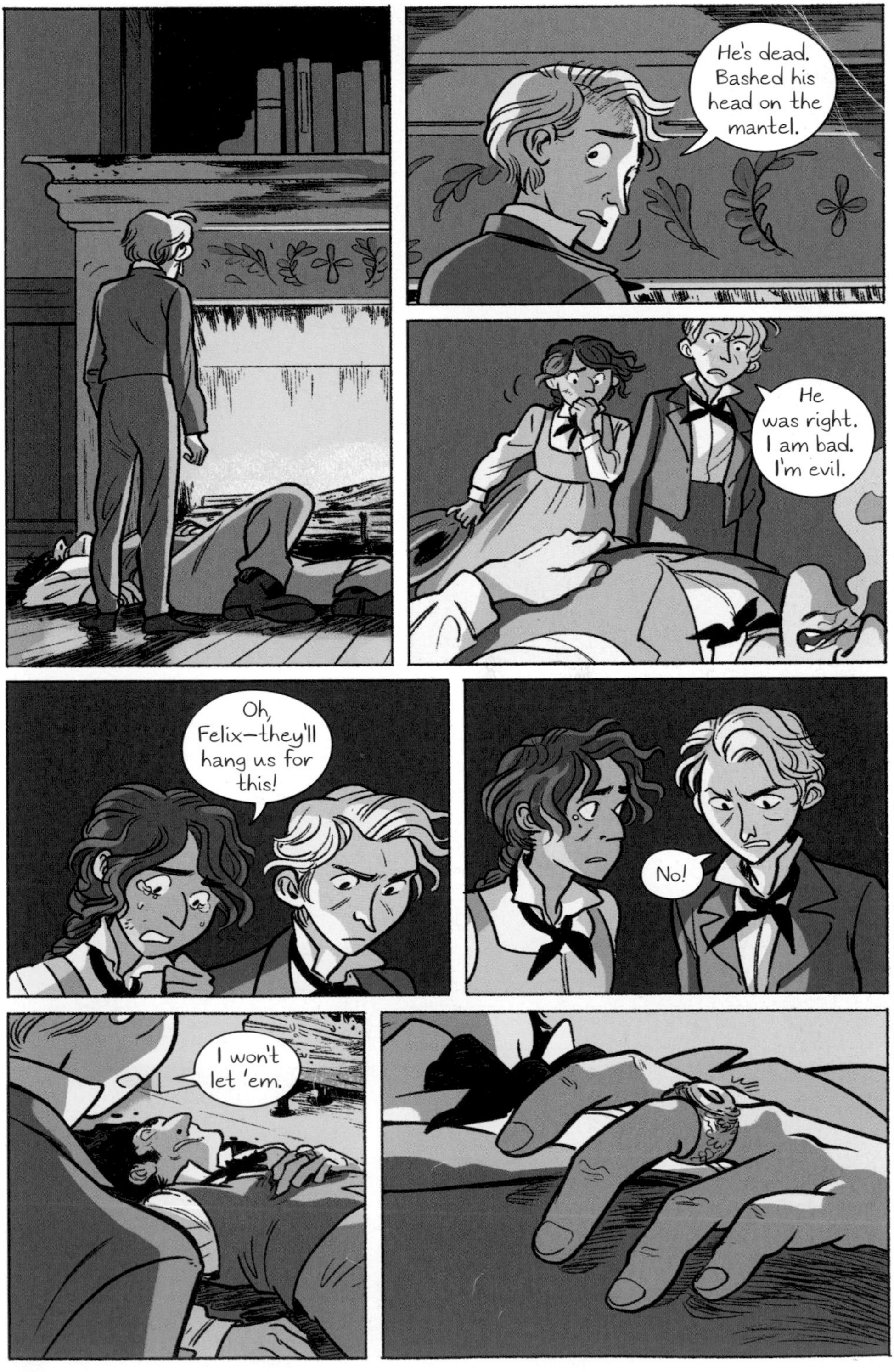
He's dead. Bashed his head on the mantel.
He was right. I am bad. I'm evil.
Oh, Felix—they'll hang us for this!
No!
I won't let 'em.

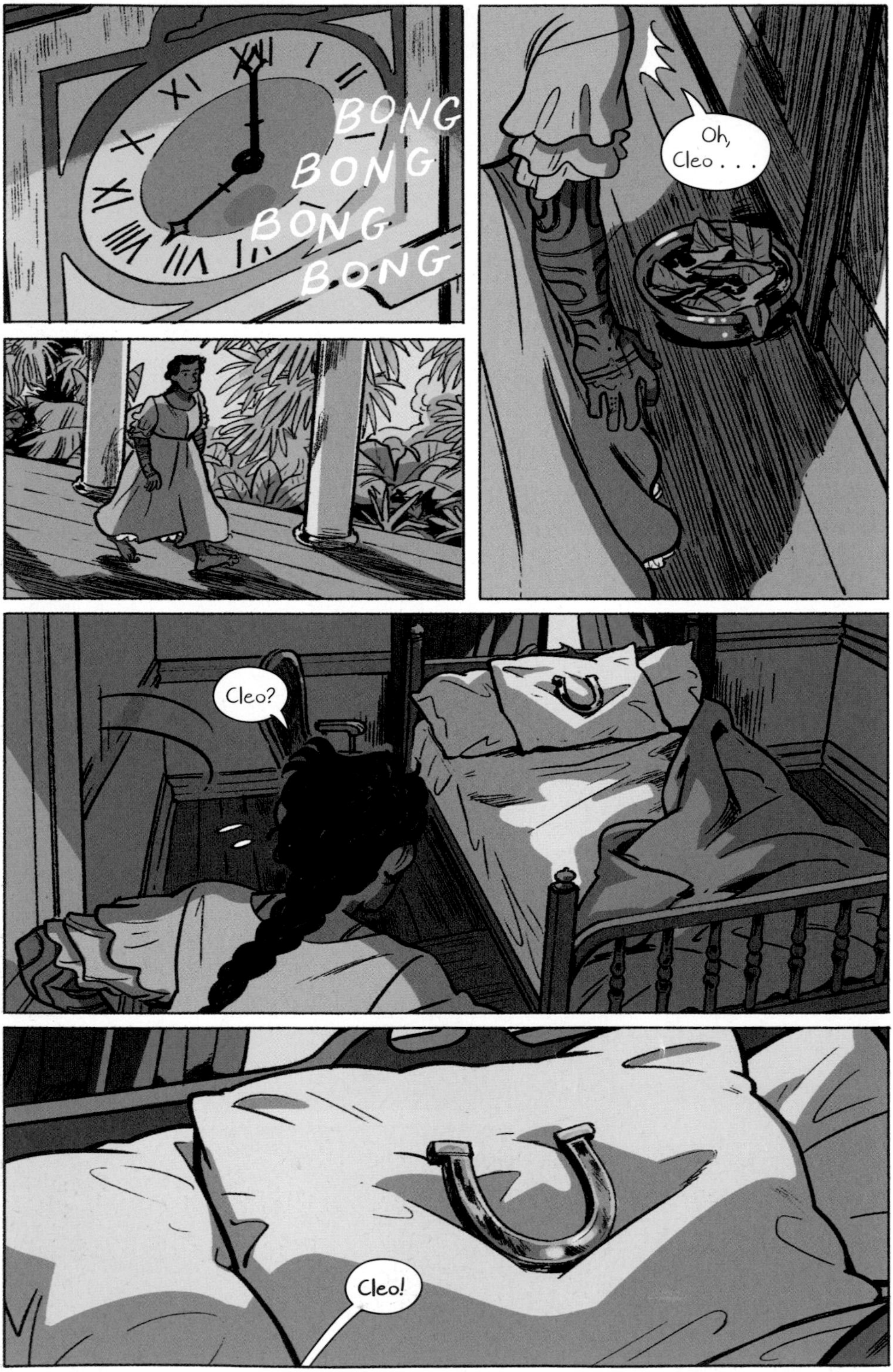
BONG
BONG
BONG
BONG
Oh, Cleo . . .
Cleo?
Cleo!

179

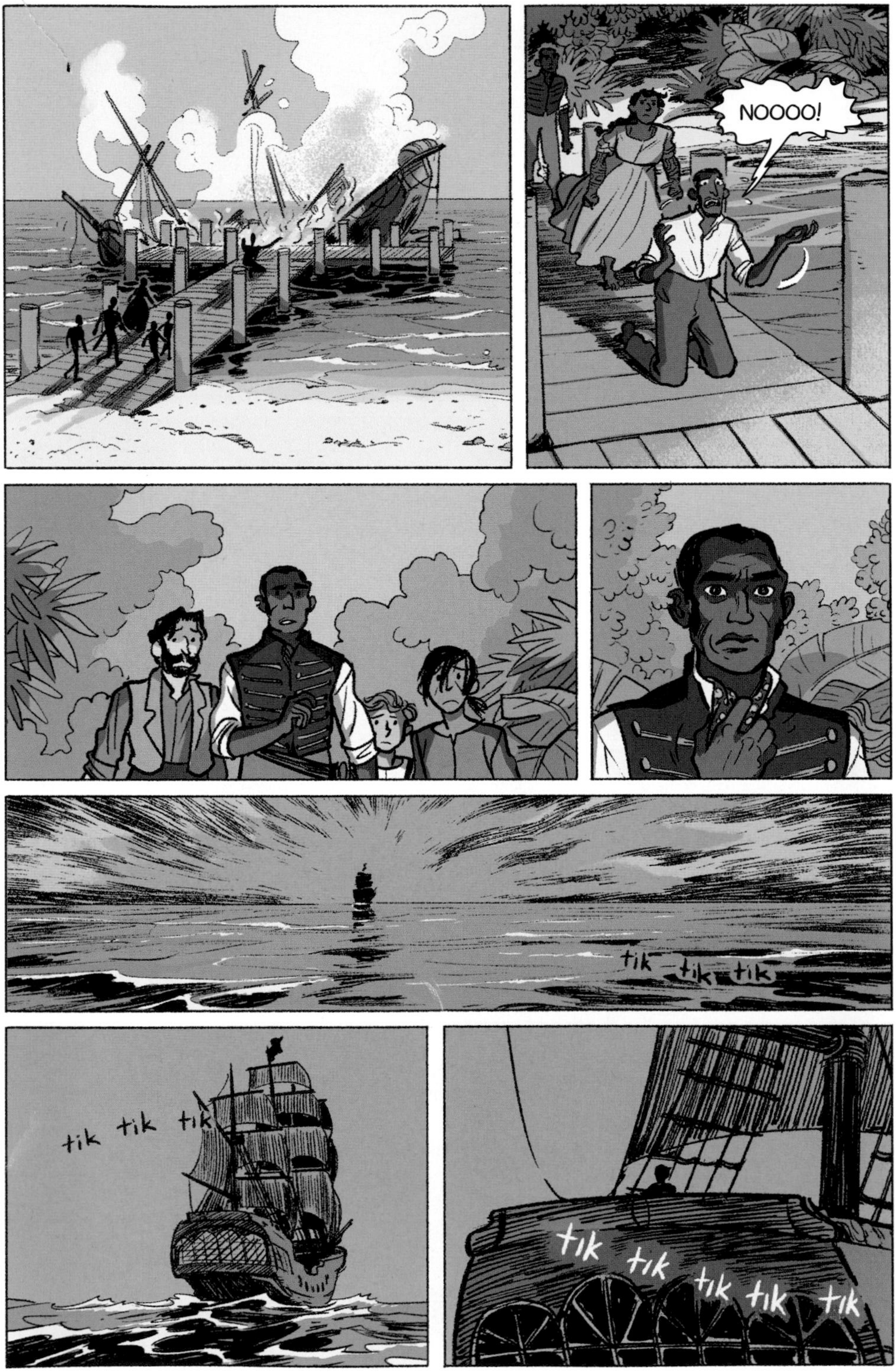
NOOOO!
tik tik tik
tik tik tik
tik tik tik tik tik

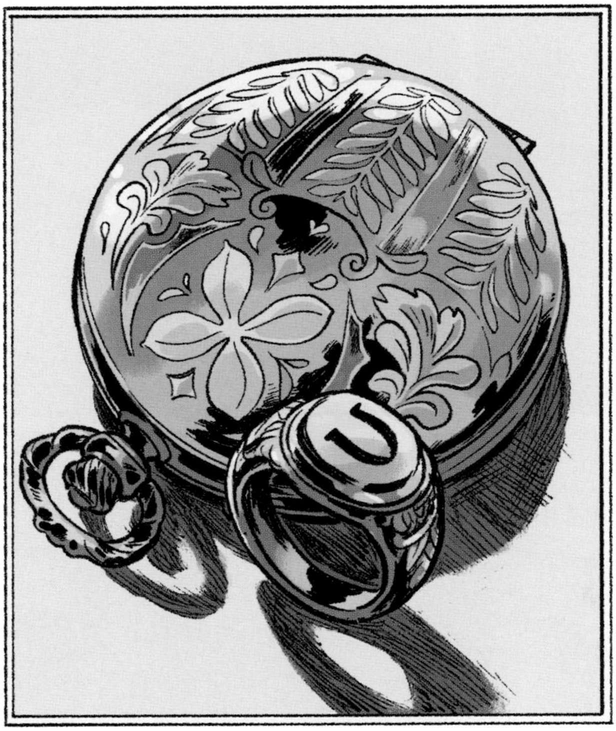

CHAPTER TEN

ETERNITY

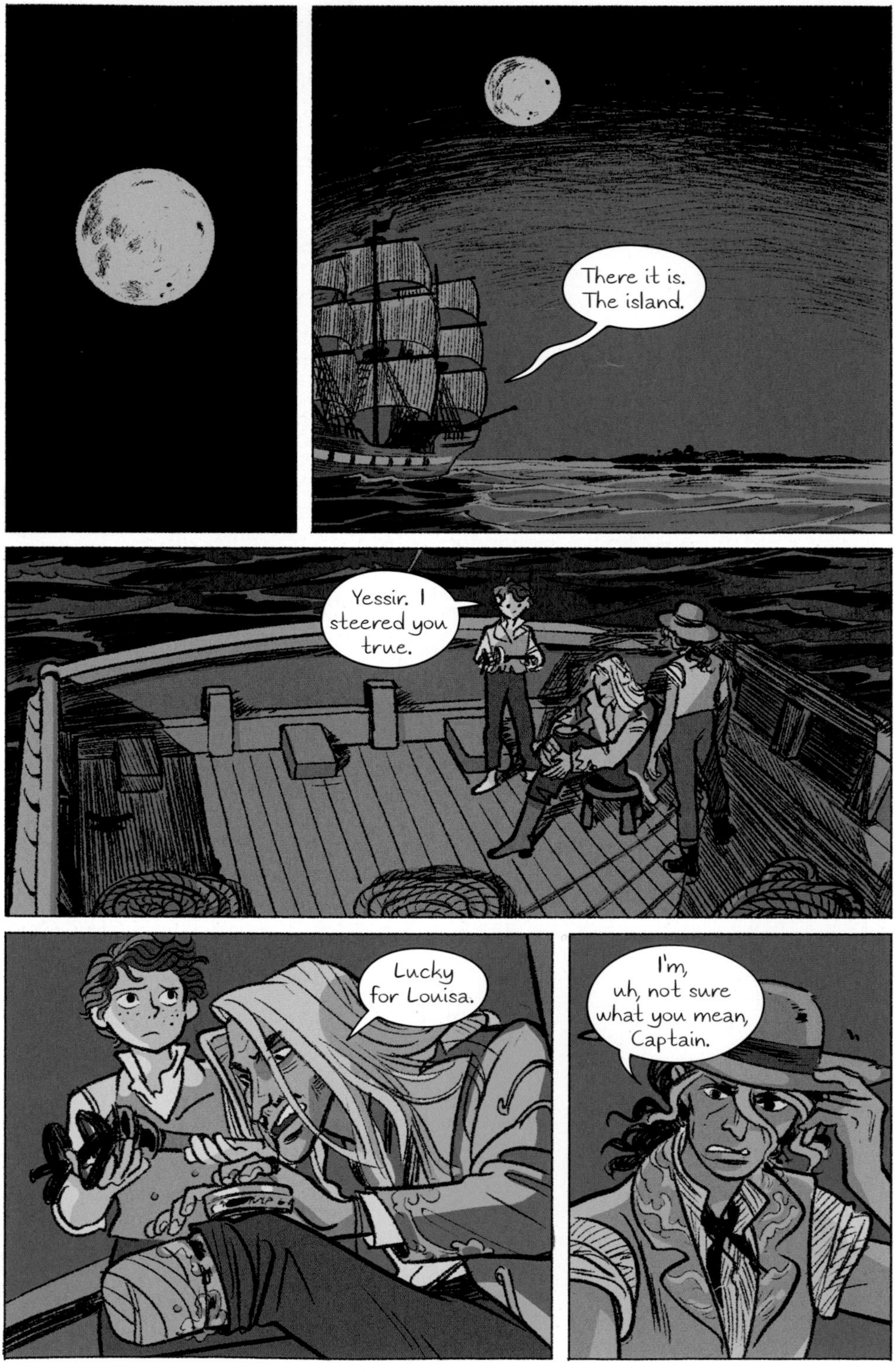
There it is. The island.
Yessir. I steered you true.
Lucky for Louisa.
I'm, uh, not sure what you mean, Captain.

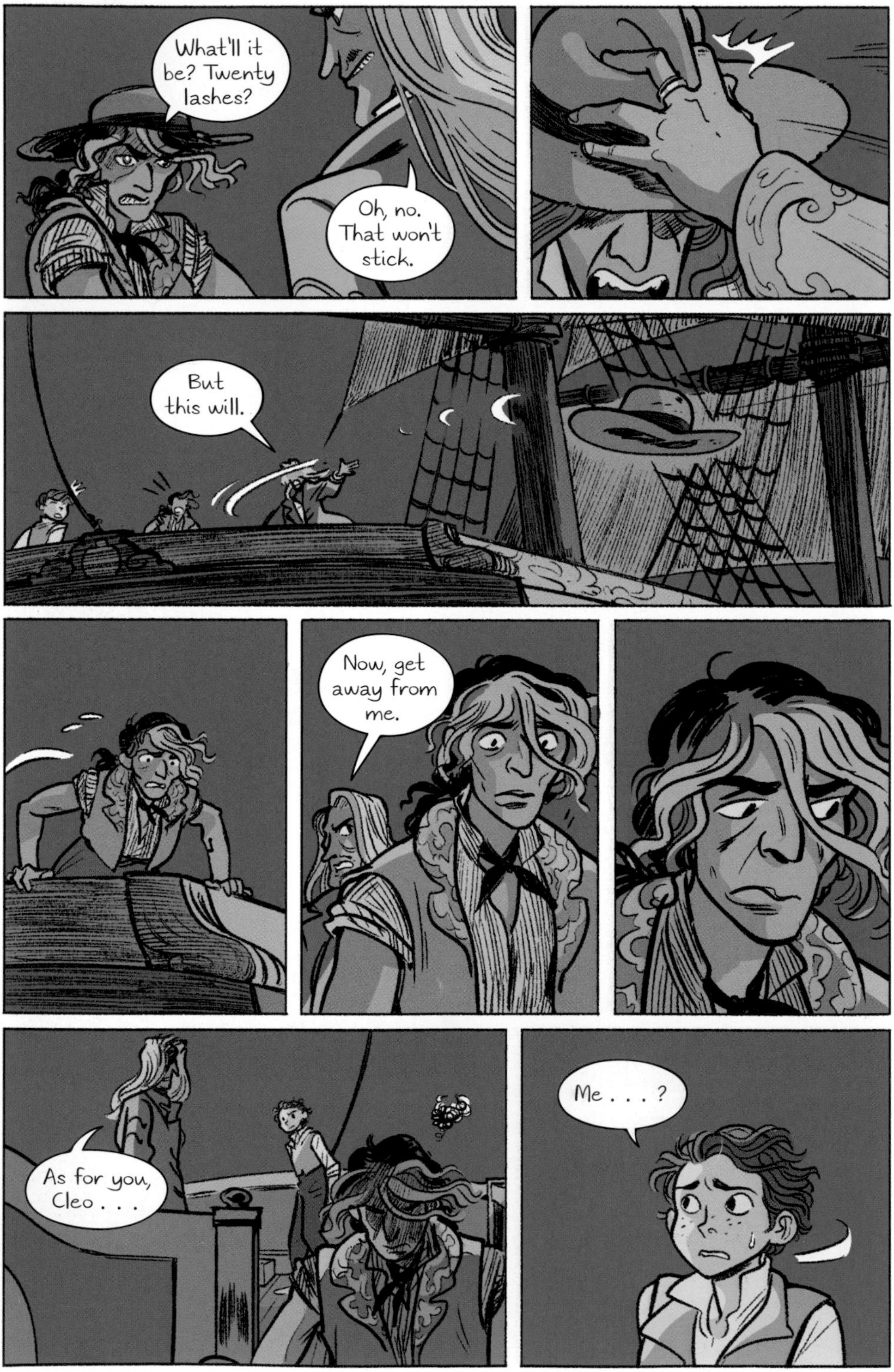
What'll it be? Twenty lashes?
Oh, no. That won't stick.
But this will.
Now, get away from me.
As for you, Cleo . . .
Me . . . ?

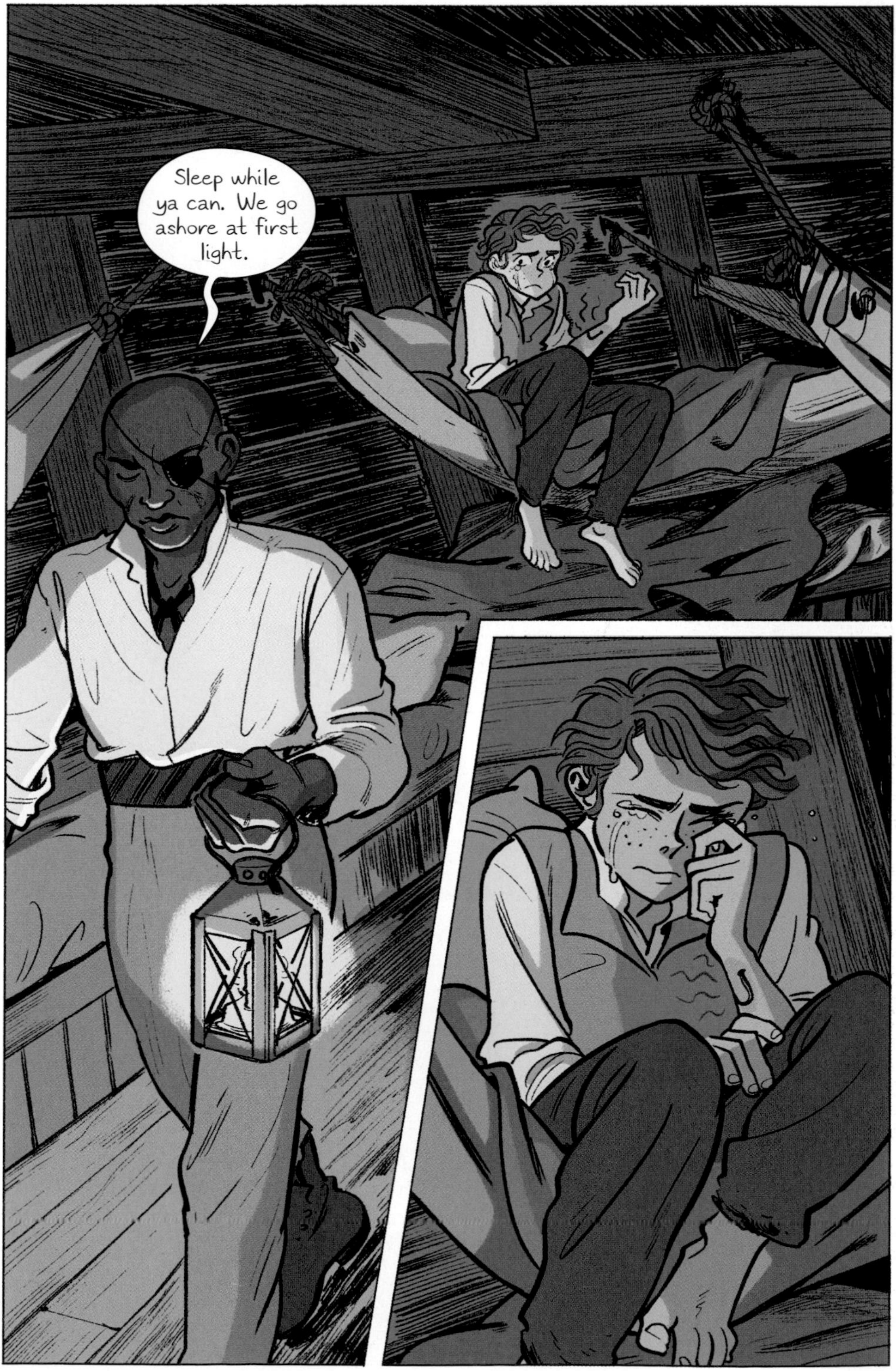
Sleep while ya can. We go ashore at first light.

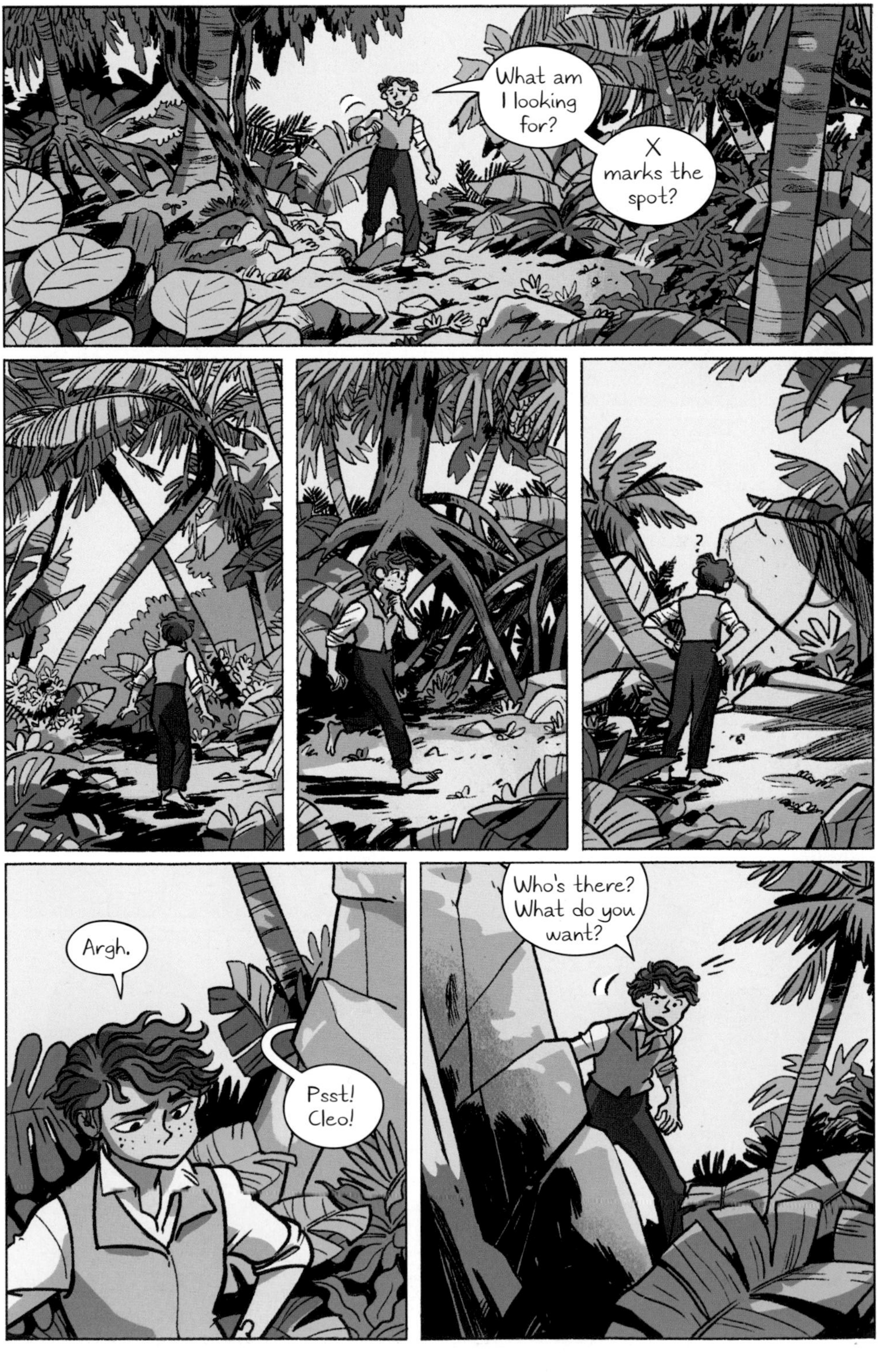
What am I looking for?
X marks the spot?
Argh.
Psst! Cleo!
Who's there? What do you want?

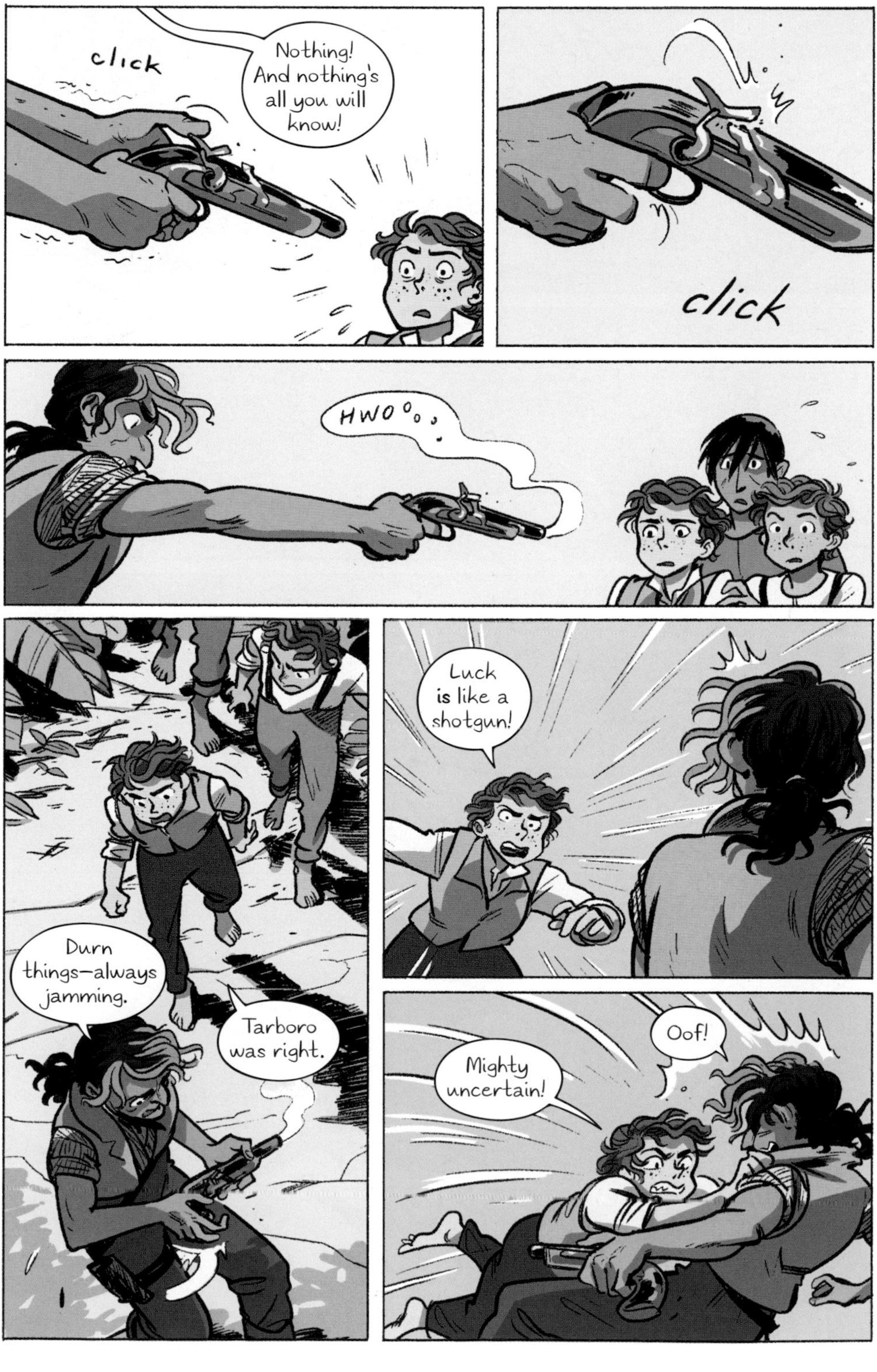
click
Nothing! And nothing's all you will know!
click
HWOooo
Luck is like a shotgun!
Durn things—always jamming.
Tarboro was right.
Oof!
Mighty uncertain!

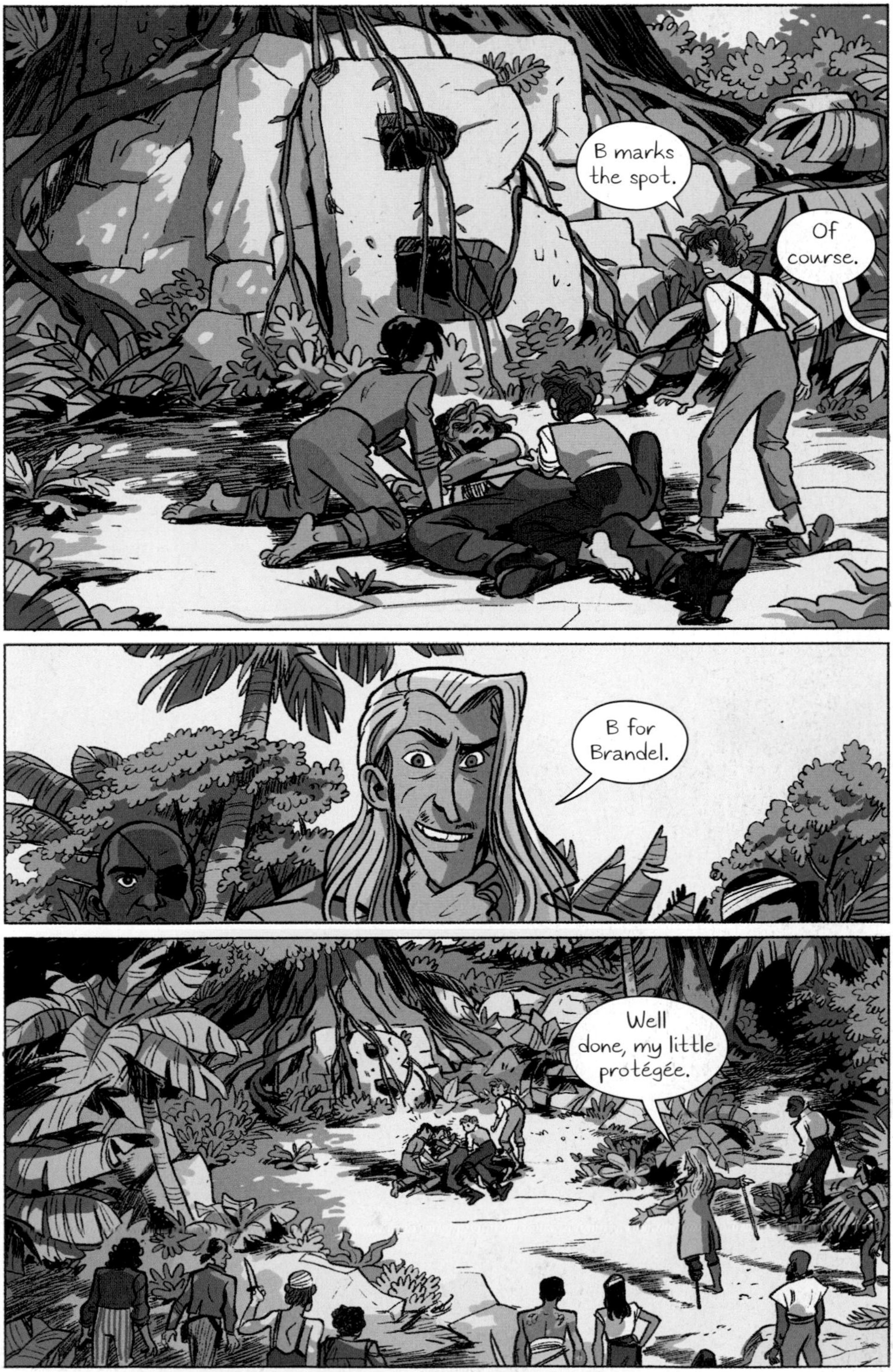
B marks the spot.
Of course.
B for Brandel.
Well done, my little protégée.

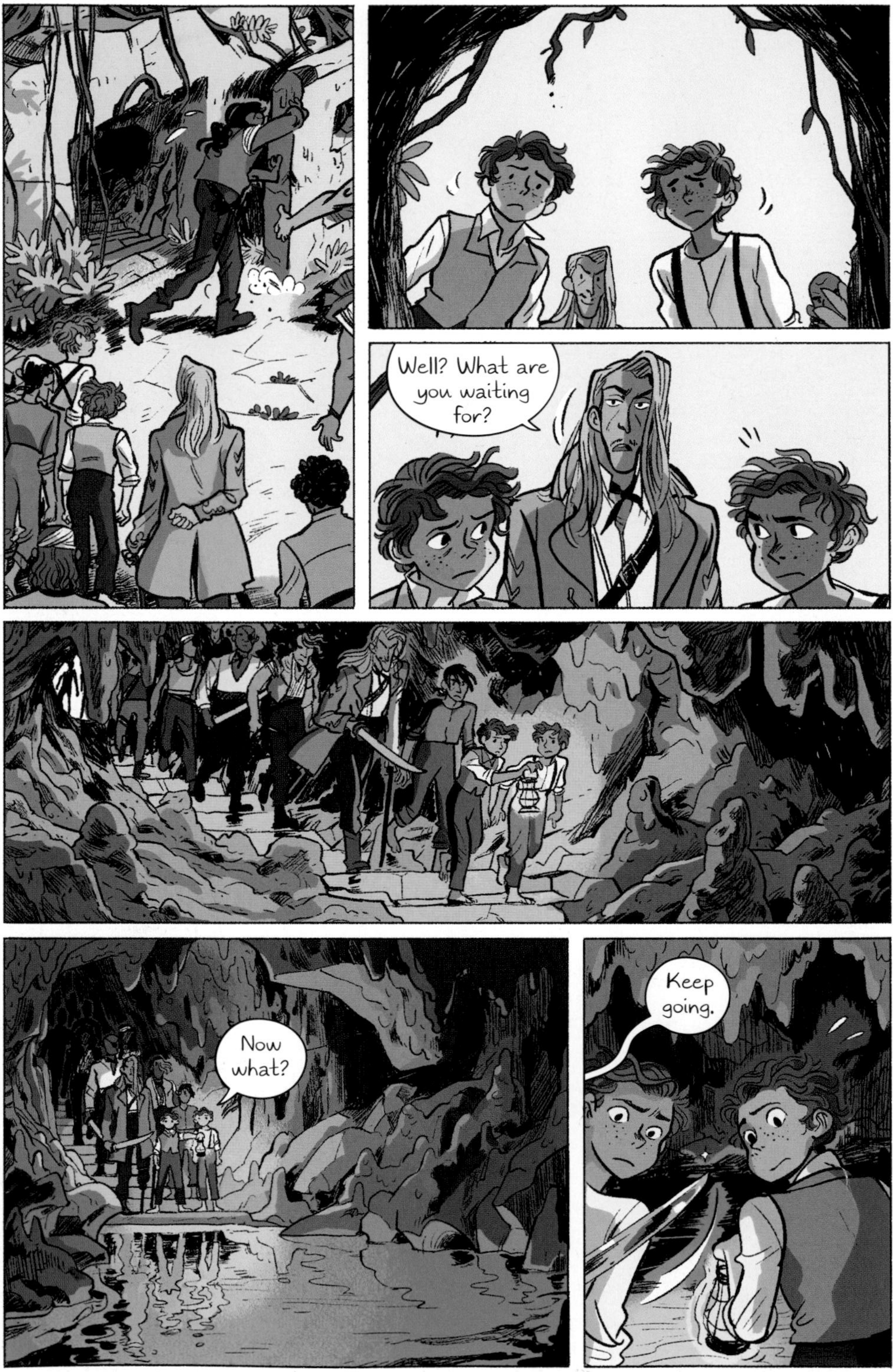
Well? What are you waiting for?
Now what?
Keep going.

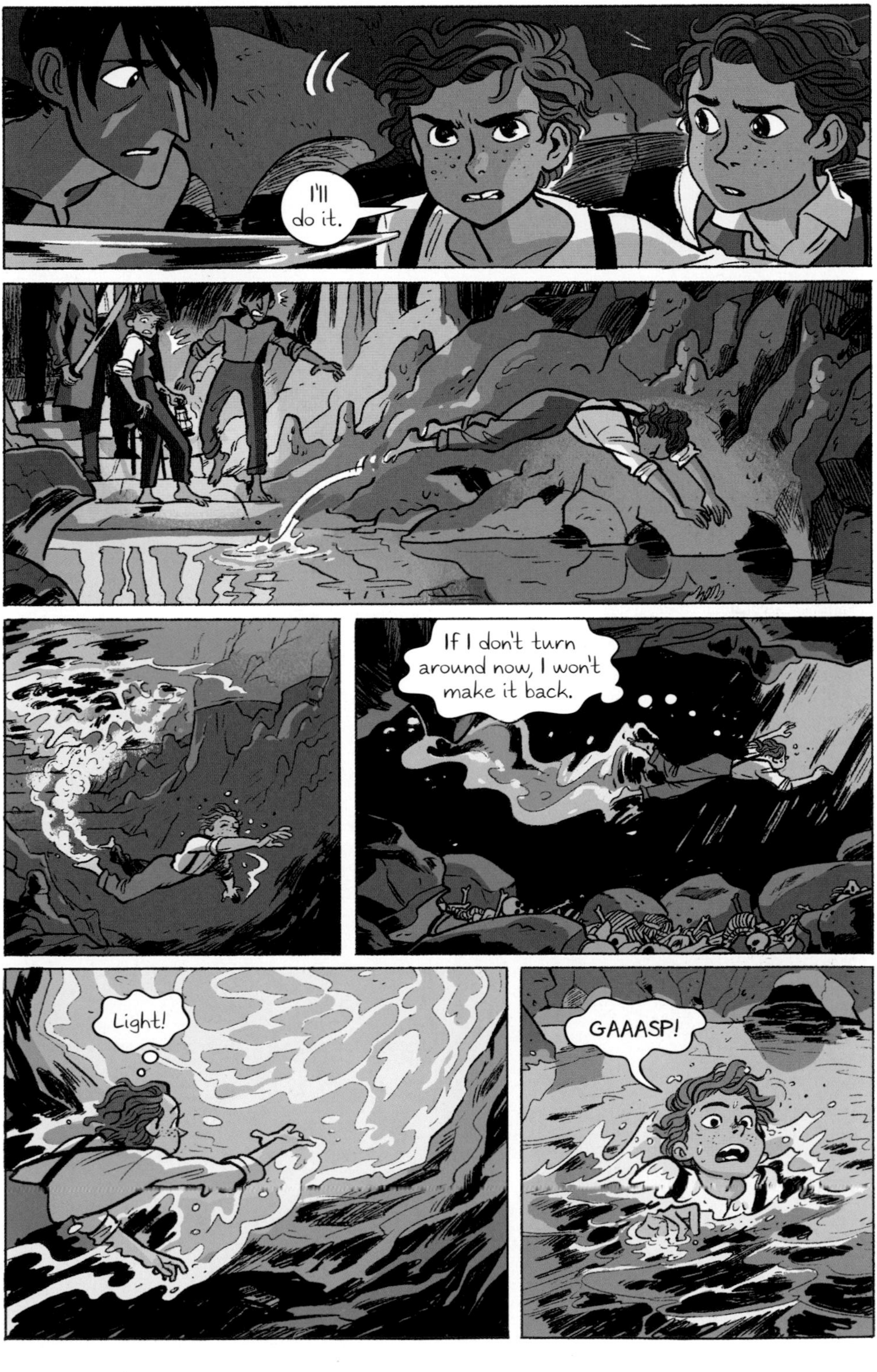
I'll do it.
If I don't turn around now, I won't make it back.
Light!
GAAASP!

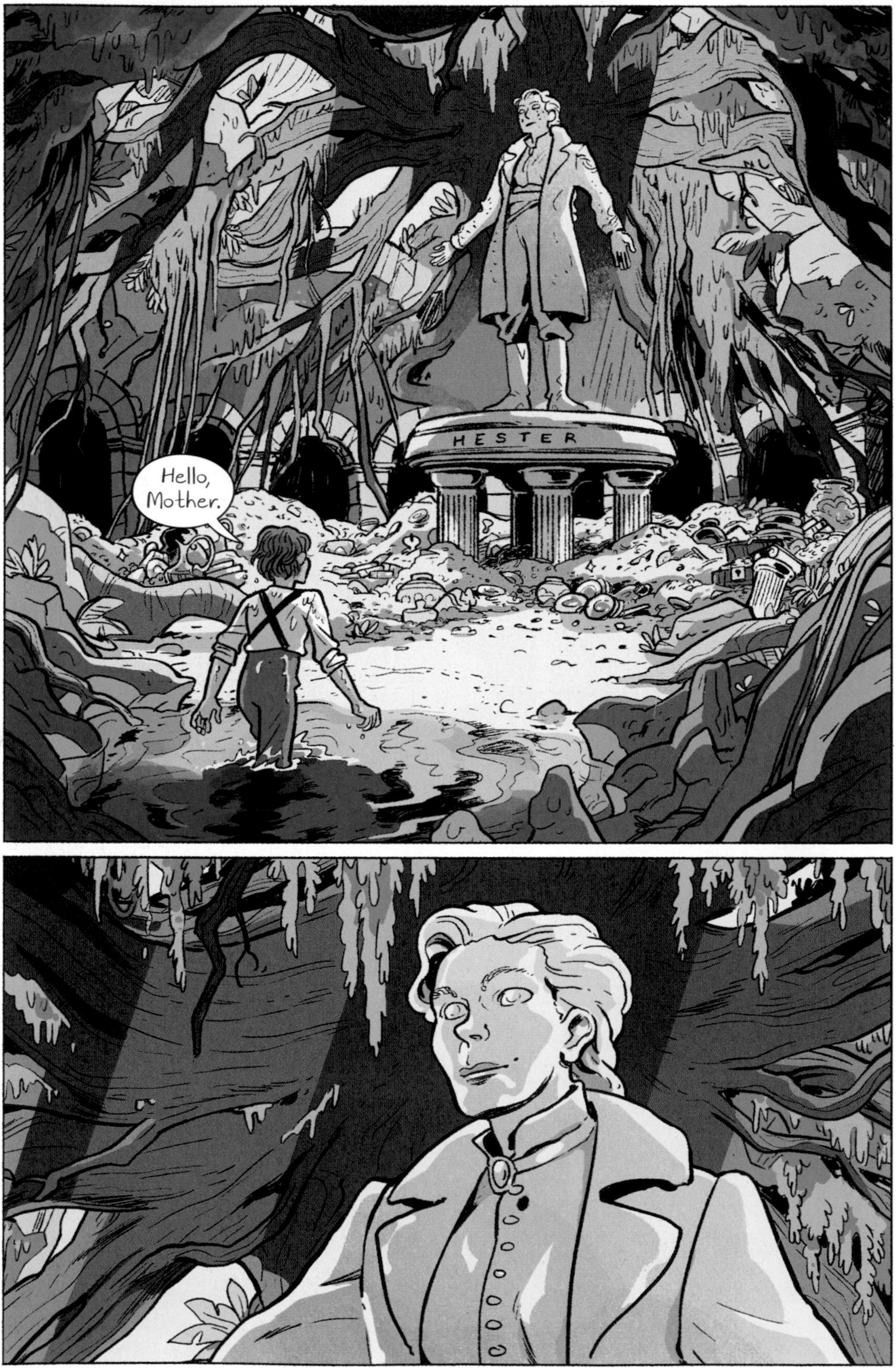
HESTER
Hello, Mother.

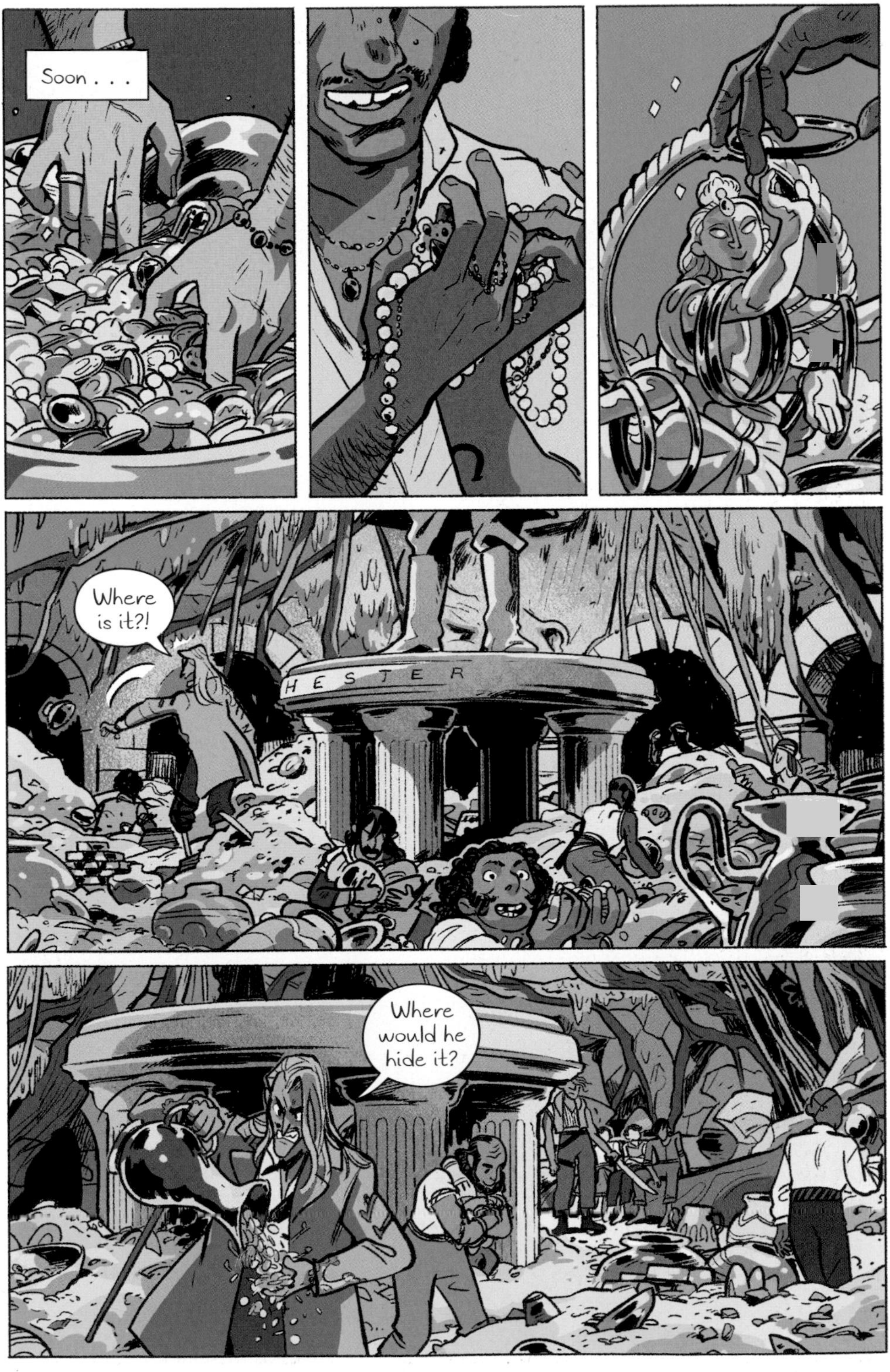
Soon . . .
Where is it?!
HESTER
Where would he hide it?

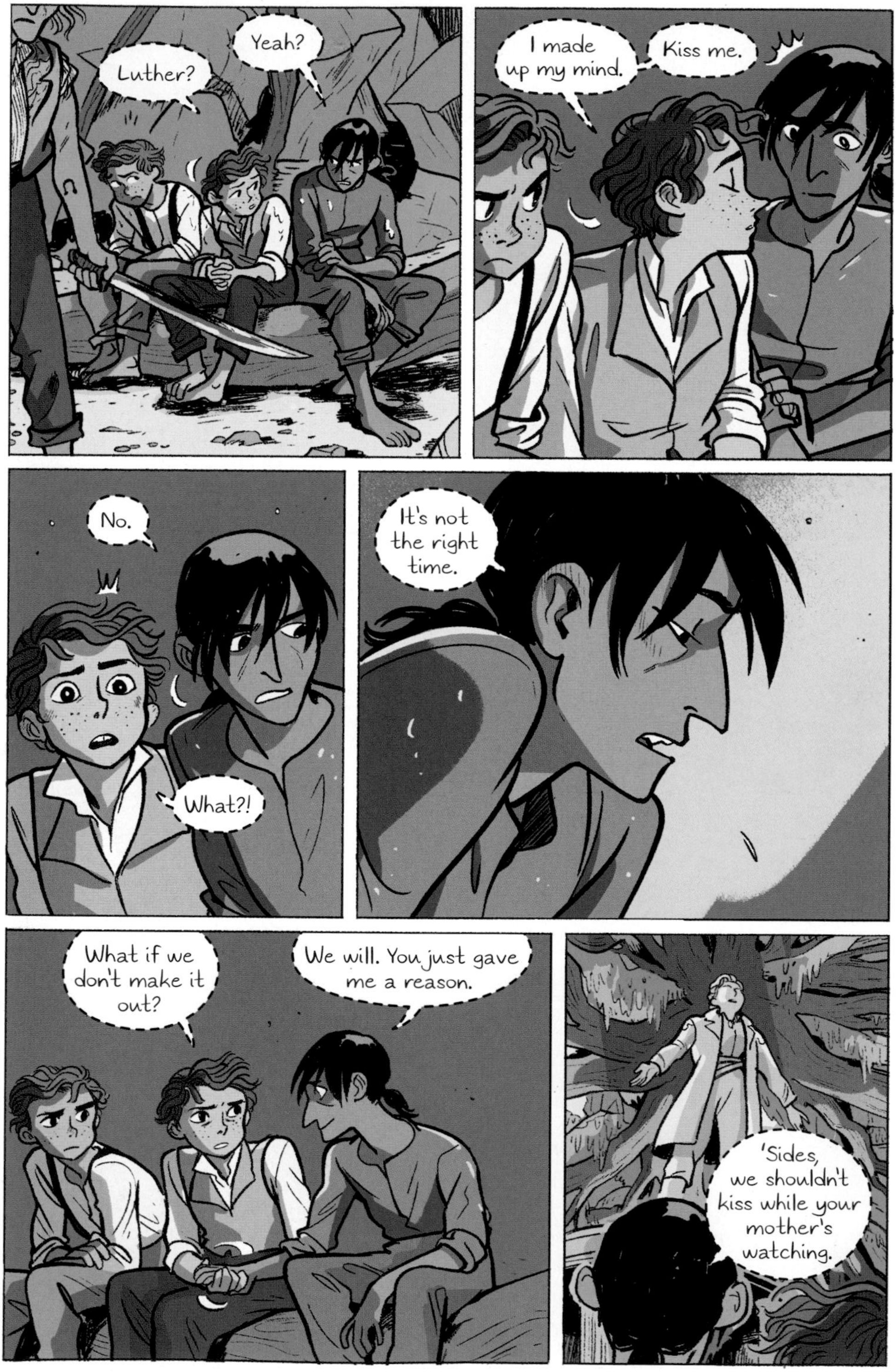
Luther?
Yeah?
I made up my mind.
Kiss me.
No.
What?!
It's not the right time.
What if we don't make it out?
We will. You just gave me a reason.
'Sides, we shouldn't kiss while your mother's watching.

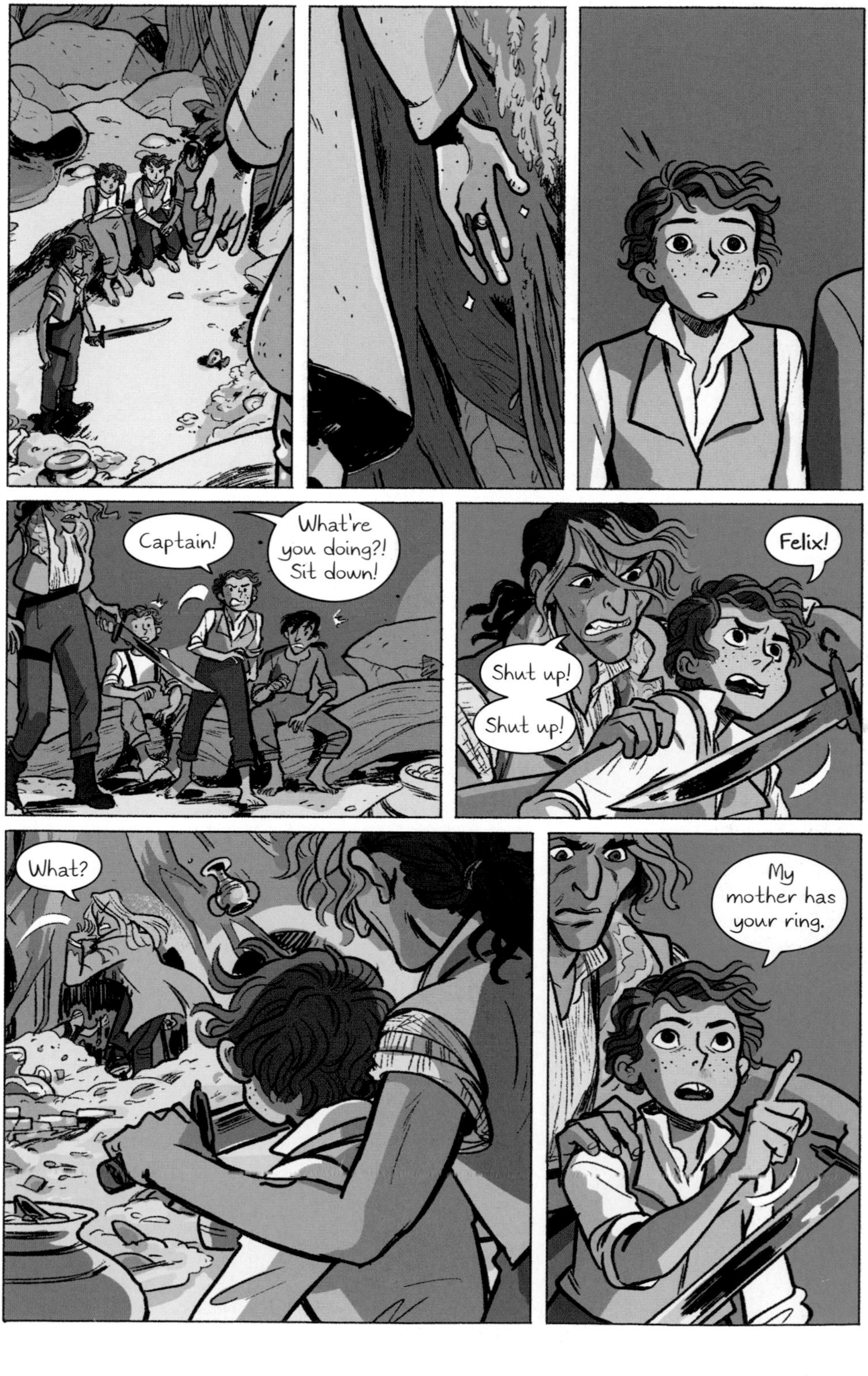

Captain!
What're you doing?! Sit down!
Felix!
Shut up!
Shut up!
What?
My mother has your ring.

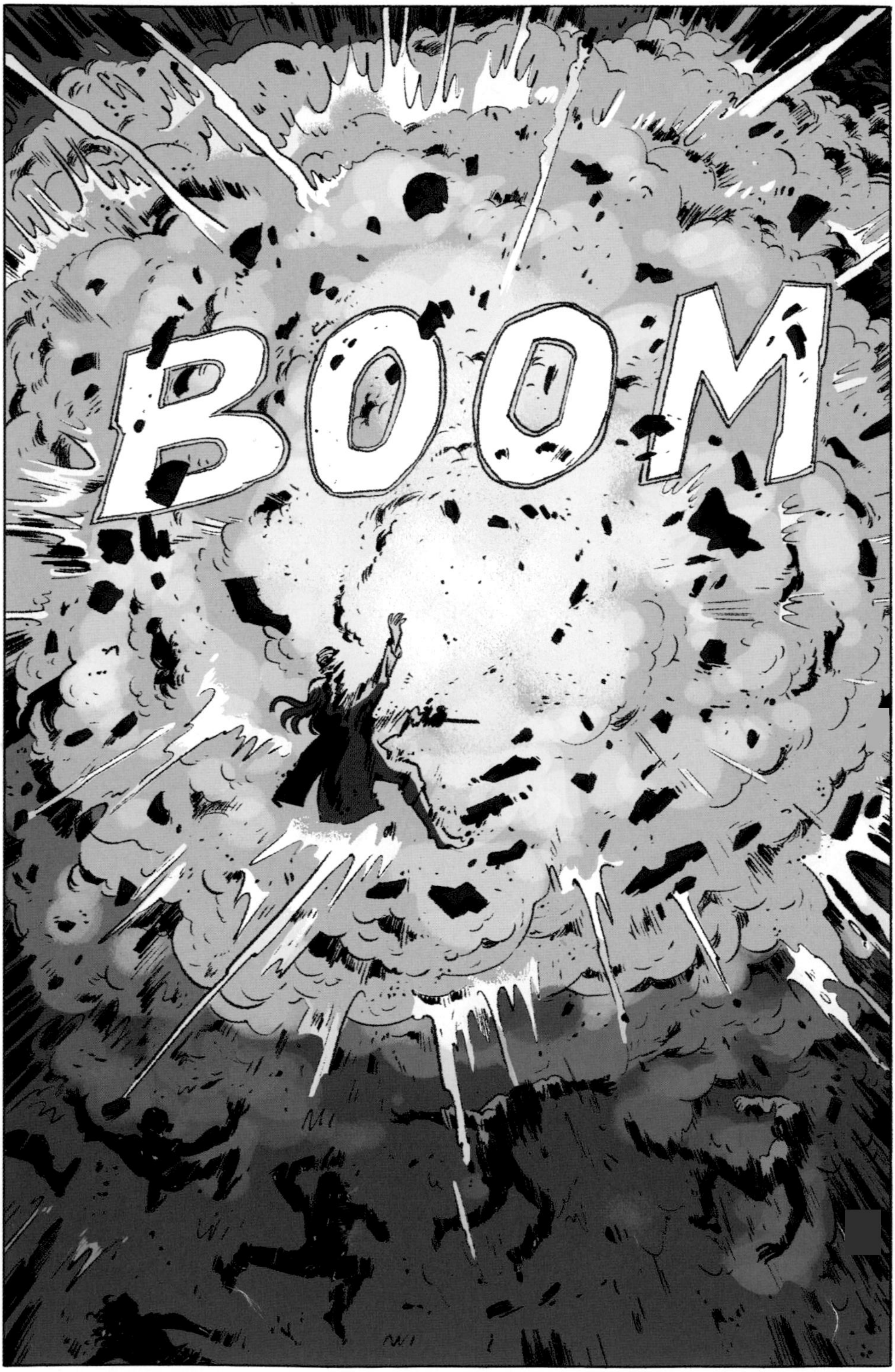
BOOM

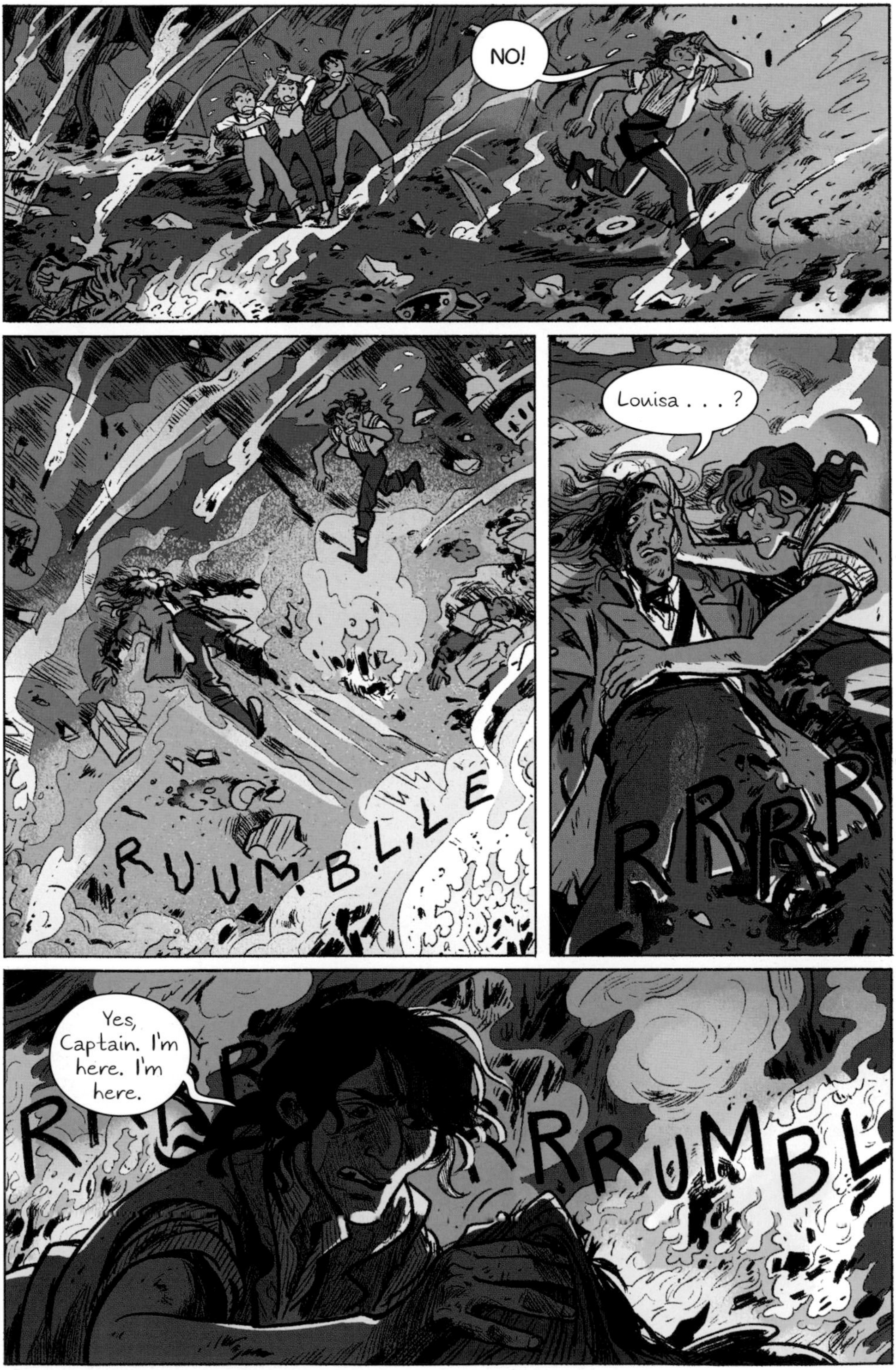
NO!
RUUMBLLE
Louisa . . . ?
RRRR
Yes, Captain. I'm here. I'm here.
RRRRRRUMBL

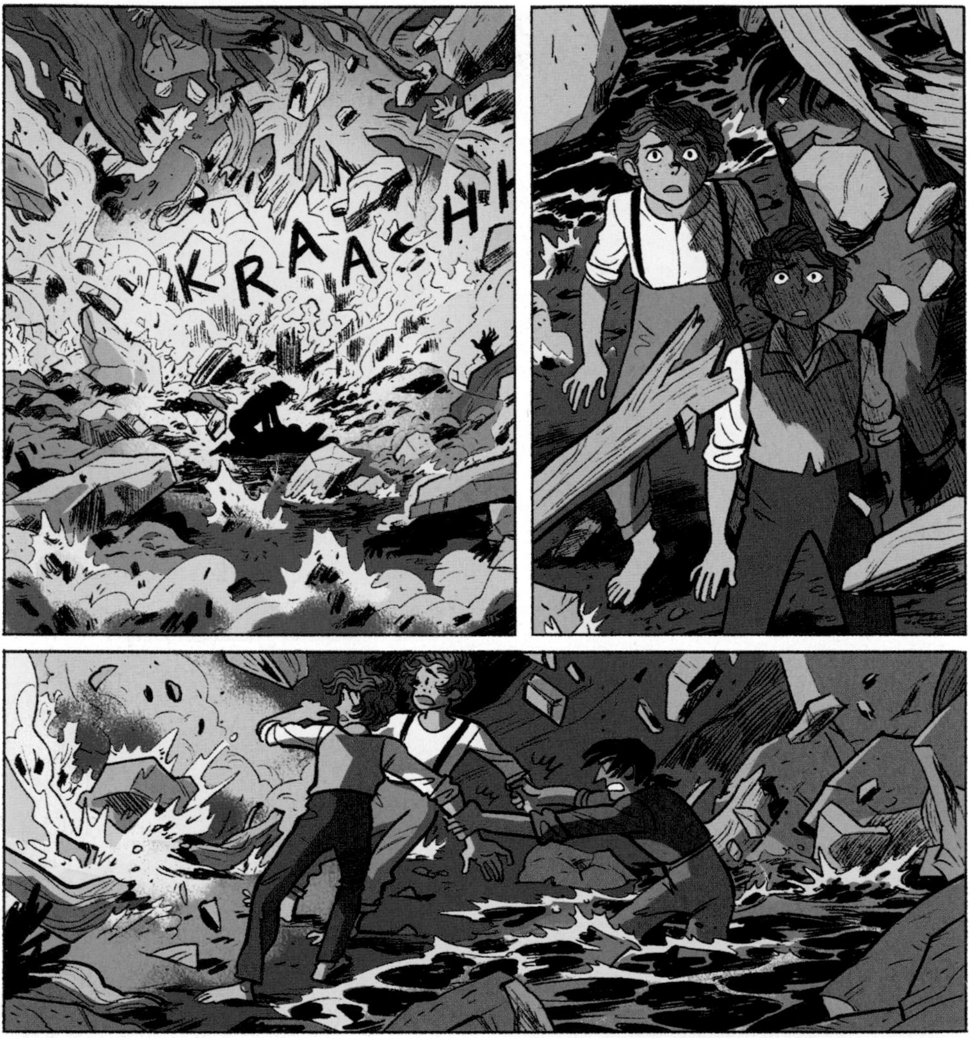
KRAACHH

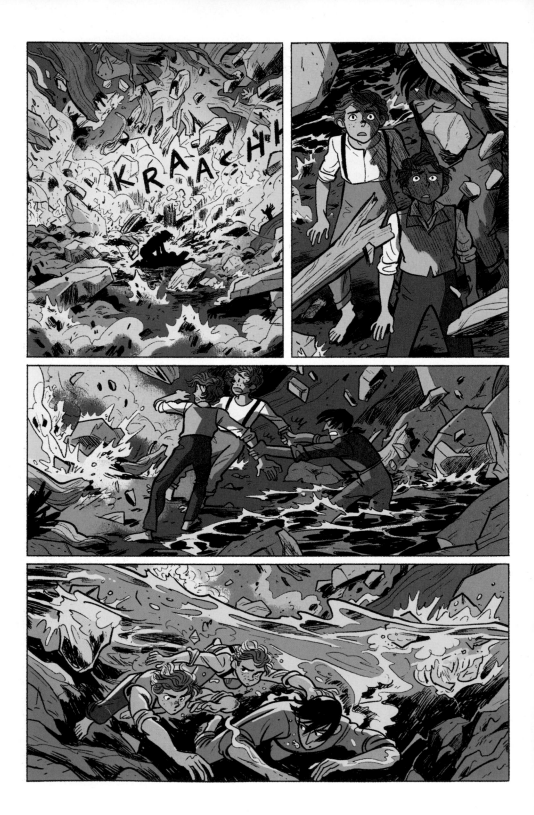

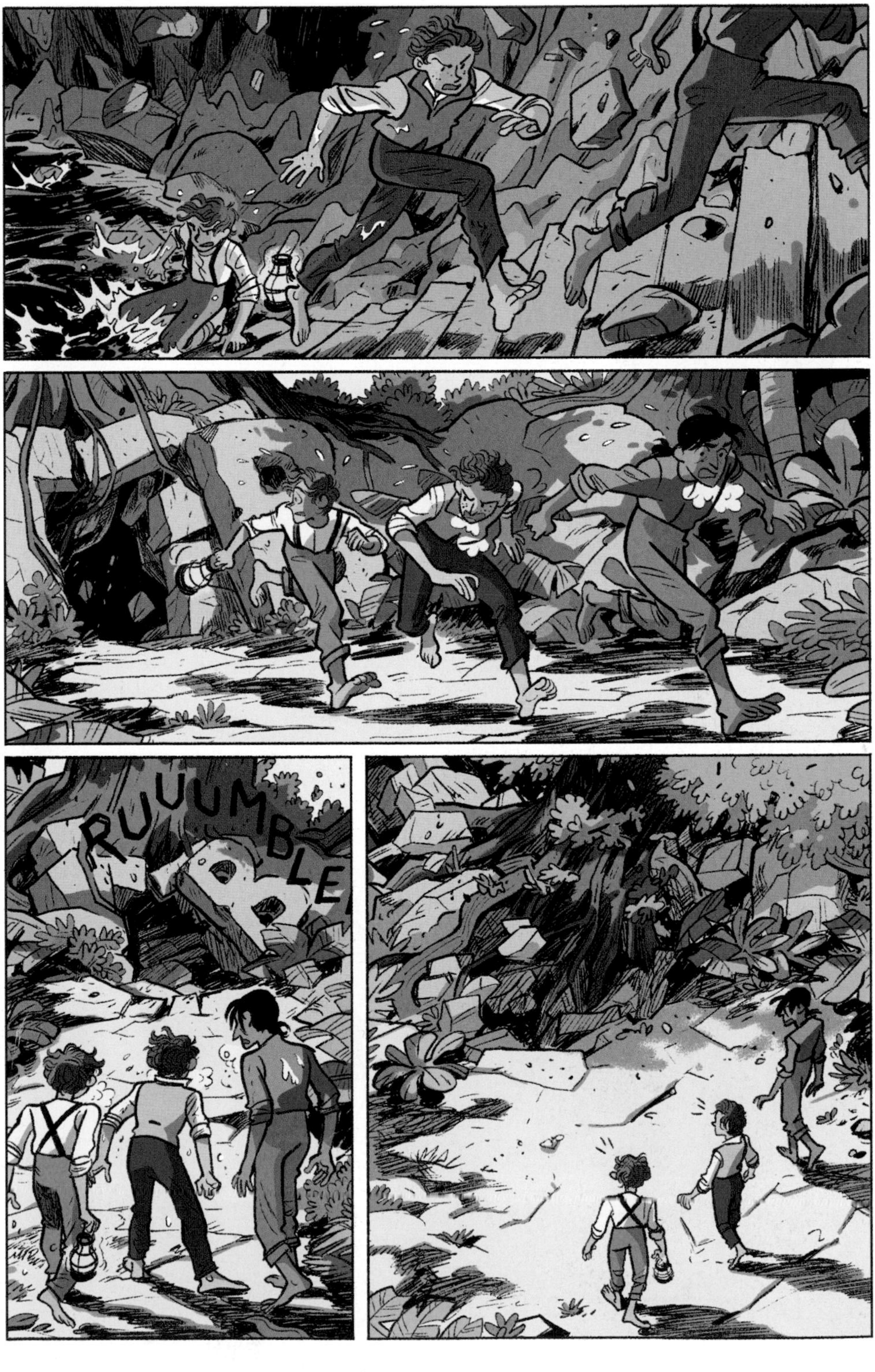
RUUUMBLE

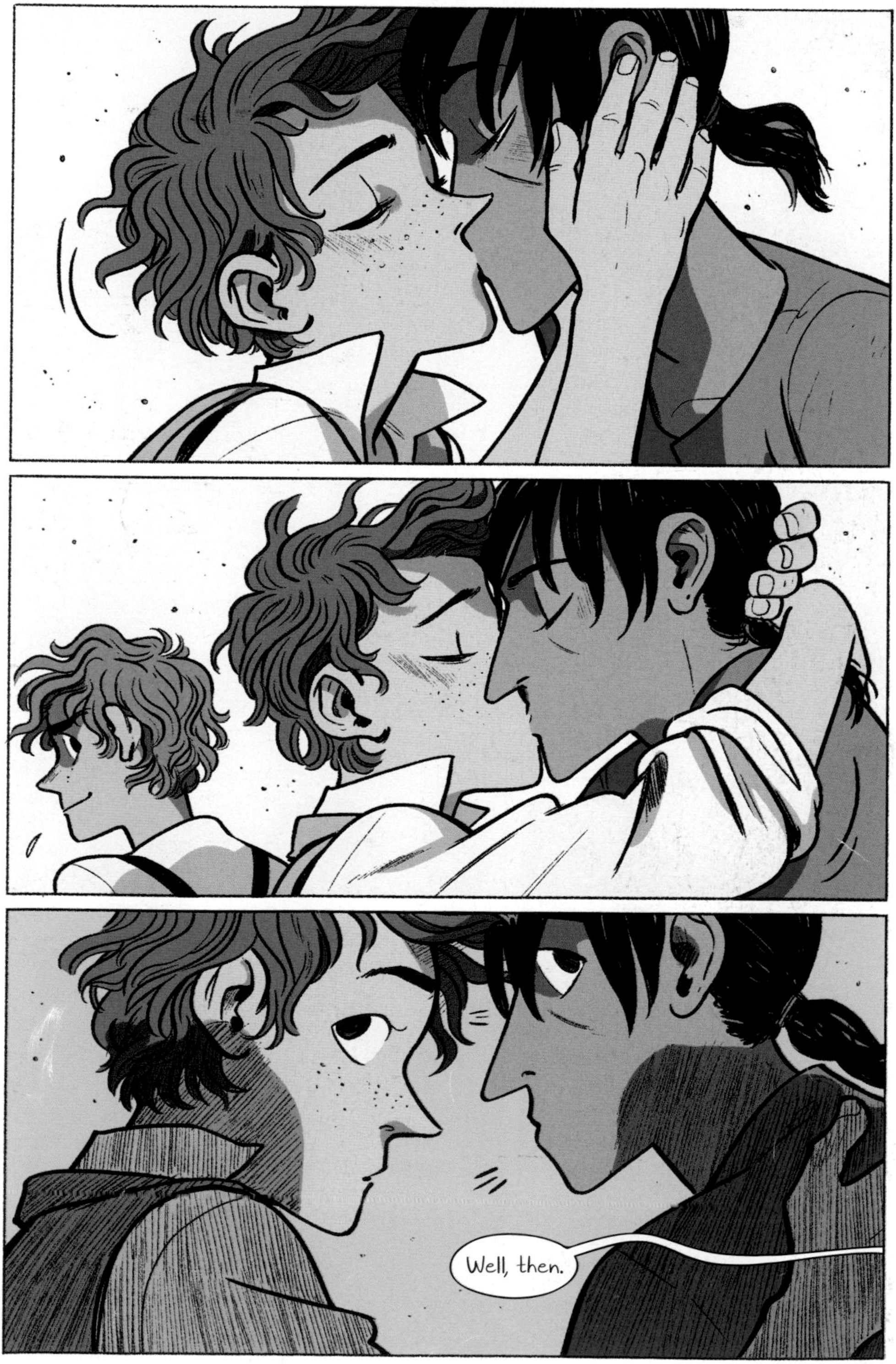
Well, then.

212

CHAPTER ELEVEN
ECHOES

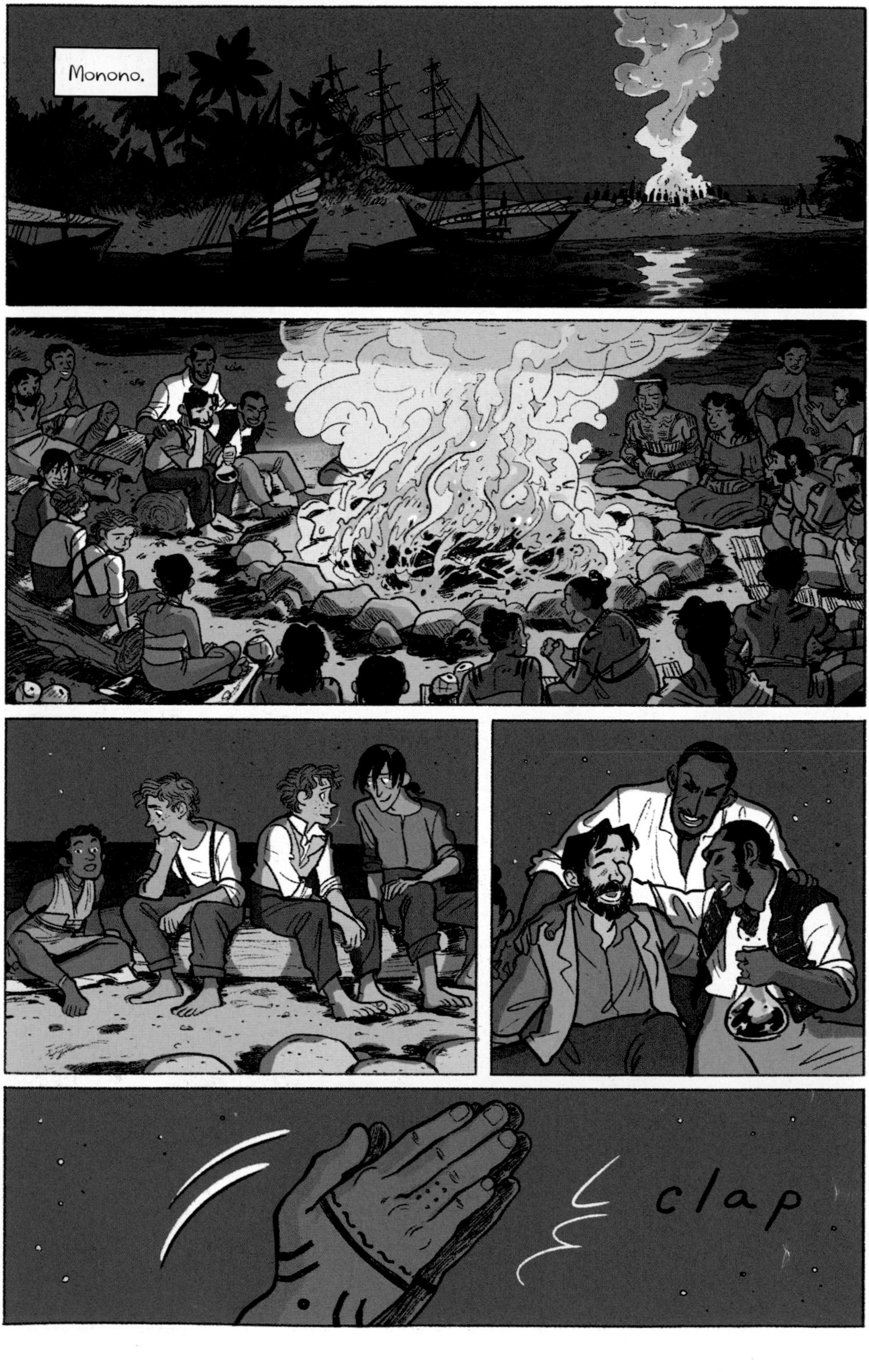
Monono.
clap

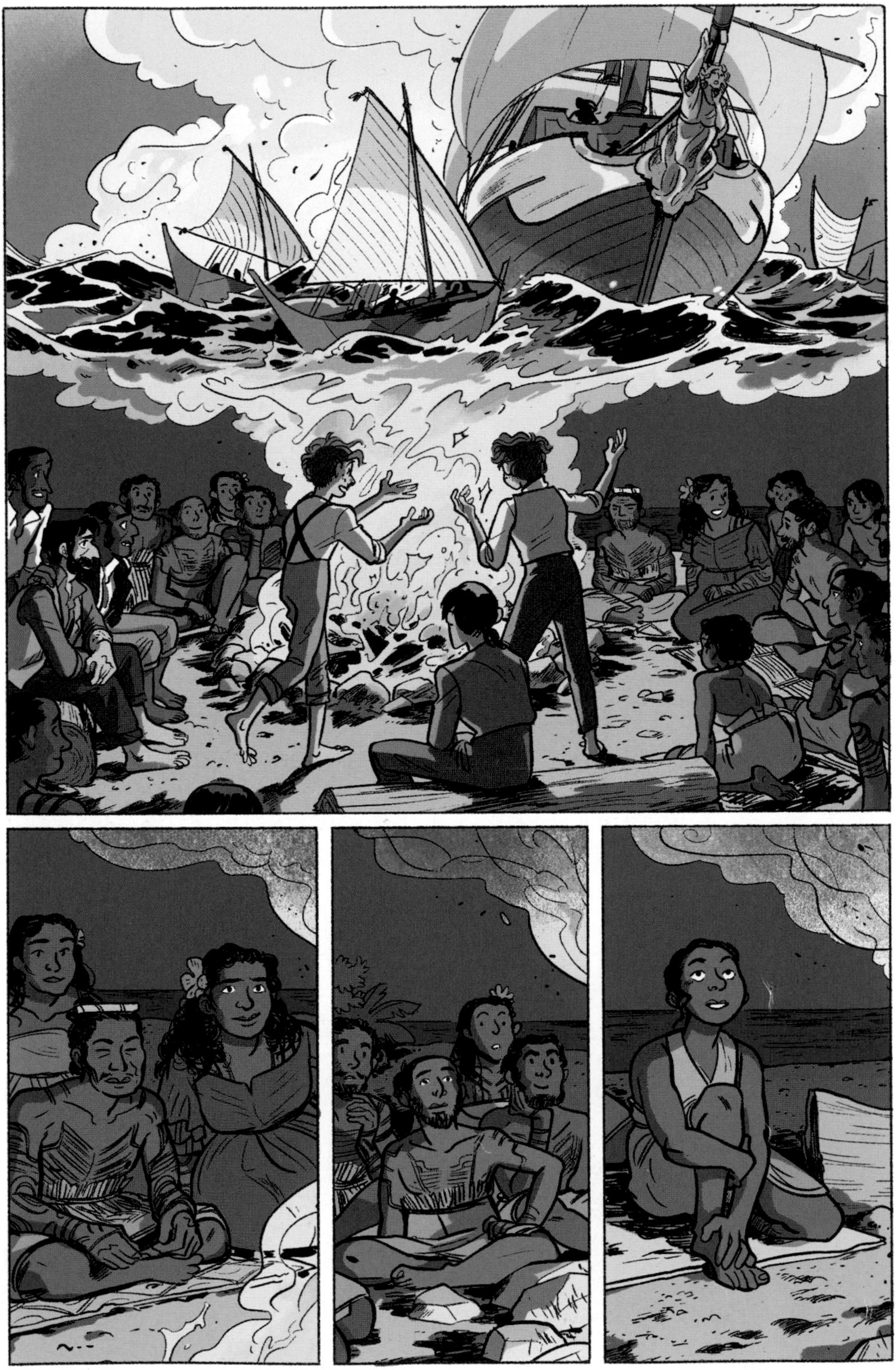

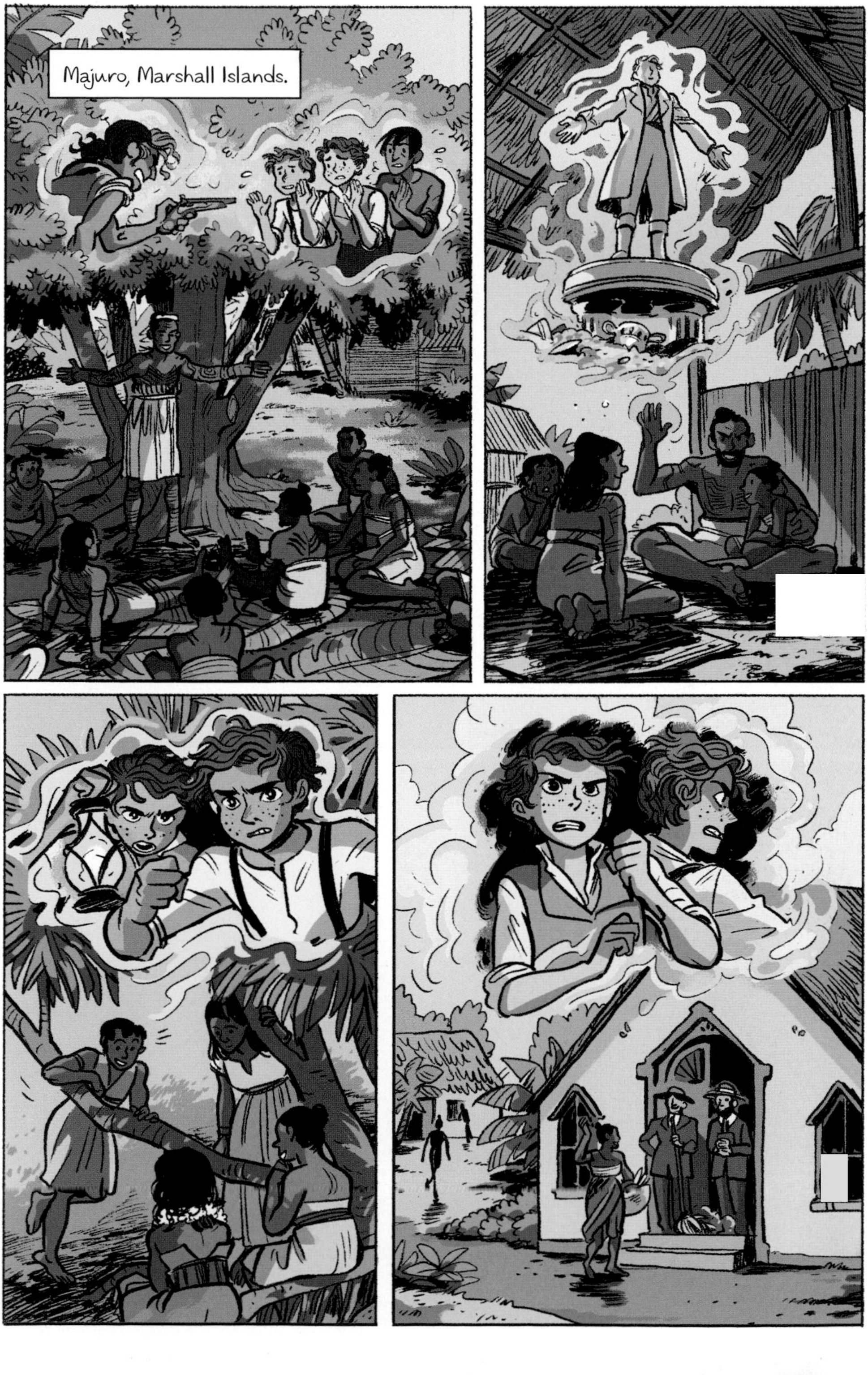
Majuro, Marshall Islands.

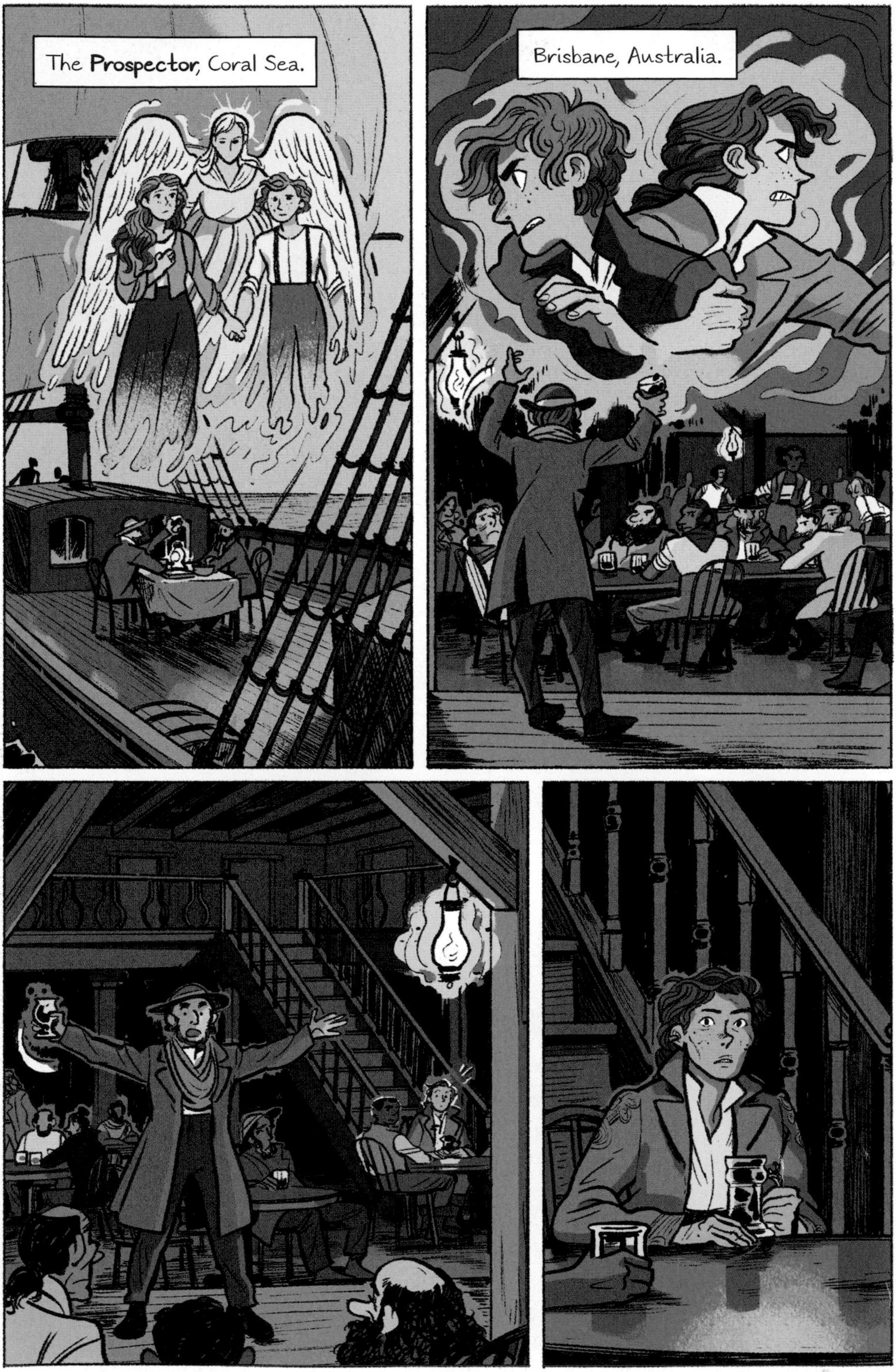
The **Prospector**, Coral Sea.
Brisbane, Australia.

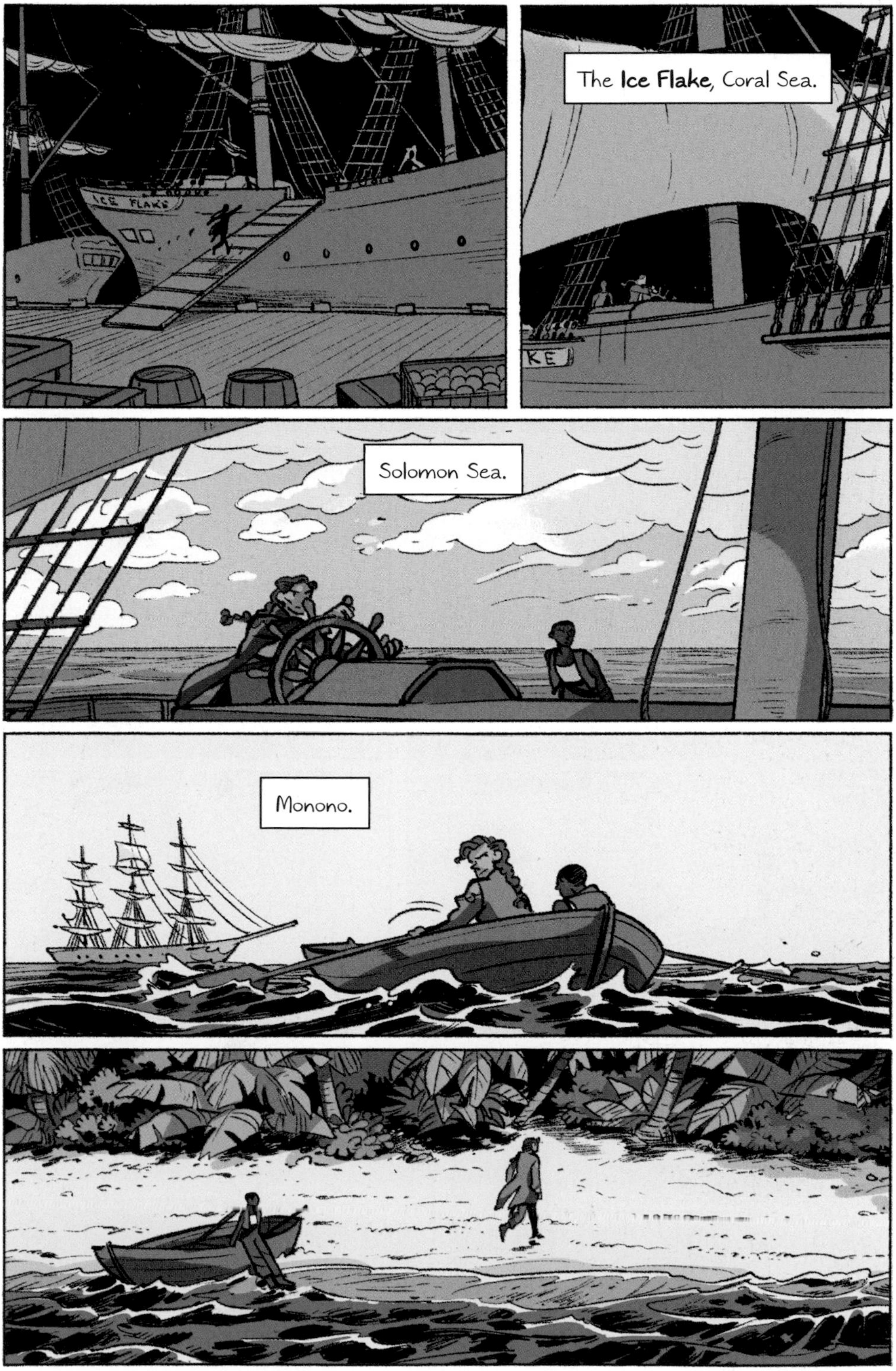
ICE FLAKE
The Ice Flake, Coral Sea.
KE
Solomon Sea.
Monono.

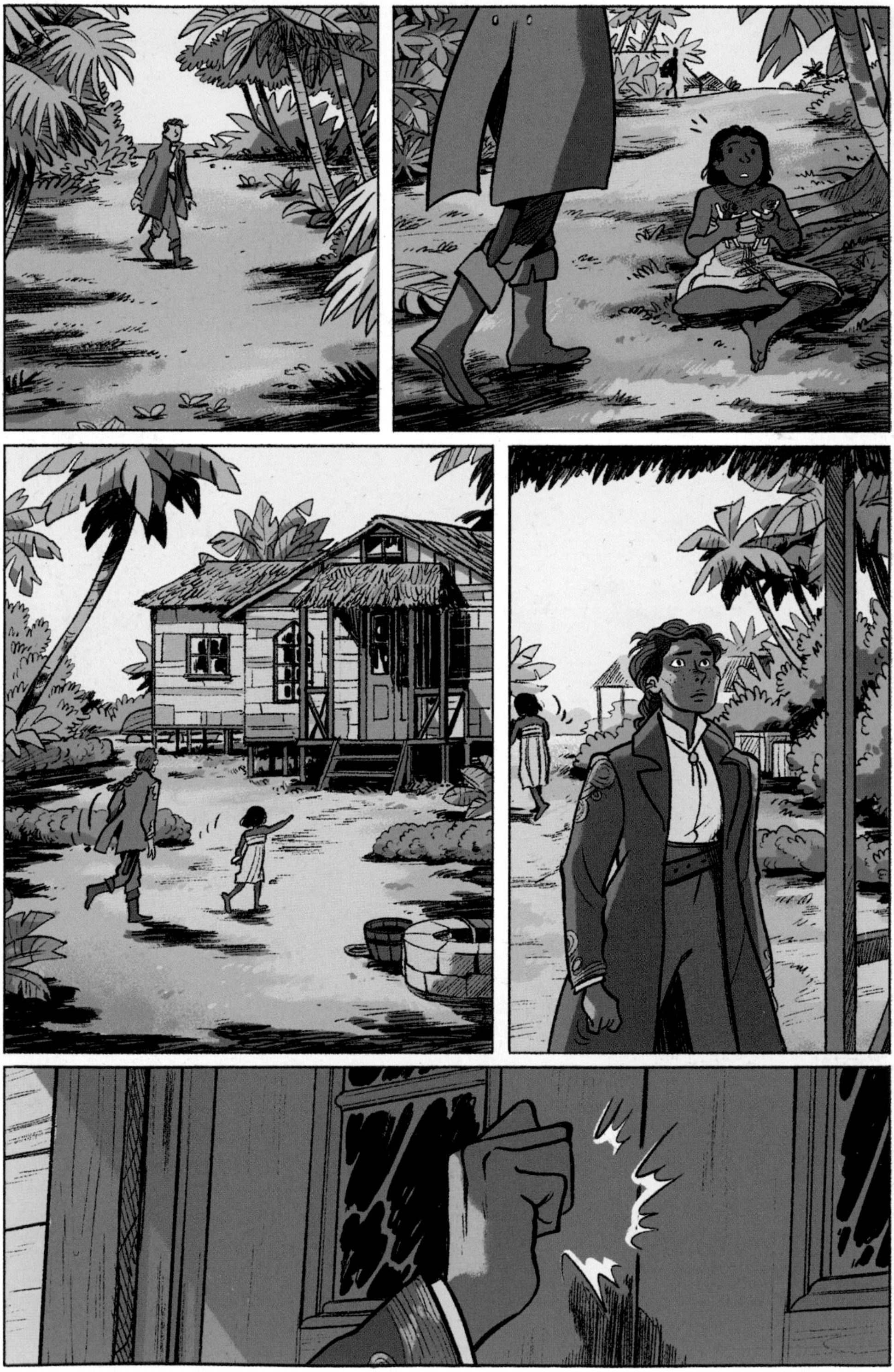

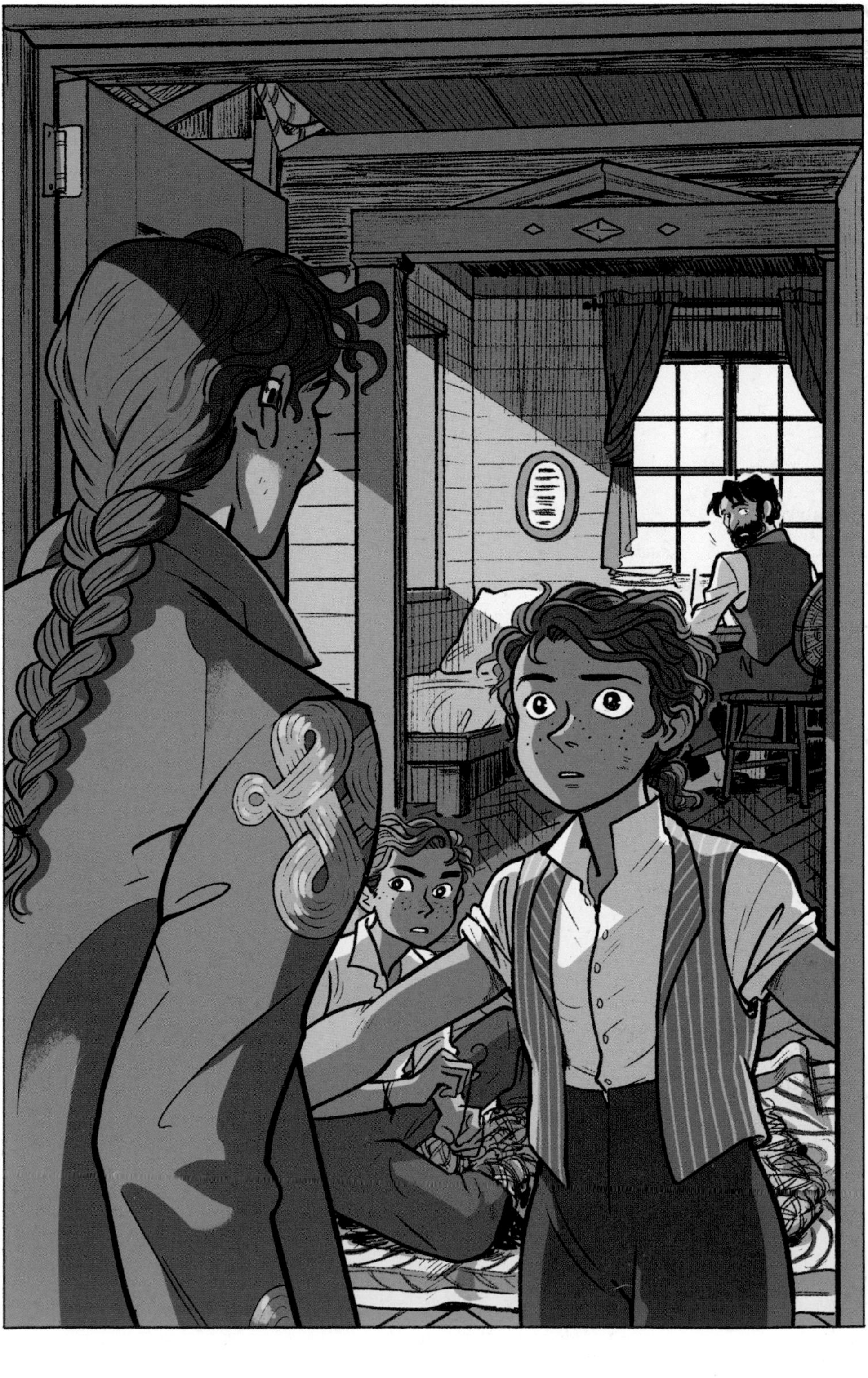

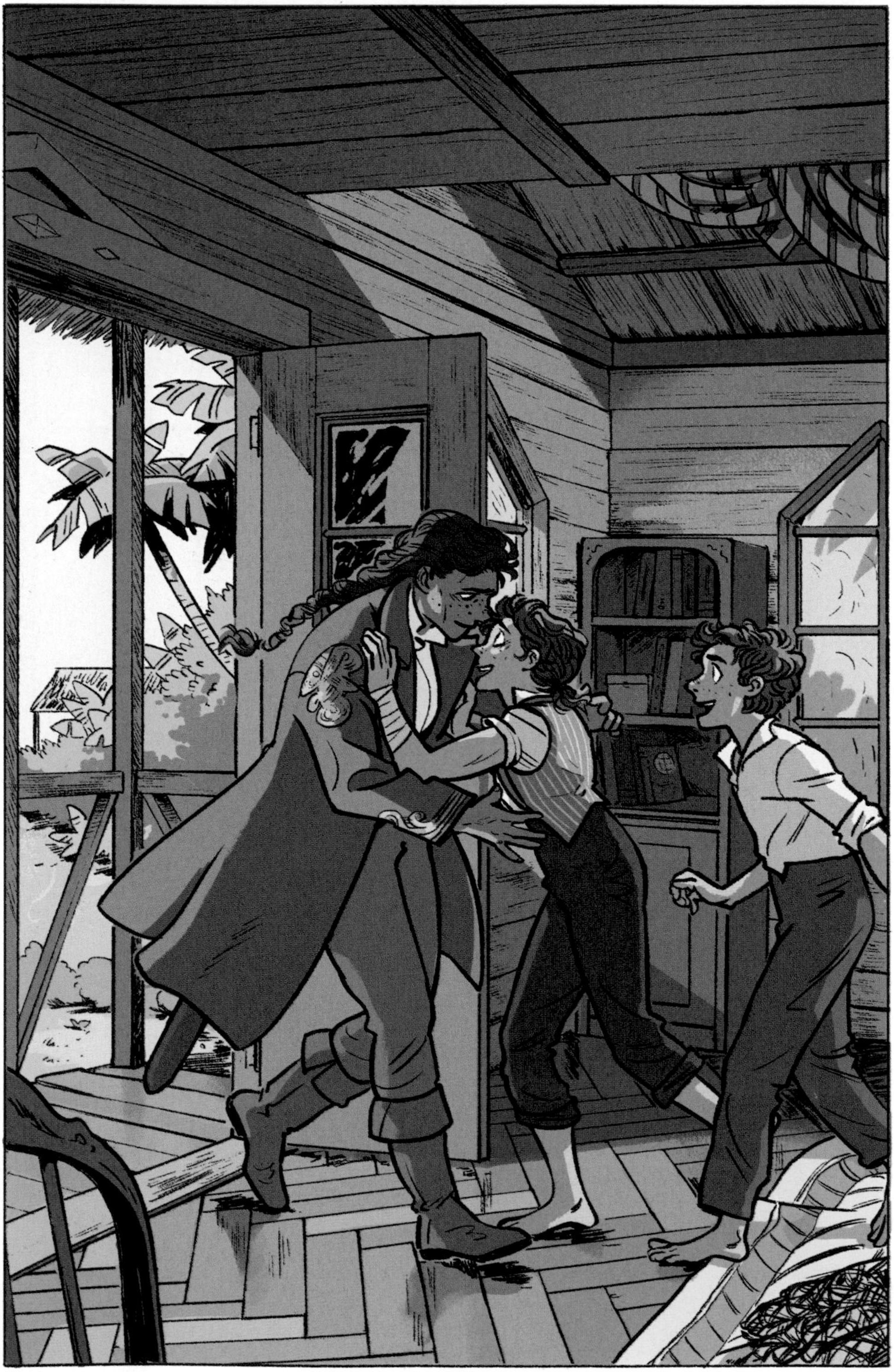